THE HAVENS COVE

By
Estelle E. Falardeau

* * * * *

Edited, Revised, and Published
By
Brenda Falardeau

Copyright © 1998 by Estelle E. Falardeau
Revised Second Edition

All rights reserved. No part of this book may be reproduced, stored in a retrieval system, or transmitted in any form or by any means without the prior written permission of the publisher, except by a reviewer who may quote brief passages in a review to be printed in a newspaper, magazine, or journal

This book is a work of fiction and any resemblance to persons, living or dead, places, or events is purely coincidental. The characters are productions of the author's imagination and used fictitiously.

ESTELLE E. FALARDEAU

Acknowledgments

I'm dedicating this book to my two best friends Carolyn Pack and my sister Pauline Sherman. Both of them constantly encourage me in my goal to become a writer. Also to both of my daughters "my pride and joys" My oldest daughter Brenda for being right beside me in editing my book, adding her own creative parts to the book, and getting it published and my daughter Debbie for being our sounding board.

My sincere thanks to Jolaine Johnson and Carol Smith for the final proof reading of this book.

Chapter One

Sarah Saint James was standing behind her desk, looking out her office window observing the many activities going on. Washington Street was buzzing with vendors selling their wares. Their carts were full of tantalizing items; decorated T-shirts, designer ties, all types of copper items, and a multitude of one of a kind gadgets. Crowds of shoppers filled the streets. A well-dressed businessman was buying a bag of honey-roasted peanuts from the peanut vendor. A lone man, his hair tide back in a ponytail wearing oversized jeans and a T-shirt, was strumming his guitar. In front of him, the lid of his guitar case stood opened with a few coins scattered inside. A woman in a light blue business suit and white sneakers dropped a five dollar bill in his case. Nodding his head, he kept on playing his guitar. The bag lady carrying a paper bag and a green plastic trash bag half filled with soda cans was rummaging through the trash collecting more cans. She picked up two cans of Pepsi cola and placed one in the trash bag, and drank what was left in the other hand. Wiping her mouth with the back of her hand, she threw the empty can in her bag and continued walking. "Poor soul," Sarah thought. The bag lady wore a black dress, two unmatched shoes, one flat and the other a high heel. She had long brown matted hair, two circles of red rouge on her cheeks, and several front teeth were missing. Sarah loved Boston, but she felt sorry for the abundance of homeless people that made the streets their home. She donated money, and worked at the shelter twice a month. With her hectic schedule that's all the time she could spare.

It was early in the morning and the temperature was eighty-five and climbing. Sarah was looking forward to going home to Newport Rhode Island for a couple of days. The weather promised to be perfect for the weekend, and she really needed a few days off. She planned to have a fourth of July clambake for her family and a few friends. The buzzer on her phone rang Sarah picked it up. "Yes, Nora" "Sarah, Jake Lamark is here to see you." "Please send him in Nora." Sarah walked over to the door to greet him. "Please come in Mr. Lamark."

Sarah walked over to her desk and sat down. She motioned for Jake to take a seat. He didn't wait for her to speak. "Miss Saint James," he said professionally. "I have an offer here, that you just can't refuse." Taking the offer out of the breast pocket of his suit coat and placing it on the desk in front of Sarah, he continued. "My buyer is now offering you and your Cousins twenty million more for the Newport Property, bringing the amount to a grand total one hundred and twenty million dollars. I cannot see how you can reject this offer." He said sharply. "Think of what you can buy with that much cash." Sarah felt chills throughout her whole body, has she sat there and listened to Mr. Lamark. She knew it was a lot of money and her Cousins would greedily accept this offer. Clearing her mind and glaring at Mr. Lamark, Sarah responded impatiently, "Mr. Lamark, the money doesn't mean anything to me. It can't replace the way I feel about the Haven. The only reason I would consider selling it is if my Cousins forced me into it." Adding angrily Sarah said, "If I could afford to buy their share, I would. Mr. Lamark raised an eyebrow and said, "I spoke to your Cousins earlier today, and they are very anxious to sell the property." Standing abruptly and holding out her hand, Sarah replied. "I'll be seeing them this weekend, Mr. Lamark. I'll discuss it with them. I hate to rush you out, but I have another appointment in 5 minutes." Standing and shaking Sarah's hand Mr. Lamark said. "Fine Miss Saint James, I'll be in touch."

When Mr. Lamark was gone, Sarah placed her head in her hands and thought to herself "that man makes my skin crawl." Sitting back in her chair she turned around and looked at the sky. Tears flowing, she said, "granny, what am I going to do, I don't really want to sell your Haven? I know how much it meant to you, and I feel the same way you did. I'm so confused, please help me. I must be going crazy," she thought. "Granny has been dead for a year now, and I'm still talking to her. What could she possibly do for me now? I feel so alone; it feels that everyone I love leaves me, first my parents and now granny. Shaking her head, Sarah said out loud "I've got to stop feeling sorry for myself." She turned around in her chair and grabbed a tissue from the silver tissue box on her desk. She wiped her eyes and blew her nose. Looking around her office, she thought, "Look at what I've accomplished, my business is great and I have a beautiful office."

Looking around again, Sarah sat and admired her office. It was a comfortable room, yet it held an essence of exquisite taste. It was bright. On one wall was a large hand painted picture of the Haven that a friend of her grandmother's had painted. Under it sat a black leather sofa with gold trim. Her desk was a deep mahogany, the top covered with glass, two black leather chairs, handmade and designed especially for Sarah, and behind her desk was her chair, a comfortable soft leather executive chair that swiveled. On the left side of the room was a large mirrored wall designed to make the room look bigger. Two large floor plants stood on two corners of the room, a small black glass coffee table also trimmed with gold.

The table was adorned with a vase of fresh red roses, Sarah's favorite flowers. Nora made sure there were fresh roses every week. Sarah had decorated her office herself and she loved it, her eyes going back to the picture on the wall her heart filled with love, she loved the Haven even more. Pulling herself back to reality, Sarah picked up the file from her desk that she wanted to give to Nora and took her white shoulder bag out of her draw slipping it on her shoulder. Today she couldn't wait to leave the office, it seemed that the pain over her grandmother's death would never cease. Especially now that someone wanted to buy the Haven She needed time to unwind and think. Walking to the door she looked around her office one more time before leaving. She opened the door and walked out, going straight to Nora's desk. She handed Nora the file and gave her some last minute instructions and said "I'll be at the Haven, call me if you need me and don't forget the fourth of July party this Sunday. You are coming right?" Nora smiled and answered "I wouldn't miss it for the world." Sarah smiling turned around and walked out the door. Being on the fifth floor, Sarah headed for the elevator and pressed the button. Sarah headed for the elevator and pressed the button. A few seconds later the elevator door opened Sarah stepped inside and pressed G. The elevator started to descend. When the door opened she stepped out of the elevator into the parking garage. She walked the short distance to a red Trans Am. Unlocking the door she stepped inside her car and placed the key in the ignition and turned it. The car started with no hesitation. She drove out of the garage.

Once Sarah was out of the heavy Boston traffic, she felt the tension leaving her body. She took route sixty-six along the coast, it was the scenic route. The trees were in full bloom and the landscaping on the side of the road was breathtaking. Some of the ocean views would make marvelous, photos, she thought. Driving along Sarah thought, "I have to think about the positive things in my life, not that damn Jake Lamark driving me crazy." While Sarah was driving she started thinking of Nora, she was her right hand in her office and a good friend. Nora had been with Sarah right from the beginning. Sarah had listed and sold Nora's home. Her home had been in the suburbs of Boston. A few months after her husband Ben had passed away from a long illness, Nora felt her home held too many memories and she needed a fresh start. A friend of hers recommended Sarah Saint James to her; she had sold her home, and bought another home through Sarah, and had been very satisfied with her services. The first time Nora met Sarah she liked and trusted her right away. With the money Nora made from the sale of her home she bought a condo in downtown Boston. In one of their conversations she had mentioned to Sarah how she had been an executive secretary for an Attorney, before Ben's illness and was hoping to find employment once she was settled. Sarah informed her that she was in the process of opening her own real estate office; it would be ready in two months. She offered Nora a position as the office secretary, and Nora gratefully accepted. Sarah had never been sorry with her decision to hire Nora, in fact after one year in business Nora had become Sarah's personal secretary typing her agreements and listings and one of her best friends. Nora was 38, tall and slim, with jet black hair and green eyes. Sarah admired how professional and meticulous Nora was in her work. Nora had been out on a few dates, but no one special had entered her life. She was happy with the job and she was content enough for now. Sarah went back to concentrating on her driving. She always liked taking the back roads to Newport, instead of the highway. Although some parts of the road were treacherous the view was breathtaking and she could easily control the Trans Am. Sarah was looking forward to the small gathering of friends that were coming for the Fourth of July clambake. Julie would also be joining her for the long weekend along with her Cousins Tom, and Vicki. All of them spent their weekends at the Haven in the spring, summer and fall.

As Sarah approached the estate gate she pressed the electronic switch on the visor of her car to gain entry. The gates were high, black with a gold crest in the middle of each with a letter H. The H stood for the name of the estate. Sarah thought the name fit perfectly; to her it was her Haven, since she was a little girl. Sarah had spent summers here with granny and her cousins. Granny had passed away a year ago and now someone was trying to buy the property. Sarah didn't know what to do. She felt like she was stuck between a rock and a hard place. She held a sixty percent share and her Cousins had twenty percent each, she had the final say but it still wasn't easy. The house was an attractive Victorian, over one hundred years old set high on a bluff overlooking the Atlantic Ocean, on two hundred and fifty acres of land. As Sarah was climbing up the front steps, Alfred the butler opened the door. Alfred was a distinguished looking gentleman in his early sixties; he was tall and stately with a full head of white hair. His pale blue eyes twinkled when he smiled. He'd been with granny since he was a boy. Alfred looked at Sarah with love, for she was his favorite out of all the grandchildren and he knew how much she loved and appreciated her grandmother.

Smiling, he said, "good day Miss Sarah." Sarah returning Alfred's smile greeted him. "Hello Alfred." "It's good to have you home Miss." "It's certainly good to be home. My Cousins Haven't arrived yet, have they Alfred?" Trying not to frown he replied "no, Miss." "I didn't think so. They told me they'd be here around two. Good. This will give me time to rest before lunch." "Yes; Miss. I'll let Mrs. Johnson know you'll be having lunch at two thirty where will you want your lunch in the dining room or on the patio?" "It's such a beautiful day Alfred I think I will eat on the patio." "Yes, Miss. "Oh. Alfred?" "Yes, Miss." "Please let Mrs. Johnson know that I'll see her after lunch to go over the menu for the weekend." "Will do, Miss." "Thank you, Alfred." "You're welcome Miss." Sarah walked up the large mahogany staircase to her second floor bedroom. Sarah loved the seclusion and peace she felt just being home, especially in her bedroom. Sarah remembering fondly on her twenty-first birthday how her grandmother gave her a blank check and told her to go and buy herself new furniture and redecorate her bedroom and sitting room. She smiled remembering the reluctance to take the check telling her grandmother it was too much of a big gift, and how granny just stood there looking at her in disbelief and told her she would not be happy if Sarah rejected her gift. Finally giving into her grandmother she hugged her tightly and said thank you. Admiring her room, she had it painted eggshell white. A light rose bedspread with matching pillow shams, and dust ruffles adorned the Brass bed Displayed over her bed was an oil painting of a sunset in all its splendid colors. There were matching night stands and brass lamps on each side of the bed. A white wicker dressing table and a large bureau with a full size mirror sat across from her bed. On the right side of the room was a sitting area with white Persian rugs that were scattered over the highly polished hardwood floors. A painting of her grandparents hung over the marble fireplace. On both sides of the fireplace a display of family photographs. A white love seat and chaise lounge completed the sitting area. Sarah smiled as she remembered how her grandmother's eyes smiled as she approvingly told her how wonderful her room looked. She remembered how proud she had felt and her spirits started to lift. Sarah's room was located at the back of the house. She opened the French doors that led to a balcony, and stepped out. Looking over the ocean, the view was spectacular. Wrapping her arms around herself and smiling, she thought out loud. "How could I ever sell all of this? No amount of money could give me the joy and serenity I get looking at this beautiful scenery." She felt tired and went back inside. Sarah took off her clothes, set her alarm and snuggled under the blankets and fell asleep.

"Tom, I do wish you would slow down around these curves" as she held on to the door for dear life and asked "Are you trying to kill us?" "Vicki, you worry too much! Relax, and take in the scenery. "The scenery, I can't even see anything you're going too fast. The scenery won't be so wonderful if you kill us in the process. "Tom just laughed, and kept going faster. "Please Tom I'm going to vomit all over your new Mercedes, if you don't slow down. "Tom turned, and looked at his sister and decided to slow down. She did look rather faint. Slowing down he asked, "What do you think Vicki, can we persuade our dear cousin Sarah, to sell the Haven?" "I was planning on both of us trying to convince her to sell this weekend." "Why grandmother gave her a sixty percent share and everything in the Haven; while only giving us a twenty percent share is beyond me." "Sarah has always loved the Haven. Unlike us Vicki, she sees it as her home. Well with the new offer we received today of one hundred and twenty million, I would think she changed her mind." "I'd say that amount of money is nothing to sneeze at Vicki, it will buy Sarah, any house she wants." "She can buy one with a stable for her precious horse Midnight Blue. Grandmother gave her that dreadful horse for her twenty-fifth birthday. and I really detest that horse." "If you hadn't whipped him Vicki, he wouldn't go after you every time he sees you." "He deserved that whipping; he wouldn't let me ride him." "Changing the subject Vicki, as for myself I can visualize living quite comfortably with my share of the money from the sale. I can certainly make good use of that money; I've depleted most of my inheritance. As you know we can never sell our home on Beacon Hill until one of us dies. And you know, my dear, I do like the good life. I certainly cannot see myself working for a living. That's not my style he frowned. That's why I want the sale to go through." Vicki interrupted "My divorce settlement from Sean was pretty profitable. Along with selling my New York townhouse gave me a good cushion. Like you I do so enjoy the good life. With my share of the sale, I would never have to worry again. Unlike you, my dear brother, I don't gamble my money away. Of course if Sarah was out of the picture we would have so much more money to share." "Wouldn't that be fabulous, Vicki?" Vicki smiled and thought to herself, "If Tom was also out of the picture I would have it all". Tom's thoughts were exactly the same as his sister. Vicki looked amazingly like her Cousin Sarah. Dressed alike they could have passed for identical twins. Born two weeks apart with Sarah, being the oldest, both had long Blond curly hair, blue eyes, and were both five feet six inches tall. The difference between the two girls was that Vicki was calculating, cold and very vindictive. She wore heavy make-up, long false eyelashes and very revealing clothes. On the other hand Sarah was gentle, caring and forgiving. She wore very little make-up. Her look was softer. Both girls resembled their grandmother. At thirty-one years old Vicki, had been married three times. Sarah had never been married or engaged. In complete contrast Tom, was a little over six feet tall with jet black hair, and large black eyes and two years older than the girls. As children they spent all of their summers with their Grandmother at the Haven. Their grandfather died a year before Tom was born. Sarah's, parents were both surgeons, and had a very busy lifestyle. They felt very fortunate to have their daughter in the care of her grandmother during the summer months, instead of with a nanny.

Tom and Vicki lost their father to cancer when Vicki was two years old. Devastated, their mother fled to Europe and one year later married a millionaire. The children were left home alone in Boston to live with their servants and their tough nanny. Their grandmother took them every holiday, and they spent them with her, Sarah, and her Parents. They also spent all their summers with their grandmother. Their mother came home once for Christmas. All the other years she would mail the children expensive gifts for their birthdays, and Christmas. The children would have rather had their mother then any gift she gave them. With no parental supervision Vicki and Tom pulled many stunts that got them into trouble. They became very jealous of the relationship Sarah had with her parents and their grandmother. They couldn't understand why their mother didn't want to spend any time with them. They were both very resentful. Sarah, on the other hand had very loving parents, who spent as much time as they could with her. They made a point of taking a month off in the winter for a ski vacation with their daughter. They took her to Switzerland, Colorado, and other times to the White Mountains in New Hampshire. Sarah loved her winter trips with her Parents. She excelled in all her schoolwork, and had no problems getting the time off from school. She was happy as long as they were together. Sarah was a creature of habit, even as a child. One summer when she was seven years old and playing hide and seek with her cousins, she had an accident. Tom knew Sarah, always liked to hide in the tool shed. The previous day he had found a Beehive hanging in the shed. He told Vicki what he found, and together they plotted to have Sarah locked inside. "Sarah, it's my turn to be the finder in our hide and seek game. You and Vicki go on and hide and I'll come looking for both of you." Placing both her little hands on each side of her waist, trying to look stern Sarah said, "Tom, you make sure you turn around and count to one hundred you always cheat and only count to twenty-five." "I always count to one hundred Sarah. "Well just make sure you do." Tom turned around facing the tree he put his right arm up, closed his eyes and started counting. "One, two, three..." Both girls took off in different directions. Sarah headed for the shed, once she was inside she went into the corner, and crunched down. Vicki, ran back to the shed close the door, and slid the board into place locking it. She joined Tom behind the shed where Tom had left the window opened earlier. Through The window Tom could see Sarah, crunched down in the corner. He took his slingshot out of his back pocket. Vicki handed him a rock she had picked up. He took it placed the rock in the sling and aimed it at the beehive hanging over Sarah. The beehive exploded, hundreds of bees came rushing out and began attacking Sarah; she started screaming, and ran for the door. She tried to push the door open, it wouldn't budge. The bees were stinging her everywhere she kept screaming and trying to get out. Tom and Vicki were hiding behind the shed laughing. A while later when they stopped hearing Sarah scream; Tom went and unlatched the door and Sarah fell out. She was unconscious.

Vicki, bending down over Sarah, started screaming and crying "Sarah, what happened to you?" Tom ran to get help. Just then the gardener arrived on the scene. He found Vicki, out of control. He moved Vicki aside, bent down and picked up Sarah. Vicki followed him as he carried Sarah to the house, went into the living room and laid her on the sofa. Hearing Vicki's cries, their grandmother came rushing in. She gasped when she saw Sarah lying on the sofa. She exclaimed, "My God what happened to this poor child?" "I don't know granny," Tom replied. "We were playing hide and seek, Vicki and I were hiding waiting for Sarah to find us. Finally we heard her screaming, and went looking for her, we found her on the ground in front of the tool shed and I took off to find someone to help her. "Looking at the Gardner, grandmother said, "Ed, please go and fetch the Doctor." "Yes ma'am." Sarah, had to stay in bed for three weeks, her face, head and every other part of her body were covered with welts. The doctor had told her grandmother that if she had been allergic to bee venom she would have died. After putting on such a fine acting job concerning their cousin's accident Tom and Vicki enjoyed their time without Sarah. Each night after they had their dinner Vicki and Tom would stop by Sarah's room to tell her how much they missed her. Back in their room they would laugh at how amusing Sarah, looked with all her welts and she didn't look much like Vicki. Every summer Sarah would have some kind of misfortune brought on by her cousins.

Sarah's alarm clock went off. She turned over and shut it off. She got up wiping the sleep from her eyes with her hands cupped. She went into the bathroom, turned on the shower, and stepped in. She let the water flow down her whole body and it felt so refreshing. When she was finished she felt completely refreshed.

THE HAVEN'S COVE

Chapter Two

Sarah put on a pair of white shorts and a red tank top; tying her hair back with a white tie back, she slipped into a pair of white sandals. She looked in the mirror satisfied with how she looked she headed downstairs to have lunch. Vicki and Tom were sitting at the table, on the patio, when Sarah arrived. Tom rose as Sarah approached the table. Helping her with her chair he said, "Sarah, my love, how are you?" "I'm fine, Tom, and you?" sliding her chair forward as she sat down. He said. "I'm just dandy thank you." "Thank you Tom, always the perfect gentleman." "I do try, my dear cousin." Vicki, looking at Sarah commented "Sarah, you do look a little pale. Are you ill?" "No Vicki, I'm fine. I just woke up from a nap." Taking her napkin off the table and placing it on her lap. Vicki said, "That explains the fact that you still look a little worn." Sarah ignored her last remark. Vicki, was wearing short hot pink shorts, with a matching halter top, big loop earrings, her blond hair was pulled back to one side held with a shell comb. Her feet were in a pair of hot pink backless spiked heels; her face was heavily made up. Tom wore a white Polo shirt, tan shorts, and brown loafers without socks. Alfred brought in a pitcher of ice tea and four glasses. As he was setting the glasses down, Vicki, put her hand out to stop him and said, "Alfred I want something a little stronger than ice tea." "What do you prefer instead Miss Vicki?" Arrogantly, she replied, "I'd like a Vodka Martini with a twist of lemon and one ice cube Alfred" Before he placed a glass in front of

Tom, he asked, "and you sir? Would you like something other than ice tea?" "Yes Alfred, make mine Gin and Tonic." "Yes Sir. Would you like something else, Miss Sarah?" "No thank you, Alfred." Alfred poured the tea in her glass. "Thank you, Alfred." "You're welcome Miss." The drinks were brought in and lunch was served. Lobster salad and hot rolls. While eating their meal, Tom said, "Sarah, I received a call from Jake Lamark this morning." "So did I" Vicki intervened. Tom continued, "His client is really pushing to buy this place. He offered us another twenty million dollars. It brings the total at one hundred and twenty million dollars." "Sarah placed her fork down on her plate. Her stomach was in a knot. She knew how badly they wanted to sell. If only she could find a way to buy them out. She looked at Tom. "You know how I feel about selling Tom, and I don't really want to. That man Jake, makes my skin crawl. I just feel granny would be upset with us if we were to sell her Haven. " Irritated, Vicki spoke up. "For God's sakes, Sarah, grandmother is dead and we are alive. You cannot ignore the amount of money they are offering us for this place. You would be a fool not to sell. If you want to keep this place so bad buy us out twenty seven million dollars for me, and twenty seven million dollars For Tom." "You know I don't have that kind of money, Vicki otherwise I would buy you out." At that moment Alfred interrupted them, "Miss Sarah, there's a gentleman at the front gate who claims to be your grandmother's brother?" She looked at her cousins, "our grandmother's brother? "Tom said, "I didn't know granny had a brother?" "Neither did I," Vicki said. . Sarah replied "Tell him to drive up Alfred, and escort him to the patio when he arrives." "Yes, Miss Sarah." "This is strange!" Tom said. "Granny never mentioned she had a brother," said Sarah. "Come to think of it, she never spoke about anyone, except grandfather. It's like she didn't have a life before she married him." "I have always thought that was strange?" said Vicki.

Alfred followed by the Uncle walked out onto the patio. Seeing the man behind Alfred left Vicki, and Tom, speechless they just stared at their uncle. Tom thought "he has to be granny's brother." His mother looked exactly like him and so did he. It's uncanny. While the other two sat looking stunned. Sarah stood up, extending her hand, "I'm Sarah, and my Cousins Vicki, and Tom." Taking her hand in his, he said, "I'm your grandmother's brother, Armand Saint John." "It is so nice to meet you. Please sit down and have some lunch with us." He sat down and said, "I am a bit hungry." Alfred was still standing in the doorway. Turning to him Sarah said, "Alfred, please bring our guest a place setting." "Yes miss." "Mr. Saint john, would you like a drink?" "Yes I would, Alfred. Scotch on ice if you have it?" "Yes sir." Tom, Vicki and Sarah, just stared that their uncle. Armand was a handsome man about six feet tall, well built, with jet black hair and just a speck of white on each side and piercing black eyes, the same eyes as Tom shared with his mother. Armand cleared his throat and said, "You three look as if you've seen a ghost. I didn't mean to frighten you by showing up on your doorstep." Alfred brought Armand this drink and set it in front of him, along with his plate and silverware. "Thank you, Alfred." "You're welcome, sir. Will there be anything else Miss Sarah?" "No Thank you, Alfred." Armand picked up his glass raised it and said, "let's have a toast shall we." Sarah, Tom, and Vicki raised their glasses is to his. Armand said, "To our family reunion." They all repeated, "To our family reunion," and drank from their glasses. Tom placed his glass on the table and said, "We never knew granny had a brother. Where have you been all these years? And why come around now?" "I am sure this is a shock for all of you. I didn't know I had a sister up until a few months ago. My mother died a couple of years ago she was ninety-two. I was devastated by her death. I sold the House and placed what I wanted to keep in storage and I sailed off to Europe. I stayed there up until a few months ago. When I settled into an apartment in Lowell, Massachusetts I took my things out of storage. I found my mother's strongbox in one of the trunks, there was a letter inside addressed to me. In the letter she told me I had a stepsister who was fifteen years older than me. Her name was Monique and her second husband was Matthew Thompson and they lived in Newport, Rhode Island. I decided to come and introduce myself to her." "I'm sorry, Uncle Armand, granny died a year ago in May. But I'm sure she would have loved to have met her brother," said Sarah. Vicki said, "I'm not sure about that. She never mentioned a brother or that she was married before. Are you sure you are her brother?" "Oh! I'm sure Vicki. I have a copy of her birth certificate." "Very strange" she mumbled. "Granny was seventy years old when she died, being fifteen years younger than her that would make you fifty-five?" "That is correct, Sarah." "Well now that you've found us it would be nice if you stayed with us for a while we have plenty of room." "Why thank you Sarah." "Not so fast, Sarah we don't even know this guy and you're asking him to stay here?" "For heaven's sake Tom, you look just like him. He's granny's brother. He's found his sister and lost her all in one day. He is staying with us."

"Hi everyone" "Julie, please join us. This is granny's brother, Armand Saint John. Uncle Armand this is my best friend and co-worker Julie Tate." Armand stood up and held out his hand. Julie placed her hand in his. "I'm pleased to meet you Miss Tate." "Same here Mr. Saint john." "Please call me Armand." "And you may call me Julie." "Did you have lunch Julie?" "Yes Sarah. I ate before I left Boston. I'm going up to

THE HAVEN'S COVE

my room and freshen up. I'll see you in a little while. It was a pleasure meeting you Armand. Vicky, Tom." Julie acknowledged. "It was a pleasure meeting you also Julie." Armand placed his napkin on his plate, and finished his drink "thank you Sarah, this was delicious." Alfred came in and walked over to Sarah. "Will you be in need of anything else Miss Sarah?" "Will you please bring my uncle to one of the guest bedrooms, Alfred, and see that he gets settled in." "Yes Miss." Armand rose and followed Alfred out. "Well now that we're alone we can continue our discussion on selling this white elephant." "Tom how can you call this home a white elephant?" "My dear Cousin Sarah, it's exactly what it is. We've been offered a great deal of money to part with it and that's exactly what I want to do." "So do I Sarah. You can buy something just as nice with your share of the money." Sarah was lost in her own thoughts. "How can they bare to part with this home? After spending all their summers here as children, when everything about it here is so beautiful, especially the gardens." The patio overlooked the entrance to the gardens with its multitude of colors. Granny had won so many prizes for her roses and she cared so much for everything connected to the Haven. "Sarah have you been listening to us?" Vicki screamed. "Yes Vicki I have. I just don't want to make a decision right now. I'm going to the kitchen to speak with Mrs. Johnson about the July fourth clambake." Sarah stood up and left leaving Vicki and Tom in a state of anger.

When Alfred finished unpacking Armand's luggage he asked "will you be in need of anything else Sir?" "No. Thank you, Alfred." Alfred left the room. Armand looked around the room and liked what he saw; dark cherry wood adorned the walls with a stone fireplace on one wall with a gas log. Armand flipped a switch in the fireplace and the fireplace came alive with a burning fire. He switched it back off. A large four-poster bed sat on one wall with matching night stands and lamps. A man's dresser stood on the opposite side of the room. French doors led to a deck overlooking the garden and pool area. Armand decided to go out and explore the grounds. As a child his mother spoiled him. She loved him more than life itself. He was a mirror image of her. Whatever he wanted she gave him. Has he grew older he had a very dark side. When He was fifteen years old his father died leaving him in his mother's care. When he turned sixteen and got his driver's license his mother bought him a brand new car. As the years went by his demands grew bigger, and his mother couldn't refuse him anything. However If she tried to say no he would turn around and give her a backhand, many times sending her flying backwards into a wall, always when the servants were not around. If he got angry about anything he would take it out on his mother. In her last year she was bedridden. When the servants retired for the night he would take care of her. He would sit by her bed and tell her he couldn't wait for her to die. He wanted to sell the house and collect his inheritance and travel to Europe. She understood everything he was telling her. Tears wood flow from her eyes as she wondered why he hated her so much. She had loved him so and gave him everything he ever wanted. When Armand made love to a woman he was brutal and left his partner with bruises. He never had sex with a woman more than once. One night when he felt his mother was near her end he didn't see the sense in waiting any longer he took a pillow and placed it over her face and said "good-bye mother" as he smothered her to death. The next morning one of the servants found her, rushed to knock on Armand's door and let him know his mother had passed away during the night. He acted like a distraught son, but inside he was gloating. Portraying the dutiful son a two day wake was held and a Funeral Mass for his mother she was buried by his father's side at Saint Joseph's cemetery. He placed the house on the market. Looked through his mother's artifacts and that's when he came upon the letter in his mother's strongbox and decided he would check it out at another time. Now he wanted to get the money and go to Europe.

Jake Lamark was a buyer's broker. His office was located in a small house in Newport, in a pretty rundown section of town. Jake was sitting at his desk contemplating the commission he would make once the Haven was sold. He was also thinking how grateful he was that a friend of his had recommended him to the buyer for this property. He was going to pay him ten percent of the selling price. Jake would make a commission large enough to retire, buy himself a little cabin on a lake up north and spend all his time fishing and drinking beer. Jake was fifty-six years old with a large pot belly with gray wild and greasy hair. He had small beady eyes and a large nose. His face was full of pot marks the result of bad acne as a teenager and always picking at his pimples. Jake always held a thick cigar between his lips. His office smelled like an ashtray. His secretary buzzed him. "Jake, Mr. Gavin is on the line."Jake picked up the phone, "Mr. Gavin how are you?" "I'd feel a hell of a lot better if you tell me the Saint James woman took my latest offer." "I'm working on it sir. I went to her office to see her today; she still wants to think about it." "Why is she so stubborn?" "I don't know sir?" "I want you to offer her an extra ten million in addition to the twenty million you told her about this morning. I'll have my secretary fax you my new offer and I want it presented this week-end." "Yes sir. I believe she's in Newport as we speak. As soon as I get your new offer, I'll be on my way." "See that you do, Jake. I want the Haven." "Again, I'll do my best Sir." "I'm sure you will, Jake." The line went dead. Jake hung up the phone and thought, "I want to sell that property as much as you want to buy it. I wish her Cousins owned the property outright."

Evan Taylor was a very handsome thirty seven year old male. He owned a multitude of exclusive vacation playgrounds in the Caribbean, Europe, and all across the United States. Evan always made it a point to get what he wanted. He was a sharp businessman. He was also the most sought after bachelor. Evan was blessed with exotic good looks, dark skin, jet-black hair, big blue eyes, and long eyelashes, he was 6 foot one with a muscular body. He never lacked for female companions. Although he never met a woman he would want to share his life with. He owned a vast empire and wanted children to leave it too. However most of the women he had affairs with were jet setters, and only interested in acquiring his vast fortune. Evan's father died when Evan was only four years old. His mother remarried when he was ten years old. His stepfather Phillip Taylor took an interest in Evan and loved him like he was his own son. Phillip adopted him when he was twelve. He occasionally took him on his business trips and taught him at a young age how to negotiate on the hotel's he acquired. After college, Phillip brought Evan into his business. Father and son worked side by side until Phillip died of a massive heart attack six years ago. Evan's mother lived in a townhouse on Beacon Hill in Boston. She was very active in several charities, especially the Heart Association. She gave of her time and money. She was proud of her son, but desperately wanted to see him settle down with a wife and children. Although her son was a ruthless businessman, she knew he would make the right woman a loving husband. He was gentle and kind. Her relationship with her son was built on love and trust. Kate Taylor was also a very attractive woman her hair had turned completely white when she was twenty-one years old and she had never colored it. She wore a hair short in the latest style. She was five foot three inches tall, slim and had hazel eyes. Kate dressed in the latest fashions. At fifty-seven she looked much younger than her age. Evan sat behind his large modern desk. His office was plush and very expressive. He was on the thirtieth floor in the Trump Towers building. The view of New York from his office was imposing. He stood, turned and admired the view of the city. His thoughts were on the townhouse he lived in a cross the street from Central Park. It was convenient to his office, and he enjoyed running in Central Park in the early morning. It was a nice enough place to live when he couldn't get home to Newport where he really loved to be. For the last two years it had been impossible for him to go home. He really missed it, and he missed taking long rides on his chestnut horse named Barron. When time allowed it, he spent time at his sixteen-room estate set on fifty acres. His land bordered the Haven property. Something told him it was time to take a break. He decided to take a few weeks off and go home. He needed a little rest and relaxation. He called his staff in Newport to prepare for his arrival that night. He also phoned his mother to see if she could join him. Unfortunately, she had made other plans and had to decline his invitation.

Sarah was in the kitchen in conversation with Mrs. Johnson the cook and housekeeper "We'll be twenty-four for the clambake. We'll need lobsters, clams, corn and strawberry shortcake for dessert." "Sarah, I've already placed in an order at Joe's seafood. I told him I would call him with the actual amount I'll need. He assured me a delivery by noon tomorrow. Miss Sarah, what's wrong?" Mrs. Johnson had been with the family for twenty-five years. She was a gem. She was short, heavy set with a big bust line, shot white curly hair and brown eyes. She was like a mother to Sarah. She knew her well and loved her and Sarah felt the same way about her. Mrs. Johnson was her confidant even more so since her granny had passed away. The Cousins, Mrs. Johnson just tolerated. Her daughter, Maggie also worked at the Haven as a maid. Maggie had been ten years old when her mother was hired. They lived in the back of the house in their own quarters. "Oh Mrs. Johnson, Tom and Vicki are after me again to sell this place. We were offered another twenty million dollars this morning. Of course they're thinking of the money and I can't blame them, but I have such mixed emotions. I really can't see myself selling and living somewhere else and yet I'm depriving them of their share of the money if the property was sold. I love it here, but they hate it. If I had the money I'd buy them out, but the higher the buyer goes on the offer the harder it will be for me to come up with the money." "I've known you and your cousins since you were children, and I tell you I have no use for those two imps you call your cousins." "Oh! Mrs. Johnson you mustn't say that. They are really good people. They are just a little different, that's all" "Those two have always been up to no good, Miss Sarah. When you were children do you think all the accidents you had were your fault?" "I've always been accident prone, Mrs. Johnson." "Accident prone my eye No dear, your cousins caused those accidents to happen. They thought no one was the wiser. You'll have to be careful. Watch yourself around those two. Sometimes Miss Sarah you can be so naïve. You know I wouldn't lie to you. Now if you want to sell this house, sell. If your decision is not to sell then don't let anyone influence you into selling." At that moment the phone rang and Mrs. Johnson stood up to answer the phone. "The Haven residence" "I'd like to speak with Miss Saint James." Said in a real gruff voice. "Who may I say is calling?" "Mr. Jake Lamark." "It's for you Miss Sarah, its Mr. Lamark." She handed the phone to Sarah. Sarah stood one hand cradling the phone, and the other hand resting on her hip, made a face and asked "what do you want Jake?" "Miss Saint James, I would like to see you and your cousins this afternoon. I can be there in an hour." "Mr. Lamark I told you this morning I would think about the offer over the weekend. Why are you bothering me?" "I have a higher offer to present. "Sarah raised her eyes, and said a silent "Oh No! You can tell me over the phone Mr. Lamark." "I really would like to present it in person." "Look I'm not having you come here. So you might as well tell me over the phone." "Well, if you insist Miss Saint James." "I do." "The buyer offered another ten million dollars making his full offer one hundred and thirty million dollars. How can you even hesitate at this offer, Miss Saint James? I would advise you to snatch this offer up." "What is it you don't understand, Mr. Lamark? You did your job you've read me the offer. As I told you this morning I will think about it over the weekend. Good day." "But he is offering an extra ten million." "I don't care. I told you I think about. Now leave me alone." Sarah banged the phone down. Jake took the phone away from his ear and hung up saying "I'll get you for this you high class bitch." Sarah was shaking. At that moment Julie walked into the kitchen. "Sarah, do you want to go to the beach for swim?" "Sounds good to me, I'll go up and change into my swimsuit. I'll meet you on the back porch in fifteen minutes." "Great see you in a few." "Miss Sarah." "Yes, Mrs. Johnson." "How does a picnic lunch sound for after your swim?" "Sounds wonderful, doesn't it Julie?" "It sounds like a terrific idea!"

Fifteen minutes later, Sarah and Julie picked up the basket, towels, and blanket sitting at the back door. They took the path that led to the beach. They laid the blanket down on the sand by huge rock, and then placed the basket and their towels down on top of the blanket. Taking their sandals off Julie said, "I'll race you." "You're on." They ran towards the ocean. "I won, I won," said Julie. "OH! You cheated." They laughed and splashed each other as they were wading deeper into the ocean. The tide was low and they had to walk quite a distance before they could dive in. They swam for over an hour. It made Sarah feel refreshed. When they walked back to the blanket Julie grabbed the towels and handed one to Sarah "thank you." Wiping herself off Julie said, "That felt great, didn't it Sarah? The ocean water always makes me feel wonderful." Once they dried off they sat down on the blanket. Sarah opened the basket and took out the chilled Dom Perrione and a corkscrew handing both of them to Julie. "Would you open the bottle please? You're so much better with a corkscrew then I am." "Why certainly." Sarah took out two plates, cheese, bread, crackers and some caviar. Then she took out two champagne glasses. Just as Sarah looked up the cork popped, and some of the bubbly spilled out. Sarah held up the glasses and Julie poured the champagne. "Let's make a toast Sarah". They raised their glasses and Julie said, "To our friendship and to Mrs. Johnson for this terrific snack." "I'll drink to that." They both laughed and toasted each other. They enjoyed their lunch along with some small talk. When they were finished eating, Julie refilled their glasses." We can't let this wonderful bubbly go to waste. "Sarah smiled and took a sip. She was feeling a little lightheaded. With her knees up she had both hands wrapped around her glass, looking out at the ocean, but seeing nothing. "Sarah what's troubling you?" "You remember the buyer's broker Jake?" "Jake?" "The guy that's been bugging me to sell the Haven for the last six months, he's been at the office quite a few times. In fact he was at the office this morning before I left." "Oh yes! The one you've named "Jake the snake" because he makes your skin crawl." Sarah smiled. "That's him. He called me just before you came into the kitchen." "What did he want?" "He wanted to come over and present another offer, higher than the one he presented this morning." "Gosh how much more was the offer." "With this morning's offer it came up to thirty million dollars, for a total of one hundred and thirty million dollars." "Wow For this property?" "I know. Tom and Vicki haven't even heard this latest offer and they have been on my case to sell. "Sarah, think of everything you could buy with all that money. You would never have to work again." "Julie you don't understand. This place is part of me I love it as much as granny did. The money doesn't mean anything to me." "You could buy something just as nice, Sarah." "It wouldn't be the same." Sarah stood up. "I want to be alone, Julie. I'm going for a walk. I'll see you later." "I'll take everything back to the house Sarah." "Thank you Julie." "You're welcome." Sarah started walking towards the edge of the ocean. Julie was picking up the basket when she felt someone was standing behind her. She turned and gasped. "I am sorry if I startled you, Julie." "I just wasn't expecting to see anyone else here Armand. You certainly gave me a scare." "Again I apologize for frightening you. I was just looking over my sister's property. I am amazed how big and beautiful it is. My sister did quite well for herself. It's really a shame I didn't get to meet her." "Yes it is. She was a wonderful woman." "My niece Sarah looks like she lost her best friend, what's wrong with her?" "She has a big decision to make." Armand picked up the basket, Julie carried the blanket and the towels. "Would I be intruding if I asked what decision my niece has to make Julie?" "You're bound to find out sooner or later, so I don't believe if I tell you it will make a difference." Only when they started walking up the path did Julie speak. "Sarah and her Cousins own the Haven and someone has been trying to buy the property they were offered one hundred million dollars. Sarah loves it here and she really doesn't want a sell." "I can understand she loves this place, but one hundred million dollars would set her up for life, Julie."

"That's not the half of it today she got offered another thirty million dollars. I tried to talk some sense into her, but she just won't listen. "Armand falling silent and thinking to himself he had to find a way to get control of the estate, with that kind of money he'd be set for life. "Well, I'm sure my dear niece will make the right decision, Julie." "I hope so, Armand." They had reached the porch. "Just leave everything in the corner, Armand. Mrs. Johnson will take care of it. Thank you." "My pleasure dear, I'll just look around the property a little longer." "See you later Armand." Julie continued inside.

Tom went looking for Vicki he climbed the attic stairs. He figured Vicki would be in the attic to see what prized possession they could sell when they went to New York next weekend. Since their grandmother had passed away whenever they came home they would steal one of the valuable paintings that were stored in the attic, and sell it. They brought the paintings to an exclusive antique dealer in New York, who knew Sarah very well. The art dealer had completed many transactions in the past with Sarah and her grandmother. Vicki would impersonate Sarah, right down to speaking like her, and signing her name. Dressed alike no one could tell them apart. Vicki was able to sell all the art pieces without a problem. The money was shared between her and Tom. They had found the treasures on a rainy day when they were children exploring the attic. After their Grandmother passed away and left everything inside the house to Sarah. Vicki and Tom decided the old bitch hadn't been fair, so they took matters into their own hands and remembered all the expensive art paintings that were stored in the attic. They sold one painting at a time. They had already made quite a bit of money in the last year, and didn't plan on stopping until the house was sold. They knew Sarah had never ventured up to the attic and didn't know the paintings existed. "Vicki, are you up there?" "Yes Tom. I'm here. I'm just taking out the painting I want to sell this week." "How many more paintings do we have left?" "Fourteen." "Great that gives me some extra gambling money." "Is gambling all you ever think about?" "I can't help it Vicki, it's in my blood." "Just think of all the money you would have if you didn't blow it all gambling." "Let's not go there Vicki, you spend your money the way you want to and I'll take care of mine." "Do you want me to take this painting downstairs and place it in my trunk?" "Yes, but be careful not to be seen." "I haven't gotten caught yet."

Tom started gambling when he was nine years old. He would bring his friends home after school and they played poker with their allowance. Tom knew just how to stack the cards and won everyone's money every week. Once in a while he would let one of the other guys win so they wouldn't find out he cheated. His friends thought he was so lucky. They liked hanging around with him because his parents were never home. Tom always had the cook send plenty of snacks to his bedroom for him and his friends. Vicki on the other hand didn't have many girlfriends. In fact she spent most of her spare time with boys and experimenting with sex at an early age. The rest of the time was spent looking at fashion magazines. At eighteen years old she eloped with Roger Nelson. Roger was a high school dropout, but he was very good looking, green eyes and over 6 feet tall, blond hair. His goal in life was to marry a girl with money. He found what he was looking for in Vicki. After two years of marriage Vicki got bored with Roger, and divorced him costing her family half a million dollars. Vicki vowed the next time around she would marry for money. Her second marriage lasted five years. The divorce was bitter and all she received was an eight hundred thousand dollar settlement. Her third marriage was to a successful lawyer named Paul Dixon, he was 25 years older than Vicki. They owned a townhouse in New York. On their third wedding anniversary Paul was on his way home when he was mugged and stabbed. Help arrived too late to save him. Vicki was left with a million dollars and their townhouse that was sold for five hundred thousand dollars. Vicki moved back home to Boston with Tom in the house their parents had left them.

Jake was sitting at his desk fuming, he was very angry with Sarah. His phone rang. It was late his secretary had left for the day. He picked up the phone on the third ring "Hello." "Jake, is that you?" "Who the hell else would be answering my phone?" "Well aren't we in a good mood?" "I'm not interested in your sarcasm. What the hell do you want?" "Well now I thought you might be interested in a little deal? That would make sure you sold your hot property. Sound interesting?" "Very, what do you have in mind?" "I'll meet you say in half an hour at the Black Panther bar. Do you know the place I'm talking about?" "Yes." "See you there." Jake put the answering machine on, shut the lights and locked his door. He felt better than he had all day.

It was eleven PM; Sarah was by the pool going for her nightly swim. She heard a noise someone was behind her. It startled Sarah. She turned around. "Julie you scared me." "I'm sorry Sarah. I couldn't sleep. So I thought I'd join you for a swim. I hope you don't mind?" "Not at all Julie" Without another word both girls dove into the pool.

At nine every morning when Sarah was home she rode her horse. Today she wore a pair of worn out blue jeans, a white tank top, and her riding boots. The groom had her horse Midnight Blue all saddled, and ready for her. "Good morning, Miss Sarah." "Good morning, Jimmy. Isn't it a beautiful morning?" "Yes it is, Miss." She walked over to Midnight Blue handed him a sugar cube and stroked his mane. He nuzzled her neck. "You're such a handsome devil and I love you so much. Are you ready for our ride?" Like he understood her, he raised his head. Jimmy gave Sarah a boost onto the saddle; she grabbed the reins and turned the horse around and edged him toward the beach. Once towards the beach they rode at a fast pace her hair was flying in the wind giving Sarah a feeling of total freedom. Slowing down they took the path into the woods that was as familiar to him as it was to her. She was thinking how wonderful she always felt when she was riding Midnight Blue when a shot rang over her head. Midnight Blue got spooked and bucked sending Sarah flying backwards her head hitting the base of a tree. The horse kept on going. The shooter looked down with a satisfied grin and said, "The bitch is dead." Then turned around and left.

Sarah stood up, and brushed herself off. Looking down she saw herself sprawled on the ground against the base of a big tree. "How can this be, am I dead?" "No, you're not dead," replied a voice from behind her. Startled she said, "Who said that?" As she turned around faced she was faced with a bright light. Standing in the center of the light was a very handsome man dressed in a white suit he had jet black hair and deep blue eyes as deep as the sea. "Who are you?" she asked. "What's happening to me, and why do I see myself lying on the ground? Yet I feel so alive. Please tell me." With a voice so sweet and mellow he answered, "You're in between worlds. Someone took a shot at you they missed, but your horse got spooked, and bucked you fell off hitting your head on the bottom of that tree I believe you're in a coma." "Are you here because I'm going to die?" "No, it isn't your time to die yet. I was sent here as a messenger to help you." "Who sent you?" Your grandmother, she feels responsible for what's happening to you. She knows the decision you're faced with, of course she can't tell you what to do and neither can I. She feels if you knew her background it may help you make the right decision." "This is very strange. I don't understand?" "You will." "What's your name?" "My name is Simon, Sarah." He held his hand out to her. "Come with me." She placed her hand in his. It looked like a ray of light. He said, "We will be visiting your grandmothers past. You may very well not like what you see and hear, Sarah. You must remember you can't help her or change anything. It will be like watching a film, but standing very close to everyone as if you can touch them. I will narrate some of it and we will hear and see how she lived.

Chapter Three

Monique Marie Leblanc was born September first, 1915 to Richard and Joel Leblanc. In a small town named Three Rivers, in Canada. Her family immigrated to the United States to the city of Lowell Massachusetts when Monique was four years old and her Brother Pierre was one." Simon told her.

"I would have never guessed my grandmother came from Canada, Simon. She never spoke to me of where she came from." "Sarah most Canadians who migrated to Lowell back then settled in an area they called Little Canada where everything, and everyone was French Canadian. Church, schools, food markets, banks, and it was minutes to downtown Lowell. Many young French girls came here and worked in the spinning mills and they lived in boarding houses."

Monique's family lived in first floor cold water flat on Moody Street, next door to an all-girl Catholic School. The flat consisted of five rooms, two bedrooms, dining room, Parlor, and a commode. A black cast iron stove was used to cook and keep the flat warm. The commode was off the kitchen and held a sink and a toilet. When entering the dining room the doorway was garnished with blue beaded tassels. There was a built in China closet. Monique's papa built an oak dining room table and six matching chairs. Her mama kept the table covered with a lace tablecloth. The children were not allowed in the dining room except on holidays. The parlor was arranged for Joel's sewing. The sewing machine stood in front of the window, one fitting form, and a screen for clients to change their clothes. A small mahogany pedestal table sat between two stuffed chairs.

Joel was an excellent seamstress. It didn't take long for her reputation as a great seamstress to spread. Doctors, Lawyers, and Bankers wives and their daughters became her clients. Monique, and her brother Pierre, shared the bedroom in the back of the flat. Their mama and Papa's room was off the kitchen. On the nice days Monique, and her brother Pierre, would be sitting on the back steps waiting for their beloved Papa to come home. Their Mama would get angry with Richard, for buying the children treats. She felt he was wasting their money. Richard ignored her complaints he felt five cents a week wasn't going to break their pocketbooks. After all they both made good money. They eventually wanted to buy a house. Although Joel complained about giving her children things, she didn't deny herself anything. She gave them as little as she could get away with. She constantly criticized everything Richard did. As far as she was concerned he couldn't do anything right. The only time she was nice to him was when he was building her a piece of furniture. Then honey would drip from her lips until the project was finished. While Richard was at work Joel was cruel to the children. They ignored her cruelty knowing when their Papa came home at five everything would be fine. Monique thought Papa was the most handsome man in the whole world. He was 5 feet nine, blond hair, blue eyes and a blond mustache that tickled her when he kissed her goodnight. He took turns carrying each of his children on his broad shoulders. He always tucked them in at night and told them bedtime stories. He was a great storyteller. The children thought his stories were just wonderful. Many nights Joel screaming at Richard and criticizing him would awaken Monique. Shouting how much she hated him and the children, especially Monique because she looked just like him. On those nights, Monique would shed many tears for her beloved Papa and tried to block out the sound of her Mama by covering her head with her pillow.

Joel was a tall as Richard, and as dark as he was light. She had beautiful jet black hair that was down below her back, she wore it in a bun during the day, and at night she wore it in a pigtail after brushing it over one hundred strokes. Her figure was slim with an ample bosom; her eyes were large and as black as coal. When she looked at you she made you feel like she could see right through you. She had no love for Richard or her children.

Joel married Richard for only one reason to get away from the farm she was brought up on, in a small town in Canada. She was the oldest daughter of 12 brothers and sisters, her papa had named her his "Black Eyed Beauty." Her parents were very loving to her and her brothers and sisters. The farm provided a roof over their heads and food on the table. Everyone in the family had a chore to do. Her Mama made all their clothes. They lived modestly and Joel wanted to get as far away from them as she could get. She met Richard at a barn dance. He was staying with an uncle. When he first laid eyes on Joel, he fell in love. He thought she was the most beautiful woman he had ever seen. Her black hair was tied up with a white ribbon and she was wearing a white dress. He asked her to dance, and she accepted. They danced several dances, and then went outside for some fresh air and a stroll. She talked to Richard about her dream to live in the United States. Richard who was already in love with her, promised her if she married him he would bring her to live in the United States within five years. She agreed and they were married a month later. Richard had one sister who was married. His parents had died when he was sixteen years old from the fever. He felt his sister was well married and he could migrate to the United States when the time came.

One afternoon when Monique and her brother were sitting on the stoop waiting for her papa to come home, a policeman approached them and asked the children to see their mama. Monique stood up and brought the policeman to her mama. Pierre was following behind them. By this time Pierre was six years old and Monique was ten. The policeman informed her mama that there had been an accident where papa worked. He told her that Richard had been standing under a bundle of hardwood when the strapping broke and fell on top of him, killing him instantly. Monique and Pierre ran to their room crying hysterically. The next few days were terrible for Monique; her papa was laid out in the parlor in front of the double window with the drapes drawn, giving the room and eerie feeling. Her mama had moved all her sewing equipment into her bedroom to make room for the casket, and chairs. She also made room for friends who came to pay their last respects to Richard. At night when everyone had gone home and her mama was asleep. Monique would stand by his casket and speak to him asking, "papa please get up don't leave us we need you. Don't leave us alone with mama she doesn't love us like you do." Lying on top of his chest in the casket, she cried silently. "Oh Simon it's so sad, what's going to happen to her and her brother?" "Just keep watching Sarah." Three days later Richard had a funeral mass at Saint Jean the Baptist Church and the burial was held at Saint Joseph's Cemetery. He was loved by so many people that you would have thought it was a funeral for a dignitary so many carriages were in the funeral procession. Monique and Pierre were not allowed to go to the funeral. They stayed home alone. After the funeral when all the guests had gone home. Joel brought the children into the kitchen and made them sit down at the kitchen table to go over her new house rules. Their life was about to change drastically.

"Your papa is gone and I am left alone to care for the two of you and to tell you the truth I never wanted either one of you. But as it seems at this time I'm stuck with you. Therefore, things are going to be different around here from this moment on." Monique held Pierre's hand under the table while her mama was speaking. Both children were very frightened. Their mama's eyes looked like she was shooting daggers at them. "Now that I am left with your care I will have to scrape every penny so that we don't starve. For one thing there will certainly be no more treats. Your papa was too easy with the both of you. From now on you will be allowed a portion of meat once a week on Sunday, daily your breakfast will consist of a slice of bread in a bowl sprinkled with sugar and soaked in milk. For supper you will have a slice of bread, a banana, and a small glass of milk. Monique your ten years old and old enough to be responsible for the housework, and taking care of your brother. He will be your responsibility." "Yes mama." "When school starts up again your chores should be finished before you leave in the morning, and make sure your brother gets to school on time. When your chores are done and you have nothing else to do I want you to stay in your room. I will be sewing, and my clients will be coming for their fittings and I do not want to be disturbed. Do you understand everything I have just said to you Monique?" "Yes mama." Joel looked Pierre and said, "You stop your damn crying, before I give you something to cry about. Monique, take Pierre to your room and make him stop crying, he is giving me a headache."

"Simon I can't believe this woman. She's a monster. These children have just lost their father and she's treating them like strangers."

Monique stood up, and took Pierre by the hand. She brought him to their bedroom, and they sat on the bed they shared. "Please Pierre, don't cry." "Why doesn't mama like us?" "I don't know Pierre." "I want my papa." "Papa is gone Pierre. He's not coming back he's in heaven with Jesus and his Angels. I'll take good care of you I promise." "I hate mama." He screamed. "Hush Pierre, if she hears you she will come in and spank you." "I don't care." She held him in her arms until he fell asleep.

When the children had gone to their room Joel thought, "now that Richard is gone, if I could get rid of these two little monsters my life would be perfect. They look so much like their father; I just cannot stand the sight of them." The next day was Sunday, and mama had told them she was taking them to church. Before they left she gave them instructions on how to behave. "In church one does not speak, fidget or fall asleep. Monique you will be responsible for your brother. If either of you make a sound I will take care of you when we get home." It was a beautiful morning the sun was shining and the birds were chirping. The sidewalks were filled with people on their way to Mass. Monique and Pierre encountered Mrs. Fortin one of their neighbors who lived in a little white house down the street. Her husband had passed away three years ago. She said, "Good morning children." "Good morning Mrs. Fortin." They said in unison. "My you look so lovely in your little pink dress, Monique." "Thank you. My papa bought me this dress." "You're welcome dear. And you Pierre, you look very handsome in your blue suit." "Thank you. Papa bought me this suit too." He had a big smile on his face. Then he said, "we are going to church, Mrs. Fortin." At that moment his mama grabbed his hand yanked it and said in a prim voice "come along children. We don't want to be late for Mass," nodding her head to Mrs. Fortin. Mrs. Fortin said in a low voice, "the poor little children left in the care of the likes of her. Two blond angels with a dark and evil she devil." When they arrived at the front of the church Pierre looked at Monique with his big blue eyes and said, "Monique the stairs are Soooo………. Big." "Yes Pierre they are. Now you heard what mama said you have to be quite in church." "Yes Monique. I'll be very good I promise."

Saint Jean the Baptist was a big church. The stairs were not only long but wide. The Mass was being said on the second floor and was in Latin except for the sermon, which was said in French. Once inside and seated at their pew, Pierre looked around and was amazed at the size of the ceilings with the beautiful, color of the paintings. He wondered who could reach that high to paint. He also loved the stained glass windows depicting Jesus in different scenes on both sides of the walls. When Mass started Pierre found it difficult to sit still. He could not understand the Latin and he couldn't see with the big man sitting in front of him. When the man stood Pierre stood, when he knelt Pierre knelt He followed everything the man did. When communion started Pierre whispered to Monique, "I have to use the commode "Hush Pierre, you have to wait until we get home." The children stood up to let their mother by so that she could receive communion. When Joel returned to her pew and was kneeling in prayer with her head bowed, Pierre again whispered to Monique that he had to use the commode. At that moment Joel raised her head and Monique turning just in time to see her mama give her a look that said wait until you get home. Monique turned to Pierre, tears running down his face. She looked down and saw he had wet his pants. "Oh My God" She thought. "If she sees his pants she will do something terrible to us when we get home." When they were leaving the church Joel noticed the front or Pierre's pants. She whispered to

Monique, "You walk behind me with your brother. I don't want anyone knowing you're with me." Not saying anything Monique held Pierre's hand. They were both frightened, shaking and didn't say a word all the way home. Once inside their flat Joel took off her black hat and placed it on the table, grabbed Pierre's by his shirt collar and made him take his pants and underwear off right in the middle of the kitchen. When the pants were off she dragged him into the commode took hold of Richard's shaving strap hanging on the wall and dragged Pierre back, pulled out the kitchen chair, pushed Pierre down on his stomach and started beating him on his behind with the strap. Pierre was screaming and crying, but she kept whipping him with all her might. To Monique she looked like a mad woman. Pierre's little bottom was bleeding. Monique screamed, "Mama Stop, he's bleeding." Finally she stopped, and said, "Get up Pierre. Pick up your pants and get out of my sight." Pierre picked up his pants and ran to his room. Joel turned to Monique, "get in your room, your next." As Monique walked to her room Joel was right behind her holding the strap under her arm. Once inside the room Joel grabbed Monique by the shoulders and spun her around. "So your papa bought you this lovely dress; well I don't believe you will ever wear it again." She placed both hands inside the front of the dress and ripped it down the middle letting it fall to the floor. Then she flung her on her stomach on top of the bed and began beating her with the strap. Monique grabbed the bedspread and shoved it in her mouth so she wouldn't scream. Pierre was standing in the corner holding his pants up to his mouth, as he watched in horror Joel beating his sister. He couldn't believe she wasn't crying. Joel was out of control, screaming obscenities in French while beating her daughter. Finally she stopped and told Monique "you and your brother will have nothing to eat today. Next time I take you anywhere you will know how to behave. Stay in your room." She left slamming the door shut.

Sarah was crying "Oh my God, Simon look at the welts on her back and his bottom. I would like to scratch her eyes out. This is so unbelievable." "Sarah any time you feel it's too much for you to handle we can go back. We don't have to continue." "No Simon this happened to granny. She had to live this nightmare I should be strong enough to watch it. Although my heart breaks for both of them, I'm watching a film, but it's real, not make believe. I can't understand how a mother can be so abusive to her children. Why did God let this happen to them?" "Sarah, God has no control over what people do. He gives all human beings choices. Who knows why some people choose to be cruel? There is an old saying Sarah; what goes around comes around. One way or another we all get what we deserve."

Monique lying on her bed thought, "I know there is a God, but why is he letting this happen to us?" Then she felt a small hand on her shoulder. She turned to see Pierre lying beside her. She opened her arms to him and held him close to her; he was trembling. His face was swollen from crying. She released him. "Show me your bottom Pierre." He turned around his bottom was covered with blood and welts. "Lay on your stomach Pierre, I will get something to clean you with. She got up took her robe off the hook and slipped it on. She picked up her dress rolled it up and shoved it in her drawer. She went into the kitchen filled the basin with warm water from the kettle. Took a washcloth, and some salve, and brought it back to her room. "Pierre this may hurt a little, but I have to clean your welts and wash off the blood so it won't get infected." Gently she cleaned Pierre's bottom. All the while thinking "how could a mother do this to her children?" When she was finished, Pierre turned to her, "thank you Monique.

Now you take your robe off and lay on your tummy and I'll take care of you." "It's not necessary." "I know I'm little, but really I can clean your welts, honest I can. Now you lay down on your tummy." As Monique removed her robe, Pierre started crying again looking at all the big red welts on her back. He picked up the washcloth and gently began to wipe her back. When he was through, he spread the salve on her back. When he finished she stood up and put her nightgown on. Then she picked up the basin, Pierre's pants and brought everything back to the kitchen. She put everything back, then washed Pierre's pants and underwear and hung them on the clothesline to dry. She could hear the sewing machine humming in the parlor. "Thank God," she thought "I don't have to see mama." Back in the bedroom she laid on her side in bed holding Pierre, and they fell asleep.

When they awoke the smell of roast beef filled their room. It was five o'clock. "Monique I'm so hungry, my tummy hurts and it's smells so good." "Mama said we couldn't have anything to eat until tomorrow." Pierre started crying. "But I'm so hungry." "I'll get you a glass of water." When she went into the kitchen her mama was eating her supper. It looked and smelled so good. If her and Pierre were allowed to eat their meal they would have been having meat pie not a roast Joel looked up as Monique was walking in. "I told you no food today." "I'm just getting a drink of water, mama." "Make sure that's all you take." "Yes mama." Joel's plate was filled with roast beef, mashed potatoes, string beans and hot bread. Monique's mouth was watering. When she was walking out of the kitchen holding two glasses of water she turned to Joel and asked, "Mama, do you think you could give Pierre a slice of bread? He is so little and very hungry." "Then he will remember next time not to wet his pants. Won't he? No there is not even a crumb of bread for Pierre or you now go to your room." The following Sunday Joel didn't take them to church. Instead she locked both children in their bedroom closet. The closet was locked with a skeleton key. Both children protested the first few times begging Joel not to lock them up, they kept promising to be good. Both of them were afraid of the dark. She would tell them they were bad and needed to be locked up. This went on for several months. Some Sundays she didn't let them out of the closet until supper.

One day at school Sister Dominique approached Monique in the corridor "Monique I would like a word with you." "Yes Sister Dominique." "I would like to know why you don't attend eight o'clock Mass with the other student's on Sunday." "I'm sorry Sister but my mama will not allow me to attend Mass." "Monique you need to come to church to make your first communion. Are you eleven yet?" "Yes Sister, I am." "Then you should make your first communion this month." "Yes Sister." "I will write your mother a note telling her you have to go to Mass on Sunday and that you will be making your first communion in the spring. Please wait here while I go to my desk to write a note." "Yes Sister." Sister left. Monique was getting fidgety she had to go get her brother after school, he would be dismissed in a few minutes. She wondered what her mama would say when she gave her the note from Sister Dominique? Sister returned and handed the letter to Monique. "Please Monique; give this note to your mother." "Yes Sister." "Monique you look forlorn is there something else bothering you?" "No Sister Dominique." "Are you sure, my dear?" "Well." "What is it Monique?" "Sister could I bring my little brother Pierre to mass with me on Sunday? He is only seven years old." "Yes he can come with you, but he will have to sit on the other side with the boys in his class." "Thank you, Sister." Sister Dominique, wanted to find a way to help Monique, she seemed so lost. She asked, "Monique do you like to read?" "Yes I do sister. But except for my schoolbooks; I don't have access to any other books." "How about if I took you to the library on Saturday; you could get your own library card and you could get different books to read once a week." "Smiling Monique's said, I would love to go Sister." "Fine, Saturday I'll meet you here in front of the convent say around eleven am?" "Yes Sister, I'll meet you here Saturday. Thank you." "You're welcome dear."

After months of being locked in a closet, Monique was happy to bring Pierre to church without her mother's presence. After going to the library with Sister Dominique, Monique went to the library every Saturday. She read as much as she could and she always brought a few books home to read to Pierre. She read about art, biographies and fashions. She wanted to learn everything she could. Their diets were so poor, that both children kept getting thinner. Joel wouldn't buy them any new clothes or shoes. She would go to the Saint Vincent De Paul society at the church. Everything was given to her without cost. But the clothes she picked never fit the children properly. She didn't care what they looked like. She barely acknowledged them. The only time Joel paid attention to her children was when she beat them or took their food privileges away, which was too often.

Monique made her First Communion in a blue dress that was too big for her and all the other girls snickered behind her back when they saw her. Pierre was at the church and thought his sister looked beautiful. After the ceremony, which Joel didn't attend, Monique went home took off her dress and threw it in the garbage bin then went into her bedroom and cried Pierre, sat on the bed next to her and said, "don't cry Monique, you looked beautiful today. I'm sure Jesus thought so too. Don't worry about those girls. They were just jealous, because you're beautiful and they're not." Monique sat up, wiped her eyes and hugged Pierre. "How about I read you a story?" "Can you read the book about Tarzan?" "I sure can." She took the book off the bureau. They both sat on the bed and she read to Pierre.

That summer, Monique started doing errands for Mrs. Fortin, when her chores were done. She took Pierre with her. Mrs. Fortin would give her a dime and six large oatmeal cookies. Monique saved her dimes until she had enough to buy thread, needles and scissors, so that she could take in her clothes and Pierre's. She had picked up a book at the library on how to sew. She was tired of wearing clothes that didn't fit her. They would only eat one of the cookies Mrs. Fortin gave them and the rest would be saved in case Joel made them go without supper, which happened at least once a week.

'Christmas was spent just like any other day. The children didn't receive any gifts; except for an orange, an apple, walnuts and a candy cane that Mrs. Fortin gave them. Joel would set up a small Christmas tree in her sewing room. She placed little wrapped gifts under the tree that she gave to her steady clients for Christmas. She made excellent money especially around the holidays making gowns. Yet, she wouldn't spend a nickel on her children. Their menu was still the same even on holidays. In the winter when Pierre was eight years old, he caught a bad cold. Joel gave him a spoonful of honey twice a day. It didn't help him. He Seem to be getting worse. One night he had a high fever and he had a hard time to breathe. Monique went to wake her mama. "Mama, wake up. Pierre is very ill." Joel woke up and looked at the time on her dresser it was two am. "Monique, what are you doing waking me up at this time of the night?" "Mama, Pierre, is very ill. He can hardly breathe and he's burning up. He needs a doctor." "I also need my sleep. Give him some more honey. If he's still sick in the morning, I will call the doctor." "But mama" "You heard me Monique. Now get out of my room." Monique went to the kitchen; got a basin filled it with cold water and took a washcloth. She went back to her room and started bathing Pierre. She did this all night; changing the water often and his fever still wasn't coming down. At six am, Monique went back to her mama's room. "Mama, you will have to call the doctor. Pierre is no better." Her mother sat up in bed, "are you crazy Monique? Waking me up this way?" "I'm sorry mama, but Pierre may have something your clients can catch. That's the reason I think you should get the doctor." Her mother jumped out of her bed. "You're right Monique. I'll get dressed and go for the doctor." When Monique was leaving her mama's bedroom she thought, "Anything for her precious clients. Why didn't I think of this sooner?" Joel walked into the bedroom with the doctor following behind her. He walked over to Pierre's bed and Monique moved out of his way. The doctor lifted Pierre's nightshirt and listened to his chest. He turned to Joel, "Madame your son has pneumonia." Then he turned again to Pierre and felt his stomach. He turned again to Joel and said, "Your boy is also suffering from malnutrition and he is very weak. He will have to be placed in the hospital immediately and I'm not sure I'll be able to save him." Joel, tears streaming down her face said, "I assure you doctor my son has been well fed. If he will not eat what is placed in front of him, what is a mother to do? I can't be blamed." Monique, was listening to her mother and couldn't believe what she was hearing and seeing. Joel looked like a caring mama and so appalled at what the doctor was saying. Pierre ate everything he was given and she would never allow him more than he was allotted for his meals. No matter how much he begged for more food. This last year they had taken their supper in their bedroom when Joel was entertaining her men friends. She would cook a big meal for her and her suitor. Monique would be summoned to clean the kitchen when they were finished and she was warned not to touch the leftovers. Monique thought, "When I leave this house, I'll never eat another banana."

That morning Pierre went to the hospital and died two days later. Again the parlor was set up with a casket. Late at night, Monique would sit by the casket and cry. "He looked so innocent," she thought. Then she would speak to him. "Pierre, I wish I was laying there with you. I don't know how much more I can take. I should have died with you. I'll miss you so much. I'm sure you'll be much better off where you are now. I know you're with papa in heaven. No more beatings. No more starving and no more tears. I love you, my little brother and I will never forget you. You'll always be close to my heart." She stood up, leaned over the casket her tears spilling on Pierre; she kissed him and said "Good-bye my little love; fly free with papa and all the angels."

"My poor darling granny; my heart is breaking for her and Pierre. Simon, look at Joel, isn't she terrible? Pretending she is the caring mother crying and dabbing at her eyes when friends are in the room. What a disgusting excuse she is for a woman." "Sarah, I know your heart is heavy and your tears are flowing, do you want to continue?" "Yes Simon. I do." Pierre was buried three days later at Saint Joseph's cemetery next to his father. Mrs. Fortin had heard from a friend of hers who was a nurse at the hospital, that if Pierre would have had a proper diet he would have survived. She said the poor boy was malnourished when they brought him in. Now she was worried about Monique. She was only twelve years old and she was skin and bones. Her face was sunken making her blue eyes protrude. If she fell ill she would surely follow her brother. She felt guilty that she hadn't done something sooner to help Pierre. She didn't want to see the same thing happen to

Monique. She had to find a way to help her and she had an idea of what to do.

The second Sunday after Pierre's death, Mrs. Fortin, was coming out of church when she noticed Joel and she said, "Good morning, Mrs. Leblanc." "Good morning." She answered as she proceeded ahead. "Excuse me Mrs. Leblanc may I have a word with you?" "What the hell does the old bat want?" She thought. "I can only spare you a few moments. Mrs. Fortin. I'm very busy today." "I won't take up much of your time. I know how busy you are. I just wanted to ask if I could hire Monique to do some work for me three nights a week and Saturday. You see my Arthritis has been flaring up so much lately; I can't seem to move around much anymore. Of Course I would pay her, although I can't pay her much." "How much would you pay her Mrs. Fortin?" "I can afford one dollar per week Mrs. Leblanc." "As long as it doesn't interfere with her chores it will do. What nights do you need her for?" "Monday, Wednesday, Thursday, and of course Saturdays say around one o'clock?" "I'll tell her, she can start tomorrow." She didn't wait for a response. She turned and walked away. Mrs. Fortin smiled; she would be able to help Monique. When Joel arrived at home, she walked into her bedroom, summoned her daughter, and took off her black coat and hat. She hung her coat in her closet and placed her hat in the hat box. Walking out of her bedroom she came face to face with Monique. "Yes Mama, you called me?" "Yes I did. I saw Mrs. Fortin after church today and she wants you to work for her three nights a week and Saturdays. You will be receiving a dollar a week from her. That money is to be given to me for your board and room. You start tomorrow after school." "Yes Mama." Joel felt wonderful, "this will give me an extra four dollars a month for my savings and keep Monique away from me for a few hours." On Monday, Monique was pleased to report to Mrs. Fortin.

She loved the older woman. She had always been kind to her and Pierre. Monique loved the way her gray eyes sparkled when she smiled and her white hair was always pulled back in a bun. She was sixty three years old with a slim figure that made her look as if she was younger. "What would you like me to do Mrs. Fortin?" "Why don't you polish the furniture in the parlor? You'll find a rag and some polish under the kitchen sink, my dear." "Yes, Mrs. Fortin. It sure smells good in here." "I'm cooking roast pork. "Gee, it sure smells good." Mrs. Fortin, added potatoes and string beans in her pot and placed it back in the oven. She also made a loaf of fresh bread and an apple pie for dessert. She was delighted to have someone to cook for. Since her husband passed away, she didn't cook much except to bake cookies for Pierre and Monique.

Monique enjoyed polishing Mrs. Fortin's furniture. She found her home so cozy. In her parlor there was a green overstuffed sofa with a matching chair and an ottoman. In between the two well-dressed windows stood an upright maple radio. On one side of the radio was a gray rocker with a pedestal silver ashtray by its side. White doilies adorned the arms of the sofa and chairs. In front of the sofa was an oval cherry wood coffee table; which held a candy dish full of chocolates. While Monique was polishing the table; the chocolates were making her mouth water. She was especially careful while polishing the radio for sitting on top of it was a white clock with a little girl dressed in blue sitting on a swing. She had never seen anything like it; the little girl was swinging back and forth. When she was done polishing; she walked back into the kitchen. "Mrs. Fortin, I'm through with the polishing. What else would you like me to do?" "Please set the table for two." "Oh, are you having company?" "No dear. It's just going to be me and you." Monique looked at her strange. Mrs. Fortin showed her where the fine china dishes were in the built in china closet in the kitchen. When Monique had finished setting the table, Mrs. Fortin said, "Now my dear, please sit down and we will enjoy one of our first meals together. It is so nice to have someone to cook for." Monique sat down while Mrs. Fortin took the pan out of the oven. She arranged the roast on the serving dish then added the potatoes and string beans to it. She poured some of the gravy in the gravy bowl and set everything on the table Along with the sliced bread. Then she poured them each a cup of hot tea. At that point she took her apron off, and hung it on the hook behind the cellar door, and sat down to join Monique. Mrs. Fortin made the sign of the cross Monique followed her doing the same. With their heads bowed Mrs. Fortin said grace. "Dear Lord, Bless this food we are about to eat and thank you for sending me Monique to share it with, Amen. Now we shall eat, my dear." Mrs. Fortin stood up picked up the carving knife and fork then sliced the roast. "Now dear, hold your plate up and I'll give you a few slices of pork." Monique held her plate up and Mrs. Fortin placed two generous slices of pork on her plate After placing the meat on Monique's plate she said to her "Now, help yourself to some potatoes, string beans, hot bread and gravy" When Monique took her first bite, she savored the taste of pork and said, "Mrs. Fortin, This is Soooo good I feel like I died and went to Heaven." Mrs. Fortin observed Monique eating. She ate slowly enjoying every bite. When they finished Mrs. Fortin asked, "Would you like a piece of apple pie?" "I don't believe I have room for dessert Mrs. Fortin. I ate too much of everything else, I'm full."

Monique stood up and started to pick up her plate. "Please, dear, sit down. I'll clean up later." Monique sat back down. "Did you enjoy your meal, dear?" "Yes very much." "Good. Monique, I have to be honest with you I don't have arthritis problems. I made up the story for your mothers benefit so she would let you come over here. I also knew if I mentioned paying you she would agree. I'm so sorry I didn't think of doing this for you sooner. If I did Pierre would be alive today." Tears were flowing from her eyes. Monique also started crying. They both stood up and hugged each other for a while.

When they finally sat down, Mrs. Fortin held Monique's hand. Monique began to confide in Mrs. Fortin. "Do you know Mama acts as if Pierre was never here? She took all of his things out of our bedroom after the funeral and threw them out in the garbage bin. She didn't find his teddy Papa had bought him. I hid it so that I could have something that belonged to him. Pierre died because he didn't have enough to eat. The doctor told Mama Pierre died from malnutrition, she denied it. She still feeds me the same thing I believe she wants me to die too." "I'm not going to let it happen to you, said Mrs. Fortin. Being here four times a week you will be able to have nourishing meals. Also I'll make you a lunch for school every day; that you can pick up in the morning on your way to school. While helping you; I'll also be helping myself. You see dear, it isn't very pleasant cooking for one person and it is also very lonely." "I'm so fortunate to have you Mrs. Fortin. I haven't had a decent meal since Papa died. At least once a week we went without food and when we did eat it wasn't to much." "Oh dear Jesus that woman should be sent to prison for treating you and your brother in such a manner. I'm so sorry there isn't any other way I can help you. I would like to take you away from her, but unfortunately the law protects the likes of her and not the children." "I better get going, Mrs. Fortin. It's getting late." "Yes dear. Now you make sure you stop here on your way to school for your lunch." "I don't know how to thank you, Mrs. Fortin. You are so good to me." Everyone deserves a little kindness dear." They hugged before Monique left.

"Simon what a wonderful woman thank God Granny found such a friend." Smiling he said, "Mrs. Fortin, is an Angel." From that Monday on Mrs. Fortin kept her word. She would always put a little extra something in her lunch. Monique started gaining weight, her face filled out and the color returned to her cheeks. Every morning when she picked up her lunch, Mrs. Fortin would kiss her on the cheek and give her a hug. For the first time since her father died she felt loved. Every week Monique gave Joel the dollar. Her clothes fit her better since she gained some weight. Monique was able to mend them. She was happy that she had Mrs. Fortin in her life.

Chapter Four

Evan Taylor was riding his horse, Barron, when he came upon a horse grazing. The horse was saddled. Evan looked around for the rider and he didn't see anyone. "This horse must belong to the Haven," he thought. He took the horse's reins and said, "Come along boy. I'll take you home. Maybe we'll come across your owner on the way." He pulled on the reins behind him and Midnight Blue followed. About 2 miles up the path Evan saw a woman lying on the ground. He tied Midnight Blue's reins around his saddle and jumped off his horse. He knelt down beside Sarah picked up her wrist and felt for a pulse. He couldn't seem to find it. He placed his ear on her chest he could hear a heartbeat. "Thank God, she's alive." He picked her up and sat her on his saddle getting on behind her. He held her close to his chest with one hand. Placing both reins in his other hand and rode as fast as he could to the Haven. When Evan rode into the Haven, the groomer came running towards him and said, "My God, what happened to Miss Sarah?" "I don't know. I just found her on the ground. Take care of her horse and I'll take her to the house." "Yes sir." He handed Midnight Blue's reins to the groomer and sped away. Evan rode up to the front of the house, jumped off his horse and carried Sarah up the stairs to the front door and rang the bell. Alfred answered the door and gasped when he saw Sarah in Evans arms. "Miss Sarah, what happened? Please come right in and follow me sir." Evan followed Alfred to the living room. He set Sarah down on the couch. Alfred ran out of the room calling for Mrs. Johnson. "Mrs. Johnson, come quick Miss Sarah's been hurt." Mrs. Johnson came running out of the kitchen wiping her hands on her apron. Her daughter Maggie following behind her. When Mrs. Johnson saw Sarah lying on the couch with no life in her she cried. "What happened to her, Is she alive?" "Yes." Evan answered just barely. "She needs to go to the hospital." Mrs. Johnson turned to her daughter, "please Maggie, call 911 and tell them to hurry." "Yes mother." Maggie went right to the living room phone to make the call. After the call, Maggie went to her mother and said, "Mom the ambulance is on its way and I also called Dr. Burns. He will meet you at Saint John's Hospital." While they were waiting for the ambulance, Evan introduced himself. "Mrs. Johnson, my name is Evan Taylor. I live in the house that abuts this property." "Pleased to meet you, Mr. Taylor, this is my daughter, Maggie." "Hello Maggie." "Hello Mr. Taylor." "And this is the butler Alfred." "Please to meet you also Alfred." "It's a pleasure to meet you also sir." "Do you know what happened to Sarah, Mr. Taylor?" "No I don't, Mrs. Johnson. I was riding my horse when I came upon her horse grazing. I figured he belonged here and I was on my way to return him, about two miles later I found Sarah lying on the ground unconscious. It looked to me like she had fallen off her horse and hit her head on the tree." "She is such a good rider. I don't understand how she could fall off her horse?" As they were speaking the ambulance arrived. Alfred led the two attendants carrying the stretcher into the living room. They gently laid Sarah up on the stretcher and covered her with a blanket before leaving for the hospital. Mrs. Johnson spoke to her daughter, "Maggie, please finish up in the kitchen while I'm at the hospital. "Yes mother". Evan suddenly spoke up saying "I'd like to go with you Mrs. Johnson if you don't mind." Not at all, I would appreciate the company Mr. Taylor."

When they arrived at the hospital, Doctor Burns was waiting for them at the entrance of the emergency room. When Mrs. Johnson entered Doctor Burns asked "Do you know what happened to Sarah?" Mrs. Johnson replied "as far as I know doctor she fell off of her horse and banged her head on a tree." "Please take a seat in the waiting room, while I examine her. Doctor Burns turned and walked away. Mrs. Johnson and Evan went into the waiting room. Mrs. Johnson sat on the couch and Evan picked up a magazine. "Would you like a magazine Mrs. Johnson, we could be here a while?" "No thank you Mr. Taylor." "Please call me Evan, Mrs. Johnson." "Thank you Evan." Evan took a magazine and sat in a chair opposite of her.

Two hours later Doctor Burns walked into the waiting room. Mrs. Johnson and Evan stood up. Mrs. Johnson spoke first. Doctor Burns I'd like you to meet Evan Taylor; he is the one who found Sarah. Both men shook hands. "Pleased to meet you Evan, may I call you Evan?" "Yes please do Doctor.""Thank God you found Sarah. Mrs. Johnson clearly upset asked "How is she Doctor Burns?" "She's in a coma, Mrs. Johnson." "How long will she be in a coma?" Mrs. Johnson asked. "It's difficult to say; as we speak, Sarah is being moved to a private room. She'll be given an intravenous to keep up her strength, and I instructed the nurses to periodically massage her arms and legs. It's all I can do for now. I didn't find any other damage. Saying a few prayers wouldn't hurt either." "You can go see her in a few minutes once they've settled her in her room, she'll be in room 409." "Thank you Doctor." "You're welcome Mrs. Johnson. I'll keep you informed." He turned and walked away.

Evan and Mrs. Johnson took the elevator to the fourth floor. When they walked up to Sarah's room a nurse was coming out. "Can we go in now, asked Mrs. Johnson." "Sure, go on in." she replied. They both walked to her bed. "She looks like she's just sleeping doesn't she, Evan?" "Yes, she does." Evan felt something stir inside of him the same feeling he got when he first saw her lying on the ground. He ignored it at the time. But now he couldn't ignore his feelings; it was as if he knew this woman all his life. He had to make sure she got better. He would try to be by her side every day until she came out of her coma. "How strange," he thought. Looking at Mrs. Johnson, he asked "are you almost ready to leave?" "Yes." "Then I'll call my chauffeur to pick us up." He took his cell phone out of his pocket and made the call.

After he took Mrs. Johnson home, he sent his chauffeur home explaining he would ride his horse back home. Jimmy the groomer had taken Evan's horse back to the stable and rubbed him down. Evan thanked him, climbed on his horse and rode off. As he was riding his thoughts were, "what would have spooked her horse so badly that she would have been thrown off him?" He rode back to where he had found Sarah, jumped off his horse and started looking around. He thought, "Something scared the horse, but what? Maybe a snake, but it would be long gone by now." He walked around the tree, and examined the tree with his hands, "Nothing here." Then he looked up at the front of the tree. He thought he saw something shiny "it could be the sun shining making it appear like something was there." He wasn't tall enough to reach it. He brought his horse up against the tree, he climbed on his back, standing up on his saddle he said, "Easy Barron, don't move boy." He raised his hand and felt the spot he had seen shining, it felt like a bullet. He reached in his front jean pocket and took out a small pocket knife opened it with his teeth and jimmied the bullet loose letting it fall into his hand. Sitting down on his saddle, holding the bullet in the center of his hand, he asked himself "Who would want to kill Sarah and why?" Then he rode home.

One day when Monique came home from school she heard the sound of a piano playing coming from the parlor. She went in to see where it was coming from. She saw Joel sitting at the piano and playing it. The music she was playing was beautiful. "Mama," she exclaimed, "I didn't know you could play the piano! And where did it come from?" The upright piano replaced the two chairs and the table. "Norman Saint John bought it for me, and yes I play very well I might add. If I hear a piece of music, I can play it. I play by ear. When I was a young girl we had an old piano and I played it every night after dinner." "Could I try to play Mama?" "No you cannot, don't you dare touch my piano. Do you understand?" "Yes mama." At least she thought "I can enjoy listening to the music from my room."

Norman had asked Joel to be his wife. He had a charming home on Andover Street in an exclusive area of Lowell Massachusetts. He was thirty-nine years old. He was a widower; he and his wife never had children. Norman was the president of a Mill Street bank and a very wealthy man. He stood five feet nine, dark brown eyes and brown hair. He wore his hair slicked back and he also wore goatee. Joel had made Monique sound like a monster with all the stories she made up about her daughter. When Norman proposed to Joel he had two stipulations. One was that she would no longer sew for anyone else but herself. The other was he did not want Monique living with them. Joel agreed with his stipulation and told him she needed one year to take care of everything. Her thinking was next year Monique will be fourteen and graduating from grammar school. She'd find her a husband and her and Norman would be married.

One Friday night while Joel was out with Norman it seemed to Monique like the piano was calling out to her. She walked to the parlor and sat on the piano bench feeling the piano cover with her hands. "I wonder if I have mama's gift for playing the piano?" she thought to herself. Then thought "Mama is out for the evening she'll never know." Monique opened the cover placed her fingers on the keys, her foot on the pedal and started humming a tune she had heard her mother play. Her fingers started playing to her surprise she was playing as well as her mama. Then she hummed another popular tune and played it. She lost track of time because she was so consumed by the music. She didn't hear Joel come home or enter the parlor. Joel walked over to the piano slamming the cover on Monique's hands. Monique jumped back and screamed "Mama why did you close the cover on my hands I wasn't hurting anything?" As she rubbed her hands together crying because the pain was excruciating Joel grabbed Monique by her braids pulled her off the piano and shoved her to the floor. Screaming she said "I told you not to touch my piano, now go to your room and get out of my sight!" Monique's hands were swollen she thought "Thank God it's Friday and I don't have to go back to school until Monday." Saturday morning when Mrs. Fortin saw Monique's hands she was horrified "What happened to your hands?" "Mama slammed the piano cover on my hands. I deserved it, she told me never to touch her piano." "My God Monique, no one deserves to be punished in such a manner. It doesn't matter if she warned you against touching her piano. Your mother had no right to hurt you for heaven's sake. Sit down dear. I'll get a basin of water to soak your hands than I'll rub your hands with ointment." As Mrs. Fortin was preparing the basin she thought

"Joel is such a monster, she should be horse whipped and I would like to be the one to do the honors." She brought the basin over to Monique letting her soak her hands. When she was done soaking them she rubbed her hands with ointment. Monique smiled at Mrs. Fortin and said "Thank you so much for taking care of my hands. I don't know what I would do if it weren't for you."

Monique was washing the dishes when the ice man walked into the kitchen with the weekly ice delivery for the ice box. Joel was also in the kitchen. She noticed he was taking much longer than usual. He was staring at Monique he couldn't seem to take his eyes off of her. Joel decided he was the man Monique was going to marry. She knew he wasn't married.

.It was the first week of June and Monique would be graduating from grammar school in two weeks. Monique was sitting on her bed reading a book when Joel walked into her room "Put the book down I want to speak to you." "Yes mama." Monique you will be graduating in two weeks and I will not be attending." "Yes mama." "I will however be attending your wedding the following week." "I am not getting married mama." Oh but you are my dear." Joel said with a satisfied look on her face. "You see I've found you a husband he is twenty-five years older than you and he is also very smitten with you." "I don't want to be married mama I'm only fourteen years old and besides I don't even know the man." "Oh but you have seen him often. Joel responded. However, I will keep his name a secret until your wedding day." "A Justice of the Peace will marry you in New Hampshire. No bands have to be posted and no blood tests are needed. All I have to do is sign a consent form, because you are under age. I will be getting married to Norman at a Catholic church in August. We are planning a big wedding and reception. I certainly do not need any excess baggage and you my dear are excess baggage." I am leaving my old life behind and starting a new one." With tears flowing Monique begged "Mama please don't make me do this. Why not let me go away you never have to see me again I won't come back here, I promise." You are too young I can't take that chance." Monique stopped crying and started to shake, "You can't take that chance?" and she repeated it again "You can't take that chance?" "What kind of woman are you? You are unbelievable, you would rather marry me off to someone I don't even know. I am only fourteen years old for Gods sakes!" she shouted at her mother. Joel gave Monique a warning look and said "One word of this arrangement to Mrs. Fortin and I will cut your tongue out and you will go to your new husband mute. You know I will do it!" I wouldn't put anything past you Joel, you don't deserved to be called mama. I hate you with a passion and I will never forgive you for the way you treated papa. Because of you Pierre starved to death. I hope you rot in hell!" Joel slapped Monique across the face and walked out of the room. Monique didn't feel the sting she lay across her bed and cried herself to sleep.

Mrs. Fortin was the only one who attended Monique's graduation on Sunday afternoon. Monique graduated top in her class. She was given awards for Mathematics, Spelling, French, and English. Mrs. Fortin was so proud of her. After the graduation she gave Monique a big hug. Then Monique went home as Joel had instructed her to do. Joel never spoke to her daughter the entire day. It was as if nothing had happened. Monique spent the rest of the day in her room reading a book.

Monday when Monique arrived at Mrs. Fortin's on the hutch displayed a cut strip from a white sheet in hand painted letters in blue that said **"CONGRATULATIONS MONIQUE."** The table was set with a lace tablecloth, her best

China and in the center a beautifully decorated cake. Monique's face lit up with a smile. "Oh! Mrs. Fortin everything looks so beautiful. How can I ever thank you." "We are celebrating your graduation with a feast." Mrs. Fortin picked up the cake and placed it on the coffee table in the parlor. Then she brought the platter of roast duck and placed it on the kitchen table.

Monique brought out the mashed potatoes, hot bread and salad.

Mrs. Fortin filled two champagne glasses with sherry. Monique sat down and Mrs. Fortin took her apron off and placed it on the hook.

She took her seat next to Monique. Picking up her glass of sherry she said, "Pick your glass up, dear. For this special occasion you will have a glass of Sherry." Monique picked up her glass and said, "I've never had Sherry." "There is always a first time my dear. Now hold it up like this." Mrs. Fortin lifted her arm up. "I will make a toast. Mrs. Fortin smiled and said, to my beautiful Monique, who I cherish and love very much, may your future be filled with happiness." They touched glasses and took a sip of sherry. Placed their glasses down and filled their plates. Monique had never tasted anything as succulent as the duck. When dinner was finished Monique took both their plates to the sink. Mrs. Fortin went into her bedroom and came back holding a beautifully wrapped small gift and handed it to Monique. Smiling she said, "A little gift for you, my dear." They both sat down at the table. Monique began opened her gift. Under the wrapper was a little box and she lifted the cover. A little black pouch lay there; she picked it up and untied the gold strings, pouring the contents into the palm of her hand, a gold chain with a diamond heart shape pendent. "It's so beautiful," she exclaimed. She held it in her fingers. "I can't accept this Mrs. Fortin." "Of course you can my dear. This pendant belonged to my mother. You are the only one that comes close to being like a daughter to me." Smiling she said, let's not forget you graduated with honors. With all your troubles at home, you never let your schoolwork suffer. I believe you deserve something special for your efforts. I love you Monique, as if you were my own daughter. These last two years have been wonderful for me, I will always treasure the time we spent together. Look inside the box my dear." Monique, picked up the box, and lying inside the box was a crisp fifty dollar bill. She gasped. "Please dear don't say anything, hide the money. Someday you may need it. Do you have someplace you can hide your treasures?" "Yes, papa made me a cherry wood music box, and gave it to me the Christmas before he died. It has a secret compartment. I can place my pendant, and the money inside. Mama doesn't even know the compartment exists." "Thank goodness," Mrs. Fortin said. "I will put the box with its contents in my pocket when I leave. I want you to know Mrs. Fortin that I love you very much and I appreciate everything you've done for me. Where ever I am I will try to write and let you know how I'm doing." "Are you going somewhere, Monique?" "Please Mrs. Fortin, I can't say any more. Let's just enjoy the time we have together." "Will you be coming over again this week?" "Oh yes, I'll be here."

Sarah, felt for the chain around her neck holding the diamond pendant in her fingers. Granny had given it to her along with the cherry wood music box, a few months before she died. Sarah, had worn it ever since. She knew she had to continue viewing granny's life with Simon, but my god, it was so heart breaking watching her beautiful granny as a child being physically and mentally abused, by her great grandmother.

"Sarah." "Yes Simon." "Are you ready to continue?" "Yes I am."

The last Thursday with Mrs. Fortin was very difficult for Monique. When she said goodbye to her she held her for a long time she couldn't seem to let her go. When they finally parted Mrs. Fortin had a feeling this was the last time she would see her. During the time she had been going to Mrs. Fortin the money Mrs. Fortin was paying her she would give to her mother however Mrs. Fortin also gave Monique twenty-five cents for herself. Except for buying thread, she saved the rest of the money. With the money she had saved she went to the store and bought writing paper, envelopes, pencils, a quill pen and ink. Then she went to the post office to buy a supply of stamps to take with her. Monique went home took the small valise Joel had given her. Placed it on her bed and opened it. She went to the closet and brought her music box down, opened the secret compartment to check on her money and her pendant. Closed it and placed everything she had bought including the stamps in the box. She placed the box in the valise along with her awards, a few clothes, personal items, and Pierre's teddy bear. She closed the valise, and set it by the door. Joel had been given a yellow dress with matching shoes by one of her clients. She placed them in Monique's closet to be worn on her wedding day. When Monique saw the dress she thought it was lovely. At another time she would have been happy to wear such a dress, but now she could only cringe.

Saturday morning, Joel was singing in the kitchen when Monique walked in. Joel said, "Isn't it a beautiful day for a wedding?" as she smiled at her daughter. "Would you like some bacon and eggs for breakfast Monique?" "After all these years of bread and milk for breakfast you are offering me bacon and eggs?" She looked at Joel with disgust. Still smiling, Joel said, "just think of it as your last meal as a single woman." "You disgust me Joel I'd rather starve." Taking a bite of a slice of bacon she said, "suit yourself I would suggest you get dressed we will be leaving shortly." Without a word Monique turned around and went to her bedroom to dress. She dressed as if she was in a trance she could not believe what was about to happen to her.

Norman had sent his carriage for them. Monique sat across from Joel and did not pay attention to where she was going until the carriage came to a stop at a small white house with a white and black sign in front that read JUSTICE OF THE PEACE. Joel had taken care of the marriage license earlier in the week. The driver opened the carriage door, Monique hesitated, but Joel pushed her out of the carriage and the driver caught her; saving Monique from falling face down on the ground. The driver thought, "How beautiful this young girl looks in her pale yellow dress, her long blond hair in a braid down her back. Why was she getting married so young? She can't be more than thirteen or fourteen years old." Monique looked at the driver "thank you for not letting me fall." "You're welcome Miss." When they stepped inside the makeshift chapel Monique gasped and her hand went to her mouth when she saw that the groom was the iceman. "It can't be?" She thought. Just then she looked up and he smiled at her. "Oh my god" she's marrying me off to of the iceman David Larose?" He walked over and handed Monique a bouquet of daisies. "Thank you," she said softly. He then walked over and stood by the small bald man with eye glasses who was The Justice of the Peace. He wore a black suit, white shirt, blue tie and he was holding a little black book. David was a big heavy man with a potbelly. He had devious looking gray eyes. He snuffed tobacco and he had a big red nose. His head was bald on the top with long straggling thin black hair. One of his front teeth was missing. He wore a pair of black pants held up by suspenders with a white shirt and a tan tie. Monique thought, "He looks disgusting. How can she do this to me?" The man who was doing the ceremony signaled to Monique to step forward. She froze and couldn't move. Joel grabbed her upper arm and pinched her as hard as she could to get her to move. Monique went forward. Monique was oblivious throughout the ceremony, until the man pronounced them Husband and wife. He told David he could kiss his bride. David placed his big callous hands on both sides of her face and placed a wet kiss on her lips. It was all she could do not too vomit. Then he caught her arm and walked her outside.

 The driver handed David Monique's valise. Holding the valise in one hand and Monique's arm with the other hand he headed for the wagon that would take them home. He helped Monique up onto the wagon and placed her valise in the back of the wagon. Monique looked back. Joel was smiling. Monique gave her a sharp look, turned around and promised herself she would never forgive her.

 The New Hampshire scenery was beautiful with all the trees and flowers in full bloom. A tremendous cascade of colors was there to greet you, but Monique saw none of it. She was to frighten thinking about what was ahead of her to see anything else. When they were almost at their destination David said," we are going to be living with my mother and my sister. My mother has a big house on Hall Street in Lowell, Massachusetts. I give her my wages and she takes good care of me. Now she will have to take care of you, too. But you have to do what she tells you to do and everything will be fine." Then he said, "Monique, I can't wait to get you in my bed tonight." "Why?" She asked. "It is my right as your husband to take you whenever I feel like it especially on our wedding night. He turned to her and gave her a big toothless grin. Monique could tell that this man was a little dimwitted and she was petrified of the night that lay ahead. She wasn't educated when it came too men and women together. She didn't even know what a woman's monthly menstruation was. She hadn't started yet.

When they arrived at the white Colonial house David's mother was sitting in her wooden rocking chair on the front porch. She stood up as the ice wagon came to a stop. She was a huge woman who weighed three hundred pounds with a big round blotchy face, straight short gray hair and gray eyes like her son. David, with a big smile on his face, jumped off the wagon walked around to fetch the valise and went to help Monique out of the wagon. He held her by the elbow walking up the stairs. Facing his mother on the porch he said, "Mama I want you to meet my wife Monique." She scrutinized Monique from head to toe. David continued "Monique this is Mama Larose." Clearing her throat she said, I'm pleased to meet you Mrs. Larose." "Monique is it?" "Yes. Mrs. Larose." "You will call me mama Larose, is that clear?" "Yes. Mama Larose." "David, bring her to your room and let her unpack. When she is finished bring her down into the kitchen, so that I can go over the house rules with her." "Yes Mama."

The staircase that led through the five upstairs bedrooms was dark wood. David's' bedroom was the second one on the left. He pointed to the next room and said, "That's my sister Connie's room next to our bedroom." He opened the door to his bedroom and Monique stepped in. The room was large with wide pine wood floors with scattered rugs adorning the floor. A large cast iron bed decorated a multi collared quilted spread, a small bureau with a mirror next to the bed. Next to the bureau was a straight back wooden chair. There were two small wooden tables on each side of the bed with doilies and two oil lamps. A large walk-in closet held David's clothes on one side. He placed her valise on the bed. "Monique, you can unpack and I'll sit here and watch you. I left the two first draws in the bureau for your things." He sat on a chair with his arms folded and a smile on his face. Monique opened her valise took out a few dresses she had brought with her hung them up in the closet, along with her winter coat and a couple pairs of shoes. She set the shoes on the closet floor. She opened the first draw and placed her underwear, slip, nightgown and a few pairs of stockings. In the second drawer she placed her comb, brush and her sewing kit. She left her music box and the teddy in the valise closed it and placed it in the back of the closet. "You don't have much, do you Monique?" "No David. I don't." "Oh well that will have to do. Let's go downstairs to see my Mama." Monique followed him down the stairs to the kitchen. Mama Larose was sitting in a large maple rocking chair knitting a blue and white afghan. She motioned for them to sit down at the kitchen table. Monique had never seen such a large kitchen. The maple table was 8 feet long with eight matching chairs. A black coal stove with two ovens, a large built in China closet filled one wall. Their icebox was three times bigger than the one Monique had in her house. The pantry held a black cast iron sink, five white wood cabinets from the ceiling to the large counter, and a back door leading to a large porch. "My daughter Connie is a weaver at the mills down the street. She should be home shortly. I want her to be here when I speak to you." Monique was light headed she hadn't eaten since the night before. She turned to David, and said, "I'm hungry and thirsty David, do you suppose I could have something to eat and drink?" He looked at his mother, "Mama, can I give Monique a cup of tea and a slice of bread and butter?" "Yes David you may give her tea and only one slice of bread." While Monique, was eating; Connie came into the kitchen "Hello mama Larose, and

David." She looked at Monique and said, "Hello." David quickly said, "Connie, this is my wife Monique."

"Hello Monique." "Hello Connie." Connie was 18 years old, tall, slim, dark brown hair worn in a bun and brown eyes that were sunken in, her face was pretty but drawn. Once Connie was seated, Mama Larose began to speak, "Now that David got himself a wife, it means we have one more mouth to feed and more work to do in this house. Monique, to help support yourself, Connie will get you a job at the mill and David will sign a consent form because being fourteen years old you're under age. At the end of the week when you receive your paycheck, you will cash it and hand it over to me along with your pay stub. You and Connie will be responsible for all the cleaning in this house. Also the washing and ironing. I do all of the cooking and both of you will clean up after supper. Do you understand Monique? "Yes mama Larose." Monique thought to herself "are all French mothers mean and rotten?" Connie was thinking, "Monique is so pretty and young. How is she going to handle living in this crazy house with a husband that is simple and a mother in-law who's a tyrant?"

When supper was finished and the dishes were done. David took Monique by the hand and said, "Time to go to bed, my sweet."David led her up the stairs to their bedroom. She was so frightened she was shaking. Monique went to the bureau and took the nightgown out of her drawer and laid it on the bed. Picking up the nightgown and tossing it on the chair. David said, "you are not going to need that thing tonight Monique." "What do you mean, David?" "This is our wedding night, you little fool. Take your clothes off." Monique took off her dress. He sat on the bed gaping at her. Then she took off her slip hanging them in the closet. She didn't want to turn around. Joel had never bought her a bra. All she had on was her panties. She hid her breast by crossing her arms in front of them. He got off of the bed, grabbed her arms and turned her around. Pushing her arms down He took both breasts in his hands and began sucking on one and then the other. Monique was mortified. Thinking "what is this pig doing?" Sliding her panties off he said, "You taste so good." He laid her on the bed. Monique was more frightened then she had ever been in her life. She was thinking "this animal is touching me everywhere on my body and there is nothing I can do to stop him. I hate you Joel, for putting me in this situation." David quickly undressed himself tossing his clothes on the floor. His belly was hanging out; He had a large erection he couldn't wait to shove it inside of her. He held his penis in his hand and said, "Monique look at what I have for you," as he joined her in bed. He started fondling her breast and belly. He spread her legs and climbed on top of her. She was having a hard time breathing he was so heavy for her small frame. He shoved his penis in her, never giving it a thought that she was a virgin. Monique screamed. The pain was excruciating. David covered her mouth with his hand to muffle the sound and continue until he was satisfied and came inside of her. He rolled off of her to his side of the bed and fell asleep. Crying, Monique got up grabbed her nightgown and went out into the hall into the commode to wash herself. She found a washcloth and a towel. When she started cleaning herself she noticed she was full of blood and that made her feel so dirty. When she was through she took the towel back to the bedroom and placed it on her side of the bed. She laid on the bed in a fetal position, shaken and bruised. She cried herself to sleep. She would never forget this night.

Chapter Five

On Monday David signed Monique's working papers giving his permission for her to work. Routine set in, Monique worked from seven am until three thirty in the afternoon with Connie. At night they would scrub the floors, wash and iron clothes and make sure the kitchen was clean. For the two of them their work day didn't end until late evening. Mama Larose was the only one allowed to cook and serve the food. Small portions were given to Monique and Connie however Mama and David's plates were filled to the brim. They were the only ones to get seconds. David took his mother grocery shopping once a month in the ice wagon. When she wasn't cooking she sat in the kitchen on her rocking chair knitting with a small table by her chair with bowls full of goodies she snacked throughout the day and night. She was the first one up in the morning and the last one to go to bed. Going to bed was the worst time for Monique especially when David came home from the bar drunk. He would make her take his penis in her mouth, when he was finished with her she would go to the commode and vomit. She swore that if he ever died she would never marry again. Although it didn't hurt her anymore when they had sex, she felt nothing but disgust for him.

Monique had gotten thin again from over work and poor nutrition. She and Connie had developed a good friendship walking back and forth to work together and sharing all of the household duties. Connie had confided in Monique telling her how her mother had always mistreated her. She didn't remember her father; he had died when she was three years old. She also told her of another brother she had his name was Albert; he was married five years earlier. The marriage was arranged and his wife Annette was 15 years old when they wed and he was also a tyrant to her. Albert, didn't allow his wife out of the house. If someone knocked on the door and he wasn't home she wasn't allowed to answer the door. They had three small children. The only time Connie had any contact with her sister in-law was when she and her mother delivered her babies.

Monique had been married two years when every morning she would wake up and vomit. After the fifth day she went to her mother in-law, "Mama Larose there is something wrong with me I can't keep anything down, I'm always vomiting." "How long as this been going on?" "Two weeks." "Well I'd say you are going to have a baby. It will probably be born sometime in May." "I'm having a baby, really?" She placed both of her hands on her stomach," I can't believe I'm having a baby. Mama Larose, how will the baby come out?" Mama Larose started laughing. She was laughing so loud her belly was shaking and she could hardly speak, "it will come out the same way it was made." Monique was stunned, "it can't be," she thought. Monique didn't understand mama Larose's answer she thought to herself "How is that possible?" If she had the time she could go to the library and look for a book on the subject, but she wasn't allowed to go anywhere but work. After her fit of laughter, mama Larose finally spoke, "eat a few soda crackers in the morning with plain tea and it will stop the vomiting." "Thank you." Monique took her advice and the vomiting stopped. When she told David she was having a baby, his comment was, "it better be a boy." Then he walked away.

The next day on their way to work, Monique asked Connie where babies came from. Connie explained everything to her and she was petrified. She couldn't imagine a baby coming out of her private. Monique continued to work until two weeks before she delivered. When she could no longer perform her wifely duties, David took to going to the bar every night. He would come home so drunk, he would fall on the bed fully dressed and in a short time he started snoring. Monique didn't care she was so happy not to have him touch her.

Now that she was no longer working Mama Larose, gave her much smaller portions of food and she still kept up her cleaning duties. One day while she was on her knees scrubbing the kitchen floor her water broke, when she stood up her underpants were soaked. She was scared. She screamed, "Mama Larose!"

Mama Larose came wobbling in and said, "what in tarnation is wrong with you girl?" "Water came gushing out of me while I was scrubbing the floor." "That means the baby is almost ready to be born. Now wipe up that mess, then get yourself undressed and into your bed and don't wear your nightgown. I will be up shortly." "Yes Mama Larose." Monique, cleaned up the mess, emptied the bucket and put it away. Then she went up to her bedroom, undressed and got into bed. A short while later the pains started coming they were excruciating. She held onto the bed rails to stop from screaming. When the pain subsided, she would wipe the perspiration off her face with the back of her hand. Finally mama Larose came into the bedroom she pulled the sheet off Monique and spreads her legs to see how close she was to delivering the baby she said, "The baby isn't quite ready yet. I'll be back to check you in a while." "Please don't leave me alone mama Larose, I'm so scared." "Babies are born every day Monique, you will survive." She turned and walked out of the room.

When Connie came home and her mother told her Monique was in labor, she ran upstairs to be by Monique's side. When Monique saw Connie she gasped, "Please help me Connie, it hurts so much and I'm so afraid." Connie went over to her and held her hand. She noticed she was drenched with perspiration. She let go of her hand and said, "I'll be right back." "Where are you going?" "I'm going to get a basin of water and a cloth to wipe you down." She returned promptly. She placed the basin on the night stand and began sponging Monique's face and arms. When a contraction came, Connie would hold her hand. When the pain stopped she continued to sponge her down. Mama Larose came in to check on her again. "It's time," she yelled. She then turned to Connie and said "Connie go downstairs, boil some water and bring me some rags." "Yes Mama Larose." She ran downstairs and did what she was told. The contractions were getting to be just a few minutes apart. Connie came in and placed everything her mother asked for on the dresser. She then went to Monique. Mama Larose yelled "Connie raise her up." She lifted the pillows and raised Monique up so that she was in a sitting position. Mama Larose spread her legs and tied each foot to the bedpost. "Monique push that's it push. Push some more." She ordered. Monique felt that she was going to die from the pain. Finally the baby's head was out and the rest followed. Mama Larose cut the cord, held the baby upside down by the feet and said, "it's a girl," slapped her bottom and the baby began to wail. She handed the baby to Connie, "clean her up and then give her to her mother. After your done clean this mess up too." "Yes Mama Larose." She took the baby from her and then her mother turned and left the room. "Is she pretty Connie?" "Oh yes. She is beautiful. She looks just like you."

Connie cleaned up the baby then gave her to her mother. "Connie, she is so tiny and delicate." "What are you going to name her, Monique?" "I will name her Isabelle Marie Larose. Isabelle was my Papa's mother's name." "It's a beautiful name."

When David came home, he went up to the bedroom. Monique showed him their daughter and he looked at her with very little interest. Then he asked her, "When can you start being my wife again?" "Not for a few months." "I'll move into the spare bedroom until you're ready." I do not want to be awakened by a screaming baby in the middle of the night." He turned and left the room.

Isabelle was hungry. Monique placed her breast in the baby's mouth and she suckled hungrily. "How beautiful you are my little Isabelle. I will always be good to you. No one will ever hurt you." Connie brought in a tray and set it on the night stand. Monique was starving after her ordeal. It was eight PM and she hadn't eaten since a toast and tea for breakfast. She looked down at the tray; there was a bowl of broth, a slice of bread and a cup of tea. She looked up at Connie, "I'm sorry Monique," she said, "this is all she would allow me to bring to you. Now that you have to stay in bed and can't do any work." Monique started crying, "I won't be able to get stronger if this is all I'm allowed to eat. Are all French mothers such bitches, Connie?" "My mother is, but I don't know too many so I don't know. I wish I could sneak you up some extra food Monique, but you know how she is. She stays up until we are all in bed and she's the first one to get up in the morning." With tears in her eyes she turned, and left the room. Every day for the time she was in bed her diet was the same. Mama Larose had given her some of Connie's baby clothes, blankets and a basket for the baby to sleep in. Isabelle was a good baby, hardly cried, but to Monique she didn't seem to be gaining any weight.

After one week Monique, started doing her chores so that she could have more food to eat. She would carry the baby around with her in her basket while she washed, ironed and scrubbed the floors. All the floors had to be scrubbed once a week. Mama Larose increased her food portions very little because she wasn't working. She asked David to speak to his mother about increasing her food portions. He wouldn't ask her.

The baby was three months old and she woke up for her late feeding. When Monique had finished feeding her she laid her back in her basket. Isabelle seemed listless. Monique was worried about her. Later that night when she checked Isabelle she didn't seem to be breathing. She picked her up and she felt stiff. Monique started screaming. Her Isabelle was dead. Everyone came rushing. Mama Larose asked, "What is going on here? Why are you screaming?" "My baby is dead. She's dead." She was hysterical. Mama Larose turned to David, "go get the doctor." "Yes Mama." When the doctor arrived, Monique was cradling the baby in her arms. The doctor walked over to her "please let me examine your baby." She handed Isabelle over to the doctor. He placed the baby on the bed and lifted her nightgown. When he was finished his examination, he turned to Monique and said, your baby's death was caused from malnutrition." Monique stared at him and screamed. "NO! Just like my brother Pierre." "What were you feeding her?" he asked. "I was breast feeding her." "Evidently you haven't been eating properly?" To him she seemed like she hadn't had a decent meal in months. "I'll send the undertaker over here shortly," he was saying has he wrapped the baby back up. Monique leaned on the bed and picked up her daughter. The doctor left shaking his head and thinking, "that poor young woman she looks no older than 14 years old, so thin and. drawn out. How did she end up with the likes of them?" Monique cradled her baby in her arms saying, "My poor little Isabelle only three months old and you never had a fighting chance."

She held her baby until the undertaker arrived. He gently removed the baby from her mother's arms. He then asked "Where will you be having the wake and where will the baby be buried?" Mama Larose spoke up before Monique had a chance to say anything. "There will not be a wake and the baby will be buried in Potter's Field. We are penniless." "What is Potter's Field?" Monique asked. "It's where they bury people who have no money." The undertaker answered wrapping the baby in the blanket he brought, he took her and left. When the undertaker was gone Connie asked, "Mama Larose, don't you own several plots at Saint Joseph's Cemetery?" "Yes. But I'm not about to let Monique's baby be buried there." "Why?" She is your granddaughter for God's sakes" "I'm not discussing this matter with you Connie. Now get back to your room." July twelfth nineteen hundred and Forty four Isabelle was buried in Potter's Field without a marker. The only ones present were the gravedigger, the undertaker Monique and Connie. Monique hated mama Larose and David as much has she hated Joel.

Simon had his arm around Sarah comforting her. She couldn't stop crying. "Simon, it's beyond my understanding how these people can get away with being so cruel to another human being and a granddaughter. I'm so angry I'd like to hurt them like they're hurting her." "Are you strong enough to continue Sarah? Would you rather go back?" "No Simon. I can continue. I want to see everything."

Monique had written to Mrs. Fortin every month since she had been married, except the last month of her pregnancy never giving her a forwarding address. When she went back to work she continued to write to Mrs. Fortin. She let her know what had happened to Isabelle. The only time she dared to mail a letter was when she was working. The night after Isabelle was buried; David came back to their bedroom. She looked at him with disgust and said "if you think you are going to sleep with me and get me pregnant again? I don't think so. To have another baby with you, so that baby can die too, because that bitch of a mother of yours practically starved me to death and you did nothing to stop her. Oh no. I will go back to work at the Mill, give your mother my pay and do my chores. But I will not sleep with you David. Do you understand me? If you ever touch me again I will kill you. Now get out of my room." The look in her eyes told him he'd better stay away. He left her room and never returned.

Monique went back to work at the mill the following Monday. She decided to tell her mother in-law she had to take a two dollar pay cut per week. The reason being, her past job had been filled when she left and now she had to take a job that didn't pay as much. Mama Larose didn't ask her any questions. Every payday when Monique received her paycheck, she would cash it at the pay window located at the Mill. After she cashed her check she went into the ladies room, went in one of the stalls and fixed her pay stub. The pay stub with the amount, hours and how much she made was written in pencil. She erased her stub and filled it in with the new numbers minus two dollars. She put her at two dollars in her pocket. The rest of the money and the stub was put in an envelope and sealed to be handed to her mother in-law every Friday. Each week Monique added the money to her secret compartment in her jewelry box. When she had enough money she would leave.

A year later just after her eighteenth birthday late one night there was a knock at the front door. Monique was on her way up to bed. She answered the door. Two police officers were standing there. "Who is it?" asked Mama Larose as she came trotting down to the kitchen "Mrs. Larose?" asked one of the officers. "I'm Mrs. Larose," answering him and pushing Monique out of the way. "I'm afraid we have some bad news ma'am. Your son David was knifed to death in a barroom fight tonight. We are very sorry, Mrs. Larose." "No……" Mama Larose screamed, "not my boy, my baby my David." She walked away and went up to her room. Monique thanked the officers for coming over and then she thanked God.

The wake was held in the front parlor and lasted three days. Mama Larose sat by his coffin holding David's hand and wouldn't leave his side. At the cemetery mama Larose kept screaming, "Not my boy, not my boy" Connie put her arms around her mother and said, "Come, let me take you home, Mama." She pushed Connie away, but she followed her to the carriage. Two nights later Monique took her valise out of the closet and took twenty-five one dollar bills out of her secret compartment and placed the money in her coat pocket she left the rest in her box and put it back in her valise then packed the rest of her things. She had written a note to Mrs. Fortin telling her she would let her know where she was going to be. She also wrote Connie a note telling her she was leaving and advising her to do the same. She also thanked her for being her friend. She left the note on the dresser along with her wedding ring. Then she waited until two am when everyone was asleep to leave. Monique quietly left the house.

Monique was glad she had spoken often to one of the girls at work, who went to Boston often. She had given Monique, a Brochure of the train schedule, along with directions to the train station from the Mill. Monique felt a little apprehensive while she was walking two the Lowell train station, but for the first time in her life she was free and she liked the feeling. All of her young life she felt older than her years she was eighteen years old and felt like she was forty. She imagined that nothing could happen to her that could be any worse than what she had lived through already. When she got to the station she sat on a bench and waited for the train that would take her to Boston. When she finally boarded the train, and in her seat, she felt like she was starting a new adventure. She looked at all the other passengers one by one and wondered what kind of life each of them had. Forty-five minutes later Monique was walking on the streets of Boston not knowing where she was going. It felt so good to be free. Monique didn't care where she was walking. She thought to herself, "I do have to find myself a place to live. I'll buy a newspaper and look for a place to live. Then I'll find a job. "God, I'm hungry." She spotted a street vendor selling hotdogs. She walked over to the cart. The street vendor asked, "What can I get you miss?" "I'll have a hotdog please." "What would you like on it miss?" Monique had never eaten a hotdog so she didn't know what to say. "Whatever you usually put on them will be fine." "Okay miss the works." He filled the top of the bun with onions, relish, and mustard then handed it to Monique. "Thank you." "You're welcome miss would you like something to drink to go with that? I have coffee, tea, and cocoa." "I'll have cocoa please." He handed her the cocoa and said "that will be twenty-five cents miss." She took the quarter out of her pocket and handed it to him. "Have a nice day miss." "Thank you." Monique walked over to the bench and sat down placing the valise on the ground between her legs and holding it with her feet. She took a bite of her hotdog. "Mm" she thought "this is the best meal I've had since I've left Mrs. Fortin." She enjoyed sitting there eating and watching the people walk by. She was still hungry and ordered another hotdog from the vendor. Although she hadn't slept all night she wasn't a bit tired. In fact she felt very energetic. She loved the fresh air and the sun was shining brightly. It was the middle of October and the weather was still beautiful. She finished eating threw her cup and napkin in the trash bin and started walking.

She stopped at every store and went inside to browse. Looking at dresses, shoes, handbags and she even went into the furniture store. She also enjoyed all the different sights and sounds. At the newsstand she bought a newspaper and turned to the rental section. "Maybe, she thought, "I could find a room in a boarding house for now." She wasn't paying attention to where she was walking and had lost track of time. It was getting dark and difficult to read the paper she walked over and stood under a lamp post to read. She was so involved in reading the newspaper she didn't hear two rough looking men approach her. They circled her and one of them said. "What have we got here Joe?" as he grabbed her arm, Monique said "Let go of me you brute!" "Hey Al the girl's got some spirit, I like that." Both of them started laughing Monique struggled dropping her newspaper and her valise. Al had both of her arms the more she struggled to get away the tighter his grip became and they both laughed. They were talking dirty to her. "Get away from me you pigs!" "Pigs is it?" Al said giving her a back hand across the mouth and her mouth began to bleed. "Please leave me alone she begged." They laughed and took turns slapping her around. Finally she passed out and they let her fall to the ground. Al stooped down pulled open her coat her buttons went flying and he tore her dress and slip down the middle, then took of her panties. Al said to Joe. "I'll take her first than you can have a turn." Whining Joe said "Why can't I ever be first?" "Because I'm the boss that's why now shut the hell up so I can get on with it." Al unzipped his pants, took out his penis, got on top of Monique just as he was about to rape her a black horse and carriage approached. Al was so consumed in what he was doing, he never heard it coming, Joe was so busy watching Al he didn't notice either. A man slipped out of the carriage carefully approaching them he took his pistol out of his breast pocket and shot above Al's head. "Holy shit" Al yelled as he got up and started running while trying to put his penis back in his pants. Joe took off like a bat out of hell. The gentleman walked up to Monique, covered her with his coat and gently picked her up. He called his driver over and gave him the valise. He gently laid Monique on the seat in the carriage and sat on the opposite side. "Hurry home Archie" he commanded. "Yes sir" Archie replied. As soon as they arrived at his home on Beacon Hill in Boston Archie carried in the valise and the gentleman carried Monique inside. He sent Archie for the doctor.

Evan was sitting at his desk in the library holding a glass of scotch in one hand and a bullet in the other. He decided to call his friend Chris Jennison, a police detective at the Newport police department. He placed his glass of scotch on the desk and dialed the police station. Chris and Evan had been friends since elementary school. Chris had been with the police department for the past fifteen years. For the last five years he had been assigned to the detective squad. The phone began to ring and was answered immediately. "Good afternoon, Newport police department." "I'd like to speak to detective Jennison please." "One moment I'll see if he is still here." A few minutes later a gruff voice answered "Jennison here." "Chris its Evan" "Evan my man, how are you?" "I'm fine and you?" "I can't complain I'm still chasing criminals." "Are you still busy building hotels?" "Yes but I decided to take a few weeks off and come home." "Chris I need to talk to you can I buy you a sandwich and a beer at Sam's Bar and Grill in about an hour?" "What's this all about Evan?" "I'll tell you all about it when I see you." "Okay Evan I'll see you in an hour at Sam's."

Evan was already seated at a booth when Chris arrived he waved at Chris to join him. They shook hands and Chris took a seat in the booth. "I took the liberty of ordering for us your favorite a Rueben with extra sour kraut on a bulky roll and a Budweiser." "You're alright Evan you never forget anything." The waiter approached them placing their sandwiches and beers on the table. "Will there be anything else gentlemen?" "No we're all set, thank you." Evan answered "You're welcome" said the waiter he left the two to eat their lunch. Chris took a bite of his sandwich and a swig of beer wiped his mouth with his napkin and said. "What's up Evan?" Evan set his beer on the table "Chris, are you familiar with the property that abuts mine called The Haven?" "I've never been there but I know the property you are talking about." "This morning while I was riding my horse on the path there was a horse saddled and ready to ride all by itself grazing I started to look around for its owner about two miles from where I found the horse I found the rider lying on the ground unconscious. It was Sarah Saint James from the Haven. I picked her up placed her on my horse and took her to the Haven where she was rush by ambulance to the hospital. I accompanied her housekeeper Mrs. Johnson to the hospital. The doctor told us that Sarah was in a coma. When we returned I headed home on my horse and decided to check out the site where I had found Sarah she is a competent rider and I was curious how she could have fallen off her horse. I saw I tiny speck lodged in the tree she was lying under. I climbed up on my horse and saw the bullet and I was able to dislodge it with my pocket knife." Evan took the bullet out of his coat pocket and handed it to Chris. Chris examining the bullet said. "It doesn't look like it's been in that tree very long." "That's what I thought and that is why I called you. I believe someone is trying to kill Sarah but I don't have the slightest idea why." "Evan I'll have ballistics check the bullet out. Is there anything else you can tell me?" "No but you can check with the servants at the Haven they seem to really care about her." "I'll check it out and give you a call." "Thanks." "What are friends for?" They finished their beers and sandwiches and caught up with what was going on in each other's lives, Evan paid the bill and they went their separate ways.

Evan went to the hospital to spend some time with Sarah. He couldn't believe how drawn he was to her. He had never felt this way about a woman before. He was glad he had taken a few weeks off he planned to spend as much time as he could in the hospital by Sarah's side. He was thinking "There's something so innocent about Sarah that I have this urge to protect her and I want to be with her when she wakes up. I can't believe this is me falling in love with a woman I don't really know who's lying there in a coma."

Chris Jennison was thirty-five years old six feet tall and muscular. He had sandy blond hair and brown eyes. He usually ran five miles a day to stay in shape. At the precinct he was known as a great detective because he was thorough and caught every little detail. He never married he was married to his job. Chris had several nieces and nephews whom he liked to spoil when he had time off. He was sitting at this desk reading the ballistic report on the bullet Evan had given him. He read the bullet had just recently been fired at a short range. It came from a 38 caliber handgun. Chris thought "Evan is probably right someone is definitely trying to kill Sarah Saint James or trying to scare her off." Tomorrow he would make a stop at the hospital to look in on Sarah. Then he would ask Evan to accompany him to the house to speak to the servants.

Chapter Six

"Simon, thank God that man showed up just in time before those goons raped her. She still looks pretty bad her face is all bruised." "I agree she doesn't look well at all. They certainly did a number on her." "You know Simon I believe this man that came to granny's rescue is my grandfather. He sure looks like the man in the pictures granny showed me." Smiling he said "Only time will tell Sarah. Hopefully her life will get better from here. Let's just see."

Matthew Samuel Thompson was twenty-nine years old over six feet tall and well-proportioned in all the right places. He had shoulder length jet black curly hair a moustache and deep blue eyes. He was a very wealthy man his parents had him late in life. His father made his money in oil wells. When his parents passed away a few years ago they left Matthew with a huge estate. A house on Beacon Hill and a large Victorian home near the ocean in Newport Rhode Island.

Matthew's father Samuel Thompson migrated to the United States from the slums of London. He was orphaned at eight years old with no relatives. He lived off the streets of London sleeping wherever he could find shelter. When he was twelve years old he decided he wanted to go to America. He got himself a job working for his passage on a ship headed for New York. While swabbing the deck he sometimes overheard the men talking to each other. This particular time two men were discussing oil wells in Texas. He heard how people were getting rich striking oil. Samuel decided when he got off the ship in New York he would make his way to Texas to seek his fortune. It took five months before the ship reached New York. Samuel got himself a job right away working on the docks loading and unloading cargo from the ships. His sleeping quarters were in the back of a saloon. When he felt he had enough money he bought himself a map circled Texas, and started to walk to his destination. Sometimes he would hitch a ride on a wagon. He would stop in little towns along the way and do odd jobs. It took him two years to reach Texas. Once there he found himself a job working on a rig in an oil field. For the next ten years he worked, he learned and he saved his money. He learned everything he could how to purchase land and how to set up a rig to dig for oil. Finally the day came when he had saved enough money to buy his first piece of land as well as the equipment to dig his first oil well. As luck would have it he struck oil his first time. At the age of thirty-two he had over a dozen oil wells.

He was invited once again to the Texas spring ball. In the past he always refused the invitations because he was too busy. But the invitations never stopped coming for he was handsome, rich and eligible. This particular ball he decided to attend. He was standing by the fireplace holding his drink and having a conversation with the other men. One of the men told a joke and they all started to laugh Samuel turned his head for a moment and out of the corner of his eye he noticed the most beautiful woman he had ever seen standing on the opposite side of the room. Ignoring the conversation he turned to get a better look at this woman. She was wearing a pale blue gown with white lace around the bodice. She was petite with a tiny waist. Her blond hair was piled high on her head with tiny ringlets across the front and the sides of her face. Her eyes were a deep blue as blue as his own eyes. Their eyes met and held. He thought to himself, "She's the woman I'm going to marry." He excused himself from the conversation and made his way towards her. Abby Van Doe was twenty-three years old and visiting her aunt and uncle in Texas. She lived in Boston Massachusetts. When her eyes met Samuels she felt a sensation throughout her body that she had never felt before. It was so strong it made her gasp for breath. As she held his eyes she thought he looked so dashing in his black tuxedo, his dark curly hair and eyes that matched her own. She couldn't take her eyes off him as he was approaching her. Samuel asked her to dance and she accepted. From that night on they were inseparable. They were married two months later. They moved to Boston and Samuel bought Abby a home on Beacon Hill. They had been married for fifteen years and were very happy. They had adjusted to not being able to have children. Then at thirty-eight Abby was surprised to find out she was pregnant with Matthew. They were delighted that they were finally going to have a child. After Matthew was born and as he grew his parents taught him love, understanding, respect and how to handle his wealth. At twenty-five Matthew's mother became very ill and died. His father was so heart broken by Abby's death he died two months later.

Matthew carried Monique up the stairs to the guest bedroom. He pulled the covers down and gently laid her on the bed and covered her with the blanket. He removed her shoes and tucked the blanket under her feet. Doctor Nelson arrived a few minutes later and the butler brought him to the room Monique was in. "Thank you for coming right away Doctor Nelson." "Your butler caught me just in time I was on my way out to get a bite to eat. Now what happened to this young lady Matthew?" "She was mugged and almost raped." The doctor looked at Monique and back to Matthew and said "It looks like she took quite a beating." "That she did doctor." Matthew went to stand by the fireplace while the doctor examined Monique.

Doctor Nelson cleaned the wounds on her face, arms, and legs. When he was finished he turned to Matthew "You'll have to keep an eye on her for the next twenty-four hours she has a mild concussion. I'll leave you some powder mix it with a full glass of water for the pain when she wakes up. The poor girl is skin and bones in addition to the beating she took, I also believe she is malnourished. If you could let her rest for a few weeks while tending to her nutrition issue she'll get stronger and heal much faster Matthew." "I'll make sure the young lady is well taken care of Doctor Nelson." "I'm sure you will Matthew." The doctor turned to leave saying "Goodnight Matthew" "Goodnight Doctor, I'll see you out." "Don't bother Matthew I'll see myself out if you need anything just send your butler for me."

Mrs. Johnson was sitting at the kitchen table having a cup of coffee when Julie walked in. "Is Sarah back from her ride yet Mrs. Johnson? I missed her this morning I left early to go shopping. I just got back a little while ago. I can't seem to find her anywhere. I didn't think she'd ride this late into the afternoon." "Sit down Julie I'll make you a cup of coffee." Mrs. Johnson stood up walked over to the coffee urn to pour Julie a cup of coffee. She placed the cup in front of Julie and sat down. Julie took the creamer and poured it into her coffee she lifted the spoon from the sugar bowl and added it also. She stirred her coffee placed the spoon on the table and took a sip. "Mm you make the best cup of coffee Mrs. Johnson." "Thank you Julie. I have something to tell you." "You look so serious what is it?" "There's been an accident. Sarah fell off her horse this morning while she was riding and hit her head on a tree." "Oh my goodness is she alright?" "No she is in the hospital in a coma." "What hospital is she in?" "General Hospital" "Is she going to come out of the coma?" "The doctor doesn't know he told me to pray. I've been praying since I came home from the hospital with Mr. Taylor." "Who is Mr. Taylor?" "His name is Evan Taylor he's the man who found Sarah and brought her home this morning. He lives on the property that abuts this property. He was very nice and concerned. We went to the hospital together and then he called his chauffer to take us home. He's also a very handsome man." "I'll go see Sarah tomorrow I'm worried about her. I hope she'll be alright." "So do I dear." Julie finished her coffee and left the kitchen. On her way to her room she was thinking "This Mr. Taylor sounds very interesting. I'll have to make it a point to meet him."

Julie Tate was brought up in a tenement block near the docks in Boston. She was the second oldest of four sisters. The family was poor barely making ends meet. Her father worked on the docks and didn't make much money. He loved his wife and his daughters especially Julie she was his favorite. Her father's mother also lived with them. She took care of the girls when their mother went off to work. She worked as a waitress in a local diner. When Julie's oldest sister Paula was born her father was in the navy and stationed in Hawaii at the time Pearl Harbor was attacked. Fortunately he wasn't hurt. He was stationed there for three years. When he was discharged and sent home his daughter Paula was four years old. Julie was born a year later. To her father she felt more like his first born. He gave her all the attention and pushed Paula aside. When Julie was five her Sister Diane was born and a year later Suzanne. But Julie never lost her place in her father's eyes. He spoiled her as much as he could. Julie's favorite pastime was eating. She especially loved sweets and she didn't like to share her treats with anyone especially her sister Paula. Their mother would send Paula and Julie to the market down the street and sometimes gave them a dime to buy a hostess cupcake to share between them. One particular time when their mother was giving them money to buy a treat Julie said. "Mama I want to hold the money for our treat I'm a big girl now." "You are a big girl Julie. You're ten years old now so I guess you're old enough to pick up the treat and make sure you share with Paula." She handed Julie the dime. "Yes mama I always share." "Good girl now run along and don't dally." As soon as they were inside the market Julie ran to the isle that held the cupcakes she grabbed the package and ran to the register to pay for them. She hurried outside to wait for her sister. She opened the package of cupcakes and began stuffing her mouth. She ate the both of them. She had cream all around her mouth when Paula came out of the market. Julie was holding the empty package. "What did you do Julie you ate my cupcake too" Julie stuck her tongue out at her and wiped her mouth with a tissue she had in her pocket she threw the tissue in the basket and said "Yes I ate both cakes" "That's not a nice thing to do Julie you should have saved me one." Again Julie stuck her tongue out at her. Walking home Paula was fuming. Julie had a satisfied look on her face. When they walk into the apartment Julie ran to her mother crying her mother asked. "What's the matter sweetheart?" with a heavy sigh she answered "its Paula she ate both cupcakes and didn't share a little bite with me." Paula looked at her with hate "That's not true you little liar." Their mother yelled out "Enough Paula you should know better. Go to your room and stay there. There will be no supper for you tonight you shouldn't be hungry after eating both cupcakes." Throughout their childhood Paula bore the brunt of Julies lies. Julie didn't have a problem with her other two sisters she basically left them alone. In high school Julie took up baton twirling and because she was so good at it she entered and won many competitions walking away with first prize trophies. Her father attended as many of her competitions as he could he was very proud of her. When Julie graduated from high school she decided to take a real estate course. She wanted to make some big money and real estate seemed like the way to do it. She wanted an easier life than her parents had, to her they could barely make it on their meager wages. Once she passed her real estate exam and received her license she found a job at a real estate office in Boston.

On her first day at the office she met Sarah Saint James. Sarah found it difficult to keep up a conversation with Julie the first few days. Julie talked so fast that it gave Sarah a headache. After a couple of weeks Sarah got accustomed to Julies fast pace, they became close friends and would help each other whenever they could. Sarah had a natural gift for listing properties. She and Julie went canvassing to build up their inventory of homes. Julie would knock on the door once the door was open she would freeze up and couldn't speak without stuttering. Sarah would take right over handing out her business card as she was introducing herself, Julie and the office they were associated with. Then she would ask if they knew anyone who was interested in selling their home. People were so impressed with the young women and felt as if they were very ambitious. If the people they spoke to didn't have any intentions of selling they would call Sarah and Julie at the office and give them names of friends and acquaintances that were interested in selling or buying homes. Sarah would send them a gift certificate to a nice restaurant if the lead panned out. It didn't take long for them to build a good cliental. Sarah never knew how Julie from one day to the next when she came into the office. Her hair was very thin so she always wore a different wig to work. One day she would come in with long brown hair and the next day with short blond hair etc. The more money Julie made the more wigs she acquired.

After one year Julie moved out of her parents' home and bought a condo in a nice neighborhood. Sarah helped her find furniture and helped her decorate her condo. At the beginning of their friendship Sarah felt that Julie could be cruel especially the way she spoke about her sister Paula who was now married with three young children of her own. Julie would say such horrible things that she wanted to inflict on her sister. However she never acted upon those thoughts. Sarah's first gut instincts when she first became friends with Julie, was not to trust her. As time went on Sarah forgot her first instincts and they became best friends

After five years of working for someone else Sarah decided to open her own real estate office. Julie went to work for her. When Sarah's grandmother passed away Sarah made out a will leaving Julie the business as well as half of her estate. To her Julie had become the sister she never had. She was the closest thing she had to a family besides her cousins who would inherit the other half of the estate. If Julie dated someone more than once she liked playing games on them. For example on their second date she would wear a different wig making her look like a different person. She only dated professional good looking men. She stayed away from blue collar workers she didn't want to end up like her mother living day to day. If Julie was interested in dating a certain man she went out of her way to get his attention. She always made it a point to get what she wanted. Julie saw her family on holidays and would make a phone call once in a while to stay in touch. The only one she spoke to often was her father. He made sure he called her at least once a week until he had a heart attack and passed away two years after Sarah opened her office. Julie started sending her mother a few dollars a week to help her out. That way she did not have to feel guilty about not visiting her.

Mrs. Johnson was in the kitchen wiping the counter down thinking about how Vicki and Tom had left early this morning and went their separate ways. They hadn't come back yet.

Their new guest uncle Armand wasn't around either. She thought "I don't know anything about Sarah's uncle but I hope that Vicki and Tom aren't up to their old tricks and somehow made Sarah's caused Sarah's horse to buck." She didn't trust either one of them. "Mrs. Johnson" Vicki called entering the kitchen. "Think of the devil and it always appears" thought Mrs. Johnson. "Yes Miss Vicki." "What time is our little clambake tomorrow?" "The clambake has been cancelled." Vicki walked right up to Mrs. Johnson with her hands on her hips she screamed "What do you mean by cancelling the clambake? That's the reason I came down this weekend." "First of all Miss Vicki there is no need to shout at me I am not deaf. There's been an accident Miss Sarah's in the hospital." "What happened to her?" "She's in a coma she fell off of her horse and hit her head on a tree." "Did you cancel the seafood?" "I had them deliver a smaller order." "Well that's good the rest of us still have to eat and as you know we have a guest staying here, our uncle." "I'm well aware we have a guest Miss Vicki." Without another word Vicki turned around and walked out of the kitchen. Mrs. Johnson thought "That miserable little twit. I do not believe she has a heart and what did she mean the only reason she came down this weekend was for the clam bake. She is here every weekend. Oh well." She went on to prepare dinner.

Vicki went looking for Tom she found him at the pool ready to dive in. "Tom" she called. "Wait a minute don't dive in yet I have something to tell you." He stepped down from the diving board and walked towards his sister "What is it?" he asked. "I've just had some grand news from Mrs. Johnson. We may be able to sell this place sooner than we thought." "This better be good Vicki, I'm hot and I want to take a dip." "This should cool you off dear brother. Sarah fell off of her horse this morning and hit her head on a tree. She's in the hospital in a coma, poor dear." "It would be terrific if she didn't come out of this coma and she died. We could sell the place and our financial woes would be over. Our share would be fifty-fifty split now that my dear sister would be wonderful." "Did Mrs. Johnson say what Sarah's chances are of coming out of this coma?" "No that is all the old goat told me. She cancelled the clambake for tomorrow I told her we still have to eat and I reminded her we still have a guest." "You'd better be careful little sister you don't want the old goat to think you're heartless." "I don't give a damn what Mrs. Johnson thinks. Once we sell this place we'll never have to see her again." Changing the subject Vicki said "What do you think of the new uncle we've just acquired?" "He certainly seems real he looks like mother and an older version of me. However I hope he doesn't think that he is going to get his hands on our money." "Well I for one don't trust him. We'll have to keep our eyes on him. He's not going to get a cent or a stick of furniture. If that's the reason he's here he's wasting his time." "I'm going to take a swim now why don't you change into your swimsuit and join me." "No I'm going to my room and rest for a while I'm tired. Oh Tom the painting is in the trunk isn't it? That painting should bring us a nice piece of change. I'll see you at dinner." "Vicki, do you want to go visit Sarah after dinner?" "No way, she exclaimed maybe tomorrow." "Okay." Tom turned around walked on to the diving board and dove into the pool.

Vicki, Tom, Julie and Armand were sitting eating their dinner. Vicki was telling Armand who had arrived just in time for dinner what had happened to Sarah his reply was. "I pray she will recover soon from her coma. After all I have just found my nieces and my nephew. I wouldn't want to lose any of you. To me losing Sarah would be such a tragedy I found her to be quite charming." "We are also praying our dear cousin will recover uncle Armand." "I'm sure you feel terrible Tom." They finished their meal and Armand excused himself from the table and headed to his room. Armand went out on his balcony and lit a cigarette. The sun was just setting. While he was enjoying the view he was thinking. "How can I manage to get rid of Tom and his sister Sarah will probably not recover and if she did she could be taken care of and I would inherit everything." He knew how much money was being offered for the property he had to make some type of action plan.

    The clock on the hospital wall read two am. The hospital was empty accept for the night nurse behind the desk. Her back was turned and she was talking on the phone. The killer dressed in a doctor's gown and wearing a surgical mask was standing by the entrance. The killer checked down the hall it was empty accept for the nurse on the phone. The killer carefully made its way to Sarah's room. Opening the door just wide enough to slip in he approached the bed and looking down at Sarah the voice said "I'm going to have to practice my shooting skills because if you come out of this coma I won't miss next time. I want you dead bitch and I'm going to make sure it happens" then slipped out of the room without being seen. The next day Julie went to see Sarah at the hospital. She brought her a vase of red roses and placed them on her night stand. She knew how much Sarah loved roses. She thought maybe the smell would help her come out of her coma and she'd see them when she opened her eyes. She walked over to Sarah's bed and took her hand in hers. "This shouldn't have happened to you Sarah the girl that never wanted for anything not like me." She heard the door open she turned around she almost gasped. Walking in was the most handsome man she had ever laid eyes on. He approached the bed. "Hi, I'm Julie Sarah's friend and co-worker. You must be the one that found her." She thought to herself "what's he doing here?" "Yes I am the one that found her" he said as he approached the other side of the bed. He held his hand out to Julie "I'm Evan Taylor." Holding his hand she said "Pleased to meet you Mr. Taylor." "Please call me Evan." "I'm so pleased you found Sarah, Evan. Who knows how long she would have been there if you hadn't come along." "It's fortunate I decide to come home for a couple of weeks and decided to take my horse Baron out for some exercise. She does look like she's sleeping." "I was thinking the same thing before you arrived." Julie looked at her watch "I'd better run or I'll be late for an appointment. I sure hope I'll see you again Evan." She gave him her best smile and headed out of Sarah's room. Today Julie was a long haired red head. After Julie left Evan pulled up a chair sat next to the bed and took Sarah's hand in his. Examining her small delicate fingers still holding her hand he was admiring the features of her face and spoke to her. "Sarah you are so beautiful. There is something about you that touches my heart. I don't know what it is. I have never felt these feelings before about any woman. I don't even know the color of your eyes but from the moment I saw you laying on the ground I felt connected to you. It's like I have a need to protect you from everyone and everything that might try to hurt you and nothing else in my life matters but you. It's odd but I believe I'm in love with you. I'm going to be here as much as I can until you wake up. I'm going to leave you for a little while today. I'm going with Chris he's my friend and a police detective. He asked me to go with him when he went to speak to your servants and I said yes." He stood up and kissed her on the cheek.

Matthew went downstairs to speak to his butler Jacob. He found him in the kitchen "Jacob" "Yes Sir" "Does your sister have a daughter who is a ladies maid?" "Yes Sir Mr. Matthew she sure does. The Mrs. She was working for passed away last week." "Do you think she'd be interested in working here Jacob?" "I'm sure she would be happy to sir." "Good, I want you to send for her and see if she can start tonight." "Yes Sir Mr. Matthew I'll fetch her myself." "Thank you Jacob." "You're welcome Sir." Jacob was a black African American and he had been working for the family since Matthew was an infant. He loved Matthew like a son. Matthew's parents had always been very kind and gentle to their servants and so was Matthew. Jacob as well as the other servants were very loyal and would do anything to please Matthew. An hour later there was a knock on Monique's door Matthew answered it. Jacob stood there with his niece and a big smile on his face. "Mr. Matthew I brought you my niece Jasmine. She is twenty-five years old and she will take care of the young lady." "Thank you very much Jacob." 'You are welcome Sir." He turned around and left the room. Matthew motioned for Jasmine to come closer as he said. "Thank you for coming with such short notice." "It's my pleasure Mr. Matthew. What would you like me to do?" Moving out of her way and pointing to Monique he said "Could you please bathe the young lady." "Yes Sir" "Be very gentle Jasmine she has many bruises." "Yes Sir" "Her valise is in the corner by the fireplace. See if you can find a nightgown and put it on her. When you've finished let me know I'll be in the library." "Is she sleeping sir?" "No she has a concussion." I'll be real careful with her."

Chapter Seven

"Simon it really is my grandfather I have a picture of him and granny over my fireplace in my bedroom." "Yes it is your grandfather Sarah." "He seems like a very gentle man and he's even better looking in person than his picture portrays." "Sarah have you seen enough do you want to go back now?" "Do I have to go right now Simon?" "Oh no Sarah I just thought you had enough and wanted to go home." "Simon I've never met my grandfather and I would like to know more about him now that I have the chance. Is there a time limit on how long I can stay? Do I have to go back soon?" "No Sarah only when you are ready." "Good then I'll stay."

Jasmine found a nightgown in the valise. Thinking to herself "The poor miss doesn't have much." She found the basin soap and towels in the bathroom closet. She filled the basin with warm water and gently bathed Monique. When she was finished she slipped her nightgown on her. When she was finished she cleaned everything up. Picking up Monique's torn clothes she slipped out of the room closing the door gently. She went to the library to find Matthew. "Sir the young miss is bathed and in her nightgown." "Thank you Jasmine." "Sir what do you want me to do with her clothes?" "Just give them to me." She handed him the clothes. "Did she wake up?" Matthew asked. "No sir." "Very well Jasmine that will be all for tonight. See your uncle Jacob he will show you to your quarters." "Thank you Sir Goodnight." "Goodnight Jasmine." Jasmine left the library and Matthew made his way upstairs.

He went into Monique's room placed the clothes Jasmine gave him on top of her valise. He pulled up a chair and sat by her bed. He spoke to her. "I want to know everything about you little princess. You are so young and it looks like life hasn't been good to you." He fell silent and just sat looking at her. A short while later he fell asleep in the chair. Matthew awoke suddenly. Monique was stirring and moaning. "Are you starting to wake up little one?" She thought "Where am I?" She was afraid to open her eyes. "Who does that voice belong to?" Slowly she opened her eyes and saw Matthew staring down at her. She was frightened and pulled the blanket up to her neck and asked "Who are you?" "Don't be frightened little one." "Where am I?" "You are in my home." "Who are you?" "My name is Matthew Thompson and your name Miss?" "Monique Larose" "Welcome to my home Monique." She looked up and saw that she was in a canopy bed. Looking around she saw a fire blaring in the stone fireplace. Two blue stuffed chairs on each side of the fireplace, a blue and white pitcher in a wash basin was sitting on the nightstand by the bed. "How did I get here?" "I brought you here in my buggy. Do you remember what happened?" "Yes there were two men who attacked me then I blacked out." "I was able to stop them before they raped you. They had torn your clothes off and one of them was about to take you until I shot my pistol over his head. They took off at a fast speed as if Satan himself was chasing them. Then I brought you here." Frightened she asked "Did you undress me?" "No my dear I did not. I sent for a lady's maid, her name is Jasmine. She undressed, bathe you then put your nightgown on. I left your clothes on top of your valise. I was going to dispose of them has they were all torn. However they weren't mine to dispose of. You can throw them away when you feel better. Do you have any pain Monique?" "My body is sore and I have a headache." "I had the doctor here to look in on you and he left some powder for you to take. He said it he said it would ease the pain. Would you like me to fix you a glass of the powder?" "Yes please if it is not too much trouble." "No trouble my dear I'll just be a few moments." When he returned he handed Monique the glass of mixture. She was trembling too much to accept it. "Let me help you my dear." He took his arm and placed it behind her back lifting her to a sitting position he lifted the glass to her lips. Monique drank slowly when she was finished he gently laid her down. "Thank you sir you are very kind." "You are welcome and please call me Matthew." She didn't respond her eyes closed and she fell asleep. Matthew went to his room to try and get some sleep but sleep was hard to come by. He was consumed with thoughts of Monique. He wanted to know everything about her and the urge to take care of her and protect her overwhelmed him. "Just like my father knew he wanted to marry my mother when he first laid eyes on her. I am going to marry Monique."

Chapter Eight

Chris and Evan arrived at the Haven at one o'clock in the afternoon. Alfred answered the door. Chris showed him his badge and introduced himself. "I'm detective Chris Jennison from the Newport Police Department and you've already met Mr. Taylor." "Yes I have sir when he brought Miss Sarah home." "I'd like to speak to you and the other servants about Miss Saint James accident." "Certainly please follow me gentlemen." Alfred led them into the living room. "Please make yourselves comfortable while I get Mrs. Johnson and her daughter." Chris looked around. It was a comfortable room. There was a ceramic tiled fireplace adorning the room he noticed a single log indicating it was gas. "Easy he thought just push a button and it lights up." A black baby grand piano stood in front of a bay window showing a beautiful landscaped garden. A white leather couch was centered in front of the fireplace with two matching chairs on each side. A glass coffee table was sitting in front of the couch with two matching end tables which held brass lamps. Black throw pillows were neatly placed on the couch and chairs. Above the fireplace was a large landscaped oil painting of the Haven. French doors led out to the patio, pool and the garden. Chris and Evan sat opposite each other on the chairs. Mrs. Johnson entered the room with Alfred behind her. Chris and Evan stood up. Evan introduced Mrs. Johnson to Chris. "Mrs. Johnson I'd like you to meet detective Chris Jennison from the Newport Police Department." "Please to meet you Mrs. Johnson. Please sit down I'm sure Alfred told you we had a few questions for the servants." She sat on the couch and both men sat back in their chairs. Chris took out a notepad and pen. "What is this all about detective?" Mrs. Johnson asked. "Mrs. Johnson it's about Miss Saint James accident." Chris replied. "The accident Sarah had? What would Sarah's accident have to do with the police?" Evan spoke up "May I explain to Mrs. Johnson Chris?" "Sure Evan go ahead." "Thanks." Turning to Mrs. Johnson Evan started to explain. "Mrs. Johnson when we came back from the hospital I rode my horse back home and I stopped by the tree where I found Sarah. I looked to see if I could find anything that would have spooked Sarah's horse. I searched the area and then happened to look up towards the tree to see if maybe a branch had fell. However I saw something shiny lodged in the tree. I climbed up on my horse and with my pocket knife was able to remove the object which happened to be a bullet." Mrs. Johnson was shocked but she didn't interrupt Evan. "When I went home I decided to call Chris and meet with him to discuss what I had found and to give him the bullet so he could run some tests on it." Evan looked at Chris nodding so he could take over. Chris proceeded to further explain. "I had the lab check out the bullet. Ballistics discovered that it came from a 38 caliber gun and it had been fired had not been lodged in the tree long." "Are you trying to tell me someone was trying to kill Sarah?" "I'm afraid so Mrs. Johnson" "Who would want to do such a thing Sarah is such a nice person." "Mrs. Johnson" asked Chris "Do you know of any reason someone would want Sarah dead, has anything happened recently to provoke this?" "I don't know." "Please anything you can think of even if you think it's not important tell me anyway." Mrs. Johnson started to think of everything that had happened so far over the weekend. She looked at Chris and said "Sarah confided in me that someone is trying to buy the Haven and the broker is being very persistent. In fact he called Sarah Friday afternoon and got her very upset. She told me about the offer after she got off the phone." "What was the offer Mrs. Johnson?" "The original offer was for one hundred million dollars." Chris whistled and said "Wow that's a nice piece of change." Mrs. Johnson continued "The second offer was for twenty million dollars more and the third offer came Friday afternoon for another ten million. That is why she was so upset. Also her cousins have been after her to sell." "Why would it matter to her cousins if she sold or not what do they have to do with this?" "You see detective Jennison Sarah owns a sixty percent share of the property and her two cousins own twenty percent each. Sarah also told me she would like to buy their shares but she doesn't have that kind of money." "This is starting to sound very interesting Mrs. Johnson where would I find her cousins and what are their names?" "They left this morning for New York they told me they would return on Friday. The woman's name is Victoria Dixon she goes by the name of Vicki her brother's name is Thomas Kincaid he prefers Tom. They both live in Boston in a house they inherited from their mother." Chris was jotting all of this down. "Is there anything else you can tell me about them?" "Well I don't trust either one of them" she replied "What do you mean by that statement?" "Those two are cut from the same cloth as they say they are both mean and devious and very greedy." Evan interrupted "why do you believe they are mean and devious?" "They spent all of their summers here as children. They caused Sarah to have an accident every summer they thought no one was the wiser. I'll give you an example. The summer Sarah was nine years old she fell out of the tree house. She had a chair she liked to sit in and read one day she took a book up to read when she sat on the chair she fell through the floor and ended up with a broken leg and arm. Everyone thought it was an accident including myself. Much later my daughter Maggie told me she saw Tom and Vicki going up to the tree house in the morning with a saw. You see they cut the floor just enough that when Sarah went up to read and sat down she would fall through the floor." "Nice pair" Chris and Evan said in unison. "Another thing I don't know if it's important. Since their grandmother died last year they have been stealing expensive paintings from the attic. They think no one sees them but both Alfred and I have seen them putting the paintings in the trunk of their car. I don't know what they are doing with them but I know they are taking them. They probably the paintings belonged to them however their grandmother left everything in the house to Sarah." "That certainly is enough to give them motive." Chris replied. Evan asked "Mrs. Johnson if Sarah dies do you know if the property reverts back to them?" "I believe it does Evan." "That's reason enough for a motive." Evan said. "There is something else you might want to know detective Jennison." "What's that Mrs. Johnson?" "I don't know if it's important but Mrs. Thompson's brother came here Friday and we all were shocked because we never knew Mrs. Thompson had a brother." "Where is he staying?" "Here in one of the guest rooms." "What is his name?" "Armand Saint John." "Do you know where he is now?" "I believe he went out." "How did Sarah know he was really her uncle?" "He looks like Tom and his mother." "Thank you Mrs. Johnson you have been very helpful." Chris also spoke to Alfred and received the same information Mrs. Johnson had given them. Maggie was not available at this time. Chris told the servants if he had any more questions he would get back to them. Chris and Evan left. Once outside Chris turned to Evan and said "I believe your hunch was right Evan." "Chris do you think you could post a guard in front of Sarah's room?" "I was thinking about the same thing Evan I'll get on it right away." Next Saturday I'll be coming back to pay another visit and have a talk with the cousins. Will you still be in town?" "Yes I'm taking some extra time off. My office can always get in touch with me if they need to. I'd like to be there when you speak with them." "Great I'll give you a call and let you know what time." "Okay Chris."

Vicki and Tom stopped by the hospital to see Sarah on their way to New York. Both of them were standing on each side of the bed looking down at Sarah. Vicki spoke first. "Doesn't she look sweet Tom laying there in a coma I wish she would take a turn for the worse and leave us to go to that big resting place up and beyond?" "It would make things easier for us Vicki." Vicki looked at Tom and said "If only we could get hold of a drug that would kill her we could insert it in her IV tube. It would have to be a drug that couldn't be traced. Do you know anyone that is knowledgeable in pharmaceutical drugs Tom?" "No I don't know anyone. You are having one of your fantasies again Vicki." "I know Tom but doesn't it sound wonderful." "Yes it does Vicki. Shall we let Sarah know what we are about to do?" "Yes lets" Tom looking at Sarah with an evil grin says "Sarah we are going to New York to sell one of your Rembrandts from the attic that you aren't even aware you have. I guess you should have visited the attic like we did." Vick added "Sarah I impersonate you when selling your paintings. The art dealer believes he's dealing with you because I dress, talk and act just like you. Isn't it great my little Sarah after today Tom will be able to sell the painting himself because I am giving him permission under your name of course at Antoine's Antique store all I have to do is sign your name on a legal piece of paper. They know Tom to be your trusted friend and cousin. Do you think she can hear us Tom?" "I don't know I don't care lets go we've wasted enough time with the little bitch." "Of course we have business to attend to. Bye bye cousin. We've never seen her looking so good have we Tom?" "Never" he replied as they left the room.

Jake was sitting in his office with his feet up on his desk contemplating what he was going to do with the commission he was going to make on the sale of the Haven. He did this often lately. He knew Vicki and her brother were anxious to sell. His only obstacle was Sarah and he thought. "She's not going to screw this sale up for me I'm going to make sure of it." His office was always in disarray. The top of his desk cluttered with an ashtray full of ashtray and cigar butts. With a cigar held tightly between his decaying front teeth Jake was in deep thought his priority was trying to figure out a way to convince Sarah to sell. Jake thought "Of course I can't convince her until she comes out of the hospital. Wouldn't it be nice if she just passed away in her sleep while she was in a coma?"

Chapter Nine

Jake closed his eyes inhaled his cigar deeply envisioning himself living on a small island lying in a hammock with a couple of native girls bringing him his beer, cigars and taking care of his every need. He was so deeply absorbed in his fantasy he fell backwards on his chair. The noise startled his secretary she ran into his office "Jake are you alright?" Picking himself up off the floor he said "I'm fine. Leave me alone." She left shutting his office door "Damn fool" she thought. Jake picked up his chair and set it back in place. He placed his cigar in the ashtray and decided to go out and grab a bite to eat. Walking out the door he told his secretary he'd be back in a couple of hours.

When Monique woke up it was one o'clock in the afternoon. She had to use the bathroom. She sat up and placed her feet on the floor. She felt a little stiff but her headache was gone. She looked around the room she saw a door at the far end of the room she walked over and opened the door. She had never seen such a room. There stood a large white tub with clawed legs and a gold faucet. Next to the tub was a pedestal sink that also had gold faucets. A large oval mirror hung over the sink. She tried the faucet in the sink to see if they worked. First the cold than the hot water it became very hot. She did the same thing in the tub. She was amazed she had never had hot running water or a tub. She wondered what a real bath would feel like. She went to the bathroom and while she was washing her hands she looked at her reflection in the mirror.

Her face was swollen with bruises. She lifted her nightgown she had bruises on her stomach and her arms and legs. "I'm a mess" she thought to herself. When she came out of the bathroom Jasmine was in her room. "Would you like a nice warm bath Miss? It would soothe your bruises." "I would like that very much. What is your name?" "Jasmine miss" "Thank you Jasmine for taking care of me last night. My name is Monique." "You are welcome Miss Monique. I'll fix your bath when you finish bathing I'll bring you some breakfast." Monique thought to herself "How strange, I don't know where I am and everyone here is being so kind to me." Jasmine interrupted her thoughts. "Your bath awaits you miss." Monique walked into the bathroom "Mm it smells so good and look at all those bubbles." "I found some roses scented bubble bath so I poured some in. It smells like real roses." "Yes it does Jasmine." "Let me help you with your nightgown." She helped Monique take her nightgown off. She pulled out the step stool. "Here is a little stool to help you get into the tub." She helped her in. "Enjoy your bath I will be back in a little while." "Thank you Jasmine." "You are welcome Miss" She left and closed the door. Monique went down further in the tub she thought "I think I died and went to heaven. This feels so marvelous imagine washing myself in a tub full of bubbles that smell like roses. I have never smelled roses before it smells so good. From this day on roses will be my favorite flower. After washing myself with a basin of water all my life I never knew such things as a bath tub could feel so good." When the water got cold Monique stepped out and dried herself with a white fluffy towel Jasmine had put out for her. She finished drying herself and put her nightgown on. "I smell just like a rose" Just as she was walking into the bedroom Jasmine was coming in with a tray. "How was your bath Miss?" "It was divine I'm still sore but I feel like a new person." "Get in your bed Miss and I will serve you breakfast." "I should really stay up." "Oh no miss the doctor told him you had to stay in bed for a week." Jasmine put the tray on the side table and fixed the pillows on the bed. "Come now Miss Monique, get up in your bed and I will place your tray." Monique did as she was told. Jasmine placed the tray on her lap unfolded her napkin and placed it in the front of her nightgown. She took the covers off the plates and said "Enjoy your breakfast miss." "Thank you Jasmine" Jasmine left the room. Monique looked down at the food and thought "My goodness I haven't had a meal like this since I have eaten with Mrs. Fortin." Scrambled eggs, bacon, sausages, panned potatoes, homemade bread with jelly, orange juice and coffee. She ate everything that was on her tray. "I didn't realize I was so hungry." There was a knock at the door. "Come in" Matthew entered the room. "Good afternoon Monique" He removed the tray from her lap and placed it outside the door. Monique replied "Hello" "Was everything to your satisfaction?" "It was delicious sir" "Good you look a little better today Monique and please call me Matthew." "Yes Matthew" "That's better" He pulled up a chair and sat by the bed. "Tell me Monique how did you happen to be in that neighborhood last night?" "I had bought a newspaper and I was looking at the rental ads for a place to live. I was so involved in what I was doing I didn't pay attention to where I was walking and I don't know Boston at all it's my first time here." "Where are you from?" "Lowell" Monique answered. "Why did you come to Boston?" "To find a place to live, find a job and to start a new life." "Do you have family in Lowell?" "Not anyone I want to see again." "I believe Monique that you have quite a story to tell. Am I right?" "Yes Matthew you're right." He picked up her hand and held it in his. "I want you to know Monique I would never hurt you. You can trust me. I would like you to trust me enough to tell me your story but I'm not going to push you. Let me tell you about myself first. I'm twenty-nine years old. I have never been married. I own my own business and I make a good living." He told her where and how his parents met and how in love they were for over fifty years. "This house has been in my family since my parents were married. It's mine since both my parents died a few years ago I was their only child." Monique liked listening to his voice it was gentle and sweet. He was incredible to look at. He had the most ravishing blue eyes. His nose was long and straight he had black curly hair with a touch of grey that gave him a distinguished look. She liked the feel of her hand in his. Just touching him she felt something she had never felt before and it scared her. "Do you feel you could trust me enough to tell me what happened to you?" "How do you know something happened to me?" "You are so frail and I can tell by the sadness I can see in those beautiful blue eyes of yours." "You have a kind look Matthew I believe I can trust you. I've only trusted three people in my life my papa who was killed in an accident when I was very young. My brother Pierre who at eight years old died of mal-nutrition and pneumonia He never received enough food to eat. He couldn't fight the pneumonia. "My God that is terrible please go on I'm sorry for the interruption." "Mrs. Fortin is the only other person I ever trusted. After my brother died she spoke to my mother and asked her if I could work for her three nights a week and Saturdays. She would pay me one dollar per week. My mother agreed as long as I gave her the money, which I did. I worked for her for three wonderful years." Monique decided to tell Matthew everything that had happened to her. From the time her father died up until she took the train to Boston leaving nothing out. When she was finished Matthew had tears in his eyes. He asked her "How can a mother do what she did to you and your brother?" "I've asked myself that question many times Matthew never coming up with an answer." "Now you say she's married to a wealthy banker?" "Yes his name is Norman Saint John." "Your beautiful baby daughter died because you were not given enough to eat. So much pain and you were so young." "Yes it was painful and still is when I think about it all." "Monique, would you stay with me here for a while?" Shocked Monique asked "You mean like a mistress?" "No of course not the doctor told me you needed to stay in bed for a whole week. After the week is up I would like you to stay here and I would like to start courting you. You see I plan on marrying you someday." "Marry me! I promised myself I would never marry again Matthew."

Chapter Ten

"You are too young to make such a promise. You've never seen a happy marriage. My parents were married for a very long time and they truly loved each other until the end. Now I believe they are together in heaven. Give me a chance to show you the good side of life. After six months if you still want to leave I'll help you find an apartment and a job. Does that sound fair to you?" Monique didn't answer Matthew right away. She thought about what he said and though she was afraid she finally answered "Yes Matthew I'll give it a try. I need to ask you to do something for me. I need to get in touch with Mrs. Fortin to let her know where I am. She worries about me and I truly love her." "That is not a problem give me her address and I'll send her a note telling her where you are. When you are feeling better I can arrange for a visit and she can stay as long as she'd like." "You really mean it Matthew?" "Yes of course I do." Monique was so excited at the probability of seeing Mrs. Fortin she reached up and grabbed Matthew by the neck and hugged him. Realizing what she had just done she could feel the heat rising in her cheeks. She pulled away quickly. Embarrassed she said "Oh I'm sorry." Matthew smiled and said "That's quite alright I rather enjoyed it. He stood up and said "You rest now I'll have a table set up in your room tonight and we can have dinner together rest well Monique."

Matthew went shopping and bought her some new nightgowns a robe and a pair of slippers. Monique didn't know what to say when he gave them to her. She had taken the money out of her coat pocket and given her coat and clothes that she was wearing when she was attacked to Jasmine to dispose of and she didn't have anything to replace them. Monique tried to pay Matthew for the clothes but he refused telling her to save it for something she really wanted. Jasmine came into the room after Matthew left and started Monique's bath water. Jasmine fixed Monique's bath every morning and when Monique was done Jasmine would brush Monique's long blond hair and tied it back with a ribbon.

While she was recuperating Monique and Matthew would have dinner in her room by the fireplace every night. They had deep conversations about everything. They told each other their likes and dislikes. They discussed characters in books they each had read which impressed Matthew at how knowledgeable and smart Monique was. The following week when Monique felt better and was able to go out Matthew took her shopping. He brought her to Jordan Marsh. First they visited the ladies department where she tried on dresses and picked the ones she liked. She would put them on and come out and show Matthew if he smiled she knew he liked that particular dress she would put it aside to purchase it. She picked out undergarments, stockings, shoes and a winter coat. Women were just starting to wear slacks so she picked out a brown pair of slacks with a sleek white blouse and a pair of brown loafers. Monique had never seen so many clothes in her life except for the ones her mother made for other people. Then they walked to the make-up counter and an older woman was teaching a younger woman how to apply her make-up. Matthew said "Monique have you ever worn make-up?" Monique blushing said "No I wouldn't know where to begin." Upon hearing this, the older woman turned around and said "If you'd like after I finish here I can help you." Matthew smiled at Monique while saying to the woman "Good then we'll wait." When the woman was finished she turned to Monique and said "Come sit over here." Monique did what she was told. Looking at Monique's face she said "I don't believe you need a foundation miss. Your skin is lovely. Let's start by applying a touch of rouge on your cheeks to give you a little color." She applied a light shade of rouge on one of Monique's cheeks when she was finished she handed the brush to Monique and said "Why don't you try the other cheek it's really easy and you don't need much at all." Monique took the brush from the woman and carefully applied the rouge to her other cheek. The woman said "I believe you are a natural at this. You're first try, and it looks beautiful." Grabbing the light brown eye shadow and a small brush she said "The brown will enhance your beautiful blue eyes. This is also easy to apply you just put it above your eyelid like this." Showing Monique she then handed her the brush to try. Next she picked the black mascara and said "this will enhance your long eye lashes." Dipping the brush into the mascara she showed Monique how to apply it to her eyelash. After the mascara was done she picked out a pretty pink lipstick handing it to Monique she explained how to apply it on her lips. When Monique was finished the woman said "Voila, all done you look beautiful miss doesn't she sir?" Matthew gazing at Monique couldn't believe that she could look more beautiful than she already was he answered "Yes, absolutely beautiful." "See for yourself, miss." She handed Monique a mirror Monique couldn't believe she was looking at herself. She looked so different and so pretty. The woman had a few more pointers for Monique she said "Of course you should use a moisturizer to keep your skin in good condition and a cream to remove your make-up at night." Matthew bought everything the woman recommended. He had the make-up along with everything else he had purchased delivered to his home. Monique was so happy but she said "Matthew you are spending so much money on me how will I ever be able to repay you?" Matthew looked at her and smiled "It makes me happy to buy these things for you and you don't have to worry about paying me back. Consider it a gift I'm having fun. Are you?" "Oh yes Matthew you don't know how happy you've made me."

When the packages arrived Jasmine unpacked everything. She hung up the clothes in the closet and everything else was placed in the dresser. She placed the makeup on the vanity table next to the window. That night at dinner Monique wore one of her new dresses. A dark blue linen dress with a white collar the dress hung midway down her legs. She wore matching blue pumps. Jasmine did her hair with a hot iron and curled it under. Monique applied her makeup just as she had learned. Then she looked at herself in the full length mirror. Her reflection showed a beautiful woman a woman she had no idea existed until now.

"Simon granny looks so beautiful" "She certainly does Sarah." "It's so wonderful being able to see my grandparents this way so young." "It's nice to see my granny smile. She has a beautiful smile."

Matthew was standing by the fireplace when Monique walked into the dining room. He thought to himself "She looks absolutely breath taking." Walking up to her he placed her arm in his and said "Monique you take my breath away." Looking up at him she blushed and said "Matthew how can I ever thank you I feel like a different person. Sometimes I think I'm dreaming and I'm going to wake up and none of this is real." Matthew looked into her eyes saying "This is no dream Monique it is all real, as real as you." He pulled out a chair so Monique could sit and took his place at the dining room table. They had dinner and talked late into the night. Monique was now fully healed. Being at Matthew's was good for Monique. She looked healthy and happy. She was noticing the differences in her body. Her breasts had filled out and she noticed her curves. Her new clothes accented those changes. As the weeks went by Matthew introduced her to the Opera's, Plays and he also brought her to the finest restaurants in Boston. He treated her like a queen.

Thanksgiving was right around the corner and the servants were getting things ready. Thanksgiving Day a few of Matthews close friends joined them to celebrate. Matthew's friends were taken with Monique and could tell that Matthew was in love with her. Three weeks before Christmas Monique was thinking about and missing Mrs. Fortin. At dinner that night she asked Matthew "Do you think we can invite Mrs. Fortin to spend the Christmas holiday with us?" "You write her a note Monique inviting her to stay with us until after the New Year and I'll send someone to pick her up." Monique felt like a little girl smiling she said "Thank you so much Matthew" Matthew seeing how Monique's face lit up smiled and said "I told you once, anything I can do to make you happy I will do." As soon as dinner was finished Monique excused herself. She went to her bedroom and sat at her desk. Taking her note paper out of the drawer she started her letter to Mrs. Fortin. Monique had been writing to Mrs. Fortin every week since she'd been there. She also told her how much she loved Matthew. Mrs. Fortin had asked her in her last letter if she had told him how much she loved him. Of course she hadn't. Monique was still afraid to get married after the bad experiences she had with her first husband. The marriage bed scared her the most she didn't want another experience like she had with David. Thinking of him made her shiver. Then she thought of the first time she knew she was in love in with Matthew. It was that first night when she awoke and saw this handsome face looking down at her with the kindest eyes. She fell in love with him that instant. Knowing nothing about him as unbelievable as it sounded she knew she was in love. She finished her letter to Mrs. Fortin and gave it to Jacob asking him to mail it. Jacob had already been expecting the letter and was asked by Matthew to deliver it personally. Mrs. Fortin sent her reply right away and gave it to Jacob to bring back. Monique was so surprised when he came back that evening with a letter from Mrs. Fortin saying she would love to join them for Holidays.

Monique for the first time in her life was looking forward to Christmas. She wanted to buy a special gift for Matthew and one for Mrs. Fortin. She still had the fifty dollars Mrs. Fortin had given her plus what she had saved it was still in her jewelry box which now sat on her dresser. Matthew was out and Monique decided she wanted to go shopping. She asked Jacob if he would bring the carriage around and take her. Jacob brought the carriage around and asked Monique where she would like to go first. Monique answered "Jacob could you please take me to a jewelry store." "Of course miss" Jacob led the carriage to the Jewelers located downtown next to Filenes. Once in the store it didn't take Monique long to find the perfect gift for Matthew. She asked the Jeweler to engrave it while she waited for it. After she was finished at the jewelers she walked next door to Filenes. For Mrs. Fortin she purchased a pair of fine leather gloves. She bought a scarf for Jasmine. She then went to the men's department and bought leather gloves for Jacob. Monique arrived at home before Matthew. She smiled knowing he would not know she had left to go shopping. She brought her purchases to her room where she wrapped all of them and hid them in her closet.

Mrs. Fortin arrived the following week. Monique was so happy to see her they hugged in the hall for what seemed to be hours. Mrs. Fortin was the first one to let go she said "Let me look at you" She examined Monique from head to toe, she then started crying and said "You are so beautiful Monique. I hardly recognized you. You don't look like the young girl I remember you've grown into an enchanting woman and I am so proud of you." Monique smiled at Mrs. Fortin "I feel like a different person. I believe God was watching over me when he sent Matthew to rescue me." "God works in mysterious ways my dear." Taking Mrs. Fortin's hand Monique said "Come I will show you to your room and Jasmine will help you unpack. When you've rested and have had time to freshen up we will have a chat over a cup of tea in my room." "That sounds wonderful my dear."

Mrs. Fortin was so impressed with her room. When she walked into the room she faced a lit fireplace. A four post bed was against a side wall. There was a small cherry wood desk next to the window and a brown leather chair with an ottoman. There were two doors she opened one and laid eyes on the most exquisite bathroom she had ever seen. It also had a brown oak dressing table and mirror. The other door led to her closet. She had never been in such a grand house. She felt so happy for Monique. After everything was unpacked and she had time to rest and freshen up Jasmine brought her to Monique's room. Monique was waiting for her. When Mrs. Fortin arrived she looked around Monique's room. Sitting by the fireplace there was a small table with scones and strawberry preserves that the cook had made fresh for the occasion. Also there was a teapot and two teacups with serving plates. Monique invited Mrs. Fortin to sit with her. Jasmine poured two cups of tea and asked if there was anything else they needed. Monique smiled and said "Thank you Jasmine this is perfect and thank you for getting Mrs. Fortin settled. You are free to do whatever you'd like." Jasmine smiled at Monique and said "Thank you miss."

Jasmine left the ladies to enjoy their time together. Lifting her scone and taking a bite out of it, Mrs. Fortin wiped her mouth with her napkin and said "You look so happy Monique." Monique smiled at Mrs. Fortin and said "I am. I can't wait for you to meet Matthew. He is so wonderful I don't believe there is another man on this earth like him." Mrs. Fortin took Monique's hand in hers saying if you love him I am sure he is a fine man." Changing the subject Mrs. Fortin still holding Monique's hand said "You know of course from my letter that Joel had a big church wedding three months after you left. What I didn't tell you was she had a son a year later. She named him Armand. I met her down town pushing a baby buggy when she saw me she stopped so she could show me her son. I looked in the buggy and saw a very beautiful baby. He had her black hair and black eyes he looked just like his mother. I told her she had a lovely son and I hoped that she took better care of him than she did her other two children. She then walked away. Also your mother in-law passed away just before Thanksgiving. She left your sister in-law the house." Monique was upset hearing she had another brother she said "I feel bad for him Joel hates children. Someday she'll get what she deserves." Monique was glad to hear the news about her Mother in-law "Maybe Connie can now make a better life for herself."

"Simon, just before my accident a man claiming to be granny's brother came to the house. His name is Armand. I guess he was telling the truth he really is granny's brother." Simon gave Sarah a concerned look and said "Be very careful of him when you return Sarah. I don't believe you should trust him." "I let him move into the house Simon." "When you go back send him away and don't let him return. Promise me." "I promise Simon."

When Mrs. Fortin met Matthew she loved him on sight. He felt the same way about her. Matthew loved her before he met her for what she had done for Monique. Matthew brought the ladies to an Italian restaurant that night. The following night he took them to the opera. On Saturday morning he had them go with him in search of the biggest Christmas tree they could find. After they finally found the right Christmas tree they brought it home. Jacob helped Matthew get it down from the carriage roof they brought it into the house and Jacob went to get a pail and some dirt. He placed the tree in the pail and added the dirt then watered the tree. It was a tall Spruce tree. Matthew went to get the decorations he brought out box after box. Monique had never seen so many decorations. Matthew explained that his mother would buy a new decoration every year. Matthew, Monique and Mrs. Fortin started decorating the tree. The lights came first. Matthew placed strand after strand on the big tree while Monique and Mrs. Fortin were in awe of the ornaments that they picked from the boxes. After all of the decorations were placed on the tree. Matthew shut the lights and lit the tree. Monique exclaimed "I have never seen anything so magnificent." Mrs. Fortin in awe could only say "Beautiful". Matthew smiled at both women as Jacob was bringing the tray of eggnog and goodies into the parlor. After Jacob had poured the eggnog Matthew started telling stories of when he was young making the ladies laugh. They laughed into the night. Both women had never experience such a night. It was a night filled with laughter and happiness. After the eggnog was finished and everyone was exhausted from all the laughing Mrs. Fortin was the first to surrender. She looked at Matthew and said "Matthew, you have made this a Christmas I'll never forget. Thank you so much for sharing with us. However I am tired and must retreat to my room for a much needed rest. Goodnight you two I am sure I will have sweet dreams." Mrs. Fortin left Matthew and Monique standing alone in the parlor. For the first time since Monique had been staying there they were both shy. Monique was the first to break the silence. "Matthew I will cherish this night forever. Thank you for making it so special and for having Mrs. Fortin here to join us." "Monique I hope to make every day of your life special. You are an Angel sent from above and I am so thankful you were sent to me." Monique could feel the heat rising in her cheeks with her head down she said "Thank you Matthew sweet dreams." Matthew smiled and said "You as well my angel."

On Christmas Eve they all went to midnight mass. When they returned home they had a delicious meal. After the meal Matthew gave his servants their Christmas gifts and bonuses thanking them for their service. Matthew, Monique, and Mrs. Fortin went into the parlor for a glass of wine. They were all exhausted so it wasn't long before they all retired to their rooms.

Christmas morning Monique thought she was the first to awaken. She went into the closet to get her gifts. She brought them downstairs to put them under the Christmas tree. When she entered the parlor she couldn't believe the abundance of beautifully wrapped gifts under the tree. She thought to herself "Matthew must have invited quite a few friends for Christmas dinner and he bought each one a gift. I have never seen anything like this. Where am I going to place these presents?" Monique looked around and decided to put Matthews's gift on one of the branches of the tree. She placed Mrs. Fortin, Jasmine, and Jacobs gifts on the mantel of the fireplace. After she stood one more time gazing at the beautiful tree she whispered to herself "Merry Christmas Papa and Pierre." Two teardrops fell from her eyes. She brushed the tears away and headed to the dining room. When she entered the dining room

Matthew and Mrs. Fortin were already seated. Matthew stood up and went over to pull the chair out for Monique to sit down as he said "Merry Christmas Monique." Monique sat down and replied "Merry Christmas to you too Matthew and to you also Mrs. Fortin." Mrs. Fortin smiled at Monique and said "Merry Christmas my dear Monique." Matthew returned to his seat and breakfast was served. While Monique was slicing a piece of ham she asked "Matthew, are we having many guests for Christmas dinner today?" Matthew gave Monique a puzzled look "No. Why?" Monique could feel her cheeks getting hot and replied "No reason. I was just wondering that's all." When they were finished with their breakfast Matthew escorted Monique and Mrs. Fortin into the parlor. "Ladies please make yourself comfortable you are going to be very busy for a while." Monique and Mrs. Fortin looked at each other and sat on the sofa. Matthew giving the ladies a sly smile said "I'm going to play St. Nicholas for my two beautiful ladies." He walked over to the tree and started picking out gifts bringing them one by one to Monique and Mrs. Fortin. Monique with a surprised look on her face said "Matthew all these gifts can't be for us." Matthew smiled and said "Oh but they are." "You cannot be serious." "This Christmas is going to make up for all the Christmases you have missed my Angel." Matthew piled package after package in front of them. When he was finished he said "You can start opening your gifts ladies." As Monique started opening her gifts she found skirts and blouses. She also received boots and perfume. There were more gifts to open Monique could not imagine anything else that she needed. As she opened her next gift she was surprised to see a baby doll. Monique's eyes filled with tears as she said. "Oh my I have never had a baby doll she's beautiful." Monique brought the doll to her chest and hugged her. "I will treasure this always Matthew." Matthew handed her a smaller box to open.

Monique opened her gift to find a beautifully handcrafted music box with a wind up key. She turned the key and opened the box inside was a ballerina twirling to music. She looked at Matthew and said "This is beautiful Matthew." Matthew then brought a big box to Monique and said "I had this specially made just for you. I hope you like it." Monique opened the box there stood a beautiful three mirrored vanity table with a bench. Monique gasped she had never seen anything so beautiful without thinking she got up and wrapped her arms around Matthews neck hugging him "Matthew it is beautiful thank you so much" she realized she was still holding Matthew when her cheeks started to flush. She released him and went back to sit on the sofa. She had never felt love like this. Her heart felt like it was going to burst. She thought "Could this be what it's really like to be in love." Mrs. Fortin received a beautiful brown winter coat with a mink collar and matching purse, a lovely sweater, and a wallet. When she opened the wallet she gasped inside was a one hundred dollar bill. Looking at Matthew she said. "Oh Matthew thank you so much for your gifts however I cannot accept this it is just too much" She went to hand Matthew the one hundred dollar bill. Matthew smiled and said "Mrs. Fortin you can and will accept this because you are worth much more if it weren't for you Monique may not be here today and that is worth millions." Mrs. Fortin started to blush and humbly said "Thank you Matthew." When all of their gifts were opened Monique stood and walked over to the fireplace mantel. She took the gift for Mrs. Fortin she walked over to her and handed her the gift. She smiled and said "Merry Christmas Mrs. Fortin." "Mrs. Fortin looked surprised and said "Thank you Monique." Mrs. Fortin opened her gift to find a beautiful pair of leather gloves. She smiled at Monique as she tried them on. She said "Monique I have never had leather gloves before they feel so soft and warm." Monique smiled and said "I am glad you like them." Monique then said to Matthew "There is a gift for Jacob also on the mantel Matthew I'll make sure he gets it later." Monique walked to the tree and reached for the box on the branch she walked over to Matthew handing him the box "This is for you Merry Christmas Matthew." He took the box from Monique and carefully started to open it. Inside was a gold pocket watch he carefully lifted the cover to the watch inside was an inscription it read December 25, 1947 with all my love, Monique. Matthew closed the cover and placed the watch in his vest pocket. "I will treasure this always Monique." He stood up and walked over to Monique he reached for her hand to lift her off the sofa. Gazing into her eyes he lifted her chin and moved closer to kiss her. His kiss was soft and tender. Monique's body trembled as he kissed her. She felt the heat rising through-out her body. She had never felt this way before she was excited and terrified at the same time. When Matthew pulled away Monique didn't want the kiss to stop. She gazed into his eyes and blushed. Matthew reached into his pocket and pulled out a small package he knelt down on one knee in front of Monique. Monique looked confused she had no idea why Matthew was on one knee. Mrs. Fortin smiled to herself knowing what was coming next. He opened the box and Monique gasped. Matthew smiled and in the most humble of ways said "Monique would you do me the honor of being my wife?" Monique looked terrified and at the same time she was elated. She hesitated as she thought how easy it was to talk to Matthew they had stayed up for hours talking about everything. Everything that is except for the one thing Monique was ashamed of the way David treated her and raped her. Mrs. Fortin seeing the fear on Monique's face interrupted and said "I'm going to excuse myself and give you both a bit of privacy." She opened the door to the parlor and left.

Matthew felt fear growing deep inside his stomach. He looked at Monique with questioning eyes "Monique are you going to answer my question?" Monique saw the fear in his eyes she knelt in front of him and placed her hands on his face. "Matthew we have talked late into the nights about many things our childhoods, dreams, and fears. However there is one thing we have never talked about and that is my first marriage to David. I feel I need to tell you this before I can answer your question and I hope you will understand. You see when I was forced to marry David at fourteen because my mother wanted to be rid of me. He brought me home. I was still a child. I hadn't even started my monthly. I was so afraid. That very first night he made me undress in front of him. I was so embarrassed but he just laughed. He told me he couldn't wait" At the thought Monique shivered and started hyperventilating. Matthew put the box down and held both of Monique's hands as she struggled to continue. "It was all vulgar Matthew everything that he said was vulgar. He made me get into bed and then he forced himself on me." Tears started rolling down Monique's face. "He did it over and over again until he got me pregnant. When I was pregnant he finally left me alone. I had a beautiful baby girl but she died because his mother would not let me eat enough to breast feed her. When I asked David for his help he just turned and walked away. My precious baby died in my arms of mal-nutrition. It was that day I told David not to ever come near me again or I would kill him. When David was killed I swore I'd never marry again because no man would do to me what he did." Matthew wiped away Monique's tears with his finger. "Oh Monique I am so sorry for the way he treated you. That is not love. Love is gentle and kind. Making love is when two people come to discover each other in the most intimate ways and Monique when that happens love doesn't hurt. I make this solemn vow to you now. You will never experience that pain again. I will never hurt you I will be gentle and loving. If you ever feel that I am hurting you, you must tell me and it will never happen again. However Monique I don't think that is going to happen as a matter of fact I can promise you it will not happen. No woman should ever be treated that way by her husband." Monique looked into Matthews eyes and knew he was telling her the truth she said to him "Matthew I need you to promise me something" "What is it you need Angel?" "If I agree to marry you I need it to be a new beginning for us. I don't want my past or my previous arrangement to ever be brought up to anyone. If we were to have children I would never want them to know the pain that I suffered. I could not bear the humiliation if anyone else knew." "Monique if you agree to marry me I promise you it will be a new beginning and your past will be buried along with that poor excuse of a man." Matthew picked up the box again while thinking to himself "I will treat you like the delicate flower you are "Looking into Monique's eyes he asked again "Monique I love you with my heart and soul. I promise to protect you with my life and I will never hurt you." With that said he asked "Will you do me the honor of being my wife?" "Yes Matthew I will marry you." Matthew removed the ring from the box and held Monique's hand as he placed the ring on her finger he started to explain the history of it. This ring belonged to my mother. If she had known you she would have wanted you to have it. The center stone is a ten karat solitaire surround by smaller diamonds. When he finished placing the ring on her finger he said "You will never regret saying yes to me I promise. You have made me the happiest man in the world." "When shall we set our wedding date love?" "I'd like to wait until after my birthday." "Your birthday is in September isn't it?" "Yes" "How does the first week of October sound?" "I would like to get married on

New Year's Eve 1949. I'll have a year to get prepared and get used to the idea of getting married again." "That's a wonderful idea we can start the New Year as husband and wife. A new beginning I'll make reservations to sail to Europe on the Queen Mary for our honeymoon." She gasped "To Europe?" "Yes I want to share Paris, France and London with you. We may be away for more than three months." "Oh Matthew it sounds wonderful I can't believe it." She placed her hands around his neck and kissed him. When they finally separated Matthew said "As long as I am alive you will never again have to worry about anything or anyone ever hurting you. That my love is my solemn oath to you." The rest of the day was spent in celebrating Christmas and their engagement. Mrs. Fortin was so happy for the both of them especially her Monique. She deserved a good life and she finally was going to have one. It had been a long and joyous day everyone retired early. When Monique went into her room all she could think about was kissing Matthew. The kiss they shared after she had said yes was long and tantalizing. Having never been kissed before Monique was experiencing feelings she didn't understand. When Matthew was kissing her his tongue gently ran across her lips urging them to open and accept it. She eagerly opened her lips and his tongue danced around hers. He teased her with it. It had been a slow deep kiss she instinctively explored his mouth with her tongue she had never done anything like this before. It sent shivers down her body awakening places she never knew existed. She was happy with her decision to marry him. Of course she liked kissing him but she was still afraid to sleep with him. She pushed those thoughts away after all she wasn't getting married for a whole year.

On New Year's Eve to celebrate their engagement Matthew took Mrs. Fortin and Monique to Francois an elegant French restaurant in downtown Boston. Both women looked lovely Monique wore a light blue chiffon dress with matching high heels. She wore the diamond earrings Matthew had bought her with the matching diamond teardrop necklace. Her hair was a cascade of light blond curls falling on her shoulders. When she had come down the stairs Matthew was struck by her beauty and told her how beautiful she looked. Mrs. Fortin wore a long silk purple evening gown with black pumps. Matthew also looked very handsome in his black tuxedo. The food was superb and the champagne flowed generously all night. After they rang in the New Year Matthew took his two giddy ladies home.

The following week Mrs. Fortin was heading back to Lowell. Mrs. Fortin could not thank Matthew and Monique enough for the wonderful vacation they afforded her. Mrs. Fortin said with happiness "I promise to be here for the wedding." Matthew answered "Mrs. Fortin you are welcome to stay with us again before the wedding." "Thank you Matthew." Both women cried as they held each other they reminded themselves that the tears they shed were happy ones not sad and they would see each other soon.

On Valentine's Day Matthew surprised Monique with a white baby grand piano. Monique was surprised and over joyed she exclaimed "Matthew I don't know what to say it's the most beautiful piano I've ever seen. Thank you so much." Matthew looking serious answered "When you told me what your mother had done to you when you played her piano I wanted to run out and buy you one. The reason I didn't get it for you right away is because I didn't want you to feel obligated to me for buying it for you. I wanted to wait until you agreed to marry me. Smiling he continued "Now my love play something for me please." "Oh yes Matthew I would love to. I will always play for you." Monique sat at the piano flexed her fingers and began playing a waltz she remembered hearing her mother play. Matthew stood by the piano astonished at how well she played without music or instructions. She played a variety of music she had heard. After playing everything that she could remember hearing she stopped playing. Matthew promised to buy her a Victrola and some records. She could listen to the music then play them on the piano. The following day Matthew took Monique shopping they bought a Victrola and a half a dozen records. She spent her afternoons listening to the records and at night she would play the piano for Matthew. They enjoyed their evenings together and the servants enjoyed listening to the young miss play. Since Monique had come to the house she had brought more joy to the house. The servants loved listening to her play and hummed and danced while performing their duties. They were happy before she came however her being in the house made it twice as nice. Every week Matthew bought her another record.

On a beautiful May morning while finishing breakfast Matthew said "I would like to take you to Newport Rhode Island Monique I have a home there by the ocean I just know that once you see it you will love it as much as I do." "Monique was thrilled "I've never been to the ocean Matthew." Smiling Matthew said "Then you are in for a treat my love." "Why don't you change into some slacks and bring along a jacket as it tends to be cooler by the ocean. I'll have the cook fix us a picnic lunch and we will drive down in my new Model T ford. How does that sound?" "It sounds wonderful Matthew." She ran upstairs to change her clothes. Matthew had pulled the car to the front to wait for Monique. When Monique came out of the house Matthew smiled he thought she was the most beautiful woman he had ever seen and she was his. "You look beautiful Monique" Matthew got out of the car and opened the door for Monique she stepped in. He returned to the driver's seat and they were on their way.

Monique found the ford very comfortable to ride in. It was so different from riding in a horse and buggy. The sun was shining the temperature was in the high seventies. She was mesmerized by the view of the country side. The trees were starting to bloom. She was fascinated with all the mansions as they drove through Newport. Everything was so beautiful. When they arrived at the property she saw a huge iron gate with the letter H enclosed in the center. Matthew stopped the car stepped out to open the gates then returned to the car. He drove down a dirt road for about a mile. As they approached the house Monique saw the most marvelous house she had ever seen it took her breath away. There sat a large white Victorian set high on a hill standing proudly among shrubs and trees beautifully landscaped around it. She looked at Matthew "This is breath taking." Matthew stopped the car and turned it off. He walked around the car to let Monique out. They climbed a wide white stone staircase leading to the front door. Matthew took the key out of his pocket to unlock the door explaining to her "I haven't been here in two years but I have someone come in and clean once a week. The Gardner still takes care of the property and lives in a cottage behind the house." He opened the door wide and stepped aside to let Monique enter. As she walked in she held her breath while her eyes swept over the mahogany staircase in the hall. She went in further and found French doors leading to the living room. Matthew took Monique's hand in his and said "Come I'll show you around." They walked further down the hall and stopped at a mahogany door. Matthew explained "This was my father's office when we spent our summers here." Monique's eyes opened wide as she saw all the life like animals on the walls. Looking at her expression Matthew said "My father loved to hunt." Hanging over the fireplace was the head of an elk. Matthew pointing it out said "this one was one of his trophies."

Monique responded "He is beautiful I just don't understand how he could kill him." "My father would bring the venison home to Boston and the cook knew just how to prepare it for our meals. The meat would last us through-out the winter months." Monique looked at Matthew "Do you also hunt?" "No I don't. Although I enjoyed eating the venison the way cook prepared it. I can't bring myself to kill an animal." "I'm so glad you don't enjoy the sport." The office was also furnished with large cherry wood desk with a matching chair. A large braided rug lay in front of the fireplace with two comfortable leather stuffed cherry chairs set on each side. Still holding her hand he brought her to the next part of the house. He opened the French doors that led to the living room. This room also had a large fireplace and was decorated beautifully. They continued on to the large dining room that led to the kitchen. The kitchen was enormous and well equipped. He opened the back door and they stepped out onto a porch that looked out over the Atlantic Ocean. Monique gasped "My God I have never seen anything so impressive. It takes my breath away." "That my love is the ocean. There is a wonderful view of the ocean from most of the bedrooms upstairs. Would you like to see them now?" "Yes" she said hesitantly "but could we walk down to the ocean first?" Laughing he said "Of course love there is a path that will lead us right to the water's edge." Once they arrived on the beach Monique exclaimed "Wait let's take our shoes off and put our feet in the water." He led her to a big rock where they sat and took their shoes off. Monique took off her socks and shoes then rolled up her pant legs. Matthew did the same then he pulled her up. They ran to the edge of the water laughing like children. Monique waded into the water and jumped right back out crinkling her toes. "The water is so cold. Is it always this cold?" The odd expression on her face made him smile "Yes but you'll get used to it. Once your feet get numb the rest is easy." "Oh" she said and they both started laughing again. Then she started running along the edge and Matthew chased her. She giggled "I feel so free and this could go on forever" Finally Matthew caught up with her and the both fell on the sand laughing. Matthew pushing the hair away from Monique's face kissed her gently on the lips. His kiss grew more intense. Monique responded as he parted her lips with his tongue and explored her mouth. She thought "I wish his kisses could go on forever." Matthew pulled away thinking "I want to kiss her and then make love to her right here and right now. I have to be patient I don't want to frighten her." He smiled at her and said "I could kiss you all day but I need to control myself because this could easily become something else I want you so much. However I want you to feel safe and I am sure you will let me know when you do. Only then will I be able to kiss every part of you." Monique blushed. Matthew stood and reached for Monique's hand to help her up. They walked to the rock to pick up their shoes and started walking back to the house.

"Until the death of my parents I spend many summers here. I have fond memories. My mother always felt like this was her Haven that is why my father named it The Haven. That is what the Letter H on the gate stands for. I would like to spend this summer here. Would you like that love?" "Oh yes I feel like this could be my Haven too Matthew." Matthew smiled "Good then we will spend this summer and every summer after that here at the Haven." "Does all this land belong to you?" "Yes I own two hundred and fifty acres." Amazed she said "Two hundred and fifty acres." Matthew continued "We also have a stable and a few horses. The stable boy lives in a small house behind the barn. Would you like to learn how to ride?" "I would love to learn." "I'll teach you. We will look at the rest of the house than after we will eat the lunch that cook is prepared for us." Back at the house they sat on the stairs and put their socks and shoes on. Then he showed her the second floor 10 large bedrooms each with a fireplace and a full bath. They entered one of the rooms and went out on the balcony. Matthew wanted to show Monique the view of the ocean from up here. The view of the ocean was spectacular. He then led her to another set of stairs that led to the attic. "My parents have stored many valuable paintings here." "Why are they in the attic?" "My father acquired this home sight unseen from a gentleman from his club. He won it in a card game. After the game he was given the deed and the keys. He was told everything inside went with the house. It was after mother and father spent their first summer here. Being new comers to Newport the first season they were invited to many parties at some of the most prestigious homes including the Vanderbilt home. After being at a few of these homes mother felt they were more like museums than a home. She didn't want the Haven to be that way. That is when she decided to decorate and make it a home we would be comfortable in. Mother decided she wanted all the paintings taken down. They didn't need the money so she didn't want to sell them rather she had father store them in the attic." Matthew turned on the light Monique couldn't believe all the paintings that were so neatly covered. She had read about the great artists and saw pictures of their paintings in the art books at the library never thinking she would actually see one. Monique lifted the cover on one of the paintings it was hiding a Rembrandt "Oh this is so beautiful Matthew. How many paintings would you say are here?" "I counted them once when I was a child there are twenty-four of them." "If you ever want to hang some in the house let me know." "No I feel the same as your mother. The paintings should not be hanging in the Haven we'll leave them where they are for now." "Whatever you think is best my love." He switched the light off "Let's go down and have our lunch."

The cook had a picnic lunch ready for them they took the basket out to the garden. Monique opened the basket she grabbed the table cloth and spread it on the ground under the maple tree. Matthew took out the French bread, cheese, liver pate, fruits, two wine glasses and a bottle of Chablis. Monique filled their plates while Matthew poured the wine. He handed her a glass she lifted her glass and said let us make a toast. He raised his glass to hers and said "May we have many years of happiness here at the Haven." She added "Our Haven darling." They touched their glasses and sipped their wine. After lunch Matthew brought her to the stables and introduced her to the stable boy Billy. He asked him to saddle his horse White Lightning he was a beautiful chestnut horse. He then asked him to saddle Lilly a chestnut mare for Monique. She had belonged to his mother and he knew she'd be gentle for Monique. It didn't take Monique long to learn to ride. She loved it. They rode their horses along the shore and after a while Monique spurred Lilly on and galloped through the surf. Matthew told Monique they would move into the Haven June first for the summer. Monique was very pleased.

Chapter Eleven

"Simon they make such a wonderful couple. They look so free and happy riding side by side on their horses." "Yes they do Sarah your grandmother was a very vibrant woman and felt very much alive." Sarah smiled "No one deserves it more than she does after all the hell she has been through." "You are absolutely right Sarah." "Do you know Simon I've never been in the attic I never knew about those paintings." "You can take a look at them when you get back." "I plan on it then I can sell them to buy out my cousin's shares of the Haven."

Mrs. Johnson was busy in the kitchen preparing meals. Vicki and Tom were coming up for the weekend. Her daughter Maggie was also in the kitchen washing vegetables in the sink. Maggie was a very attractive girl with long brown hair, brown eyes and olive skin. She wore the same size as Vicki and Sarah. She received all of Sarah's old clothes but she resented it. Mrs. Johnson looked at Maggie "Maggie I received a call from detective Jennison. He wants me to call him when Vicki and Tom arrive." Maggie turned to her mother "Why does he want to speak to them mother?" "I didn't tell you but last week when the detective was here. He told me he believes someone is trying to kill Sarah." Maggie looked shock "Really and that is the reason he wants to speak to Vicki and Tom?" "Yes. Have you gone to the hospital to see Sarah Maggie?" "No I Haven't mother I've been busy. Have you visited her?" "Yes Alfred and I have been going every day for just a few minutes.

I feel so bad for the poor darling. Just lying there she looks so lifeless. I can't stand seeing her that way. I love her and I've been praying for her to come out of the coma so she can come home where she belongs." Maggie was in a daze as her mother was speaking to her she thought to herself "I wish my mother would show as much concern for me as she does for Sarah. If she dies it won't be so bad. She's had everything all her life while I just stood back and watched her and her cousins get everything they ever wanted. My mother could never afford to buy me clothes like they wore. What's so bad about dying when you've had it all? I'd give anything to have her life and her money." While in her daze the water was still on and filling the sink rapidly. All of a sudden Mrs. Johnson screamed "Maggie!" Maggie blinking came out of her daze. Mrs. Johnson continued to scream "The water is overflowing and coming out of the sink. Look at the mess you've made. What were you thinking?" Maggie looking down answered "I'm sorry mother I must have been day dreaming. I'll clean it right up." At that moment Vicki popped into the kitchen looking at Mrs. Johnson she said "Mrs. Johnson we're here what time is dinner?" Vicki suddenly saw all the water on the floor and said harshly "What the hell happened here?" Maggie put her head down blushing she said "I let the sink over flow it was an accident I wasn't paying attention." Vicki gave her a pathetic look and said "Well get it cleaned up. I don't want it to ruin the floor." Mrs. Johnson looked at Vicki and said "It will be taken care of promptly Miss Vicki. Dinner will be at seven. Would you like it served in the dining room or on the patio?" Vicki answered "On the patio. Is Sarah still in the hospital?" "Yes" Mrs. Johnson said she added "and she is still in a coma." "Strange" Vicki answered with no emotion as she walked out of the kitchen. After Vicki walked out of the room

Mrs. Johnson picked up the phone and called Detective Jennison to let him know they both had arrived.

An hour later Evan and Detective Jennison were at the door asking to see Tom and Vicki. Alfred led them to the living room while he went to find Tom and Vicki. A short while later Vicki walked into the living room. Both men stood up detective Jennison spoke "Miss Victoria I'm detective Jennison and this is Evan." "Please detective, call me Vicki. Victoria sounds so formal." Evan thought to himself "She looks just like Sarah except for the heavy make-up and her disposition." Chris said "Please have a seat Vicki. We have a few questions we need answered." Vicki sat next to Evan on the sofa facing Chris who sat opposite. Chris said "I'd like to ask you a few questions concerning Sarah." Vicki looked surprised "Really?" "Why?" Chris answered "I believe someone is trying to kill her." Vicki started to fidget in her seat looking at the detective she said "For heaven's sake who would want to kill Sarah?" Tom walked into the living room and said "What's this all about someone is trying to kill Sarah?" Vicki stood up and walked over to Tom "Tom thank God you're here." This is Detective Jennison and Evan. Gentlemen this is my brother Tom." Tom looked at the men "That is ludicrous She fell off of her horse probably from galloping too fast and not paying attention." Tom exclaimed. Chris raising his eyebrow said to Tom "I'm afraid not Tom. We do believe that someone is trying to kill Sarah." Vicki sat back down on the sofa and Tom sat in the other empty chair across from her. Tom looked at Chris and Evan "I just don't believe it." Chris asked . "Vicki where were you last Saturday between the hours of 9 and 11am?" Vicki answered sarcastically "How should I know that was a week ago detective." Maybe you can try and jog your memory Vicki." She looked at her brother "Tom do you remember what I was doing last Saturday at that time?" "I don't know about you Vicki I was at the club at 8 am golfing and I didn't leave the club until after lunch." Chris looked at Tom "Do you have anyone that can verify that Tom?" Tom was highly insulted "I'm not sure why that should matter to you detective. However in answer to your question I played golf with my friend Joe Martin and then we sat and had few drinks and lunch. Are you trying to insinuate that I tried to kill my own cousin?" "I'm not insinuating anything Tom I'm just checking out everything and everyone. Now back to you Vicki. Did you remember what you were doing last Saturday?" "I must have gone shopping I'm always shopping. Don't I always go shopping Tom?" "Yes shopping is her favorite pastime." Chris looked at Vicki "Did you go shopping with anyone else?" "No I don't think so detective." Chris was starting to get irritated "You don't think so? Wouldn't you know if someone else was with you?" Vicki was clearly getting angry she said "Detective I don't like the way you're badgering me I believe I should call my attorney." "That is up to you Vicki. Of course if you have nothing to hide you shouldn't need your attorney. Then again if you are hiding something then I highly suggest you call your attorney." Vicki with a frown on her face said "I'm not trying to hide anything. She's my cousin for heaven's sake. What could I possibly have to hide?" "I hope not Vicki because if you are I will find out. Do either of you know of anyone that might want to harm her?" Tom and Vicki looked at each other and in unison said "No" Chris said "That will be all for today. I'm sure I'll have more questions and you'll both be available if I need you right?" Both Tom and Vicki nodded. Chris and Evan got up and Chris said "We'll show ourselves out. Thank you for your time." When they got into the car Chris started it as he was driving down the driveway he turned to Evan and said "What do you think of those two?" "They were nervous as hell I don't know what they are trying to hide however I do know they are hiding something." "I feel the same way I'm going to have them followed for a while to find out what they are up to." "That's a good idea Chris and I think I'll hire a private investigator to check into their backgrounds etc. I'm sure between the two of us we will find out just what it is these two are hiding." "Evan, have you gone back to the hospital to see Sarah?" "Chris I have to tell you this I have been spending all of my waking hours by Sarah's bedside." "Why?" "You are going to think I've lost my mind but I feel a strong connection with this woman. I believe I'm in love with her." Chris glanced over at Evan "Maybe you have lost your mind. How can you be in love with someone you've never spoken to for that matter you've never even seen her with her eyes open?" "I asked myself the same thing and yet I can't stay away from her. I've never felt this way about any woman and what's worse it's taking her so long to get out of that damn coma. You've seen Sarah, Chris don't you think her cousin Vicki looks just like her?" "Now that you mention it yes she does. I noticed the resemblance when I was questioning her except the cousin wears a ton of make-up and tight sexy clothes. Her blue shorts and halter top didn't leave much to the imagination if that's your type." They both laughed "I wouldn't put her in my little black book Evan she seems a little too rough for me. Where do you want me to drop you off?" "At the hospital please. Chris I just thought of something you might want to speak to her friend Julie Tate she works for Sarah she seems like a nice person. I met her at the hospital maybe she can help you out." "Thanks I'll look into it and I will put that tail on Vicki and Tom. Mrs. Johnson told us they had been stealing the paintings I'd like to know what they are doing with them." "My guess is they are selling them." "That is what I was thinking."

Evan walked into the hospital and took the elevator to the second floor. When the elevator stopped he went to the nurse's station. He asked the head nurse if there were any changes in Sarah's condition. The nurse informed him that there had been no changes. Then he asked if she had any visitors. The answer was always the same Alfred and Mrs. Johnson came and stayed for a few minutes. Also her secretary Nora and her friend Julie called every day. He couldn't understand why her cousins didn't visit her. The guard was still posted in front of the door when Evan walked in. The nurse he spoke to thought how lucky Sarah was to have such a caring man by her side.

Julie was working long hours at the office. With Nora's help she was taking care of Sarah's transactions plus her own work. Nora was worried sick about Sarah. She called the hospital daily to see if there were any changes in Sarah's condition. She couldn't get to the Newport hospital to see her and that bothered her all she could do to help Sarah was pray. Whenever she had a few moments she said a silent prayer for Sarah to get well. Nora thought in spite of the fact that Julie is working hard she looked very happy and didn't seem to mind that Sarah was in a coma. In fact she acted as if Sarah wasn't coming back and the business belonged to her already. She didn't like that at all. Julie also checked on Sarah daily she thought "If Sarah doesn't come out of this coma almost everything of hers will be mine the business and the inheritance Sarah is leaving me. Not bad for a kid from the wrong side of the tracks. When all of this changes my sister Paula will die of envy." What Julie didn't realize was that Paula was very happy and content with her life. She was a registered nurse she worked a couple of nights a week at a Boston hospital to supplement her husband's income. Of course Julie didn't understand that kind of happiness she was too busy enlarging her bank account and her status.

Matthew and Monique spent a remarkable summer at the Haven. To make sure Monique felt at home Matthew bought another Victrola and a black baby grand piano for her so she could enjoy playing her music. He wanted both homes to have whatever made her happy. He continued to buy her records every week. They picnicked and swam in the ocean daily. One day while out exploring they found a cave while off the beach. It seemed pretty deep. They decide to go in and explore it. The further they went in the more they had to crouch down. Finally they saw a light at the end of the tunnel when they emerged from the cave they couldn't believe what they were seeing. There stood a cove with a beautiful garden and wild flowers with a natural spring heated waterfall. The scene was simply exhilarating. Looking at Monique, Matthew said "who would have thought there was such a beautiful place around here." "Matthew it is so beautiful. You've been coming here your whole life and you never knew about this paradise." "No love never. We found it together and it will remain our secret cove. When we have children we won't tell them about our find. This can be our secret hideaway where no one will find us." They both entered the water. They couldn't believe how warm it was. Matthew taught Monique how to swim there because it was so calm. Then they would sit on a rock under the waterfall and just enjoy the warm water flowing down upon them. They dreamed of their future together. They played and laughed it was like their little piece of heaven. They spent a lot of time there throughout the summer. During the summer they rode their horses every day. Matthew also introduced Monique to the finest seafood restaurants. He showed her how to eat a steamed lobster as well as opening steamed clams. He would get different seafood dishes and have her try them all. Most of which Monique loved. Carnivals often came through-out the summer. On one lovely summer night Matthew brought

Monique to her first carnival. He brought her at night because he wanted her to experience seeing it all lit up. Monique was like a little girl again. At first she was in awe and then they went on every ride, played all of the games. Then Matthew bought her first fried dough. As she ate it she had white powder all over her face. Matthew laughed as he wiped the powder off of her face. They shared candy apples, cotton candy, French fries. They ate so much they would have to walk their horse's home. They were walking by the fortune teller's tent. Matthew asked her if she'd like to have her fortune told. Monique told him yes saying she may as well experience everything at least once. They walked into the dark and were greeted by a heavy set woman dressed in a long multi-colored caftan her head dressed with the same colored turban. She also wore long gold looped earrings and a dozen gold bracelets on both wrists. She was sitting at a small round table covered with a gold laced cloth. A crystal ball sat in the center of the table. The only light was coming from a candle in a gold candle stick sitting by the crystal ball. The woman said "Please come in and sit down. Maura will tell you your fortune for just five dollars." Matthew took out his wallet he took out a five dollar bill and placed it in her palm. She took the money folded it and placed it in her cleavage. She then placed her hands with long red fingernails around the crystal ball. She started "The crystal ball shows me that you are very much in love. It also shows me that you will marry in the New Year. You will have two children both girls. Your life together will be very happy. Do you have any questions for me?" Monique answered "No I don't" "Then your reading is finished." Monique stood up and she and Matthew left the tent. After they left the tent the gypsy thought "I wish all young couples I read had a happy future like they do." Holding Matthew's hand Monique looked at him "How do you suppose she knew we were getting married?" "I don't know love she must be truly gifted." It was getting late and both Matthew and Monique were getting tired. Matthew asked "Have you had a good night love?" Monique looked at him and smiled "This was one of the best nights of my life!" Matthew looked and questioned "One of the best? What was the other?" Monique stopped and held Matthews other hand she gazed into his beautiful eyes and said "The day you asked me to marry you was the very best day of my life." Matthew slowly bent his head and brought his lips to Monique's kissing her tenderly he then said "It was the best day of my life when you said yes. Come let's get the horses and return to the Haven." She smiled at him and they both walked to their horses. After the stable boy brought their horses to them they galloped back to the Haven.

On the day they were returning to Boston Monique was standing by the open window in her bedroom. Suddenly a white dove flew in and perched itself on the window sill cooing at her. "Why good morning my little friend did you come to wish me well on my return home?" The dove looked up at her as if it understood and cooed again. "Will you come back to visit me when I return next summer?" The dove cooed one more time and flew away. "It's funny" she thought "The doves visit has made me feel so at peace." As they were leaving for Boston Monique asked "Matthew when we have our daughters I would like them to be born here. I like the house in Boston but I love the Haven I feel so at peace here." "Whatever pleases you Monique. If you want our children to be born here then they shall be born here." "Thank you Matthew." While Matthew was driving he was thinking "We had a wonderful summer we had so much fun getting to know each other better spending many nights walking on the beach. Kissing in the moon light her kisses left me breathless again and again. I'm glad we decided to wait until our wedding night to make love. I believe by then she will be ready to come to me with no fears. I'm a patient man and I love her too much to jeopardize our relationship." The rest of the ride home they talked about how much fun they had and looked forward to next year.

When they arrived home Jacob and Jasmine were there to greet them. Jasmine spoke first "Miss Monique I have missed you! How was your holiday?" Monique hugged Jasmine "It was wonderful I have plenty of stories to share with you." Both women giggled and walked toward the door as Jacob and Matthew started to unpack the car. Jacob turned to Matthew "I trust you had a good holiday also sir?" Matthew smiled at Jacob "I have never been happier Jacob. She loved the place and we intend to spend all of our summers there." Jacob smiled "I am so glad Matthew that you have finally found happiness. There is no greater man who deserves it." Matthew wrapped his arm around Jacobs shoulder "Thank you Jacob it means the world to me that you approve." They both grabbed the luggage and brought them into the house.

Matthew had a lot to catch up on with his job and before long the holidays were quickly approaching and there was a wedding to prepare for. Thanksgiving had come and gone it seemed like the months were just flying by. After Thanksgiving one evening while Matthew was sitting beside the fireplace Monique was sitting at her piano. She had suddenly stopped playing Matthew noticed and was watching her. Monique suddenly felt dread creeping up on her in the pit of her stomach. She was afraid something awful would happen to spoil her happiness. When she felt that way Matthew always seemed to notice the change in her. Matthew could tell that Monique was starting to feel terrified. He walked over to her and placed his hands on her shoulders and said "Love I promised you that you would never have to be frightened again God wants you to be happy. That is the reason he sent you to me he knows how much I love you and that I will always protect you. Please believe me and believe it in your heart." Monique staring at the music said "Oh Matthew I do believe you. Sometimes I just can't explain how happy you make me and I'm afraid it won't last. You know me so well you can tell when I get these awful feelings." "Yes love I can feel when you are unhappy." "I shouldn't let myself get this way especially after what happened to me the day we were leaving the Haven." "You didn't mention anything to me?" "On our last day at the Haven a white dove landed on my window sill and cooed at me. I said hello to the dove it was beautiful and it looked at me like it understood me. I did talk to it a little bit and each time it cooed. When it cooed for the last time as I said goodbye I felt such an inner peace I cannot describe it." "I believe my love the dove was a sign from God letting you know that everything in your life will be fine. Just think in two months we will be married. Think of your wedding day and the trip we will be making to Europe. Of course Mrs. Fortin will be here for Christmas and she will stay for the wedding and you know how much she loves you. Think only happy thoughts I command it!" They both started to laugh. Monique turned to look at Matthew with a sly look on her face "You command it do you?" She said raising her eyebrow. She then grabbed the collar of his jacket to pull him down to her face and kissed him. Matthew wanting her to know how much he loved her, and wanted her, deepened the kiss. He parted her mouth open and slowly slid his tongue across hers. Monique opened her mouth fully to take all of him in. They kissed exploring each other's mouth. He felt his manhood harden and he knew if they didn't stop he wasn't going to be able to control himself he wanted her so much. He suddenly pulled away and Monique opened her eyes and looked at him questioningly he said "Love if I hadn't pulled away I wouldn't be able to control what happened next and I made you a promise and I intend to keep it. But please know I could kiss you all day and all night and make sweet love to you just as much. Monique blushed she had felt the stirring deep inside of her and didn't quite understand it but she didn't want Matthew to stop. Now that they had stopped she had a flashback of David throwing her on the bed and spreading her legs forcing himself inside of her. Monique shuddered at the thought and made herself remember she was with Matthew not the animal. Monique bringing herself back to the present thought "I love this man so much. I love him with my body and soul."

A week before Christmas Mrs. Fortin arrived. Monique was so excited that she stayed by the door waiting for the carriage to come. When the carriage arrived Monique opened the door and ran out to greet Mrs. Fortin. She helped her out of the carriage and then wrapped her arms around her saying "I have missed you. I am so glad you are here!" Mrs. Fortin smiled and placed her hands on Monique's face "Let me look at you. My you look more beautiful than the last time I saw you. I have missed you also my dear girl. You'll have to catch me up on everything since we've last written to each other." Monique smiled "I have lots to tell you. Let's go inside before you catch cold." Mrs. Fortin and Monique walked into the house as Alfred was getting her luggage from the carriage. When Matthew arrived home he greeted Mrs. Fortin "I am so glad you are here I hope the ride wasn't too rough for you." Mrs. Fortin smiled and hugged Matthew "The ride was fine and thank you for sending your carriage to come and get me. You are truly a wonderful man Matthew and I am so glad that you will be my dear Monique's husband." Matthew blushed. "I am glad too." Looking at Monique he said "I love her with all that I am. Come let's go enjoy dinner I'm sure we have plenty to talk about." They all walked into the dining room as dinner was being laid out on the table for them. Matthew had told cook to find the finest roast to serve for dinner with Mrs. Fortin's favorite apple cobbler for dessert. During dinner they talked about everything that had been going on since Mrs. Fortin had last been there. Mrs. Fortin talked about some of the things that had been going on since she had left. They all talked late into the evening. Matthew was the first to retire. "If you'll excuse me ladies I have a very busy day tomorrow. I could stay up all night and talk with you two however I wouldn't make it to work in the morning." He bent down and gave Monique a kiss on the cheek goodnight love I'll see you tomorrow." Monique smiled "Rest well." Matthew gave Mrs. Fortin a kiss on the cheek also "Again I am so glad you are here. I hope you sleep well." Mrs. Fortin smiled "Goodnight Matthew sweet dreams." Matthew smiled and headed for the foyer. He climbed the stairs like a boy he was happy and all was right in his world. Mrs. Fortin and Monique didn't last too much longer. Mrs. Fortin kept yawning and finally Monique said "I think it's time that we retire you've had a long journey and I'm sure you must be exhausted. We will talk more in the morning." They both retired to their rooms.

Chapter Twelve

The days flew by and Christmas was wonderful. Matthew once again spoiled Monique and Mrs. Fortin lavishing them with gifts. This year the women were prepared and had many surprises for Matthew as well. It felt like the day had just started when it ended late in the evening. Mrs. Fortin wished the day could last forever. The week coming up would be busy preparing for the wedding. They had decided on a small informal wedding at Saint Patrick's Chapel. They were only inviting a few friends. Monique was so nervous. When she and Mrs. Fortin were alone she voiced how scared she was. "Mrs. Fortin I love Matthew so much and I am so afraid." Mrs. Fortin asked "What are you afraid of dear?" "I'm afraid I won't be a good wife because of all the things David did to me I don't know how to make love as Matthew calls it. I get these feelings in my stomach when he kisses me. What does it all mean?" Mrs. Fortin sighed and took her hand. "My dear sweet Monique how innocent you were when your mother sent you away. I am sure she never even explained to you about making love." Monique shook her head no. Mrs. Fortin continued. "When you really love someone you will not be afraid and making love will come naturally to you. I know you may find this hard to believe but do you trust me Monique?" Monique shook her head and answered. "I trust you completely. You are the mother I never had. Sometimes I forget and want to call you mother. You are the only person I have ever felt close to up until now. I feel very close to Matthew too. Do you think

Mrs. Fortin that I could call you Mother?" Monique was blushing and didn't realize she was holding her breath. Mrs. Fortin looked at her lovingly "I would be honored to have you call me Mother my dear child." Monique hugged Mrs. Fortin and for the first time said "Mother I love you." With tears in her eyes Mrs.

Fortin replied "I love you too and I couldn't have been blessed with a more perfect daughter." They hugged again. Mrs. Fortin made sure Monique felt comfortable with her answer and told her not to worry everything would be just fine. They finished the last of the details two days before the wedding. The night before the wedding Monique and Mrs. Fortin stayed at a hotel. She didn't want Matthew to see her until their wedding day. The day of the wedding Monique woke up early she watched Mrs. Fortin sleep and smiled as she thought "how I wish you would have been my real mother." Mrs. Fortin was starting to awake she looked over at Monique's bed it was empty she sat up and looked around the suite suddenly she saw Monique sitting in a chair beside the window. She smiled "How long have you been up dear?" "I awoke a few hours ago I have butterflies in my stomach. I am so excited." Mrs. Fortin smiled and climbed out of the bed "Well we may as well get ready for the big day!" Monique jumped up "I already washed. I wasn't sure how to do my hair. Could you help me with that mother?" "Well you see dear when I booked us here at the hotel I knew there was a hair salon on the first floor. I made arrangements for the both of us to have our hair done. We are due down there in fifteen minutes." Monique giggled like a child "ooh let's go down there now." Mrs. Fortin laughed "Well I think I should put something on rather than my night gown. It wouldn't look to good if I went down there looking like this." Monique laughed "I'll just sit here and wait while you change." Mrs. Fortin went into the bathroom to wash and change. After she was changed she came out of the bathroom "Okay dear I believe I'm more presentable now. Shall we go?" Monique got up and wrapped her arm in Mrs. Fortin's arm "Yes mother." Mrs. Fortin smiled "Let us go become beauties for the day." They walked out of the suite and to the elevator. When they entered the elevator Mrs. Fortin pressed the first floor. When they got off the elevator they walked to the left and straight to the salon. Once in the salon Mrs. Fortin was greeted by a young lady. "May I help you?" Mrs. Fortin smiled "My daughter and I have an appointment." "May I have your name please?" "Yes Mrs. Fortin and Monique." "Just one moment I will let Bridget know you are here." "Thank you." The young lady disappeared into the salon. When the curtain opened Mrs. Fortin and Monique were greeted by an older woman. She was very well dressed and wore a black apron over her clothes. She greeted the two women. "Hi I'm Bridget you must be Mrs. Fortin and Monique." Both women nodded yes. "Who would like to be first?" Mrs. Fortin smiled at Bridget "Why not do the brides hair first after all this is her big day." Bridget smiled she escorted Monique to the sink. "Please make yourself comfortable while I get a towel." When Bridget returned she had a towel and a black cape. She placed the towel around the back of Monique's neck as she was placing the cape she asked Monique "What time are you getting married?" "We are getting married at six pm. We are having a candle light wedding." "Oh my how romantic" Bridget replied. Bridge finished washing Monique's hair and escorted her to a chair in front of a mirror. Monique was looking all around taking it all in. She had never been in a beauty salon before. Bridget was fluffing Monique's hair as she asked "Are you wearing a veil or a hat?" "I'm wearing a white box hat with a veil in front." Bridget replied. "Hmm with that type of hat I believe that a

French twist would look lovely especially with your beautiful blond hair. What do you think?" "You are the expert so I'm leaving it in your hands." "Very well then let's get started." Bridget worked on Monique's hair while Monique watched the transformation take place in the mirror. When Bridget was done she said "What do you think?" Monique smiled "It's absolutely beautiful. I feel like a princess." Bridget looked at Monique through the mirror "May I have the honor of doing your make-up at no extra charge?" "Yes" Monique smiled "That would be lovely." Bridget brought Monique over to the make-up table. "I'll just get my case." Monique sat down and waited for Bridget to return. Bridget returned with her case. "This is going to be delightful. You have such beautiful skin." Monique blushed. Bridget took her time applying the make-up to Monique's face. As she was finishing up she looked at Monique and said "What a beautiful bride you are going to be and what a lucky man your groom is." Monique blushed again and said "Thank you" When Bridget handed her the mirror Monique looked into it and gasped "Oh my. Is this really me? I look so different." Monique went to touch her face and Bridget pushed her hand down gently "Don't touch it dear we wouldn't want that beautiful face all smudged." Monique walked into the waiting room and took Mrs. Fortin's breath away. "My dear you look absolutely stunning. I cannot wait to see the look on Matthew's face when he first looks at his bride." Bridget smiled and said "She is a beauty he's a very lucky man. Mrs. Fortin if you'll join me we'll get you ready." Mrs. Fortin got up and followed Bridget into the back. Bridget worked on Mrs. Fortin's hair for another forty-five minutes. When Mrs. Fortin walked to the waiting room Monique smiled brightly "Mother you look so beautiful we are going to be just smashing together." Mrs. Fortin paid Bridget and slipped her a generous tip. "Thank you so much Bridget. You've done a wonderful job on both of us." Bridget tucking the tip in her apron pocket said "Thank you it was a pleasure meeting both of you." Looking at Monique she said "Congratulations and I hope you have a very happy life." "Thank you." Monique answered. They walked out of the salon arm in arm Mrs. Fortin said "I am famished. Are you hungry dear?" Monique answered "Now that you've mentioned it my stomach is rumbling." "How about if we go have lunch before we head up to the suite to get you dressed?" "That sounds wonderful. You know we skipped breakfast." "Yes I was just thinking about that. No more skipping we wouldn't want you passing out at your own wedding." "Oh dear!" exclaimed Monique "That would not be good at all." Still arm in arm Mrs. Fortin said "I know a lovely café a block away let's go there and have lunch." They walked out of the hotel with their heads held high. Both women looked stunning and the bride wasn't even dressed yet. They went into the café and ordered lunch. They both attacked it like it was their last meal. Mrs. Fortin looked at Monique and said "Goodness that was delicious. How was yours dear?" "Monique smiled "It was wonderful I'm so full I hope I fit into my dress." They both laughed. Mrs. Fortin paid the bill and they headed back to the hotel. They entered the hotel and went over to the elevators. They took the elevator up to their suite. It was a little after three pm and the ride to the chapel would take them at least thirty minutes. Mrs. Fortin noticing the time said "I'll go and get ready and then we will get you ready. It won't take me long why don't you start with your stockings dear. I'll be out in time to help you with your corset." "I will gather my stockings and corset and start putting them on." Mrs. Fortin went into the changing room to change. It didn't take her long. After she was finished she headed back into the main room where Monique was fighting with her corset. "Here let me help you with that dear." She tied her corset. Mrs. Fortin grabbed the bag hanging in the closet which contained Monique's wedding attire. She unzipped the bag and held a white lace and ivory satin dress, with a full skirt and pearl embroidery. She reached up for the round box that contained the hat. Monique had opted for a hat instead of the traditional veil. Her hat had a veil attached. Mrs. Fortin brought the gown and hat over to where Monique was standing. She helped Monique into her dress. After Monique had her dress on Mrs. Fortin reached into her luggage bag she pulled out a blue garter walking over to Monique she said "I brought you this blue garter I wore it many years ago when I married. I am giving it to you to wear today so that you may be just as blessed as I was when I married my love." Mrs. Fortin had never talked of being married and now was not the time to ask questions. Monique figured she could talk to her about it when they returned from their honeymoon. She took the garter and placed it on her right thigh "This is beautiful." Monique smiled. "That is not all I have for you dear. I bought you a present a while ago for your wedding day" Mrs. Fortin reached into her pocket and pulled out a long blue velvet box handing it to Monique she said "Here dear open this." Monique took the box with trembling hands she opened the box. Inside was a white pearl necklace the pearls had been imported from France. Monique put the necklace in her hands and marveled at its beauty. "Mother please put it on for me. It is beautiful thank you so much." "I'm glad you like it dear I wanted something special as you are special to me." Mrs. Fortin took the necklace from Monique she went behind Monique and placed the necklace on her neck and then clasped it. After she placed the necklace on Monique's neck she said "Well we have something new and something blue now we need something borrowed." Reaching to the breast of her dress Mrs. Fortin removed a small gold ribbon watch and said "I'll let you borrow my ribbon watch it was a gift to me by my dear husband." She put in on Monique's dress. "Now let's put your hat on dear." Monique lowered her head so Mrs. Fortin could put her hat and veil on. She placed two bobby pins on each side and then said "There now let me look at you." Monique turned to face Mrs. Fortin "What do you think Mother?" Mrs. Fortin smiled "I think you are the most beautiful bride I have ever seen. You look absolutely stunning. Here have a look for yourself." She turned Monique to face the full length mirror that was on the other end of the room. Monique couldn't believe she was looking at herself. "I think I'm dreaming and I'm going to wake up soon." She said to herself out loud. Mrs. Fortin laughed. "This isn't a dream dear it is really true and you look like a princess." Looking at her watch Mrs. Fortin noticed the time was five fifteen. She looked at Monique "We must hurry Matthew is sending a carriage for us at five thirty." Monique took her white cape from the closet and draped it across her shoulders. Mrs. Fortin retrieved her coat and her bag. She put on her coat and looked at Monique again. "Are you ready dear? I believe I hear wedding bells from afar." Monique took a deep breath "I think I'm ready. Shall we go?" Opening the door to the suite they walked into the hall. Mrs. Fortin pressed for the elevator. While they were waiting Monique was thinking "I can't believe this is happening it feels like a dream. If it is a dream I don't ever want to wake up." The ding of the elevator brought her back to the present. As they stepped into the elevator there were a few people already in there when they saw Monique each remarked about how beautiful she looked and congratulated her on her wedding. When they got to the first floor they saw a white carriage through the glass doors. Monique looked at it "What a beautiful carriage whoever is riding in that today is one very lucky person." She smiled. As they went through the glass doors there was a very distinguished looking gentleman standing next to the carriage. He looked over at them and asked "Are you Miss Monique?" Monique looked surprised and hesitantly answered "Yes I am sir why?" The gentleman bowed and said "Madame your carriage awaits you. I have been sent here by Matthew to take you to your wedding." Monique was shocked and didn't know what to say Mrs. Fortin stepped forward "Good evening sir please excuse my daughter I think she is a little nervous." The coachman smiled "I understand. Miss Monique may I help you into the carriage?" He held out his hand for Monique to take she put her hand in his as she climbed onto the carriage. Mrs. Fortin followed. Monique couldn't believe how beautiful this carriage was she thought "Could this evening get any better?" The coachman went to the front of the carriage to retrieve something as he came back to the door he held a beautiful bouquet of red roses. Handing them to Monique he said "These are from Mister Matthew I was told to give them to you after you were in the carriage." Monique blushed she reached for the roses and smelled them "These are my favorite flowers thank you sir. Look how beautiful they are mother. The smell is filling the carriage." Mrs. Fortin smiled "They are very beautiful dear almost as beautiful as you." The coachman closed the door to the carriage and climbed onto the front. He turned the horses around and headed for the church. As they drove through the streets of Boston they could see all the people getting ready for the New Year's Eve celebration. The city was bustling. This was one of the biggest celebrations of the year. At midnight everyone would be yelling Happy New Year and the champagne would start flowing. Monique smiled as she watched children playing, vendors setting up their carts and couples holding hands. As they started to leave the heart of the city things were quieter. She admired the scenic view of the drive. She finally had the church in sight. The butterflies started to come and she was nervous. As the carriage reached the church it stopped. The coachman opened the door to the carriage and helped Monique and Mrs. Fortin out of the carriage. He then opened the door to the church foyer Jasmine was there waiting for them and took their coats. Jasmine whispered something in Mrs. Fortin's ear she nodded then said to Monique "I will be right back dear." She followed Jasmine. They reached a small room off the chapel Jasmine opened the door and there was Matthew looking so handsome in his white tuxedo. Mrs. Fortin went over and gave him a kiss "Is everything alright Matthew?" Matthew smiled "Yes everything is wonderful. How is the bride to be?" "She is nervous however she is doing fine." "Good I wanted to ask you considering Monique's father is no longer living I was hoping that I could ask you to walk Monique down the aisle. Would you mind?" Mrs. Fortin smiled "I would be honored. Monique asked me last night if it was okay for her to call me mother and I was honored that she asked me. This seems fitting that I shall walk her down the aisle as her mother. Thank you Matthew for asking me." He placed a kiss on Mrs. Fortin's cheek "Thank you for loving my soon to be wife as your own. You are truly a remarkable woman." "She is easy to love Matthew but I don't have to tell you that you already know. I'll leave you to finish getting ready and I'll see you in a few minutes." Mrs. Fortin returned to Monique. Monique looked at her and asked "Is everything all right?" Mrs. Fortin answered "Well Matthew just asked me to do the honors of walking you down the aisle. How you do you feel about that?" Monique smiled softly "I could not think of a better person to have that honor. I will be proud to walk with you down the aisle." Mrs. Fortin smiled

The wedding march began to play and Mrs. Fortin looked at Monique and said "Are you ready?" Monique wore a big smile on her face and said "I am ready and I cannot wait a minute longer." Mrs. Fortin laughed and offered her arm to Monique and they started down the aisle. The first people Monique saw were Jacob and Jasmine. They smiled when Monique walked near them and Jasmine remarked how beautiful she looked. When Matthew saw his bride walking down the aisle he thought "She is the most beautiful woman I have ever known and I am the luckiest man alive. Thank you God for sending her to me." As Monique approached the alter she looked at Matthew and thought "He is so handsome and kind I can't believe my good fortune to be marrying such a man. I am a new woman. My past no longer exists that girl is dead and I'm alive. Thank you God for sending me Matthew." As they reached Matthew Mrs. Fortin turned lifted Monique's veil and kissed her on the cheek. She took her hand and placed it in Matthews hand and kissed him on the cheek also. She said "God bless you both and may you always be as happy as you are now." She turned to walk to the pew as she was walking she dabbed her eyes to catch the tears of happiness that were falling. Matthew and Monique turned to the priest and the ceremony began.

Chapter Thirteen

Sarah said "Simon" Simon answered "Yes Sarah?" "I believe I'm ready to go back now." Simon looked at Sarah carefully "You have seen enough?" "Oh yes. I basically know the rest of her life story. Some evenings I would sit in the swing with granny on the back porch and she would describe to me the places that she and my grandfather visited in Europe. She told me many stories. After viewing her young life I feel closer to her than I did before if that's possible." Simon smiled "That's very possible Sarah after you have witnessed the kind of hell she went through." "I still cannot understand some of the things that happened to her and my uncle Pierre." Simon still looking at Sarah said "I'll tell you something Sarah your uncle Pierre is very happy. He is with all the people who loved him. Sometimes he is sent on an assignment like I am doing with you." Sarah nodded in understanding and said "It is good to know that when I am finished with this life I will be with the people I love. Although I am rather glad I do not have to go right now Simon." Simon gave Sarah a serious look and said "You have to be very careful when you go back Sarah. There is danger all around you. Be careful of who you trust." Sarah replied "I will Simon. How long have I been gone?" "Two weeks" Simon answered. "Everyone must be worried about me." Simon chose his words "I am sorry to say not everyone Sarah. Some would like it if you never returned." Sarah looked surprised "Who Simon?" Simon sighed "I'm not at liberty to give you that information Sarah you will just have to be careful." Sarah looked disappointed "I'll be very careful." Simon said "Sarah." Sarah answered "Yes Simon?" Simon asked "When you return will you deliver a message for me?" Monique nodded "Absolutely Simon anything I can do for you I will do." Simon continued "When you meet my son give him this message from me. Tell him I'm sorry that I passed on when he was only four years old. You see I was a salesman and I was killed in a train derailment. I want him to know I love him and his mother very much and how very proud of him I am. I am proud of all of his achievements and the man he has become. Also tell him his second father Phillip is also here and he is very happy."Sarah looked at Simon thoughtfully "Simon what is your son's name?" Simon looked down "I am not allowed to give you that information either Sarah." Sarah looked at Simon in disbelief "How can I give him your message if you do not tell me his name?" Simon sighed. "My dear Sarah you will know him as soon as you meet him." "But Simon what if I do not meet him?" Simon kissed her on the forehead and said "Goodbye Sarah." Without another word he faded away. Sarah was upset and started to call "Simon, Simon come back!" She stopped for a minute and then said in a low voice "Simon please come back?" As she was calling Simon's name she felt herself going back into her body.

Evan was holding Sarah's hand as she was calling someone named Simon. Her eyes started to flutter open. She felt someone holding her hand. When she opened her eyes she looked up and said "Simon, you didn't leave me I was so afraid I would never see you again." She took his hand and brought it to her lips a tear fell from each eye. The touch of her lips on his hand gave him a chill. Evan was mesmerized. He didn't want to move she was so beautiful and she had a voice like an angel. Staring at Evan she said "What is the matter with you Simon and why aren't you speaking to me. What happened to your white suit?" Evan found his voice "I am not Simon." Sarah looked at Evan in disbelief "Don't be ridiculous of course you are Simon. I have spent the last two weeks with you do you think that I do not know you?" Evan thought to himself "She must be hallucinating she's been in a coma for two weeks." Sarah continued "Don't you remember you asked me to give your son a message telling him how much you loved him and his mother. You told me how sorry you were that you died when he was four years old in a train derailment. You told me how proud you are of his accomplishments. Are you remembering any of this?" "You also said you were proud of the man he has become. Let's see what else did you say? Oh yes that his second father Phillip is with you and is very happy." Evan sat there with a shocked look on his face thinking "She is talking about my father and my step-father" Sarah interrupted his thoughts saying "Now Simon how do you expect me to give that message to your son if you won't even tell me his name it's impossible!" Evan once again found his voice. "Sarah" Sarah interrupted "I see you found your voice Simon." Evan looked at Sarah and gently said "Sarah I am not Simon. I am Evan Simon's son." It was Sarah's turn to look shocked "I must be cracking up!" She closed her eyes tight and opened them again "You still here?" Evan chuckled to himself "Yes I am." Sarah was now confused "Where am I and how did I get here?" Evan answered "You are at Saint John's Hospital Sarah" Evan started to explain what had happened to her two weeks ago. "I was riding my horse Baron when I came upon your horse grazing in the woods. I looked around and couldn't find the rider. About two miles away I found you unconscious I picked you up and brought you and your horse home. Maggie called the ambulance and I brought Mrs. Johnson to the hospital. Since that day I have been spending all of my spare time here with you." Sarah looked more confused "Why?" Evan smiled "It's the craziest thing Sarah I don't know why and you may think I'm foolish but since I first laid eyes on you I feel connected to you." Sarah looked at Evan "After what I have been through I don't think you're foolish. Was your father named Simon?" Evan replied "Yes it was." Did you have another father named Phillip?" Evan replied "Yes he married my mother when I was twelve years old and adopted me. He died a few years ago. Sarah I'm confused. What happened to you while you were in a coma?" Sarah looked at Evan "You're confused! I feel like I've been with you for the last two weeks and yet it can't be. You look exactly like Simon only he was wearing a white suit and you're in a blue polo shirt and jeans. When I fell off my horse I banged my head on a tree I stood up and brushed myself off. Looking down I saw myself lying there. I thought I was dead until a man told me I wasn't dead. I was in between worlds. He called me by my name and introduced himself as Simon. He told me he was sent to help me he was wearing a white suit and a white light engulfed him. He looked exactly like you!" Evan looked astonished "This is amazing. Why was he sent here to help you?" Sarah answered "Someone was trying to buy the Haven and I didn't know if I should sell. In my heart I didn't want to sell but my cousins who each own a twenty percent share want me to sell. My grandmother was worried about me. That is why Simon was sent to help me. You see my grandmother would never speak about her past but now I know why it would have been too painful for her." Evan raised his eyebrow "What did Simon do to help you?" Sarah replied "He took me back into her past. It was like watching a video. I saw my grandmother whose name was Monique as a child her brother my uncle Pierre, my great grandmother and my great grandfather. My granny's father was a wonderful man however he died when granny was nine and Uncle Pierre was six. Then my great grandmother made life for them pure hell. My Uncle Pierre died of pneumonia and malnutrition when he was eight years old. My great grandmother married granny off to an idiot living with his mother who was as wicked as my great grandmother. Granny had a baby girl who died when she was three months old of malnutrition because granny wasn't given enough food to eat while breast feeding her baby. Her mother in law would not let the baby be buried in the plots she owned instead she had her buried in Potters field. It was the most appalling story I have ever seen and what was worse was that it was real. The worst part of it all was there was nothing I could do to help granny." Sarah started to sob uncontrollably. Evan stood up and sat at the edge of her bed. He pulled her into his arms and held her. Tears began to flow from his eyes. A while later Sarah stopped crying looking up at him she said "I'm sorry Evan." Evan let go of her and handed her tissues from her nightstand and kept a few for himself they wiped their eyes and Sarah blew her nose. Evan looked at Sarah "Sarah you have nothing to be sorry for." "I know but it all sounds so unreal so crazy your father, my grandmother. Do you believe what I just told you?" Evan replied "We've never met yet you wake up and call me by my father's name Simon. You repeat the message he gave you thinking I was him. There is no possible way you would know how my father died or how old I was when he died. Oh yes Sarah as strange as your story sounds I do believe you." Sarah smiled "Thank you Evan." Evan looked at Sarah "Do you believe in fate Sarah?" Sarah replied "I guess I better say yes after everything I've experienced in the last two weeks." Evan gazed into Sarah's eyes "I have no doubt that it was fate that led me to you that day in the woods. I hadn't been home to Newport for over two years. I just happened to be riding my horse when you had an accident." "Evan, because of the time I spent with Simon I feel like I've known you forever. This might sound silly but I truly feel we are soul mates." Evan spoke up "It's not silly Sarah I felt the same way from the moment I saw you lying on the ground. I've never felt this way about any woman." Sarah smiled "We both must be crazy Evan." Evan smiled back "We can't be it feels too right. How are you feeling now Sarah?" "I feel a little stiff but it's just as if I've just woken up from a nap and I want to go home." Evan replied "You'll probably be a little shaky from being in bed for two weeks." Sarah gave Evan a serious look "I don't know about shaky but I'm starved." Evan stood up "I better let the nurse know you are awake." Sarah touched Evans arm "Evan before you go I don't want anyone else to know what happened to me." Evan grabbed Sarah's hand "I won't tell another soul. I don't think they'd believe us anyway." They both laughed and Evan walked out of the room to tell the nurse that Sarah was awake.

    Up from above Simon and Monique are looking down at Sarah and Evan. Monique spoke first "They do make a lovely couple don't they?" Simon smiled "Yes they do Monique." Monique turned to Simon and with concern said "I wish there was some way I could keep her safe." Simon put his hand on Monique's face lifting her chin to look at her he said "My son will watch over her. You know there is nothing else we can do to help her it is out of our control." Monique sighed "I know Simon all we can do is hope for the best." Simone responded "It's true that is all we can do. However I am counting on the best for our two angels on earth. Let's go Monique it's time for us to go back."

    Evan found the head nurse at her station pre-occupied. Evan interrupted "Excuse me" Looking up she asked "Mr. Taylor is everything alright with Miss St. James?" "Could you call Dr. Bennett she is awake." The nurse said with excitement

"That is wonderful I will page him right away." Evan smiled and said "Thank you."

When Evan had walked out of the room he had left the door open Sarah noticed there was a police officer sitting outside her door. As Evan came back into the room Sarah asked "Why is there a police officer sitting at my door?" Before Evan had a chance to answer Dr. Bennett walked in. Approaching Sarah's bed he said "Sarah you certainly gave us a scare. How are you feeling?" Sarah looked at Dr. Bennett "I'm fine really I'm just a little stiff and I'm starved." Turning to Evan Dr. Bennett asked "Mr. Taylor would you mind stepping out of the room while I examine Sara?" Evan replied "Not at all Dr. Bennett." Evan left the room. Sarah thought "Evan Taylor what a nice name for such a handsome man. I can't believe myself I'm in love for the first time in my life with a man I don't know anything about where he works or where he lives and I don't care." "Sarah, Sarah" "I'm sorry Dr. Bennett what were you saying?" "Do you have a headache?" he asked. "No I don't." The doctor leaned over Sarah with his stethoscope and listened to her heart. Then he checked her pulse. He took a small flashlight out of his breast pocket shined it in each eye to see if her pupils dilated. He took the blanket off of her and said "Sarah please lift your right leg." She lifted her leg without a problem. He made her do the same with her left leg again she lifted her left without a problem. He covered her back up with the blanket and said "Everything seems to be fine." Sarah replied "So I can go home?" Dr. Bennett smiled at Sarah "Hold on young lady you have just woken up from a coma. I'd like to keep you overnight just to make sure everything is okay. If all goes well I promise you can go home tomorrow." Sarah sighed "If I have to. But you promise I can go home tomorrow?" Dr. Bennett raised his eyebrow "I said I promise only if everything goes well tonight." Sarah replied "Okay Dr. Bennett." "I'll see you in the morning Sarah." As Doctor Bennett opened the door he said "Mr. Taylor you can go back in now. I'm afraid our patient may need a little ray of sunshine. I told her she'd have to wait until tomorrow to go home. She wasn't too happy about that." "Is she okay?" Evan asked with concern. Dr. Bennett smiled "Yes, she seems fine however I want to make sure she's a hundred percent before I send her home." "Okay Thank you doctor I'll make sure she smiles." As Evan opened the door to walk back into Sarah's room again she noticed the police officer outside her door. "Evan why is there a policeman in front of my door?" Just as he was about to answer the nurse walked in carrying a tray. Evan placed the tray table towards Sarah. The nurse placed the tray on the table and said "It's good to finally see you awake." Sarah smiled "Thank you." "I brought you some food I am sure you must be starving. Be sure to take your time eating if you eat too fast it could make you sick. Enjoy!" The nurse left the room. Sarah lifted the cover "Evan, look at this food! Two dry pieces of toast, a small bowl of jello, and a cup of black tea. Gross!" Evan chuckled "You Haven't had solid food for two weeks maybe if they gave you something more solid you wouldn't keep it down." She sighed "you're probably right." She took a bite of her toast and made a face. Evan smiled looking at Sarah he said "Now about the policeman outside your door. Let me explain why he is here. After Mrs. Johnson and I brought you here I went back to the Haven with her and rode my horse home. I kept wondering what spooked your horse to make it buck. I went back to where I found you and started looking around. I found a bullet lodged high up in the tree. It probably just missed you but was enough to spook your horse. I took it out with my pocket knife." She nearly choked on her tea and placed the cup down. "A bullet, are you trying to tell me someone took a shot at me? That is preposterous." "Please let me explain Sarah." "No, I remember Simon told me someone took a shot at me and spooked my horse Oh my God! I'm sorry Evan please continue." Evan rubbed the back of his neck and continued "When I arrived home it kept bothering me so I called a friend of mine his name is Chris Jennison. He's a police detective in the city. We met for lunch and I told him what happened and gave him the bullet. He had it checked out and found out it had been shot very recently. We both felt like someone was trying to kill you and you needed protection. Chris had a policeman stationed outside your door." Sarah was upset "Why would someone want to kill me?" Evan looking concerned said "That is exactly what we are trying to find out Sarah." Sarah was very shaken by what Evan had just told her. As Sarah finished her meal she pushed her table aside. Looking at Evan she said "I have to stay here one more night Evan I know this is a lot to ask will you stay with me? I feel safe when you are here. Evan smiled "Of course I will. While it is still early let me run home and shower and I will be back before night fall. How's that sound?" Sarah smiled "That sounds fine and Evan? Thank you." Evan kissed Sarah on the forehead and told her he'd be back soon. As Sarah lay there she suddenly felt exhausted. She closed her eyes thinking about everything Evan had said and who would want to kill her. Sarah drifted off to sleep.

Sarah started to dream. It was nighttime she was riding her horse through the woods when from out of nowhere came a masked person in a hooded black cape riding a black horse. The person started chasing Sarah. Sarah started sweating and she urged Midnight Blue to go faster. She felt her heart pounding as she rode faster and faster. She couldn't see where she was going and it seemed like the masked person was gaining speed. Unbeknownst to Sarah there was a cliff in front of her ending the path. Before she realized what was happening Midnight Blue stumbled over a boulder throwing Sarah over the edge of the cliff. Screaming Sarah reached out in front of her and caught a branch that was sticking out. As she held on for dear life she started screaming. The hooded figure just looked down and started to laugh. The more the person laughed the louder Sarah screamed. Evan ran into Sarah's room when he heard the screaming. All of a sudden Sarah could hear a voice calling to her. "Sarah it's me Evan. Wake up Sarah you're okay I'm here. Please open your eyes Sarah." Sarah's eyes started to open as her eyes focused she saw Evan leaning over her with fear in his eyes. "Evan? What's wrong?" Evan let out his breath not realizing he was holding it and wrapped his arms around Sarah. "I ran down the hall because I heard you screaming. You were having a nightmare. Do you remember what you were dreaming about Sarah?" "All I remember was someone was chasing me. I don't know who it was and the next thing I knew I was hanging over a cliff. It was horrible Evan." Evan held her tighter "I'm right here Sarah and you are safe. Would you like a drink of water?" "Yes please" Evan poured Sarah a cup of water and held it to her lips while she sipped it. "Are you feeling a little better now?" Sarah shook her head. "Yes I am so glad you are here." She reached for Evans hand and held it. Evan smiled softly "I will be here all night. Try and rest. I'm not going anywhere." Evan pulled up a chair next to Sarah's bed and held her hand. Sarah drifted off to sleep. Evan smiled when he saw how peaceful she looked. He thought to himself "Don't you worry Sarah I won't let anything happen to you again."

The next morning Dr. Bennett came into the room he saw Evan asleep in the chair holding Sarah's hand. Sarah was just waking up "Good morning Sarah. Did you sleep well?" Evan almost jumped out of the chair and Dr. Bennett chuckled.

Sarah rubbed the sleep from her eyes and smiled "Yes doctor I slept like a baby." Dr. Bennett smiled "I'm sure you did with this young man protecting you all night." Evan blushed "She had a nightmare and I wanted her to get a good night's sleep so I stayed here beside her all night." Dr. Bennett looked over at Evan "You are a good man to sleep in that uncomfortable chair and watch over Sarah all night." Evan could feel his face getting flushed "She's worth it Doctor." Dr. Bennett nodded and then looked at Sarah. "Let's get you checked out so we can see if you can leave today." Sarah smiled "That's fine with me." Dr. Bennett removed his stethoscope placed it on his ears and warmed the end with his hand. Placing the drum on Sarah's chest he listened to her heart. He asked her to take a few breaths then he placed the drum on her back asking her to take a few more breaths. He removed his light from his pocket and checked Sarah's eyes. When he was satisfied he asked "Sarah did you have any headaches last night? Do you have one this morning?" "No doctor Bennett my head feels fine." Doctor Bennett raised his eyebrow "I think it's safe to send you home Sarah. However I want you to rest when you get home. Tomorrow you can start taking short walks. Until you feel stronger I don't want you to do anything strenuous. Eat good meals, walk a little and rest. I do not want you to go to work or to ride your horse and if you have any problems I want you to call me immediately okay?" "Can I swim in the pool?" "Yes, again in moderation. I will send the nurse in to remove your IV and to make a follow up appointment with me. After you've had some breakfast you are free to go home." He turned to Evan "I'm counting on you to make sure she follows my directions Evan. I know how Sarah likes to rush things." Evan smiled "You bet Doctor Bennett I'll make sure she follows everything you said and more!" Doctor Bennett smiled at the both of them and left the room. A few minutes later the nurse arrived with a tray for Sarah. "I've brought you your breakfast Miss Saint James." "Thank you" Sarah answered. "Doctor Bennett said I could remove your IV so let's do that first so that you can eat your breakfast while I get your paperwork ready." "Okay" The nurse removed the IV from Sarah's arm placing a Band-Aid where the needle had gone in. "That should feel a little better. I'll be back with your paper work soon." Sarah lifted the lid from her tray. This morning she was given scrambled eggs, juice, toast and a cup of tea. "This looks much better than last night's dinner and I'm starving!" As Sarah was finishing up her breakfast the nurse came back with her paperwork. The nurse smiled "I see you ate all of your breakfast Sarah. I trust it was better than last night's dinner?" Sarah smiled "Much better" "Okay I have a few papers for you to sign and here is your appointment with Doctor Bennett in two weeks. Also here is a list of signs to watch for if you develop any of them please call Doctor Bennett immediately." "Thank you nurse" Handing Sarah a pen she pointed "Sign here and my dear girl you can go as soon as you are ready." "Thank you so much for your kindness nurse." The nurse smiled at Sarah "It was my pleasure taking care of you Sarah." The nurse left and closed the door behind her. Sarah looked at Evan "Evan do I have any clothes here?" "Yes, Mrs. Johnson brought you a pair of jeans, a tee shirt and sneakers. Your under garments should be in the top drawer of the dresser. I'll get your things for you." Evan grabbed the stuff out of the closet and the dresser handing them to Sarah he said "Are you strong enough to dress by yourself or would you like me to get the nurse to help you?" Sarah smiled "No I think I can manage." I'll bring the car around to the front while you get dressed. Tell the nurse when you are ready and she will take you down. I'll meet you in front of the hospital. I'll see you in a bit." Sarah smiled "okay." Evan walked out the door.

While Sarah was getting dressed she started thinking about everything Evan had told her she thought to herself "Why would someone want to kill me? I have never done anything to hurt anyone." Remembering what Simon said she thought "Simon was right I have to be really careful and I'll have to keep my eyes and ears open. I need to make sure I stay alert and not trust anyone. That is of course except for Evan and Mrs. Johnson I know she would never hurt me." Evan walked out the door. While Sarah was getting dressed she started thinking about everything

While Evan was getting the car he took the time to call Mrs. Johnson to let her know Sarah was awake and fine and he would be bringing her home shortly. Mrs. Johnson was happy to hear the good news and told Evan she couldn't wait to see Sarah and she was going to start preparing her favorite meal. Evan drove to the front of the hospital and waited. Five minutes later the nurse was pushing Sarah in the wheelchair to the exit. Evan got out of the car and walked to the passenger side of the car and opened the door. As the nurse helped Sarah out of the wheelchair Evan held Sarah's arm and gently led her into the seat. Thanking the nurse Evan placed the seatbelt on Sarah. He smiled "Are you ready to go home Miss Saint James" Sarah smiled "Oh yes I am more than ready." Evan smiled and walked over to the driver's seat got into the car looked at Sarah and said "Home it is!"

When Evan approached the front of the house Alfred rushed out the door and down the stairs to open the car door for Sarah. Alfred smiled and said "Miss Sarah it is so good to have you home." Sarah smiled back "It's good to be home Alfred." Alfred asked "Are you feeling alright miss?" Just a little stiff I'll be okay thank you Alfred." As Alfred helped her up the stairs Mrs. Johnson was standing at the front door with tears in her eyes. Sarah fell into her arms and Mrs. Johnson hugged her tightly. "I prayed so hard for you to get well thank the good lord my prayers for you were answered." "Thank you for all of your prayers Mrs. Johnson I'm hoping we can talk later right now I need to go to my room and just rest. I guess I'm a little weaker than I thought." Sarah's legs buckled Evan was standing behind her and caught her before she hit the floor. He picked her up and carried her. "Just lead me to the direction of your room Sarah." "Up the stairs please." She directed him to her bedroom he placed her on her bed. Sarah sighed "I don't know why I am so weak, I felt so good when I woke up." Evan replied "You hurt yourself pretty badly when you fell and have been in bed for quite some time. It will take a few days for you to start feeling like yourself again and gaining strength. Are you still hungry?" "I'm starving." Evan asked "How do a couple of poached eggs on toast sound?" "That sounds delicious along with a glass of milk." "I'll ask Mrs. Johnson to fix your breakfast for you on my way out. Please get some rest Sarah and watch yourself." "Will you be coming back?" "You couldn't keep me away! I'm going home to make a few calls. When you finish eating why don't you take a nap and I'll be back this evening." "Yes after I have something to eat and take a nap I should feel much better." "I'll see you later" Evan kissed her on the forehead and left.

Sarah thought "I can't believe everything that has happened to me in the last few weeks. Going back in time and seeing granny's life and the misery she suffered. Who would believe mothers could be so cruel. Knowing granny I would have never imagined the terrible life she had as a child. I definitely know now I do not want to sell the Haven. It meant too much to her and it means too much to me. I'll have to think of a way to buy Vicki and Tom out." Remembering what her grandmother had done Sarah thought "I almost forgot about the paintings in the attic. I'll sell them they must be worth a fortune. I'll make sure to go up there as soon as I'm strong enough." Closing her eyes Sarah heard her door open. Mrs. Johnson entered her room with her breakfast on a tray with a single red rose in the middle. Sarah propped herself up. Mrs. Johnson walked over and placed the tray in front of Sarah. "Here you are Miss Sarah just like you like them. Would you like anything else?" "No thank you Mrs. Johnson this looks delicious." Mrs. Johnson smiled "I'll be up to collect your tray later Sarah, enjoy." Mrs. Johnson left the room. Sarah ate her breakfast enjoying every bite. When she was finished she placed the vase on her nightstand and the tray on the floor. She fluffed up her pillows laid her head down and fell asleep.

Chapter Fourteen

Vicki was lying on her stomach on a lounge chair with no top. A pitcher of margarita mix was sitting on the cart along with Tom's drink. Vicki was sipping her Margarita while Tom was sitting next to her dousing her back with suntan lotion. Tom saw Alfred walking towards them and whispered to Vicki "We've got company." Alfred approached them and said "Miss Vicki, Master Tom I have some good news. Miss Sarah is home from the hospital she's a little weak but she is fine." Vicki looked up at Alfred "Where is she now?" Alfred responded "In her room resting Miss Vicki." Tom put on his fake smile and said "Thank you for letting us know Alfred." Alfred said "Your welcome sir." Alfred turned around and went back inside. Vicki waiting until Alfred was inside said "Great the bitch lives." Standing up and wiping his hands on a towel Tom said "We really have to convince her to sell Vicki, I want my share of that money especially since the last and final offer was received last week for two hundred million dollars. We have until August thirtieth to give them our decision. I want the fifty million in my pocket." He picked up his margarita and drank it down. Taking the pitcher he refilled his glass then walked over and sat in a chair under the umbrella table. He continued "Although we are making good money selling the paintings Vicki it's not as much as what we will get when this place is sold. Thank goodness the dumb bitch didn't know there were paintings in the attic because she's never been up there." Vicki smiled "You're right she doesn't even know they exist." She raised her glass "Here's to the dumb bitch." Tom raised his glass and said "I'll drink to that." He raised his glass to his lips. Vicki spoke first "Tom what can we do to convince her to sell." "I don't know take another shot at her?" "Tom did you try to kill Sarah?" "No and if I did I would not tell you. Believe me I've thought about it but I didn't do it." "That reminds me Tom did you put the painting I left by the attic door in the car?" "Yes I did this morning." "Terrific Monday we'll go to New York to sell it." "Vicki how many paintings are left?" "After we sell this one there will be seven left." "I want to make sure we sell the other paintings before the house is sold." "We will dear brother."

Sarah was having a nightmare someone was chasing her she was running until she couldn't run anymore. She found herself on the edge of a cliff with a drop off to jagged rocks and the ocean below. There was no escape from her pursuer. The pursuer caught up to her and pushed her forward. Sarah was falling and screaming she woke up screaming. She sat straight up in her bed; her body was soaked in perspiration. "It was only a bad dream" she thought "Thank God." She got out of bed and went into the bathroom to take a shower. The water felt good against her skin. She washed her hair and stayed in the shower a little longer letting the warm water rush over her. Still she couldn't shake the nightmare. She turned off the water and wrapped a towel around her hair slipping into her white robe. She decided to call her office to get her mind off the dream. She brought her portable phone on the balcony.

Sitting on her lounge chair she dialed her office. Nora answered on the first ring "Sarah's residential collections Nora speaking may I help you?" "Nora it's me Sarah." "Sarah thank God! Are you alright? Where are you?" "I'm fine and I'm home I'm just a little weak from being in bed for two weeks." "You're not planning on coming to the office are you?" "No the doctor wants me to take it easy for a couple of weeks. Anything earth shattering happening that I should know about?" "No everything has been running smoothly. Julie went to your closings on the six new homes you sold. All went well. One of the buyers Mr. Boalter gave Julie some movie passes for you. He said they were good at any of the cinema's he owns." "What a sweet man. How are the Lantern townhouses doing?" "Two are closing on Monday, one is closing Wednesday, the other two are closing the following Wednesday. You can afford to take some time off Sarah. Julie and the other agents can handle the properties for a while and I can handle everything else. You know business always slows down in July and August." "You're right if I have to take some time off this is the perfect time to do it." "Sarah last week a detective Jennison stopped by and spoke to everyone who works for you including me. He had me a little worried. Do you know anything about this?" "Yes unfortunately they think that someone is trying to kill me." "Oh my God the detective didn't say anything like that to us. He just asked us some questions. Sarah you should be careful in case some weirdo is trying to kill you." Laughing Sarah said "Maybe it's a buyer who isn't satisfied with the house I sold him." "Sarah this is nothing to laugh about it's very serious." "I'm just teasing you Nora please don't worry the police are taking care of it. Changing the subject is Julie around?" "Yes she's in I'll buzz her and tell her you are on the phone. Sarah welcome back to the world of the living again please be careful I don't want anything else happening to you." "Thank you Nora." Julie answering her line said "Hello Sarah" "Julie it's good to hear your voice." "Good to hear my voice you're the one that's been in a coma for two weeks. I for one am very glad to hear your voice." "Touché you are right of course. Nora just gave me the low down on what's been happening in the office.

Thanks for going to my closings." "It was my pleasure after all what are friends for are you feeling alright?" "Yes just a little weak. The doctor wants me to take a few weeks off." "Take as long as you need, you know it's slow this time of the year with everyone on vacation. I haven't put anything else under agreement in the last couple of weeks. I've been working on the deals we have going now. I'm also working on getting a new development of two hundred homes." "That sounds really good. Did you make up your package on advertising and the figures?" "I sure did boss lady." "Good are you planning on coming up tonight?" "No I can't I'll come up next Thursday and make it a long weekend." "That will be great. It's already the third week of July summer is going by too fast. I have to make up for the weeks I lost." They both laughed Julie said "That sounds like something I'd like to do. I missed you so much! The last time I saw you we went swimming and had a picnic lunch on the beach." "We'll have to do it again next weekend Julie. If you need me for anything please call otherwise I'll see you next Thursday." "Alright then see you next Thursday." Sarah hung up phone took the towel from her hair and shook her hair out. She went inside and checked the clock it was five o'clock. Sarah went down to the kitchen to let Mrs. Johnson know Evan would be joining them for dinner and could she serve it at 7:30. Mrs. Johnson replied "Your cousins and your uncle will also be here for dinner. Your cousins arrived last night." "That's fine I'm looking forward to seeing them. Something smells good what are we having for dinner?" "We are having baked lamb, brown potatoes, and strings beans. For dessert we are having strawberry shortcake." "Mm sounds delicious. My taste buds are already getting activated. I better go back upstairs and get dressed." Sarah went back to her room she went to her closet and she looked at her light blue sundress "not too fancy yet cool and comfortable" she also grabbed her bolero jacket that matched her dress. Mrs. Johnson told her the temperature wasn't going to change much and it had been a hot and humid day. However it was always a little cooler living by the ocean this dress would be perfect. She wore tan nylons under her dress because her legs were so white then she slipped on a pair of comfortable sandals. Sarah thought "I need to work on my tan. Well I'll have plenty of time now that I have to rest for the next few weeks." She brushed her long blond hair pulling it to the back she attached a barrette to keep it from falling. She applied some make-up looking in the mirror she thought "Not bad for a girl who just got out of the hospital at least I look more alive than I did earlier." She went downstairs she saw Alfred "Alfred could you get me a glass of ice tea please?" "Yes miss" When he handed her the tea she asked "Alfred could you let me know when Mr. Taylor arrives I'll be in the garden until then." "Yes miss and might I say you look lovely this evening." "Thank you for the compliment Alfred and for the tea."

Sarah walked into the garden the flowers with the multitude of colors were breath taking. The flowers were mixed with a variety of plants. She sat on the white concrete bench and sipped her tea. Sitting in the garden made her feel like she was on an exotic island. She closed her eyes then opened them again. She started speaking to her grandmother "Granny I could never bear to sell the Haven. I love every part of this place too much to ever let it go. There is nowhere on this earth that I could be as happy as I am here. Everything is right here for me the greatest peace I've ever known is right here. I know how you felt living here Granny because I feel the same way. I'll find a way to buy Vicki and Tom out." She closed her eyes again. Evan had come in the garden while she was speaking and had heard everything that she said. He looked at her in the middle of the exotic garden and thought "She's speaking to her grandmother and she wants to buy out her cousins shares if she can't come up with all the money I'll offer to help her out. But I won't mention it unless she really needs my help. Sarah doesn't realize what a beautiful picture she makes sitting on that bench dressed in light blue in the middle of all this color. She looks like an angel." Evan walked slowly over to where Sarah was sitting he didn't want to frighten her he gently called her name. "Sarah" Sarah opened her eyes and saw Evan standing in front of her she raised her eyes to look at him her stomach started to flutter she thought "God he is so handsome" Evan was dressed in a light grey suit jacket with a white shirt and grey striped tie. He wore grey pants that matched his jacket. Sarah couldn't get over how he filled out his jacket. He was solidly built and toned. She thought to herself "I wonder what it would feel like to run my hands across that wonderful chest." Evan looking at Sarah called her again "Sarah?" coming out of her daze she blushed. "Hi" was all she managed to get out of her mouth. Evan flashed a smile "Alfred told me where I'd find you may I join you?" Sarah still blushing said "Yes you may." He sat next to her on the bench. "Your garden is beautiful Sarah" "Thank you, we have a gardener but up until granny's death she worked with him constantly telling him where everything should be and how to take care of it." She pointed to the left "See those roses?" "Yes they are beautiful" "Granny entered her roses in the Newport Rose Competition every year. She always came away with the first prize up until the year she died. She was so proud of her roses." "I can see why" Evan replied "How are you feeling tonight Sarah?" "Much better thank you. I'm not weak like I was earlier. Evan what did you do about the guard that was posted in front of my room?" "I called Chris and told him we didn't need him at the hospital anymore because you had gone home. Would you feel safer if I asked Chris to post a guard here to watch over you?" "No I don't think it's necessary I won't be riding Midnight Blue for a while I should be safe enough here." "If you change your mind you will let me know won't you Sarah?" "I will, I promise. Just to let you know my cousins and my uncle will be having dinner with us tonight." "That's fine with me. Sarah I have to tell you when I walked into the garden and saw you sitting here you were a vision of beauty. You took my breath away." Surprised Sarah didn't know what to say she felt the heat rising to her face. Sarah looking away from Evan said "What time is it?" Evan looked at his watch "it is seven thirty." "We better head to the patio dinner should be ready I hope you like baked lamb." Evan smiled "It's one of my favorites." Looking at Evan Sarah replied "Then you are in for a treat. Mrs. Johnson cooks the best lamb. I've had lamb in some of the best restaurants but none compare to hers." They stood up Sarah led Evan to the patio. The table was set and everyone was already seated. There was a look of surprise when Sarah entered accompanied by Evan. Vicki raising her eyebrow glanced at Tom. Tom rose from his chair, walked over to Sarah kissed her on the cheek and said "Thank God you are okay welcome back. You look great." Tom pulled out Sarah's chair "Please sit down." As she sat down she said "Thank you Tom." "You're welcome my dear cousin." Evan sat on the opposite side of Sarah. Sarah looked at her uncle "Uncle Armand I'd like you to meet Evan Taylor. Evan this is my uncle Armand." Evan extended his hand to Armand. Armand reached over to shake his hand and said "It's a pleasure to meet you Evan I hear you are the one who found my niece." Evan replied Yes sir I'm glad I found her." "Thank you for finding our Sarah." Evan smiled "It was meant to be." Sarah started to speak "Vicki, Tom I'd like you to" Vicki lifted her hand to stop her "We've already met Sarah. Hello Evan." Evan replied "Hello Vicki." Vicki eyed Evan and wondered "What the hell is he doing here." Maggie walked in and started to serve the salad. Armand turned to Sarah "You look better Sarah. How are you feeling?" "I feel much better thank you uncle Armand." After everyone finished their salads Alfred started to remove the plates as Maggie served the lamb. Maggie was smiling but inside she was fuming she hated serving Sarah and her cousins. Sarah took a bite of the lamb turned to Maggie and said "Maggie tell your mother that this taste absolutely delicious." "I will miss Sarah thank you." Maggie turned and headed for the kitchen. Evan looked at Sarah and said "You were right Sarah this is the best lamb I've ever tasted." After finishing the main meal again Alfred removed the plates. A few minutes later Maggie arrived with dessert. She served each of the guests then the family. After she finished serving she asked "If there is anything else you need please let me know." Sarah replied "Thank you Maggie this looks great!" Vicki took a bite of her dessert and put her fork down. Lifting her napkin she dabbed both corners of her mouth and looked at Sarah. "Sarah, both Tom and I received a call from Jake Lamark while you were in the hospital. He told us the buyer was making a final offer." Everyone stopped eating and focused their attention to Vicki. Vicki continued "He's offering two hundred million dollars and giving us until August thirtieth to give him our decision otherwise he will look somewhere else to build his resort. Tom and I want to sell and you had better make your decisions soon or buy us out or we will get an attorney involved to look after our interest. Isn't that right Tom?" Tom replied "Yes that's right Vicki. We are all done pussy footing around with you Sarah we want our share of the money." Evan stared at them with disgust. Armand could not believe the amount of money they were being offered while thinking "How can I get rid of the three of them so I can inherit it all?" Armand knew Jake from Lowell. He knew if he got rid of his nieces and nephew he would have no problem dealing with Jake. Sarah took a sip of her wine setting her glass on the table she looked at Vicki and Tom with anger and said "I would have never discussed this matter in front of our guests but seeing as neither of you care who knows our business I may as well continue. This is certainly a large amount of money but I have made a decision. I am not selling the Haven I will find a way to buy you out. As soon as I feel better I will work on it. Now if you'll excuse me." She stood up to leave the patio with Evan right behind her. After Sarah left the patio Vicki turned to Tom "Where is she going to get that kind of money to buy us out?" Tom replied "Who knows maybe her new boyfriend has money. What do you say we blow this joint and go out for a couple of drinks." "Great idea let's go." They both stood up and Vicki said "Goodnight uncle Armand" "Goodnight Vicki." After they left Armand was right behind them. He decided to follow them.

Sarah went into the living room and sat on the couch. Evan sat next to her. Facing Sarah he asked "Are you alright?" "I'm a little shaken up. I'd like to go for a walk on the beach would you like to come with me?" Evan looking concerned asked "Are you sure you feel up to it?" "Yes the ocean has a calming effect on me. It helps me to think." Evan smiled "If it will make you feel better let's go." When they got to the beach Evan took his shoes and socks off and rolled up his pants. Sarah removed her sandals and asked Evan to turn around while she removed her pantyhose. The placed their stuff on a large rock. Sarah held out her hand to Evan as he took her hand they walked toward the ocean. They were just in time to see the sunset coming down over the horizon. They stood there for a while each lost in their own thoughts. Evan spoke first

"The sunset is beautiful tonight." Sarah smiled and looked at Evan "Yes it is. I love it when the colors all come together. Shall we walk now?" They walked in silence. After a while Evan said to Sarah "Sarah I'm sorry Tom and Vicki put you on the spot on your first night home especially in front of me and your uncle." Sarah responded "They are so determined to sell all they can think about is the money. It's such a large amount it's not like they are destitute. They both received an inheritance when their mother died and Vicki received a big settlement when her third husband died last year." Evan stopped to face Sarah. "Sarah I don't know them. Vicki's looks are identical to yours but it stops there. She has a very rough exterior and a sharp tongue. They seem like two very greedy and selfish people. If I were you I wouldn't trust either one of them." Sarah replied "I don't know if I would go as far to say I shouldn't trust them." Evan looking into Sarah's eyes said "Remember what you told me Sarah." "I told you many things Evan" "One of the things you mentioned was that Simon told you to be careful who you trusted." "Yes he did." Sarah was upset "Let's not talk about this anymore." Evan smiled at Sarah and put his arms around her. "I would rather be doing this instead." Bringing his face closer to Sarah he lowered his head and kissed her lips softly. As the kiss became more passionate he spread her lips with his tongue. Sarah moaned as his tongue searched out hers. He thought she tasted like sweet nectar. Sarah's body leaned in closer to Evan as she wrapped her arms around his neck. As her excitement built she ran her hands up and down his back feeling his muscles wanting to feel more. Evan suddenly stopped kissing her. Their breaths were heavy. Looking into her eyes he said "Sarah I love you." "I love you too Evan." Pushing herself away from him she said "This doesn't make any sense. I'm in love with a man I just met this morning. Except for your name and the fact that you found me I don't know anything about you. I don't know where you live or what you do for a living. How did you find my home anyway?" Evan smiled "That's easy I own the house next to yours. I also own a chain of vacation resorts in the Caribbean, Europe, and the United States. My office is in the Trump tower building in New York. I own a townhouse across from Central Park the same building Jacqueline Kennedy lives in. I'm thirty-seven years old. I've had a few brief affairs and much to my mother's disappointment I've never been married. Is there anything else you'd like to know about me Sarah?" Sarah stood there in shock. Shaking herself out of it she asked "Does your mother live with you in your townhouse in New York?" "No my mother lives in her own townhouse in Boston. She spends a lot of time doing charity work especially for the Heart Association. Every so often she comes to one of my hotels and we spend time together. Other times she joins me here in Newport. You'd love my mother Sarah and I'm sure she'd love you too." Sarah smiled "It sounds like you are close to your mother. If she is anything like you I'm sure I'd love her too. Okay she said my turn. I'm thirty-two years old. Never been married or engaged and you may not believe this but I've never had sex with anyone I'm still a virgin." Evan was stunned to think this beautiful woman had never been intimate with a man. He asked her "Isn't there anyone you felt you wanted to sleep with?" Sarah tilted her head to the side with a baffled look she replied "I told you all about granny's past life except for after she married my grandfather. Once during one of our conversations she told me I should never give myself to anyone unless I truly loved him and he truly loved me. She said if I waited for that special someone lovemaking would be the most beautiful experience I would ever have when I became one with my true love. Whenever I dated someone and he started pushing me to have sex I would stop seeing him."

Evan replied "Your grandmother was a very wise woman and I am a very lucky man to have found you." "Yes she was and yes you are" Sarah smiled. They both started laughing Evan leaned in and gave Sarah a kiss. Hand in Hand they started walking back. The stopped at the rock to pick up their things and headed to the house. Once they were back at the house they went to the pool deck. "Evan would you like a brandy?" He looked at his watch "I can stay for one drink then I have to leave." Sarah called Alfred on the pool intercom "Alfred could you please bring two brandy's to the pool side? Thank you." They sat at one of the tables. Alfred came out with their drinks placing them on the table Sarah asked "Where is everyone else?" Alfred answered "Vicki and Tom went out for the evening and your uncle went out also. Will there be anything else miss?" "No thank you Alfred." Evan felt relieved at least they wouldn't bother Sarah again tonight. Picking up his glass he took a sip and placed it back down and said "I'm leaving for Boston early tomorrow morning. My mother called me earlier and asked if I would escort her to the Heart Association Ball tomorrow night I couldn't refuse she doesn't ask that much of me. The following day I'm going back to my office in New York." "You are?" Sarah look disappointed "If you were still in the hospital I would stay here but I feel if you stay around the house you will be safe with Alfred, Mrs. Johnson and Maggie to be close to you." He took a business card out of his coat pocket and wrote a few things down before he handed it to her. "Here is my card with my personal number, my mother's number and my cell number. If you need me at any time Sarah please do not hesitate to call me. I'll call you every night when I get to New York." Sarah took the card "I'll miss you but I would not want you to disappoint your mother. I know what it takes to run a business it takes up most of your time." "I guess you do. You are usually pretty busy yourself."

Evan was admiring the pool and said "The pool looks pretty inviting doesn't it?" "Yes it does it's a heated pool I usually take my swim at eleven o'clock every night before I go to bed." "Are you going to take a swim tonight?" "Yes of course I wish you could join me." "I wish I could too maybe another time." Evan finished his brandy and started to put his socks and shoes on "I really must go Sarah." "I'll walk you to the door." They both stood and headed for the house. At the front door Evan kissed Sarah and said goodnight "I'll talk to you soon." "Okay have a safe trip." Sarah closed the front door headed upstairs to her bedroom to change into her swimsuit.

Chapter Fifteen

Vicki and Tom were on their way home. Tom was driving they had just left the club. Vicki said "Thanks Tom this was nice. It was great to get away for a while. Of course I thought I would have to call a cab to get home that red head sure had the hots for you she was all over you on the dance floor." Tom chuckled "I would never leave you stranded Vicki she was alright for a few dances but she really wasn't my type. She was too aggressive." All of a sudden Tom's car was hit from behind. He yelled "What the Hell?" Vicki was scared "What is that car trying to do Tom?" "It looks like it's trying to push us off the road." "Is he nuts can you see who it is?" "No and this road is so treacherous Vicki do you have your seatbelt on?" "Yes. Oh my God Tom he's trying to push us over the cliff." The other car was a black Lincoln town car and their uncle Armand was behind the wheel. While he was trying to push Tom's car off the road he was thinking "I'll get rid of both of them and then I'll take care of Sarah. Then everything they have will be mine. After all I'll be the only living relative." He finally got the Lincoln alongside of Tom's Mercedes "Now just one good swerve and bye bye Tom and Vicki" Just as Armand was about to sideswipe their car Tom stepped on the gas. Armand swore "Damn I missed them!" Tom yelled to Vicki "Hold on I'm going to try to get way ahead of it." She said "This guy must be drunk." Just as Tom sped up he looked at the other driver surprised he said "This is no drunk driver Vicki its uncle Armand!" Vicki was shocked "Why is he trying to kill us?" "Why? For the money of course Sarah was right for a change we should have never had discussed the money we were offered in front of our dear uncle." Tom finally got his car ahead of Armand's. Armand was still in the other lane when suddenly a big tractor trailer truck was heading right for him from the other direction. He didn't see the truck in time the impact sent the car flying over the edge exploding in a ball of flames. Tom saw everything in his rear-view mirror "Well" he said 'That takes care of him." "Why Vicki asked?" 'That truck just hit him head on sending his car over the edge in a ball of flames I'm sure he didn't survive that. We won't have to worry about him anymore." "Thank goodness" she said "Now if we could get rid of Sarah this easily we would have it made." "My dear sister how right you are."

Sunday afternoon Sarah was lounging by the pool in a blue two piece bathing suit getting some sun and reading a murder mystery when Vicki and Tom approached Tom said "Good afternoon Sarah" not taking her eyes off the book she answered "Hi." Vicki was wearing a black thonged bikini. Tom had on beige swimming trunks. They each grabbed a lounge chair and put them beside Sarah. Tom sat down and said "Sarah we have something to tell you." Sarah replied "If it's a repeat of last night's performance I don't want to hear it." "No it's not. I must say you were right about one thing." Sarah looked up "Oh and what was that?" "Not discussing our business in front of others." Sarah put her book down "What do you mean Tom?" "Last night Vicki and I went to a club downtown around one am when we were driving home someone tried to push us off the road." "Oh my do you know who it was?" "Yes uncle Armand." Sarah was initially shocked "Are you sure?" "Yes when he pulled alongside of us I got a good look at him." Sarah thought "He's just like his mother." 'He was trying to send us over the edge of the cliff I got away from him but not before I saw who it was. As I got ahead of him I saw a tractor trailer coming straight at him he didn't see it in time. The impact of the truck sent his car flying over the edge in flames. I don't believe we will ever see him again." "Thank God you and Vicki are alright." "I'll say I've already told Alfred to pack Armand's things and put them in storage." "Should we call the police?" Sarah asked "No Sarah we didn't even know he existed up until a few weeks ago so why should we bother." Sarah sighed "I'm happy that both of you are alright." Vicki replied "So are we. Want to take a swim brother?" "Sure." They both got up and dove into the pool leaving Sarah in her thoughts. She picked up her book but couldn't concentrate. Sarah thought "Uncle arrived the day before someone took a shot at me he's probably the one who tried to kill me?" She shuttered "I've had enough sun for today." She picked up her things and said "Hey you two I'm headed into the house I've had enough sun today. I'll see you at dinner." They both replied "Okay." She went into her room and decided to nap before dinner. It wasn't long before she was fast asleep. Her sleep was full of nightmares Armand and his mother. How mean she was to her grandmother and Armand as a baby in a carriage.

 A couple of Jennison's men had been following Vicki and Tom for the last week when they would leave the Haven to go home. Monday they found themselves in New York still trailing Vicki and Tom. Tom was carrying a big covered painting they went inside Antoine's Antique Shop one of the undercover agents followed them inside. Once inside the shop the agent started looking around making look like he was interested in making a purpose. Mr. Antoine sized the agent. He was tall well dress in a light blue suit, white shirt and navy blue tie and shiny black shoes. He had brown eyes, brown hair and a good haircut. Mr. Antoine decided he looked like a serious buyer and went over to Tom and Vicki. "It's so good to see you so soon after your last transaction Miss Sarah. But of course it's always a pleasure doing business with you and your cousin Thomas." Antoine shook Tom's hand and looking at Vicki said "You look lovely as always my petite." Vicki was wearing a light pink chenille two piece suit a white bag and white heels. She wore her hair in a twist. She wore very light makeup and pink lipstick. "Thank you Antoine" she said. "What treasure have you brought me today Miss Sarah?" "A painting that once belong to the Russian czar" "How would you know the painting belonged to the Czar my dear you are too young to know such a thing." "See for yourself Antoine." Tom lifted the painting onto the counter then he gently pulled the cover off. When Antoine set his eyes on the painting he was stunned and exclaimed "Mon Dieu it is the portrait of Czar and his wife and their children painted the year before they were brutally murdered. It is priceless!" "You will pay me a great deal of money for this little gem won't you Antoine?" "Oui Mademoiselle Sarah" The undercover agent was paying close attention to the transaction that was taking place. He was standing behind a large antique clock. Antoine had completely forgotten someone else was in his shop he was so excited about his find it would bring him big money at Christi's auction. "Miss Sarah I will pay you one million dollars for this painting." "Antoine you know you will make much more money when you sell the painting at Christi's in the fall. I want three million dollars." "Please Miss Sarah two million." "Come Thomas take the painting we are leaving." "Miss Sarah wait you drive a hard bargain I will pay you the three million." "Make the cashier's check out to my cousin Thomas Kincaid" "Whatever you say Miss Sarah." Antoine had his secretary make out the purchase agreement while he went to the bank to get the cashier check. When he returned Vicki signed Sarah's name to the bill of sale and handed the check to Tom. Tom placed the check on the inside breast pocket of his jacket. Vicki said "Thank you Antoine we will see you soon." They left the shop and the undercover agent followed. Antoine was so interested in his paintings he didn't see anything else. When the agent got back into his car he told his partner everything that had taken place at Antoine's. "Those two have a good scam going on. This Antoine really believes he's dealing with Sarah. Let's report this to Chris ASAP."

Monday Sarah had spoken to Evan on the phone for two hours. She told him what happened to her Uncle Armand he felt the same way she did that Armand had tried to kill her. They talked on the phone every night. Friday when she spoke to Evan she told him she wasn't feeling good she was skipping her swim and going to bed early. They only spoke for a short time and she was in bed by nine thirty. In the shadows someone was waiting for Sarah to take her nightly swim. "I'm not going to miss you this time Sarah. I can do a lot with the money that you are getting once you are gone and this place is sold. I'll wait all night if I have to; you always take your nightly swim." The time was 11:30 Vicki was so wound up she couldn't sleep she kept tossing and turning. Tom had to go out of town on Tuesday for business and told Vicki he would meet her at the Haven on Friday night. He still had the check she was hoping he hadn't done anything stupid like cashing it and spending the money. She didn't trust her brother. She got out of bed and decided to go for a swim. She thought a few laps around the pool should tire her out. She thought "I hope Sarah finished her swim I'm in no mood for small talk with her tonight." She slipped on her bathing suit tied her hair in a ponytail. With no make-up on she looked exactly like Sarah. She put on her white robe and went downstairs. The house was quiet everyone was in bed. Vicki walked onto the patio that led to the pool there was just enough light she didn't bother turning anymore lights on. She sighed "Thank God the bitch isn't here." She took off her robe and placed it on a chair. She slipped her sandals off she walked to the pool stuck her foot into the water it felt warm. "Thank goodness the pool is heated" she thought. She walked over to the diving board stepped up and walked to the edge. She stood on her tiptoes ready to dive in when a bullet pierced her heart. Vicki grabbed at her chest with both hands fell head first into the pool. The shooter saw Vicki grab her chest and fall head first into the pool. "You are dead now Miss Sarah." The shooter made the escape through the woods slipped through the gate got in the car and sped away. No one in the house heard a gunshot. The next morning when the gardener arrived he saw something floating in the pool. He went closer to get a better look and saw the back of Vicki's body thinking it was Sarah. He blessed himself and ran into the house to the kitchen to get Mrs. Johnson. Hysterical he shouted "Mrs. Johnson Mrs. Johnson" "What in God's name is wrong with you Mr. Santos?" "It's Miss Sarah come quick." Mrs. Johnson followed Mr. Santos to the pool. When she got there she saw a body lying face down in the water the pool was red stained with blood. She screamed "Oh my God Miss Sarah my poor baby." Sarah was standing in the patio doorway "Mrs. Johnson what's the matter?" Mrs. Johnson spun around "Miss Sarah?" "Yes" Sarah answered "You are not dead?" "I hope not." Mrs. Johnson went over and placed her arms around Sarah. "Thank the good lord you are alive. It is Vicki in the pool and she is dead." Sarah in shock "Vicki's dead?" "Look in the pool" Mrs. Johnson moved aside for Sarah to see. "Oh my God in heaven what happened to her?" "I don't know Mr. Santos just found her floating there and came to get me. Both of us thought it was you." "Please Mrs. Johnson, Mr. Santos don't touch anything I'll call the police." Sarah ran upstairs to her room took the card Evan had left with her and called him. She was relieved he was at his office early. He answered the phone on the first ring. "Evan Taylor speaking" "Evan its Sarah something terrible has happened." Evan sat straight up "Are you alright Sarah?" "Yes I'm fine it's my cousin Vicki we found her dead in the pool just a few minutes ago." "You didn't touch anything did you?" "No I came right in to call you I need detective Jennison's phone number." "I'll call Chris for you and I'll be there as soon as I can. I love you Sarah." "I love you to Evan please hurry." She hung up the phone. Sarah thought "I need to wash quickly and get dressed before the police get here." Sarah gathered her clothes and jumped in for a quick shower she was dressed in less than fifteen minutes and headed back downstairs to the pool deck.

Chapter Sixteen

Twenty minutes later detective Jennison arrived with some of his men and the coroner. Alfred showed everyone to the pool area except detective Jennison. As he arrived Sarah was coming down the staircase. She was dressed in Jeans and a light green T-shirt. Her hair was pulled back into a ponytail. Detective Jennison walked over to her and introduced himself "Miss Saint James I'm detective Chris Jennison." "Nice to meet you Detective Jennison please call me Sarah." "It's unfortunate we had to meet under these circumstances. Please call me Chris. Please Sarah, stay inside while I check things out. Why don't you go fix yourself a cup of coffee" "I'll be in the kitchen with Mrs. Johnson if you need me for anything." Chris proceeded to the pool area. The body was already on the stretcher and the coroner was leaning over Vicki's body looking up at Chris he said "She was shot in the heart at a pretty close range Chris." Chris replied "What is the time of Death Jim?" "I'd say between eleven thirty and midnight. I'll know more after I do the autopsy." "Jim, could you get the bullet to forensics ASAP please?" "I sure will Chris." They loaded the body into the coroners van Jim waved to Chris got in the van and left. In the meantime the officers were checking in the garden area and the woods for any kind of clue that would lead them to the killer. Chris headed back into the house and went straight to the kitchen. Sarah, Mr. Santos, Maggie and Mrs. Johnson were at the kitchen table drinking coffee Mrs. Johnson stood up and asked "Would you like a cup of coffee detective Jennison?" He smiled at Mrs. Johnson "I'd love a cup thank you Mrs. Johnson." Chris sat down and took out his notebook and pen from his shirt pocket. Mrs. Johnson asked "Cream and sugar detective Jennison?" Chris replied "Black please." Mrs. Johnson handed him his cup of coffee and sat back down. "Thank you." Mrs. Johnson replied "Your welcome detective." Chris took a sip of his coffee and asked "Who was it that found the body?" Mr. Santos replied "I did sir." Chris looked at Mr. Santos and asked "Who might you be sir?" "I'm the gardener Joseph Santos." "Could you walk me through exactly how you found the body Mr. Santos?" "It was nine o'clock when I arrived for work that is my usual time. I was walking towards the garden I looked over at the pool area and saw something floating. I went over to have a closer look I saw the body. My first thought was that it was Miss Sarah. I ran to the kitchen to get Mrs. Johnson." Chris interrupted "At that time you thought it was Miss Sarah in the pool?" "Yes I did." Chris rubbed his chin thinking he asked "Why would you think it was Sarah?" "Sarah always goes for a swim late at night." Chris looked over at Sarah "Is that true Sarah?" Sarah replied "Yes detective." "What time do you usually take your swim?" "Usually at 11 o'clock before I go to bed." "Did you go for a swim last night?" Sarah sighed "No I didn't I was feeling a bit under the weather. At nine o'clock Evan called me we talked for a short while after we hung up I went to bed." Chris jotting down notes on his paper asked "What time did you go to bed?" "Nine thirty." "Do you always go for a swim at the same time every evening?" "Yes I'm pretty much on schedule with my nightly swim when I am home." Chris turned to Mrs. Johnson and asked "Mrs. Johnson when you followed Mr. Santos to the pool and saw the body who did you think it was?" "I thought it was Miss Sarah." "Why did you think it was Sarah?" Mrs. Johnson replied "Because she is a creature of habit when she is home. She rides her horse every morning at nine o'clock unless the weather is bad. She takes a swim every night at 11 o'clock weather permitting." "Thank you Mrs. Johnson." Chris looked around "Does anyone know where Vicki's brother is?" Sarah answered "I went to his room after I got dressed he wasn't there and his bed looked like it hadn't been slept in. I don't know where he is." Alfred walked into the kitchen followed by Evan. Sarah stood up and ran over to Evan "I'm so glad you are here." He held her in his arms and speaking to Chris asked "What happened?" Chris gave Evan a strange look and said "Vicki was shot at close range in the chest approximately between the hour of eleven thirty and midnight. I'll know more after the coroner does the autopsy." Evan led Sarah back to the table they took a seat. Mrs. Johnson got up to get a cup of coffee for Evan. "Mr. Taylor would you like cream and sugar in your coffee." Evan replied "Just cream please" Mrs. Johnson poured the coffee and added the cream. Placing it in front of Evan he said "Thank you" Sitting back down she replied "you're welcome Mr. Taylor." Chris resumed his questioning turning to Maggie he asked "Maggie did you hear or see anything last night?" "No I was in bed by nine o'clock I didn't hear a thing." Mrs. Johnson thought "She wasn't in bed I checked in on her a little after ten and she wasn't in her room. She wasn't even in the house why is she lying?" Chris calling Mrs. Johnson again repeated her name "Mrs. Johnson" "Yes detective" "Did you hear or see anything last night?" "I went to bed around ten thirty I wear a hearing aid and when I go to bed I take it off so I can't hear a thing." Chris looked at Sarah next she replied "I didn't hear anything either." "Sarah is there anyone else staying in the house?" "No my friend and co-worker Julie was supposed to come here Thursday but she couldn't make it she will be arriving tonight." Wrapping up his questions Chris closed his notebook and put it back in his pocket. Looking at Sarah he said "When Tom comes back home would you tell him I'd like to talk to him please?" Sarah replied "Yes I will." Chris stood up and said "I think I have everything I need for now. I'd like to ask that you all keep yourselves available for more questions." Turning to Evan he said "Evan can I speak to you privately for a few minutes?" Evan answered "Sure Chris." Sarah looked at both Chris and Evan and said "Why don't you use my office Evan you know where it is." They left the kitchen and headed to Sarah's office when they entered the office Chris closed the door behind him. "Evan, are you going to stay here at the house with Sarah?" Evan answered "Yes I was going to ask her if I could stay in one of the spare bedrooms until we find the killer. Do you think this is related?' Chris giving Evan a serious look said "Yes, I believe whoever killed Vicki believed they were killing Sarah. I think it is a good idea if you stay here. I wouldn't let her out of your sight." Evan sighed "I won't I love her too much to let something happen to her." Chris continued "I'm also going to post a few of my men around the property." Evan replied "That's a good idea." Chris lowering his voice said "What I am about to tell you has to stay between you and I. I don't want to tell Sarah just yet." Evan nodded "You know me Chris I would never jeopardize your trust in me." Chris continued "remember I told you I was going to have Vicki and Tom followed when they left on Monday?" "Yes" Evan answered. Chris smiled "Monday we hit pay dirt my men followed them to New York they went into Antoine's Antique Store. One of my men went inside the shop. Vicki dressed like Sarah was negotiating with Antoine on an original painting of the Russian Czar and his family. Antoine paid them three million dollars and Vicki forged Sarah's name on the bill of sale. She then had Antoine make the cashier's check out to Tom." Evan was angry he remembered what Sarah had told him about the paintings. Looking at Chris he said "Chris, they stole that painting from the attic. Now that Vicki is dead Tom is three million dollars richer." "My men told me they went straight home to Boston after the sale. They never stopped at a bank to deposit or cash the check. Tom is probably walking around with the money and he doesn't have to share it with his sister now." "You've got that right my friend. I believe if you find Tom you'll have your killer." "You may be right Evan. I have one more question I'd like to ask Sarah." Evan opening the door said "I'll go and get her for you." Evan went to the kitchen to get Sarah she wasn't there he asked Mrs. Johnson "Do you know where Sarah went?" Mrs. Johnson replied "I believe she is in the living room." "Thank you." Evan smiled at Mrs. Johnson and walked to the living room. As he approached the door he notice Sarah was staring out the window almost as if she wasn't there. He tapped on the door so he wouldn't startle her. Sarah jumped Evan walking into the room said 'I'm sorry I didn't mean to startle you." Sarah sighed "It's not your fault Evan I'm just a little jumpy." Evan held out his arms to embrace Sarah he knew this was getting to her. Holding her he said "Chris would like to ask you another question." Sarah looked into Evans eyes "Alright" Evan could see the pain and confusion in her eyes and he hated it. He hated that someone would want to hurt the woman he loved who never hurt anyone in her life. Holding her hand he led her out of the living room and to her office. After they entered the office Chris went and closed the door. Chris looking at Sarah with concern asked "Would you like to sit down? You look a little pale." Sarah shook her head "No thank you Detective I'm fine." Chris thought "It's no wonder Evan is in love with this woman. She is beautiful. Even with everything that is going on in her life right now she still manages to have a soothing

THE HAVEN'S COVE

voice." Chris smiled at Sarah "Okay we can stand I'm sure this must all be getting to you. I have one more important question for you though now that Vicki is deceased what happens to her share of the Haven?" Sarah decided she needed to sit down. Finding the nearest chair she sat. Thinking she said "If anything happens to any one of us the share is divided between the remaining two." Chris looking at Sarah said "Let's see if I understand this right. Now that Vicki is gone you and Tom each get another ten percent?" "Yes" she replied. Thinking Chris said out lout "So that would make your share seventy percent and Tom's thirty percent?" Sarah nodded "That's correct." Chris sat in the chair opposite of Sarah. "I'm sorry Sarah I should have said I have a few more questions not just one." "That's not a problem. I'm happy to answer any question that will help you find Vicki's killer." Chris continued "What is the name of the broker who is trying to get you to sell your property?" "His name is Jake Lamark." 'Where is his office?" "Here in Newport let me give you his business card." Thank you that will help a lot." Sarah went over to her desk and opened the top drawer she found the card and handed it to Chris. "Thank you Sarah. When the coroner is finished with the autopsy what funeral home would like the body sent to?" "Ask them to send it to Monahan's Funeral home please." Chris nodded "Thank you Sarah I have no more questions for you today. I think you need to get some rest after all you did just come out of the hospital." Evan walked Chris to the door before Chris walked out he turned to Evan "I'll get back to you as soon as I have more information." "Thanks Chris" After Chris left Evan walked back over to Sarah who had sat down again and began rubbing her shoulders. Sarah sighed and began to relax while Evan rubbed her shoulders.

Chapter Seventeen

Tom had spent the day in bed with his mistress. He then took the Saturday two am shuttle to Las Vegas. He had an unbearable urge to gamble he figured he had enough money to play Baccarat where the stakes were high. He felt lucky he could triple the three million dollars he was carrying. He wouldn't have any trouble cashing the check in Vegas. He was known in

most of the casinos as a high roller and treated as such. When he arrived in Las Vega he went to his favorite resort and they had the luxury suite all ready for him. He went up to his suite kicked off his shoes and flopped on the bed thinking to himself "Maybe I'll take a nap before I go down and play." He slept for a few hours and later in the afternoon he started playing Baccarat. He was on a roll and counting the money he was adding to the three million. He hoped his luck would last.

Detective Jennison paid Jake Lamark a visit at his office. When Chris arrived he said to his secretary "I'm here to see Jake Lamark" The secretary asked "Do you have an appointment?" Pulling out his badge Chris said "I believe I don't need an appointment with this. Now would you mind showing me the way to his office" She buzzed Jake to let him know there was a detective here to see him. Jake told her to show him in. The Secretary got up from her desk looking at Chris she said "Follow me." Chris followed her to Jakes office. When the door opened Jake was standing behind his desk and said "Yes?" Chris introduced himself "I'm detective Chris

Jennison from the Newport Police Dept. I would like to ask you a few questions." Jake sat in his chair staring at the detective finally he broke the silence "So what do I owe the pleasure of Newport's finest?" Chris staring back said "My visit concerns the Haven property you are trying to sell." Jake looked shocked "What about it? Since when do the Newport Police get involved with selling a property? As far as I know selling property in this state is not a crime." Chris trying to control his temper said between clenched teeth "No but murder is Mr. Lamark." Jake stood up "Murder! I didn't kill anyone!" Chris sat down and made himself comfortable he enjoyed watching Jake start to sweat. "I didn't say you did now did I are you hiding something?" Chris didn't like the look of this guy he looked slimy there was something about him that screamed crook and he wasn't going to tell him who the victim was. Jake frowned "So what the hell do you want with me?" Chris remaining calm said "I want the name of the person who is trying to buy the Haven." Raising his voice and getting perturbed Jake said "I can't give you this information it's confidential." Chris with a smug look on his face asked "Are you an attorney or maybe a therapist? You will either give me the information willingly or I'll be back here with a search warrant. Which do you prefer?" Jake huffed and stood up reaching into his drawer he pulled out a set of keys he walked over to the file cabinet and unlocked it. Chris was watching him when he unlocked the cabinet Chris said "Do you have something to hide Mr. Lamark that you have to lock your files up?" Giving Chris a dirty look he opened the drawer and as he handed Chris the file he said "I have nothing to hide detective I don't like people going through my things." Chris took the folder and opened it. As he looked through the file to make sure everything was there he closed the file stood and said "I'm going to have your secretary make a copy of everything in this file." Jake now angry said "Why do you need a copy of everything in that folder you got what you wanted that should be enough." Chris looked back at Jake as he started for the door and said "Well it isn't and I'm not going to go through this file and these papers in five minutes I need time to look things over. I can still get that warrant if you'd like?" Chris walked out the door and went to the secretary's office handing the folder to her he said "Could you please make me a copy of everything in this folder." The secretary looked at the folder and back at Chris "Everything?" she said with a look of shock on her face. She thought to herself "He doesn't pay me enough to do this." Chris smiled at the secretary and said "Yes everything I'll just wait right here while you do it." Chris watched her carefully making sure she copied every paper in that file. After she was finished she gave Chris the copies he grabbed the stapler on the desk and stapled the pile of papers together. Turning to the secretary he said "Thank you." He walked out of the office. Jake was angry with the detective but happy that Sarah was finally eliminated. Thinking to himself "He won't find anything damaging in that file only the buyer's name address and phone number and all the offers that have been made. Have fun reading detective" he said with a smirk.

Sarah and Evan were still in her office. Evan still rubbing her shoulders said "Is this helping to relax you. I feel the tension leaving." Sarah smiled "It feels wonderful and yes it has helped. Thank you so much Evan you are so thoughtful." Evan stopped rubbing Sarah's shoulders and smiled "You make it easy to want to help you. You are so easy to love Sarah and I'm one lucky man." Eric looked at Sarah and with a serious tone he said "Sarah I would like to move in here until they find the killer. I don't want you left alone. Do you have a room that I can stay in?" Sarah looked relieved "Yes the room next to mine. I'm glad you are going to stay I feel so much safer with you here." "I'm going home to pack the things that I'll need I won't be long. Chris has some of his men posted around the property. I'd like you to stay inside until I get back." "I will." Evan kissed Sarah and left. Sarah decided to call Julie at home to let her know what had happened to Vicki. Julie answered on the first ring. "Hello" "Julie its Sarah" "Hi how are you?" "Not very good we had a tragedy here Vicki is dead. She was shot while taking a swim last night." Julie was shocked and said "That is terrible. Are you okay?" "I'm pretty shaken up" "Tom must be devastated." "Tom doesn't know I don't know where he is." "Do you still want me to come up tonight? I hate to see you alone." "No I need you there because I'm sure when the press gets a hold of this they will be here like a swarm of flies. I need you to do damage control for the office. Do you think you can handle them?" "Don't you worry I'm sure I can handle them." "Evan is going to be moving in until they can figure out what the hell is going on here. In a few days when it calms down if you have time you can come then." "Okay. Sarah, I'm so sorry about Vicki. Call me if you need anything and I'll be here." "Julie, would you call Nora to let her know what happened." "Sure I'll call her as soon as we hang up." "Thank you Julie I'll talk to you soon." Julie said goodbye and Sarah hung up the phone. An hour later Evan was back he looked at Sarah and said "I'm all set. I have everything I need and I am not leaving your side until this is over." Sarah hugged Evan "Thank you I don't know what I would do without you." Evan smiled "You never have to worry about that."

The next day as Sarah and Evan were eating breakfast Alfred brought the Sunday paper in and placed it on the table in front of Sarah. The headlines read **"Vicki Dixon Murdered"** the article described in detail how Vicki was found lying face down in the swimming pool at her summer home in Newport Rhode Island. Sarah read the paper and handed it to Evan to read. She was upset "This place is going to be crawling with media Evan I just want to prepare you. Evan after reading the article put it down and looked at Sarah "Don't worry Sarah I'm used to the press it's not going to bother me. I just don't want you to be stressed more than you already are." "I'll try to stay calm I promise." After breakfast Evan went to the window "Well you are going to get your chance to try and stay calm because dozens of reporters and cameramen are gathering outside the estate gate. All of a sudden the phone started to ring Alfred came in and told Sarah it was channel 5. "What do you want me to say Miss Sarah?" "Tell them no comment Alfred and you don't have to answer the phone anymore today." "Yes miss."

TV stations and reporters from all around wanted to get comments from Sarah. Finally after two days of harassment they started to leave her alone apparently there was a more pressing story about a movie star living in Newport who had overdosed and they didn't know if it was suicide or murder. Sarah was glad the attention was drawn away from her family.

The pool area had been cleaned up and it looked as if nothing had happened there. After the police investigation Sarah hired a professional cleaning service and instructed them to make sure that nothing could be seen and if it had to be replaced to replace it. She didn't want to have any reminders about what happened. The pool had been drained and power washed it also had a fresh coat of paint. It was already filled and looked inviting. It was a beautiful day the sun was shining there was not a cloud in the sky. Sarah and Evan were taking a walk through the garden as they were walking Evan would stop to move the flowers and bushes to look at the ground beneath them. Sarah finally said "Evan what are you doing?" Evan replied "I'm just looking around maybe the police missed something." "Like what?" "I don't know anything really." "Okay I'll help too." Sarah started to poke around looking on the ground in between the bushes then she saw something she bent down to pick it up. "Evan I found something." "What did you find?" "a button" She held it out in the palm of her hand so he could see it. The button was silver usually one you would find on a sweater. Then she said "I've seen someone wearing a sweater with this type of button but right now I can't remember who it was." "Sarah, do you mind if I hold on to it?" "No here take it." Evan slipped the button in his shirt pocket. They looked around for a while longer but didn't find anything else. They turned around to go back to the pool area when they got to the patio Alfred came out to meet them. "Mr. Taylor I have a message for you to call detective Jennison as soon as possible." Evan smile "Thank you Alfred and please call me Evan" "Very well Mr. Evan your welcome." Evan looked at Sarah and said "I need to make this phone call it must be important if he's calling me during the day." Sarah asked Evan "would you like to use the house phone? "Yes if I may" "use the one in my office you'll have privacy there." Evan bent over and gave Sarah a quick kiss on the lips "I'll be right back don't go anywhere." "I won't." Sarah smiled as she watched Evan walk into the house she thought to herself "We've only known each other for a short while and I feel like I've known him my whole life. I am glad he is here it makes me feel so much safer."

Evan headed toward Sarah's office. He closed the door behind him went over to her desk sat down and picked up the phone. He dialed Chris's number Chris answered on the first ring "Detective Jennison" "Hi Chris its Evan you called?" "Hi Evan I have some news for you." "Oh?" "Forensics just came back on the bullet that killed Vicki it was fired from the same gun that tried to kill Sarah." Evan frowned "Are you kidding me you mean that bullet was meant for Sarah?" Chris sighed "I'm afraid so. It looks like Sarah is in a lot more danger than we thought. I don't think this killer is going to stop until he or she kills Sarah. Could you tell Sarah that Vicki's body has been sent to the funeral home, do you know if she's heard from Tom yet?" "No she hasn't heard anything from him yet." "Okay, ask her to please let me know as soon as she does." "I will call you as soon as she hears." "Talk to you later." "Okay and thanks Chris for the info I'd better get back to Sarah she's alone on the patio. Later." Evan hung up the phone he ran his hands over his face "how am I going to tell Sarah she's the target. This just keeps getting worse and where the hell is that cousin of hers I want to talk to him." Evan stood opened the door and walked toward the patio.

Sarah was wondering what was taking Evan so long as he walked onto the patio. She said "Hi I was getting worried what took you so long?" Evan sat across from Sarah reaching for her hands he held them for a minute as he ran his thumb across her skin. He had a concerned look on his face. Sarah could sense something was wrong "Evan what's wrong?" Evan sighed "There is no easy way to tell you this so I'm going to repeat what Chris said to me. Sarah, honey, forensics came back on the bullet that killed Vicki. It was from the same gun that tried to kill you." Sarah turned white "What does that mean exactly?" Evan looked Sarah in the eyes "That means that the bullet was meant for you not Vicki." Sarah let go of Evans hands and abruptly stood up she was shaking. She walked over to where Evan was standing. Evan wrapped his arms around her as she said "Why is someone trying to kill me?" Evan held her tighter "I don't know sweetheart but Chris is an excellent detective he will find the person behind this." "I'm so scared Evan" Sarah was shaking uncontrollably "I'm not going anywhere and you will not be alone at any time until the killer is caught." "What about your business? You just can't stay here and ignore your responsibilities. That's not fair of me to ask that of you." "I have a young executive I've been training as my assistant he's very eager to get started I will call him later I'm sure he'll be excited that he's finally going to get his chance." Sarah looked into Evans eyes "Are you sure?" "Yes I'm sure. Also Chris told me that they have transferred Vicki's body to the funeral home." "I can't believe I haven't heard from Tom you would think that he would have heard it on the news or read the newspaper by now. I hope nothing has happened to him." "I hope not either. Are you going to have a wake and a funeral mass?" "I really don't know I can't make a decision until I hear from Tom he doesn't even know yet because if he did he would have been here already?" "I understand hopefully he will contact you soon." "Let's go inside I need a cup of tea" "Okay" Evan and Sarah went inside and to the kitchen so Sarah could have a cup of tea. While Sarah was sipping the tea Mrs. Johnson had made for her, the phone rang Mrs. Johnson went to answer it. She came back into the kitchen "Miss Sarah it's the funeral director and he would like to speak to you." "Thank you Mrs. Johnson." Sarah went to the phone "Hello" "Hello Miss Saint James this is Arthur from Saint Laurens funeral home. I'm sorry to disturb you but we have just received your Cousin Vicki's body and I wanted to know what you had planned for services." "I'm sorry Arthur but Vicki's brother doesn't know yet and I can't make any arrangements without him. Right now we can't find him. Is it possible to hold everything off until I get in touch with him?" "We can't hold the body that long Miss Saint James for obvious reasons." Sarah sighed "Could you hold it until at least Friday? If I haven't heard from Tom by then I will make the arrangements." "That's fine Miss Saint James I will expect to hear from you on Friday." "Thank you so much." Sarah hung up the phone and went back into the kitchen. Evan saw how exhausted and worried Sarah looked and he knew he needed to take her mind of things for right now. He smiled at Sarah and said "What do you say we go for a swim at the beach. It's still beautiful outside let's take advantage of it. Besides you need to clear your mind for a while please say yes." Sarah smiled "That's a good idea it's almost lunch I'll have Mrs. Johnson fix us a picnic basket for lunch. I'll meet you on the porch in twenty minutes." "Alright it's a date see you in twenty minutes." Evan went to his room to change into his swimming trunks. He took the button out of his shirt pocket and placed it in the top drawer of his night stand. He changed into his trunks and put a tank top on. He was ready. He went downstairs to wait for Sarah on the porch. Sarah came downstairs she had on a baby blue bikini and matching cover-up. She walked on to the porch and smiled at Evan "I'm ready" she said just when she finished saying that Mrs. Johnson came out with the picnic basket "Here you are Miss Sarah and I even put a bottle of fine wine into the basket in case you both wanted something a bit stronger than water." Mrs. Johnson winked at Evan "Have a good time." She left the porch. Sarah went over to the porch cabinet that held the towels, blankets and whatever else was needed for the beach. She grabbed two towels, a blanket and sunscreen. She closed the door smiled at Evan and said "I think we have everything we need." Evan smiled "Okay let's go!"

Chapter Eighteen

Sarah and Evan were walking along the beach the sun was shining brightly. As they were walking Sarah stopped all of a sudden looking at Evan she said "I would like to show you a cave that I went into when I was in the past. I want to show you some of the things I experienced when I went back in time. Is that okay with you?" Evan looked at Sarah as he raised an eyebrow he said "Umm sure I'd love to see it." Sarah smiled "I know it sounds farfetched and unreal but I never knew about this cave until I was shown it." Evan smiled "Whatever you want to do love. I'd love to share some of what you saw and besides maybe I'll feel closer to my dad." Sarah grabbed Evans hand and started leading the way. After walking for quite a while Evan finally said "Just how far is this cave of yours?" Sarah smiled "Not too much further it's just around the bend over here." As they followed the beach it lead to the right as they turned Sarah smiled "See here it is" She said with excitement. The cave was tucked in between some trees and surrounded by huge boulders. As Sarah entered the cave first she told Evan "Keep your head down there are quite a few Stalactites here in the beginning." Evan crouched down so he wouldn't crash into anything. "Sarah its dark in here did you bring a flashlight?" Sarah reached into her bag pulling out a flashlight "Yes here it is I'll turn it on." They walked a short distance and came upon another opening Sarah went out the opening she turned off the flashlight as Evan followed he looked around him in wonder "Sarah this is beautiful." She smiled "My grandfather showed this to my grandmother the first summer they stayed here. If I hadn't gone back into the past I would have never known about his place." Sarah took the blanket and laid it on the ground. Evan placed the picnic basket on the blanket and put the towels in the corner. He took Sarah's hand and walked to the edge of the water when his feet touched the water he was surprised "Sarah this water is warm." "Yes it is." Taking her cover-up off and tossing it in the sand she grabbed Evans hand. "Let's swim out to that waterfall there is a flat rock there where we can sit under it." "Okay" Sarah smiled "I'll beat you there" Evan smiled back "Oh you think so huh?" Evan grabbed Sarah by the waist and turned her toward the sand he put her down and dived into the water. "I think I'm going to beat you there!" he said laughing. Sarah laughed "That's okay I'll give you a head start" she said with a smirk on her face and dived in after him. Sarah caught up to Evan she was a strong swimmer they both laughed. Sarah swam ahead leading the way to behind the waterfall. They reached the rock together out of breath they both climbed on the rock from behind the waterfall it looked so magical. As they sat there Evan moved closer to Sarah and wrapped his arms around her waist pulling her closer to him. "This is amazing Sarah if the people that wanted to buy the Haven knew about this it would be worth a lot more" Sarah sighed "Do you see why I can't sell this place? My grandparents loved it here and it's where they fell in love. This place is not only beautiful it's a part of my family history and heritage. There is no amount of money worth that." Turning to Evan Sarah looked into his eyes "This could be our very own paradise." She smiled softly inviting Evan to kiss her. Sarah turned around to face Evan their faces were inches apart. Evan looking into Sarah's eyes leaned forward and kissed her. Sarah parted her lips as their kiss became more passionate. Evan slid his tongue down her neck and nuzzled her neck softly a moan escaped from Sarah. She felt something that she had never felt before and didn't want it to stop. She tilted her head giving Evan more access to her neck. Evan started kissing lower he moved one of her bikini straps aside and kissed her shoulder and his hand slid the other strap down he made his way over to kiss her other shoulder as he started moving toward her breast he paused and looked at Sarah "Do you want me to stop?" in a raspy voice Sarah replied "No I don't ever want you to stop." Evan lifted his head to look into her eyes "Sarah if I don't stop I'm afraid that I won't be able to control myself. I know this is your first time and I do not want to do anything that you will regret." Sarah looked at Evan with longing in her eyes "Evan I have never felt this way about any man. I want you and I don't want you to stop anything." With that she bent over and kissed Evan again only this time their tongues searched each other's mouth their kisses becoming more urgent. Evan smiled at Sarah and said "I want to take this slowly I want us to remember this moment for the rest of our lives." He slid the straps of her bikini top down while caressing her shoulders and reached in back and untied her top letting it fall. He kissed her breast while his other hand slid in front to caress her other one. He licked his way down to her nipple and feeling in harden took it into his mouth and lightly sucked and flickered his tongue around it. Sarah gasped as his tongue made love to her breasts. Her hands rubbed his back and slid to the front to feel his chest. He felt so muscular. She wanted to feel all of him. Evan gently laid Sarah down and started kissing her stomach as he reached her bikini his hand slid over the top grazing her lips. Sarah gasped Evan slowly pulled down her bikini bottom, his hand massaged her slowly. Sarah instinctively spread her legs she wanted to feel his hand massage the pulsating button that was swelling with need. Evan spread her lips and started to slide his finger back and forth causing Sarah to arch into his hand. Evan stopped looking at Sarah he said "Not yet love I want you to enjoy every feeling" He moved on top of Sarah and let his manhood just rest there he wanted her to get used to the feeling. He kissed Sarah again as he felt her wetness on him. Slowly he led his manhood to her opening and slid into her. Sarah gasped at the instant pain she felt. Evan stopped and waited knowing the pain would subside he let Sarah lead. He kissed her neck down to her nipple at that point Sarah started to move her hips Evan joined her. Sarah felt something building she couldn't explain but she never wanted it to stop. Meeting each of Evan's thrusts with more intensity than the last she could feel herself climbing. Evan whispered in her ear "I want us to climax together love." Sarah wasn't sure what he meant but as she grew nearer and nearer it was impossible to hold. She let out a cry and she arched her back wanting and needing him to fill her Evan knew it was time thrusting deeper and faster they cried out together as they both reached an orgasm it seemed to last forever. They both collapsed their bodies drenched in sweat and their hearts beating wildly. Evan slid off of Sarah and wrapped her in his arms "I love you Sarah Saint James I have never loved anyone the way I love you." Sarah looked into Evans eyes "I have never loved anyone as much as you either. I don't think I've ever been in love until now." She rested her head on his chest listening to his heart beat knowing that this was the man she was going to spend the rest of her life with. Evan finally broke their silence "I didn't hurt you did I?" Sarah had tears in her eyes "Evan these tears are from the happiness I am feeling and no you did not hurt me. It hurt at first but just at first then I felt no pain just you." Evan smiled "I am so glad that I didn't hurt you I was worried for a moment." "No need to worry my love I would have told you if you were hurting me." Sarah rested her head again and closed her eyes. Evan closed his eyes they drifted off to sleep. They only slept a half hour when Sarah suddenly sat up disorientated she looked at Evan watching him as he still slept. Reaching up she traced the outline of his face with her fingers when she got to his lips Evan awoke and kissed her finger. "How long have we been asleep?" he asked "Not long. I don't know about you but I am starving! Is this what making love does to you if so I'm going to gain a lot of weight!!" Evan laughed "I am starving too and I'm sure we burned enough calories that we don't need to worry about weight." Sarah chuckled "Want to race back?" Evan grabbed his trunks and dove into the water Sarah Yelled "Hey that is not fair!" Sarah grabbed her bikini and jumped in after him. They swam back to the beach. They both were laughing as they grabbed towels. Evan started to dry off Sarah's naked body and Sarah did the same. When they were dry they both sat on the blanket wrapped in towels. Sarah opened the picnic basket and took out the bottle of wine, thankfully Mrs. Johnson had put it in a wine cooler container it was still cold. She handed the bottle to Evan. She took out the wine glasses and put them on the blanket. Next she took out the container of potato salad then she took the sandwiches out. Mrs. Johnson had made them Italian subs they looked scrumptious. She then pulled out a tossed Salad with Italian dressing the bowls were underneath. For desert Mrs. Johnson had made chocolate chip cookies Sarah's favorite. Evan opened the wine and Sarah held the glasses as he poured some in each glass. Sarah opened the sandwiches and put them on the plates along with a serving of potato salad. She then put some tossed salad in each bowl. She handed Evan his plate, bowl and cutlery along with a cloth napkin. Evan picked up the wine glasses and handed Sarah hers "Here is to a day we will never forget" they tapped each other's glass than took a sip of the wine. Sarah smiled "I will treasure this day always." She looked over to the waterfall and Evan's eyes followed hers and he smiled. They both lifted their subs and started eating. When they were finished Sarah gathered all of the dirty dishes after Evan had scraped them off she placed everything but the wine back in the picnic basket after she took out the cookies. Sarah said "Mrs. Johnson knows these are my favorite cookies. You know Evan I don't know what I'd do without her she's been like a mother to me." Evan smiled "I know what you mean James has been like a father to me too." Looking back at the waterfall Evan was thinking he looked at Sarah "You know what I know you call the house the Haven how would you feel if we name our alcove the Haven's Cove?" Sarah had a huge smile on her face Evan loved when she smiled like that she said "Evan that is a wonderful idea and although nobody else will know what we are referring to we'll know." Evan smiled back "Precisely!" Evan raised his glass and Sarah raised hers Evan smiled and said "To us and our Haven's Cove" they tapped their glasses together and each sipped the wine. Both of them lost in thought they sat in silence for a while. Sarah was looking at the waterfall and you could see the peacefulness on her face. Evan noticed how relaxed and beautiful she looked. Still looking at Sarah he said "I never knew one could feel this much joy after making love. Making love to you Sarah has made me realize just how much joy I have been missing in my life. I also will remember this day always." Sarah looked at Evan and smiled a smile that reached her eyes. Her heart was over flowing with love. She hadn't known how much you could truly love someone. Evan reached for Sarah's glass and put both glasses out of the way and somewhere safe. He moved over to Sarah letting his towel fall he reached for Sarah's towel and untucked it letting it fall to the ground. He placed both hands on her face and started to kiss her as the kisses intensified once again the made passionate love. After they made love they lay spent in each other's arms. Sarah sighed "Thank you so much." Evan looked at Sarah raising an eyebrow he asked "For what love?" Sarah smiled "For this unforgettable day and helping me to forget all the tragic events if only for a while." The sun was starting to set Sarah turned to Evan "I think we should head back although I could stay here forever with you." "I believe you are right however I think we should put something on before we go back it wouldn't be good for Chris's men to see us in our birthday suits." They both started to laugh. Sarah and Evan put their bathing suits back on and packed the rest of the picnic basket back up. They folded their towels and then folded the blanket together. After making sure nothing was left behind Sarah got her flashlight out as the entered the cave. They came out on the other side climbed over the boulders and were back on the beach. They held hands as they walked back along the beach to get to the house. By the time they arrived at the house it was dusk. When they walked into the house Sarah brought the picnic basket into the kitchen and thanked Mrs. Johnson for a wonderful lunch. Mrs. Johnson smiled "You're quite welcome. Did you both have a good time? And did you have sunscreen on you were gone all afternoon." Sarah chuckled inside "Yes we had sunscreen on. We had a wonderful time." "Mrs. Johnson could see the glow of love on Sarah's face "Well you better get changed I hope you are hungry dinner will be soon." "We are heading up there now to change for dinner." Sarah kissed Mrs. Johnson on the cheek "Thank you for always taking good care of me. I hope you know just how much you mean to me." Mrs. Johnson blushed "There, there child no need to thank me now off with you I have cooking to do." Mrs. Johnson paused "I love you as if you were like my own Sarah" after she said that she turned and went back to cooking. Sarah smiled left the kitchen and met Evan at the stairs. "Shall we go change for dinner?" "I think that would be a good idea all of a sudden I'm starving again!" They both gave each other a knowing look and smiled Sarah said "Me too. I'll see you after my shower." "Sounds good." They both went upstairs to their rooms.

Once in her room Sarah slipped out of her bikini and went into the bathroom she turned the water for the shower on. Jumping into the shower she smiled has she thought about the events of today when she thought of Evan making love to her she got chills up and down her arms. The thought of his hands on her made her want for more she couldn't get enough of Evan. Shaking her head she said to herself "Snap out of it you need to wash and get dressed silly." After her shower she dried her hair and went to pick out her clothes. As she looked through her closet she came to a light yellow sundress with blue and white daisies on it taking it off the hanger she held it in front of herself and went to look in the mirror. "Yes I think this will look great." She changed into her dress and went to put her make-up on.

In the meantime across the hall Evan went into his bathroom ran the water and jumped in the shower. He kept telling himself he had to stop thinking of Sarah or he would never be able to go down to dinner. He loved her so much it scared him yet excited him at the same time. After showering he went to his closet to pick out clothes for dinner. He decided on a pale yellow Caribbean shirt one of his favorites. He picked out a tan pair of Bermuda shorts to go with it. He finished getting dressed and went back to the bathroom to gel his hair he wanted to make sure he looked extra good tonight. After putting on his favorite cologne Evan was ready for dinner.

Evan and Sarah came out of their rooms at the same time. Sarah took Evan's breath away "You look beautiful" he said smiling at Sarah. Sarah smiled "you look pretty handsome yourself. Are you ready for dinner?" Evan held out his hand to Sarah "After you my lady." Sarah smiled as they walked down the stairs to dinner. When they reached the bottom of the stairs Alfred met them "Dinner will be served on the patio tonight. Mrs. Johnson thought it was too nice of an evening to waste." Sarah smiled at Alfred "Thank you Alfred we will go out there now." "Very well Miss Sarah dinner will be shortly would either of you care for a cocktail before dinner?" Sarah replied first "Alfred could I have a glass of Merlot please?" "Yes Miss and you Mr. Evan?" "I'll have the same thank you Alfred." "Very well I will bring your drinks to you in a few moments." They both said together "Thank you Alfred" Sarah looked at Evan and they both started to laugh. She hadn't felt this giddy since she was a teenager. They walked out onto the patio the table was already set and it was only set for two. Sarah looked upset "I see my cousin is still missing. What the hell is wrong with him? I also think it's rude that he just disappears and doesn't tell anyone where he is." Shaking her head Sarah went to sit Evan got to her chair before her and pulled it out for her. "I don't know much about Tom but I can understand you being upset about this after all it's not like this wasn't big news." Sarah sat "Exactly where ever he is he must not have a television or newspaper or and I'm trying not to believe this. He does know and just doesn't care." Evan sat across from Sarah "Don't let yourself go there Sarah it will just upset you more. I'm sure he has a good explanation for being away this long." Alfred came out with their drinks placing the drinks in front of Sarah and Evan he said "Dinner will be just a few more minutes. If you need anything just let me know." Evan said "Thank you Alfred." After 10 minutes Alfred brought out dinner Baked Lamb and rice with asparagus. After Alfred placed their plates down he topped off their drinks and asked if there was anything else they needed. Sarah said "it smells so good. "Thank you Alfred I believe we are all set. Evan do you need anything?" "No thank you I am good. "Alfred please tell Mrs. Johnson it looks delicious." "Yes Miss" Sarah and Evan started eating their dinner. When dinner was finished they were sipping their wine. Sarah had been quiet through the whole meal. Evan looked at Sarah she had a sad look on her face "Sarah you were quiet through all of dinner and you look sad. What are you thinking about?" Sarah sighed "I'm thinking about my parents I miss them so much especially at a time like this." Evan asked "Would you like to tell me about them maybe it will make you feel a little better?" Sarah smiled softly "Yes I'd like that."

Sarah took a sip of her wine before she began. "Both my parents were doctor's heart surgeons to be exact. They met while they were in medical school. They did their residency at Boston Memorial Hospital both of them ended up staying there after they were married. As a wedding gift my grandparents gave them their house on Beacon Hill in Boston fully furnished. My grandparents at the same time moved here at the Haven year round. Three years later I was born. My mother took a two year sabbatical to take care of me. When I was older she told me she took that time to make sure we had enough time to have a good bonding experience and she didn't want to miss out on all of the new things I'd be doing or discovering as a baby. When her two years were up she hired a nanny to take care of me and went back to work with my father. The three of us had a close relationship. They spent most of their time off with me. I spent my summers here with granny and they always tried to get here as many weekends as they could. We always had a wonderful time together they were very loving. My parents were very much in love and they weren't afraid to show each other affection. Six years ago they went to a medical convention in the Caribbean they stayed in a little villa by the ocean. One night there was a terrible storm while they were sleeping a tornado swept their villa into the ocean. My parents never knew what happened which was a blessing. Divers found their bodies five days later. They were flown home and buried in the small cemetery we have on the property beside my grandfather. That's another reason not to sell the property. I would have to have their bodies dug up and buried somewhere else. Then my Granny dying last May it seems everyone I love dies." Evan felt sad for Sarah "I'm sorry Sarah." A volcano of tears erupted from her beautiful blue eyes. Evan set his glass down took Sarah's glass out of her hand and set it beside his. He took her in his arms and held her until she stopped crying. His shirt was drenched with tears. He took his handkerchief out of his pocket and dried her tears. Sarah looked up "I'm sorry Evan for letting myself get out of control." Evan held her a little tighter "You have nothing to be sorry for. You have had to handle so much pain for the last few years alone. I promise you darling you will never have to handle anything else alone again." "Thank you." Evan asked "Shall we go inside?" "Yes the mosquito's are starting to have a feast." Evan held Sarah around the waist and led her inside. When they got to the stairs Sarah grabbed Evans hand and led him up to her bedroom.

Evan closed the door to Sarah's bedroom and kissed her gently on the lips. Their kiss grew more passionate. Evan lifted Sarah in his arms and walked over to her bed. He put her gently on the bed and then lay beside her. Evan started to kiss Sarah. He placed small kisses on her eyes, her nose and her cheek. He put his face near her cheek and kissed her with his eyelash. Sarah laughed "That tickles" Evan smiled "Do you know what that is called." "No" Sarah answered. "Those are butterfly kisses made especially for the woman you love." He bent his head again and kissed her again with his eyelash. Sarah giggled. He kissed her on the lips again using his tongue gently on her lips. She opened her mouth as his tongue searched for hers. When their tongues met it was as if they were dancing. The kiss was so intimate. Evan removed the straps of her sundress and started caressing her neck. Kissing and licking moving further and further down, he lowered her sundress exposing her breasts. Looking at her breasts her nipples were pink and erect waiting for his caresses. He took one breast into his mouth while kneading the other. He teased her nipple kissing, licking, biting gently then made his way to the other breast. As he was teasing her nipples he looked up into Sarah's eyes and said "I love you more than words can say my beautiful Sarah." "I love you too I never knew what loving a man meant until you made love to me. Make love to me Evan." Evan lifted Sarah's sundress over her head taking off his own shirt while Sarah unbuttoned his shorts and pulled the zipper down. She placed her hands on the inside of his shorts and boxers and pulled them down to expose his erection. Sarah blushed as she reached for Evans erection and began stroking it. She had never seen a man naked and she wanted to explore every part of Evan. As she gently stroked, Evan let out a small groan. He loved the way she was touching him. After a bit more stroking he grabbed Sarah's hands and held them over her head while he kissed her deeply. He used his mouth and his hands as he tantalized her. He kissed her abdomen and lowered himself to kiss further down when he reached her hips he licked the sensitive sides coming closer and closer to her pelvis. With his leg in between hers he urged her to spread her legs. Sarah was feeling embarrassed as she spread her legs she did not know what to expect. Evan feeling her reluctance said "Honey I will never do anything that will hurt you and if you ever feel uncomfortable just tell me and I will stop." Sarah nodded feeling the heat rise on her face. She was struggling with how good it felt and how embarrassed she felt. She said to Evan "You don't have to stop I trust you." Evan gave Sarah a sexy smile as he resumed. He used his fingers to spread her lips. He could feel how hot she was. Lowering his face he ran his tongue along her button. Sarah gasped and grabbed the edge of her bed holding on to the sheet. He sucked on her button nibbling and kissing and licking. Sarah moaned. Evan could tell Sarah wanted more as she arched her hips toward his mouth he kissed her swollen button and kissed his way up to her mouth. He kissed her deeply, she could taste part of herself on his tongue and as strange as it felt she wanted him more. He positioned himself on top of her as he entered her he moaned she felt so good surrounding him. They were now one and he wanted to stay like this forever. He started to move his hips slowly at first then a little bit faster. Sarah was meeting his thrusts their bodies were sweating has they moved in rhythm. Evan reached down to caress her button as he thrusted harder and faster. Sarah was going crazy she felt as if she were going to explode. Just when Evan thought he couldn't hold back anymore Sarah said his name and they came together this one lasting longer and more intense than the others. When they had finished Evan stayed inside of Sarah as their breaths were shallow and their hearts beating fast. He lay there for a bit longer and then gently rolled off of Sarah he didn't want to hurt her with his weight. They held on to each other as if it were their last time together. Each of them felt a love so deep so indescribable tears started to fall from each of their eyes tears of happiness that they had finally found their soul mate. Neither one of them knew what the other was thinking but they were both thinking the exact same thing. Sarah reached up to wipe away a tear from Evans eye as Evan reached to wipe one from her eye. He knew without a doubt that she was his soul mate and he would protect her with his life. This was the woman who he wanted to marry and have children with. They both fell fast asleep in each other's arms.

The next day was Friday Sarah and Evan awoke just the way they fell asleep. Evan woke up first leaning on his elbow he just watched Sarah sleep. Sarah finally woke up and said "Good morning. How long have you been awake?" Evan kissed her lightly on the nose "Good morning love and I've been awake long enough to watch how beautiful you are while you sleep. Just when I thought you couldn't get any more beautiful than you already are." Sarah blushed now it was time to come back to reality. "Evan today is Friday I really wanted to wait for Tom to make arrangements. Other than me Vicki was the only relative Tom had. His mother was killed in a boating accident ten years ago. I do not have a choice I have to call the funeral director today." "You need to do what you have to do. It's going to be okay." "I think we will have the services at Saint Paul's Church on Monday morning and the burial here in the family cemetery. Hopefully Tom will be home by then. I'll call the funeral director right after breakfast." "Okay while you do that I'm going to check in with the office to see how things are going." Sarah nodded she was making a mental note to put the Obituary in Sunday's Boston Globe and in the Newport Herald. Sarah smiled at Evan "As much as I'd like to stay here with you all day we need to get up and have breakfast. I'm going to jump in the shower. Meet you in fifteen minutes for breakfast?" Evan sighed "You are right I guess we do have to get up. I'm going to head to my room to shower and yes I'll meet you in fifteen minutes downstairs." Evan gave Sarah a slow kiss on the lips put his legs over the bed while he was trying to find his boxers. He finally located them at the end of the bed. He put them on and went to his bedroom.

Evan met Sarah downstairs in the kitchen. Mrs. Johnson smiled at the both of them "Good morning." Both of them answered "Good morning" "What would you both like for breakfast?" Sarah replied "I'm easy we just need to make it a fast one because I have to call the funeral director today to make arrangements." Mrs. Johnson replied "How about fried eggs and bacon with toast. I already have cooked bacon and it will take no time to make the toast" Sarah smiled "Okay that sounds good" Mrs. Johnson made eggs and toast. She heated the bacon. She gave both Evan and Sarah their breakfast. Sarah had poured her and Evan a cup of coffee. As they were eating breakfast Mrs. Johnson asked "Have you heard from Tom yet?" "Sarah sighed "Not a word and quite frankly I'm a little upset that he didn't bother to tell anyone where he was going." Mrs. Johnson sighed "That boy has never been responsible I guess he'll never change." Sarah nodded "I don't think he'll change either." Sarah and Evan finished breakfast Sarah looked at Evan "I'm going to head to my office to call the funeral director" Evan hugged Sarah "I'm going to run home for a few minutes to check on work. You are not going anywhere right?" "No I didn't plan on it." Evan looked concerned "Please do not leave the house not even to go in the yard until I get back." "I won't I'll wait for you." Evan gave Sarah a kiss said goodbye to Mrs. Johnson and went out the back door. Sarah looked at Mrs. Johnson "I'll be in my office if anyone needs me." "Alright Sarah just remember what Evan said." "I know." Sarah walked out of the kitchen to her office. She closed the door and went to her desk to pick up the phone. She dialed the funeral directors number he answered on the second ring "Hello Saint Laurens funeral home may I help you?" "Hi is this Arthur?" "Speaking how may I help you?" "This is Sarah Saint James I'm calling about making funeral arrangements for my cousin Vicki." "Thank you for calling

Miss Saint James. Let me get my notebook and a pen." He grabbed his notebook and a pen "Okay I'm ready" "I'd like to have a mass on Monday morning at Saint Paul's church and the burial will be here at our family cemetery. Hopefully her brother Tom will be home by then." "Okay Miss Saint James I'll get in touch with the church and arrange that." "Thank you Arthur and thank you for your patience." "Not a problem Miss Saint James this is never easy on families." "No it isn't" "I'll give you a call to confirm the arrangements after I get in touch with the church." "Thank you" "You're welcome have a nice day." "You too Goodbye" After Sarah hung up the phone she called the Boston Globe and the Newport Herald. She gave them all the information they needed and asked that it be put in Sunday's paper. Both papers agreed. She hung up the phone and put her head in her hands and thought "I wish this wasn't happening."

THE HAVEN'S COVE

Chapter Nineteen

Tom was down two million dollars he had been up to seven million then his luck took a turn for the worse. He hadn't slept for days he decided to take a break and get some rest he would try again later after he had rested. He knew his luck would come back it had to. He went up to his room opened the door placed the "Do Not Disturb" sign on the door closed it and locked it. Tom decided to take a quick shower before going to bed. While in the shower he kept thinking to himself "My luck has to change half of that money is Vicki's she'll kill me if she finds out I lost it all." He rinsed off wrapping a towel around his waist he went over to the bed put on his boxers and pulled the covers down it didn't take him long to fall asleep as he was exhausted. Tom slept until Sunday afternoon when he awoke he was starving. He ordered room service. While waiting for room service he took another shower shaved and got dressed. There was a knock on the door just as he was finishing. "Who is it?" "Room service, Mr. Kincaid" Tom opened the door to let him in. "Just set it over near the window." Tom took out a five dollar bill and tipped the waiter. "Thanks" he said as he closed the door. He sat down to eat. After finishing his meal Tom felt a lot better he said to himself "I think I'm feeling lucky today." Tom went to the elevator pushing the button he waited until it reached him. Once inside Tom pushed the button to the lobby. While he was headed to the baccarat table at Caesar's Palace he heard his name being called. "Tom" he turned to see who was calling him it was Frankie Dangelo one of his gambling friends. Tom stopped as Frankie reached him he asked "Tom what the hell are you doing here?" Tom raised his eyebrow looking at Frankie like he had two heads he said "What the hell do you mean by that remark I came here for the same reason you do, to gamble." Frankie looked at Tom with surprise and said "Well I wouldn't be here if my sister had just passed away." Tom turned white in shock he asked "What the hell are you talking about Frankie?" Frankie looked at Tom realizing his friend didn't even know about his sister. "How long have you been here Tom?" Tom answered "A week ago Saturday morning why?" Frankie shook his head "Have you seen the news or even bothered to read the newspaper?" Tom was now upset "No I have been playing baccarat up until yesterday. I was tired I went to bed in the early afternoon and did not wake up until a few hours ago. What is this bull about my sister?" Frankie was carrying a newspaper under his arm "I bought the Boston Globe this morning to read on the plane" He grabbed the paper under his arm he flipped through it to the Obituaries and then handed the paper to Tom "You might want to read this." Tom took the paper from Frankie looking at it he said "Oh my God it can't be possible it's Vicki. I have to catch the next plane home! Thanks Frankie if you hadn't of ran into me I would have never known. I'll see you later" "Okay Tom I am sorry to hear about your sister." So am I Thanks Frankie." "Tom left in a hurry he waited for the elevator. Going back to his room he picked up the phone and made reservations to catch the next plane home. After he hung up the phone he grabbed his suitcase and started to pack thinking he said "I don't have to worry about Vicki or her share of the money for the painting we sold. That's a relief since I lost most of the money. In any case it should have been Sarah that died not Vicki. Now if something was to happen to Sarah everything would be perfect all the money would be mine." He finished packing his suitcase and took the Elevator to the lobby outside the hotel he waved for a taxi. A taxi stopped in front of him "To the airport please." The driver replied "Yes sir."

The murderer didn't dare call Jake to tell him the wrong woman was dead afraid of what he would do. So far Jake hadn't called which meant he did not know yet. In the meantime Jake bought the Sunday Herald he ordered a large cup of coffee and headed for his office. Jake never watched Television and the only time he read the newspaper was on Sundays. He was enjoying his coffee while he read the articles in the paper until he got to the obituary page as he took a mouthful of coffee he noticed Vicki's name he choke spitting out his coffee he screamed "The damn idiot killed the wrong broad."

Julie had arrived at the Haven late Friday afternoon. After Alfred took her suitcase he said "Miss Julie, Miss Sarah is in the living room she is expecting you." Julie thanked Alfred and went straight to the living room. When she walked into the living room she found Sarah sitting on the couch with Evan she was surprised to see him there. When Sarah noticed Julie she stood up and walked over to her giving Julie a hug she said "I'm glad you're here Julie." They held on to each other for a minute "I'm here to help you Sarah everything is going to be fine." Sarah took Julie's hand "Come I want you to meet Evan." Evan stood up and said "Thank you darling we've already met. Hello Julie nice to see you again." Julie faked a smile "Hello Evan." Julie looking at Sarah said "Don't look so shocked Sarah we met while visiting you in the hospital." Sarah smiled "That explains it. Please sit with us Julie." Sarah and Evan sat back down on the couch Julie took the opposite chair facing the couch. Julie spoke first "So Sarah when is Vicki's funeral and where is Tom?" Sarah looked sad "The funeral is Monday morning with a mass at Saint Paul's church. Vicki will be buried in the small cemetery behind the garden. I haven't heard from Tom since this happened. I don't know where he is I'm hoping he'll be here on time for his sisters funeral." Julie gave Sarah a strange look "Don't you think its senseless Sarah to have Vicki buried in the family cemetery while you are in the process of selling this property. You are only going to have to move her along with the rest of your family when the place is sold." Sarah somewhat perturbed that Julie asked that question replied "I have definitely decided I'm not selling Julie." Julie was shocked "You have? Do you think you've made the right decision Sarah?" Sarah was clearly upset that Julie was questioning her "I certainly do think I'm making the right decision. I thought that you'd be happy about it?" Julie regained her composure "That's really up to you it's your property however I do remember that Tom really wants to sell. Of course I'm happy for you." Sarah looked at Julie "I'm going to buy Tom out all he really cares about is the money." Julie smiled "I'm sure you know what you're doing Sarah. I'm not worried about your decision besides I've kind of gotten attached to this place since I've been coming here with you." Changing the subject Julie said "What time is dinner?" Sarah replied "Seven o'clock" Julie replied "That sounds great would you mind if I go and take a nap before dinner I'm a little tired." Sarah replied "No of course not the drive here can be overwhelming. I'll see you at dinner." Julie stood up and said "Chow" both Sarah and Evan at the same time said "Sleep well." Sarah and Evan watched Julie walk out of the living room. Evan was playing the event that just happened before him over in his mind he thought to himself "Something is just not right I can't put my finger on it but I feel it." He held Sarah's hand and noticed the baby grand piano he looked at Sarah and said "Do you play the piano like your grandmother?" The black baby grand piano still adorn one corner of the living room it looked as new now as when Monique's husband bought it for her years ago. Sarah had made sure to take care of it having it tuned and cleaned every year. Sarah smiled "Yes I can play. But I read the notes I don't play by ear like granny did. Would you like me to play something for you?" Evan smiled "I'd love to hear you play do you mind?" "No of course not it will take my mind off things for awhile." Sarah walked over to the piano and sat on the bench. She opened the book of sheet music that was sitting on the lyre. She then opened the cover to the keys. She flipped the page to the song "The Rose" she began playing it on the piano and singing. Evan walked over to the piano and pulled a chair closer to Sarah. He listened in amazement as she played and sang the song. When the song was finished Evan stood up and went to kiss Sarah on the cheek "That was so beautiful Sarah I didn't know you could sing." Blushing she said "I'm full of surprises." She played a few more songs and Evan joined her in singing until it was almost time for dinner. Sarah smiled at Evan "Thank you for having me play. It always makes me feel better whenever I sing and play. It helps my soul. I must say you are not a bad singer yourself!" Evan smiled "You are not the only one with a few surprises." They both laughed Sarah took Evans arm "shall we go and get ready for dinner?" Evan smiled "Lead the way Madam" Sarah and Evan went upstairs to change for dinner.

 Sarah and Evan entered the dining room at the same time. Evan held a chair out for Sarah than took the chair beside her. Julie came down noticing Evan was practically sitting on Sarah's lap she smiled and took the seat across from Sarah. Sarah smiled when Julie sat down "How was your nap?" Julie smiled "It was great and so peaceful." Sarah replied "This place can lull you to sleep with just the sound of the ocean. I'm glad you slept well." Everyone was dressed in semi-formal attire. Evan wore a white lightweight suit with a light blue shirt opened at the collar. Sarah thought he looked so handsome in his suit the contrast made his tan stand out. She wore a short fitted dark blue satin sleeveless, backless dress that tied like a choker around her neck. She wore a pair of white pumps her only jewelry was her studded diamond earrings and her grandmother's pendant. Evan thought she looked stunning the color of her dress made her blue eyes even brighter. He also loved the way her hair curled down to her shoulders. Julie was wearing a very revealing low cut pink dress she wore a pearl necklace and matching earrings. Her hair was jet black long and straight. She also looked stunning. Looking puzzled Evan thought "Earlier her hair had been short and brown. I almost didn't recognize you Julie you look lovely." She laughed and touching her hair she said "Do you like it Evan?" "Yes it's very becoming." Julie smiled "Why thank you Evan. When I go out on a date my date never knows if I'm going to be a blond, brunette or a red head. It makes my life so much more exciting." Evan smiled and thought to himself "You still can't hold a candle to Sarah" The large cherry would table sat twelve people however the servants set the table for three tonight. A buffet table adorns one side of the room. French doors were opened on both sides of the fireplace opening up to the patio and pool area. Maggie appeared with a tray carrying piping hot French onion soup. She placed a bowl in front of each of them. Sarah smiled "Thank you Maggie." Stiffly Maggie replied "Your welcome Miss Sarah." After Maggie left the dining room Julie asked "What's wrong with Maggie tonight Sarah she doesn't seem like herself?" Sarah sighed "She's probably upset like the rest of us over Vicki's death." Julie nodded "Of course you must be right it's not something you get over quickly." Julie tasted a spoonful of soup then placed her spoon on her plate and said "Mrs. Johnson makes the best onion soup it's simply delicious." We are lucky to have her she's an excellent cook she has made Veal Marcella with angel hair pasta, chocolate mousse for desert." Julie laughed "After I've eaten here all weekend Sarah I have to starve myself all the next week or I would look like a blimp. Sarah laughed "You are absolutely right Julie I usually do the same." Maggie came in with the tray of Veal Marcella and placed a plate in front of each of them. Evan smiled "This looks and smells delicious" They ate their meal in silence as everyone was enjoying it. After Maggie picked up the dinner plates she came out with the tray of Chocolate Mousse she asked "Would anyone like coffee?" Sarah, Evan, and Julie answered together "Yes please" Maggie smiled "I'll bring it right out." After they finished their Mousse Sarah suggested they have their coffee on the patio. They all headed out the French doors onto the patio they sat at one of the tables. Sarah took a sip of her coffee and placed it on the table she looked at Julie "Julie how is everything going at the office?" Julie smiled "Don't you worry Nora and I are taking care of everything. You just stay home and take care of what you have to do most of all take care of yourself." Sarah sighed in relief "Thank you Julie it's good to know I can count on you and Nora." Looking at Sarah Julie said "I won't be able to stay for Vicki's funeral on Monday I have a nine am closing. I can cancel or try to get someone to take my place if you really need me here." Sarah replied "Of course not I will be fine you go to the closing." Alfred appeared on the patio "Miss Sarah you have a phone call." Sarah stood and said "Thank you Alfred, please excuse me while I take this call." Sarah walked into the house. While Sarah was gone Julie asked Evan "Would you like to come clubbing with me tonight? I know a lot of good spots where we can have some fun." "I bet you do"

Evan thought Julie continued "We could have a couple of drinks a few dances and who knows what else the night will bring. We really can't ask Sarah to join us she's not well enough and after all her cousin has just been murdered. What do you say?" Evan gave Julie a serious look "There is something I should tell you Julie. Sarah and I are involved in fact I'm going to marry her." Julie gasped in surprise "Congratulations. Oh God I'm sorry Evan I didn't know or I wouldn't have asked you to go anywhere. I think I'll go out anyway it's a shame to waste a perfect evening. Will you tell Sarah I'll see her tomorrow?" Julie stood blew Evan a kiss and left. When Sarah returned to the patio she asked "Where's Julie?" She sat down picked up her coffee and took a sip. Evan looked at Sarah "She told me to tell you she'd see you tomorrow. Sarah looked confused "She went to bed already?" "No she went clubbing" Evan replied with disgust in his voice. Sarah missing the tone of Evan's reply said "It's just like her she can't stay still." Evan took Sarah's hands in his he asked "Sarah how long have you known Julie?" "Nine years" Evan continued "Do you trust her?" Sarah raised her eyebrows "Yes with my life." Evan didn't know how to say this to Sarah without hurting her he got a little closer as he said "Sarah my love you are very naïve." Sarah was surprised "Evan why are you saying that?" with a serious tone Evan said "Because there is something about that woman I just don't trust." Defending Julie Sarah said "When you get to know her better you'll feel differently. You'll love her just as much as I do." Evan sighed "If you say so my love." In the back of his mind he thought "I'll be keeping my eye on her."

Chapter Twenty

Maggie had been fuming since they had discovered Vicki's body. Her mother wanted to know why she had lied to detective Jennison. While she was filling the dishwasher she thought "Mother doesn't realize that I am thirty-four years old. She thinks she has to know my every move. It's none of her damn business or detective Jennison's what I do with my time. If she cared about me as much as she cared for her precious Sarah things would be better around her. What do I care? Someday real soon I'll be out of here can't be soon enough for me." Maggie finished loading the dishwasher closed it turned it on and went out.

Tom arrived Sunday night while Sarah, Evan and Julie were sitting at the patio table finishing dinner. Tom asked Alfred where Sarah was he indicated she was out on the patio. When Tom walked out on the patio Sarah stood up in surprise and exclaimed "Tom where have you been?" Tom started turning red "I was in Vegas I didn't know about Vicki's death until this afternoon when I met a friend of mine. He showed me the obituary in the Boston Herald. As soon as I knew I took the first plane home." Sarah sighed in relief "Thank God Tom I was afraid you'd miss the funeral and the burial." Tom looked at Sarah with anger "About the burial Vicki isn't getting buried she wanted to be cremated her ashes are to be scattered over the ocean. She didn't want a funeral mass. That is what she told me she wanted." Sarah couldn't believe Tom's attitude and now she was angry "Well Tom had I been able to get in touch with you we could have made those arrangements. However, you weren't around and nowhere to be found so I had to make the arrangements myself. If you want to change the arrangements which are supposed to be tomorrow then you can get in touch with the appropriate people. The numbers are on the hall table by the phone." Tom scowled "I'll do that now and after I am finished I have a few questions I want to ask you." After Tom left the room Julie stood up "I hate to eat and run but it's a long ride back. I have that early closing in the morning." She bent down and kissed Sarah on the cheek "Drive careful Julie." "I will. Chow" Julie left the patio and went to her car. Meanwhile Tom cancelled the funeral he then made arrangements to have the ashes delivered the next day at one in the afternoon. He then made a call and rented a boat for the same time the next day. After he was finished he hung up the phone he yelled for Alfred "Yes Mister Tom?" "Alfred, get me a double scotch on the rocks and bring it to the patio. Hurry up about it" "Yes sir" Alfred thought to himself "You little snob I'd love to tell you to get it yourself!" Alfred left to make Tom his drink. Tom thought to himself "Now to talk to the bitch and find out what happened to my sister." He marched out to the patio and straight to Sarah. Standing over Sarah he demanded "What the hell happened to my sister?" Evan stood up quickly "Tom why don't you sit down and we'll explain it all to you no need to badger Sarah." Tom sat down "Whatever start explaining." Sarah looked at Tom "First of all Tom you need to calm down and remember we couldn't find you." "I get that but it doesn't explain what happened to my sister." Evan turned to Tom lowering his voice he said "Your sister was murdered." Just as he finished saying that Alfred came with Tom's drink "Your drink Mister Tom" Tom grabbed the drink from Alfred's tray waved him off and took a sip letting it slide down his throat he took another sip and said "How exactly was my sister murdered?" Evan explained with little detail how Vicki was murdered and how the bullet was meant for Sarah not Vicki. Tom took another sip of his scotch looking at Sarah he said "So my sister took a bullet that was meant for you. What the hell?" Sarah's face was flushed she didn't know what to say she asked "What arrangements did you make Tom?" "She's probably getting cremated as we speak her ashes will be delivered tomorrow morning I've rented a boat and I'll bring her ashes out in the ocean." "Tom we'd like to go with you" "Fine make sure you are ready by one I'll be at the pier. Tom stood up finishing his drink he slammed the glass on the table and left the patio. Evan looked at Sarah "I'm sorry you have to go through this. Just know that I am with you and I'm not leaving your side. For a guy who spent the last week in the casino without a care he sure is arrogant. Sarah sighed "That's Tom sometimes he is heartless." Evan looked at Sarah and said how about we take a drive along the beach and get out of here for a while?" Sarah smiled "That sounds like a great idea it's a beautiful evening." Sarah and Evan left the patio and headed for the garage.

The next day Sarah and Evan met Tom at the pier at one. Tom was already in the boat when they arrived. Sarah said "Hi Tom" Tom ignored her and said "Let's go, I want to get this over with." Evan helped Sarah in the boat. Tom started the boat and took off fast Sarah landed into Evan's arms. Yelling at Tom she said "Was that necessary? I'd like to stay in one piece please." Tom replied "Fine I'll slow down." Tom went out far enough so that you could barely see land. He turned the boat off. He picked up the black urn opened the lid and threw the ashes into the water with not so much as a prayer he said nothing. Then he tossed the urn into the water and started the boat. Sarah was clearly upset she thought to herself "I'm glad he isn't my brother." Tom turned the boat around and headed back to the pier. Evan thought "What a cold hearted bastard you think he was throwing kitty litter over board instead of his sister's ashes." When they arrived at the pier he turned the boat off tied it to the dock and jumped onto the pier before Sarah and Evan even had a chance to get off the boat. He went to his car and took off. Evan helped Sarah get out of the boat and drove her home neither one of them spoke on the way home. When they arrived back at the house Tom's car was already there. And there was another car parked in the driveway. When they went into the house Detective Jennison was waiting for them in the living room. After his men had reported back to him about Vicki's and Tom's activities in New York Chris had sent his men back to Antoine's to get copies of checks and receipts for all of the art they had sold to him. Antoine was warned not to say anything and not to sell the painting of the Czar's family.

When Tom walked into the living room Chris stood up "I'm sorry for your loss Mr. Kincaid" Tom replied with no emotion "Thank you detective." At that moment Sarah and Evan walked in. Chris said hello to Sarah and Evan and asked them all to have a seat. "I have to ask Tom some questions but the two of you can stay." Sarah and Evan sat on the couch and Tom sat on the chair. Chris looked at Tom "I know this is a bad time but I need to ask you a few questions." Chris stood by the fireplace. "Tom can you tell me where you were last Friday between eleven pm and twelve am?" Tom replied "I went to a few bars for a couple of drinks. Then at one I drove to the airport and took a shuttle to Vegas." "Is there anyone who can verify that you were at these bars?" Sarcastically Tom replied "I don't know maybe the bartenders" Tom was getting agitated and angry Chris asked "What were the names of the bars you went to?" Tom now angry answered "The bars I went to were all on Main Street in Newport: The Golden Oasis, English Pub, and the Press Club." Chris was writing all the information in his notebook. He looked at Tom and asked "Tom did you kill Vicki?" Tom frowned "Don't be an ass detective of course I didn't kill Vicki." Chris then asked "Where were you not last Monday but the Monday before?" Tom started to shift in his seat. Sweat was pouring down his back. "I don't remember I guess I was just hanging around." Chris said "Let me ask you again Tom. Where were you on the Monday two weeks ago from today and I suggest you tell me the truth. You see I know where you were." Tom stammered "New York that's right I was in New York." Chris asked "Were you alone?" Tom looked around "No Vicki was with me." Chris went over to stand by Tom 'What were you and Vicki doing in New York?" Tom was now nervous. Sarah and Evan were staring at him. In a barely audible voice Tom said "Selling a painting." Chris said "What was that you said and can you speak up I didn't hear you?" Tom cleared his throat and said "Selling a painting." Chris looked at Tom "What painting was that?" Tom replied "The Russian Czar's family" Chris asked "Was it your painting or Vicki's?" Tom was visibly sweating now "Uh" Chris pressed on "Who did the painting belong to?" Sarah couldn't believe what she was hearing she started shaking. Evan took her hand in his. Tom answered "It belonged to my grandmother. We found it in the attic." Chris asked "Did your grandmother leave the painting to you and Vicki?" "No everything that is in the house was left to Sarah. But she didn't know about the paintings she never went up in the attic." Chris asked "How much did you sell the painting for?" "A couple of hundred thousand" Chris stared at Tom "You are lying Tom wasn't it more like Three million dollars?" Sarah gasped "Oh My God!" Tom gave Sarah a smug look and answered "Yes I guess it was" Chris walked back over to the fireplace "Where's the money Tom?" Tom closed his eyes "I gambled it in Vegas" Chris asked "All of it?" "All but one million" Sarah interrupted "Tom I can't believe what I'm hearing." Tom snapped at Sarah "What the hell do you care Sarah you'll have enough money when we sell this place" Chris spoke up "I'm sorry Sarah but there is more. They sold over a dozen paintings to Antoine's Antique Shop. Vicki was posing as you forged your signature on all the bills of sales on this last sale Vicki had the check made out to Tom." Evan was still holding Sarah's hand he thought to himself "She told me about the paintings but with everything that happened she hadn't taken the time to go up in the attic." Sarah spoke up "Just so you'll know Tom I'm not the complete idiot you think I am. I know there are close to two dozen paintings in the attic worth a lot of money. I was planning on selling them to buy you and Vicki's share of the Haven. You make me want to vomit Tom you are no better than a snake." Tom stood up and said "Shut up Sarah you were supposed to die not Vicki" Chris spoke up "With that statement Tom you are under arrest for the murder of your sister Vicki and Grand Theft." Tom looked at Chris in disbelief "You can't arrest me." Chris walked over to Tom placed both his hands behind his back cuffed his wrists then read him his rights. "Tom you have the right to remain silent anything you say could be held against you in a court of law. You have a right to an attorney if you can't afford one the court will appoint one for you." Chris took Tom outside Sarah and Evan followed them two of Chris's men were looking in Tom's car Tom yelled "What the hell are you looking for in my car?" "The gun you shot Vicki with" Chris answered. "They're wasting their damn time Jennison you won't find a damn gun in my car because I didn't kill her." One of the men found a gun wrapped in a brown paper bag under the driver's seat. "I found a gun Detective it looks like the same caliber that shot the victim." "Someone put it there Jennison I swear that gun isn't mine." Chris said "Let's go Tom" Tom turned to Sarah "Help me Sarah I'm innocent." Sarah turned away from him walked back into the house and up to her bedroom. Holding her hand Evan walked along side of her she let his hand go, she threw herself on the bed and cried. Evan lay beside her and held her close they fell asleep that way. The next day the headlines read Thomas Kincaid arrested for the murder of his sister Vicki Dixon and Grand Theft.

ESTELLE E. FALARDEAU

Chapter Twenty One

The phone rang in Jakes office his secretary was out so he picked up the phone on the first ring. Without giving him a chance to say anything the caller said "Jake it's me" Jake answered "Hello my friend." "Did you see the headlines in today's paper?" "Yes I did I have the paper right here. I make sure I buy a copy of the newspaper every day now." "So you know they've arrested Tom for Vicki's murder" "Yes" "I wiped the gun clean and placed it under the driver's seat in Toms car" "I'd say that was pretty clever my friend" "Thank you Jake" "I suggest you don't try to do anything to get rid of Sarah for a while we have to wait until things cool down. The police will probably take the guards off the property now that they have their killer. I want her to feel safe for a little while. Who knows maybe she'll decide to sell." "That wouldn't help me Jake" "It wouldn't give you as much money but it would take care of you" "The deal is two million Jake and I want it." "Well for God's sakes make it look like an accident don't use a knife or another gun." "I know what to do just let me know when." "Later" he said as he hung up the phone. Another call came in it was the buyer for the Haven his office had called him in Europe informing him of Vicki's death now the arrest of her brother. He told Jake to stay away from Sarah and to let her have time to grieve. He knew he had given them until August with his last offer now he wanted to present the same offer at the end of September good until the end of October.

Jake agreed with the buyer. Jake hung up the phone and thought "I'll wait until September and if she still doesn't budge she'll be sorry."

The next day while they were having breakfast Sarah asked Evan if he would go up into the attic with her after breakfast she wanted to see how many paintings were left. Evan told Sarah that he would go with her as soon as they finished. They finally finished breakfast and Sarah said to Evan "Are you ready to go into the attic?" Evan replied "Yes I'm ready when you are." He grabbed Sarah's hand and squeezed it gently to reassure her everything would be alright. They left the dining area and set out for the attic. They walked up the stairs to the attic Sarah opened the door and both of them walked in. Sarah switched the light on so that they could see. Sarah looked around the attic it was the first time since she had been a child that she had gone in there. As she looked around she spotted the trunks she had seen in the past. She pointed them out to Evan "Those are the exact trunks I saw in the past." Evan looked at Sarah "Are you sure?" Sarah smiled "I'm very sure they are in the exact same place as I saw them and they look exactly like the ones in the past. She thought to herself "I'll have to come back up here someday to see what old treasures are hidden in these trunks. As they walked further into the attic they came to all the paintings. Sarah went over and started to count them. She exclaimed "Evan there are only seven paintings left and when I saw them in the past there were twenty-four of them." Evan frowned "I believe your cousins must have sold them. Chris has copies of all the receipts I'm sure he'll be happy to give you copies. I hope you are going to press charges against Tom" Evan hesitated "You are, aren't you?" Sarah looked over at Evan "I want to see the receipts to see how much money they received I'm sure it wasn't the full value. Then I want to make a deal with Tom to have him sign over his share of the Haven to me. If he doesn't sign then I will press charges either way the Haven will be mine. Of course he's already in jail for killing his sister I don't know if it will make much of a difference. He will probably be in jail for the rest of his life. I still can't believe he killed Vicki thinking it was me. It is so hard for me to understand. I really thought we were close and that they loved me as much as I loved them. Now even though Vicki is dead they both turn my stomach. I think of all the things that happened to me in the past that were caused by them." Sarah shuddered as chills suddenly went through her body. Evan went over to Sarah and wrapped his arms around her holding her close he said "Well at least now they have Tom in custody you can go on with your life. Chris called me this morning after Tom went to court the judge would not set bail and the trial date is in March. He's going to have a long time to think about what he has done and you my love will now be free and safe." Evan held Sarah until she stopped shaking Sarah smiled at him "That is such a relief." They looked around the attic some more before the heat started getting to them. Sarah looked at Evan whose shirt was drenched in sweat she could see the outline of his muscular chest she felt a tingling in her body as she looked at him. "I don't know about you Evan but I'm ready to leave before I pass out in here." Evan turned to Sarah her hair was clinging to her forehead he reached up and pushed it to the side she was sweating and he tried not to look at the wet spots along her chest. "Yes I'm more than ready. I feel like I'm being cooked." They laughed as they descended the stairs back into the main house. Evan was still hot from their excursion "Sarah, how about a swim in the pool?" Sarah smiled "That sounds like the perfect idea to cool us off." She thought to herself "in more ways than one" "I'll go and change into my swimsuit and meet you by the pool." Evan nodded "Sounds good to me." They both headed upstairs to their rooms. Once in her room Sarah grabbed her blue bikini and as she was putting it on she said a silent prayer "Dear God thank you for sending Evan to me. He makes it so much easier to cope with everything that has been happening to me." She tied her hair back in a ponytail and went out to meet Evan by the pool. When she got out there he was already in the pool swimming laps. It was a hot summer day perfect for swimming. When Evan saw Sarah he stopped swimming watching her walk towards him he thought "She is so beautiful I am so lucky God sent me an angel. I don't understand why anyone would want to hurt her she doesn't have a bad thing to say about anyone." As Sarah reached the pool she smiled at Evan "How's the water?" Evan smiled back and sent a playful splash her way "It's perfect!" Sarah laughed and dove into the pool. When she surfaced she sent a splash over to Evan "That's for splashing me!" She said playfully. Together they swam and splashed while laughing. They chased each other around the pool. At one point Evan caught Sarah and wrapped his arms around her waist. Looking into each other's eyes they became serious. Evan pulled Sarah closer to him as he gently kissed her lips. He pulled back looking into Sarah's eyes he said "You are absolutely beautiful" he lowered his head again and this time he kissed her more passionately. Sarah parted her lips as Evan slid his tongue inside her mouth Sarah sought out his tongue and their tongues played and searched each other's mouth. Evan moved his hand to the front of Sarah's stomach as he gently felt his way up to cup her breast in his hand. Sarah's nipple hardened the minute Evan touched her. He played with her nipple through the cloth of her bathing suit. Sarah wrapped her legs around him drawing him closer she could feel his erection through his trunks. She wrapped her arms around his back feeling his shoulder muscles and sliding her hands down she found the edge of his trunks. She slid her hand inside his trunks and Evan groaned at her touch. He lowered her bikini top and took her breast into his mouth sucking her nipple and flicking it with his tongue. While holding her up with one hand he moved his hand to her bikini bottom and slowly pulled it down. Sarah moved her legs from Evans waist to let her bottoms fall down into the pool. She wrapped her fingers around the band of his trunks pulling them down to his knees, using her feet she pushed his trunks all the way down letting them float to the bottom. Evan moved them to a shallower part of the pool. Sarah wrapped her legs around him once again pressing herself against his manhood. Evan slowly glided his hands massaging Sarah's lower lips. Sarah let out a moan. Evan kissed Sarah again more deeply this time as he spread her legs feeling the moist heat inside of her. He pulled her closer as he gently pressed himself into her. When his manhood entered Sarah she moaned louder she couldn't believe how good he felt inside of her. She had never wanted anyone the way she wanted him. Their hips started moving in the water slowly at first Evan wanted this to last forever. Evan started thrusting deeper as Sarah met his every thrust just as forcefully. Sarah's head went back as Evan took her breast into his mouth she couldn't hold back any longer as Evan thrust faster he could feel her throbbing around his manhood he knew she was ready together they climaxed until they both collapsed in the water. Evan was still inside of Sarah when they finally came down. He smiled at Sarah and said "I have never felt this way about any woman nor have I wanted anyone as much as I want you. I love you Sarah" Sarah looked into his eyes with a soft smile she said "I know exactly what you mean. I love you so much Evan I never believed in love until I met you. You are a gift from heaven." Evan slid out of Sarah and they both floated in the pool awhile longer. Evan swam to the bottom retrieving his trunks and Sarah's bikini they slipped their swimsuits back on. Sarah looked at Evan "What do you say we go take a shower and get ready for dinner." Evan wiggled his eyebrows "Together?" "Of course and if you are really good I'll let you wash my back" Evan laughed and splashed Sarah laughing as he was climbing out of the pool he said "last one there has to massage the first one" Sarah jumped up on the cement and yelled "Hey no fair you are cheating." As she grabbed her towel trying to dry off as she ran inside.

With no one in sight they ran upstairs to Sarah's bedroom they took their wet suits off leaving them on the floor Sarah turned the water on and they both entered the shower. Sarah grabbed the soap and started to slather Evan's back she ran the soap all along his body not missing a spot when she got to his erection she soaped it longer as Evan threw his head back and groaned. She took the shower head off and started rinsing him. She let the water rinse him thoroughly while she still rubbed his manhood. Evan let out another groan as she rubbed harder and faster until he emptied himself all over Sarah and the shower. Groaning he grabbed the shower head and rinsed Sarah off along with the shower. He placed the shower head back on the mount. He grabbed the soap and gave Sarah a sexy smile in a low voice he said "Now it's my turn." He lathered Sarah's back massaging it until he felt the tension leaving and her relaxing. He turned her around and starting from the top he ran the soap along her breast lathering them he tickled and massaged them as he moved the soap down to her spot. He lathered her and dropped the soap rubbing his hand creating more suds Sarah moaned he moved with expertise as he massaged her breasts and her sensitive spot. He took the shower head and rinsed her off carefully while still massaging her breast. After he rinsed her off he used his foot and slid it to Sarah's foot spreading her legs. He slid his hand down to her sensitive spot again and gently slid his fingers up to her throbbing knob. He massaged her until she thought she was going to die. He teased her with his fingers exploring all of her until Sarah yelled out his name as the spasms took over her body. She collapsed against Evan as he ran the shower over her rinsing her again. He placed the shower back on the mount and as they stood under the running water he kissed Sarah passionately. Sarah smiled as she playfully pushed him away "If we don't get out of the water we are going to look like prunes for dinner!" She laughed. Evan turned the water off grabbing a towel he wrapped it around Sarah before he grabbed another one and wrapped it around himself. "Are you sure we have to go to dinner? We could always go for a third round" He smiled sexily Sarah giggled "We need to keep up our strength if we are going to keep doing this! Come on let's get dressed." Evan feigned a hurt smile and said "Okay if we must." He opened the door to Sarah's room "Meet you in the dining room as soon as I'm dressed." Sarah nodded "Okay" She smiled as he closed the door. Leaning her back against the door she smiled as she thought how much she loved this man that she'd only known for a short while. Shaking her head from her daydream Sarah went to the closet to pick out her clothes for dinner. Meanwhile Evan was in his room getting dressed for dinner he was thinking "I love Sarah more than life itself. I want to wake up every morning and go to sleep every night with her by my side. She is the woman I want to marry but I can't ask her yet because too many things have happened. I'd like to kill that bastard Tom for everything he's done to her but if I did I wouldn't be any different than him and there is no way I am like that man. I'm going to have to ask Sarah if she knows what happens to people like Vicki and her great grandmother who spend their lives hurting so many people. They all seem like monsters to me." Tom finished getting dressed he looked in the mirror as he combed his hair. After he finished combing his hair he did a once over and smiled into the mirror "You are looking handsome tonight I must say" He turned opened the door into the hall and went downstairs to the dining room where Sarah was already sitting drinking a glass of water. She smiled up at him and said "I thought women were supposed to take longer than men to get dressed" She giggled while Evan sat down and wiggled his eyebrows. Maggie brought in their appetizers. After their appetizers she brought in their dinner. When they had finished dinner and Maggie brought out desert Evan said "Sarah would you mind if we took our coffee out to the garden area it's so peaceful there at this time of the evening." Sarah smiled "Of course not" pushing her desert aside she said "I am too full for desert anyway. Shall we go?" Evan pushed his desert aside grabbed his coffee stood and held out Sarah's chair "After you Miss" he smiled. Together they went outside.

Sitting in the garden Sarah and Evan set their cups of coffee down on the tables that were on both sides of them. Sarah looked at Evan with concern "You seem bothered by something. Is something wrong?" Evan looked pensive as he answered "Yes as a matter of fact I do. I was wondering what happens to people when they die and they have been so cruel all of their lives. Like your great grandmother for example." Sarah thought a moment before answering Evan "It's funny you should ask me that question. I asked Simon the very same thing when I saw how badly my granny and her brother were being treated." Evan raised his eyebrow "What was the answer he gave you?" "He said their souls are sent to a different place where they are taught to become a better person. He also said it isn't a very pleasant place. They are drilled constantly. Sometimes they are there for many many years in our time span. When they are ready they are re-born into another life where they have to lead a better life the second time around to be able to go to the light and join the others when they die." Evan looked at Sarah "That's amazing" Sarah continued "Simon also told me everyone receives what they give out here on earth when they die. If someone has done good things all of their lives then good things will come to them a thousand folds. The same goes if they have been evil. It's like the old saying what goes around comes around. Life goes full circle." Evan sighed "It's good to know they won't go unpunished Sarah." Sarah sighed "Yes it does help you to forgive more I guess." "Yes, I guess it does." They drank the rest of their coffee in silence. As darkness set upon them and the mosquito's were starting to feast they decided to go back into the house. It was getting late and both of them were exhausted. "Evan I think I'm going to bed early I'm exhausted. You can join me if you would like? You look exhausted too." Evan smiled "I'd like that then I could hold you all night and wake up with you in the morning." Sarah smiled and held out her hand Evan reached for her hand and together they walked upstairs into Sarah's room. They dressed for bed and fell asleep in each other's arms.

It was morning Sarah and Evan woke up and made love again before breakfast. After their showers they went downstairs to the kitchen to have breakfast with Mrs. Johnson. They said their good mornings and Sarah talked to Evan while they waited for their breakfast. "Now that the police have the killer in jail, I feel safe enough to go back to work. In fact I have decided to go back tomorrow. I just can't stay here and be idle." Evan looked at Sarah "Yes I understand although I feel that I could stay right here locked in your arms forever." Sarah smiled softly "I feel the same way but it's not very practical my dear." Both of them laughed they could hear Mrs. Johnson chuckle near the stove. Sarah told Evan "I'll be staying in Boston from Monday until Friday then I'll be back for the weekends." Evan sighed "I guess I'll go back to New York however I'll come back on Friday night too." Mrs. Johnson served breakfast while they were eating Evan eyeing Sarah said "We better not lose any precious time since we won't be together until Friday night." Mrs. Johnson Chuckled as Sarah and Evan finished their breakfast. They got up from the table thanked Mrs. Johnson and went directly to her room. They stayed in bed making love that whole day each of them missing the other already and they hadn't left yet. They fell asleep in each other's arms. The next morning Sarah awoke she reached over to hug Evan but felt nothing. She opened her eyes and looked over to where he slept there was a red rose and a note on his pillow. The note said "I left early to beat the traffic. Miss you already. See you Friday. Love, Evan" Sarah smiled while she held the rose in her hand smelling its fragrance. It was time for her to get up. Sarah got up got a vase from her closet and put the rose in it and placed it on her dresser. She took a shower she put on a lightweight beige business suit on with matching heels. She did her hair in a French twist. When she finished she went downstairs to have a cup of coffee with Mrs. Johnson. The aroma from the kitchen smelled delicious. Mrs. Johnson was standing at the stove stirring a pot of jam she made jam every year at this time. She noticed Sarah walk in "Are you happy you are going back to work Miss Sarah?" As she poured a cup of coffee she answered "Yes I am however I'll be back on Friday night and so will Evan." Smiling Mrs. Johnson said "What would you like for breakfast this morning? After all you must be starving you missed dinner last night." Sarah blushed "I was too tired to eat. This morning however I am famished! I'll have some of your wonderful banana pancakes a few slices of bacon one egg and a glass of orange juice please." While Mrs. Johnson was pouring the batter into the skillet she asked "Are you sure you are well enough to go back to work Miss Sarah?" "Yes, I feel fine." After Mrs. Johnson finished making breakfast she placed Sarah's in front of her. Sarah inhaled deeply "This looks and smells so good Mrs. Johnson why don't you join me?" Mrs. Johnson smiled "I've already had my breakfast but I'll have another cup of coffee with you." Mrs. Johnson poured herself another cup of coffee and sat across from Sarah. Maggie entered the kitchen got herself a cup of coffee and joined them. Sarah poured syrup on her pancakes and took bite. "Mm these pancakes are delicious." Maggie waited until Sarah had swallowed and then asked "Have you heard anything about Tom?" Sarah answered "Evan spoke to Detective Jennison he told him they are holding him without bail." "Thank the good lord" Mrs. Johnson said. "I always felt that those two were up to no good and I was right. Let him stay in his cell and rot that is where he belongs. To think him and his sister were stealing all those priceless paintings and selling them." Maggie asked "What are you going to do now Sarah?" Sarah looked at Maggie "I'm going back to work Maggie." "Do you think that's wise?" 'Yes now that Tom is in jail I don't have anything to worry about." Maggie also asked "After everything that has happened are you going to sell this place?" Sarah said in a stern voice "I'm definitely not selling. You and your mother don't have to worry you'll always have a home at the Haven." Maggie responded sarcastically "Great" Mrs. Johnson added "I know your granny would be so please with your decision not to sell." Sarah smiled remembering her grandmother "I feel the same way I love it here as much as she did."

Chapter Twenty Two

Sarah finished her breakfast wiped her mouth with her napkin as she stood she said "Breakfast was delicious as always I need to get going I have a long drive." "Drive careful Miss Sarah" "I will Mrs. Johnson see you on Friday." "She's gone Maggie thought how lucky can she be. Vicki is dead and Tom is in the slammer this place will be all hers witch!"

Sarah drove the highway to get to Boston faster. Friday she would take the scenic route when she returned home. Sarah drove for an hour and a half when she finally pulled in the parking lot she was already miserable. "I wish I could have just stayed home. I love being there and I loved being with Evan. I am so grateful that I met him." Sarah smiled to herself as she got out of the car and reached for her briefcase. Closing the door and locking the car she said "I'm back" Sarah walked over to the office door. Opening the door she was met by Nora. Nora was so happy to see her she was about to place a file in the file cabinet instead she dropped the file on her desk rushed over to Sarah giving her a huge hug. She said to Sarah "I'm so glad to see you I feel like you have been gone a long time." Sarah wrapped her arms around Nora to hug her back they stepped back and Sarah said "It does feel that way Nora. There have been so many things that have happened since I've been gone and so many changes in my life." Nora asked "Sarah would you like a cup of coffee?" "Yes please and make one for yourself and we can catch up." Nora walked into the small kitchen while Sarah walked into her office. She put her briefcase down opened her bottom drawer and dropped her purse in it. She turned and looked out her window she thought to herself "Nothing has changed Washington Street is still buzzing with people. The vendors are still selling their wares. The only thing that has changed is me. I feel so different." As she turned back to her desk Nora walked in with two piping hot mugs of coffee she set one down in front of Sarah "Thank you Nora" "Your welcome Sarah" "Nora let's take our coffee over to the couch and sit." They both sat down on the couch. They both sipped their coffee. There was a vase of roses in the center of the table Sarah bent down to smell them. Nora spoke up "I replaced the roses every day like I always do for you Sarah. I knew you'd be back I just didn't know when." "Thank you for your faith in me Nora." Nora reached for Sarah's hand and held it and asked "How are you really feeling Sarah?" Sarah sighed. Nora knew her so well. "In one month my life has changed so dramatically. I still can't believe it. You must have read the Boston Globe." Nora nodded "I did. It was a shock for me to read that Tom had killed his sister and stole your art collection." Sarah frowned "You don't know the worst of it Nora. I was the one he was supposed to kill. Killing Vicki was a mistake he thought it was me." Nora's mouth dropped open in shock and she held Sarah's hand tighter "Oh my God Sarah that is terrible. I can't believe this Why would he want to kill you?" Sarah responded with sadness "They wanted me out of the way so they could sell the Haven and collect all of the money." "Sarah can I ask you a question" "Yes" "How did you fall off of your horse I know you are an excellent rider." Sarah sighed "While I was riding Midnight a shot rang out and spooked her and she bucked and threw me off of her back I fell and hit my head on the tree. That shot was meant for me. There was a bullet found in the tree right above me." Nora gasped "How horrible" Sarah looked at Nora "There was something good that came out of all this." Nora raised her eyebrow "Oh?" Sarah smiled "I fell in love with the most wonderful gorgeous man you'd ever want to meet. He is the one that found me and brought me to the hospital." Nora smiled "That's wonderful! I can't wait to meet your knight in shining armor!" They both laughed Sarah took on a more serious look "Nora how have things been here at the office?" Nora sighed "Things have been a little strange around here." Sarah raised her eyebrow "What do you mean?" "Well it was Julie." Sarah frowned "What about Julie?" Nora was trying to choose her words carefully but there was no easy way to say this so she just said "She acted like nothing had happened and then she took over the office like it was her that owned it." Sarah looked at Nora "I'm sure she was just trying to keep things normal. I did leave her in charge of the office so it doesn't surprise me that she treated it like it was her own." Nora faked a smile "Yes I'm sure that's what it was. Well I think I need to get back to work there are a lot of things to be filed and typed today." Sarah smiled "Yes I believe I have a lot to catch up on." They both stood and Nora headed to her office and Sarah walked to her desk. Once Nora was at her desk she thought "I sure hope Sarah was right and I was wrong about Julie." When Sarah sat down at her desk she was also thinking "I wonder if Nora was right? She can't be. I'm sure when Simon told me to watch out for people he didn't mean Julie. I'm positive he meant Vicki and Tom." It was difficult for Sarah to concentrate she kept thinking about being killed. Thinking about Vicki and then Tom she couldn't understand why they hated her so much she had only loved them. What had she ever done to make them feel that way about her? A rush of tears flowed from her eyes down her cheeks and she couldn't stop them she put her arms on her desk and put her head down on them where she let herself sob. She was crying so much she never heard the knock on her door. Julie walked into her office as soon as she saw Sarah she ran to her. Julie gently reached out to touch Sarah on the shoulder "Sarah, What's the matter?" Sarah sat up shocked and wiped her eyes with the back of her hands sniffling she said "Julie I didn't hear you come in" Julie said "I knocked but you didn't answer so I just walked in. Is there anything I can do for you Sarah?" Sarah tried to smile "Just be my friend." Julie smiled "You know you can always count on me to be your friend." Julie took a tissue out of her suit pocket and handed it to Sarah. Sarah took the tissue dabbed her eyes then blew her nose. Julie was wearing a light green business suit with matching pumps and a long curly blond wig. She pulled a chair over to Sarah's desk and sat across from Sarah. "What's wrong Sarah? How foolish of me to ask such a question. You've been in a coma, your cousin Vicki was murdered by her brother, and they stole from you. You have had more to handle in one month than most people have in a lifetime. I guess if I were in your shoes I'd be crying too." Sarah looked at Julie "The worst part of this whole scenario is I was the one that was supposed to be killed not Vicki." Julie looked shocked "You?" Sarah responded "Yes me" Julie asked "Why?" "For money" Julie sighed "I'm so sorry Sarah" Sarah sighed "So am I." Sarah straightened herself up on her chair "Enough of me feeling sorry for myself" Julie pushing her chair away said "I've listed the Chauncey home development in Newton, MA with two hundred upscale homes to be built, the first one being the model home. I spent a lot of time preparing the package that will entice the buyers. The model home should be ready in six weeks. Would you like to see the package?" "Sure I would." "I'll be right back" Sarah thought "Nora is so wrong about Julie." Julie came back into Sarah's office holding a package. She placed it in front of Sarah. Sarah began flipping the pages astonished at what she was seeing. "This is great Julie everything is done in such excellent taste." Julie smiled "Thank you that's because I had such an excellent teacher Sarah" Sarah smiled "Thank you Julie you've' been very busy while I was away." "Yes I have been. If you don't need me for anything else Sarah I really have to get back to work." "No I'm fine." Julie stood and took the package from Sarah "If you need me just buzz me." Sarah responded "I will thank you Julie." Julie went back to her office. Her office was identical to Sarah's she had copied every detail except for the painting of the Haven. Her coffee table held a statue of Greek lovers instead of roses.

Sarah spent the next few days looking over and organizing her books. She did her own bookkeeping she was four months behind. She never usually let them fall that far behind. Before her accident she had been too busy to do them. She was going to start with April and May. Before Sarah realized Friday was here. It was a beautiful August day the temperature climbed to eighty degrees and no humidity. Sarah couldn't wait to get home. She did as much paperwork as she could before she knew it, it was four o'clock. Sarah cleaned off her desk grabbed her purse from her bottom draw and decided to leave her briefcase at the office. She walked out of her office and said to Nora "Have a nice weekend Nora I'm headed home I'll see you on Monday." Nora smiled "You too and drive careful. See you Monday." Sarah smiled as she left the office and went straight to her car getting in she started it and headed home. She knew it would be a longer drive taking the scenic route but decided it was worth it. Sarah drove two hours listening to her radio and singing along while she drove. Before long she was pulling into the driveway of the Haven. Evan was on the porch waiting for her when she arrived. She was so happy to see him she shut the car off opened and slammed the door running onto the porch into his waiting arms. She rested her head against his shoulder "Oh how I have missed you Evan." Evan smiled "I missed you too sweetheart." Evan bent to kiss Sarah. The kiss turned into a passionate one and as they got deeper into the kiss Evan accidently rang the doorbell with his Elbow. Alfred opened the door surprising Evan and Sarah stuttering he said "I'm sorry sir, miss" The both started laughing and entered the house "My mistake Alfred" Evan said they ran up the stairs laughing. Alfred was glad to see Miss Sarah so happy it had been a long time since he'd seen that smile. Evan closed Sarah's bedroom door and locked it. He turned to Sarah and took her in his arms. "God how I missed you Sarah, when we're apart I feel like a part of me is missing." Sarah snuggled closer to Evan "I feel the same way." Evan started to caress her face tracing her lips with his finger. He kissed her neck working his fingers slowly down to the buttons on her blouse he began undoing the buttons. He gently slid it off of her shoulders. He reached around and unclasped her bra letting it fall to the floor he bent and took her nipple into his mouth he caressed each nipple that way. Unzipping her skirt he slid it down along with her white silk panties. Sarah stepped out of her shoes she stood there naked and as Evan's eyes took in her body he thought "I have never seen anyone so beautiful than my Sarah." She took off the large pin holding her hair up she shook her hair letting it fall over her shoulders. She was tanned from all of her time spent at home and to him she looked like a golden goddess. "My turn" She whispered. Evan took his shoes and socks off. Never take her eyes from his she placed her hands inside of his suit coat and slid his coat off of his shoulders letting it fall to the floor. She slowly undid his tie and taking both ends of his tie she pulled him to her and kissed him passionately. She pulled away from him twisting the tie around her hand she slid it off and let it drop to the floor. Slowly unbuttoning his shirt she placed her hands on his bare chest sliding them up to his broad shoulders and down his back. His shirt fell to the floor. Sarah caressed his back thinking "What a ravishing body he has. I love every inch of him." Then she teased him by taking her tongue and licking around his nipples. Evan groaned "You are driving me crazy Sarah" She looked up at him and said "Be patient my love." She untied his belt unbuttoned his pants and slowly slid his zipper down his pants fell to the floor. Evan stepped out of them. He stood with his boxers on and his erection told Sarah everything she wanted to know. She slid her hands to the inside of his boxer's edge and pulled them down freeing his erection. Evan lifted Sarah in his arms and carried her over to the bed where he gently laid her down. He got in the bed beside her. The sun filtered in from the French doors bathing them in sunlight as they made sweet passionate love. They stayed in bed most of the weekend enjoying each other's bodies and making love over and over again.

Chapter Twenty Three

Tom was walking back and forth in his cell. He had spoken to Mr. Nolan his attorney when he was arrested and told him his situation. Tom asked him to represent him. Attorney Nolan informed him he wasn't a criminal lawyer and recommended a well-known attorney from a very prestigious firm Elliot Blackwell from Blackwell and Stone. Blackwell was known for winning some of the hardest criminal cases he ever tried. He was supposed to meet Tom at four o'clock it was four thirty and he hadn't arrived yet. His cellmate said "What's the matter pretty boy your lawyer forget about you?" Tom didn't answer him he gave Tom the creeps his name was big Dan he was in for man slaughter. Big Dan was five eight and weighed two hundred and seventy five pounds. His arms were huge from lifting weights. He wore no shirt in his cell his body was covered in tattoos his back had a big tattoo of a snake pit. His chest had different faces of the devil. His nipples were pierced there were holes where the two gold earrings had hung because the police had confiscated them when he was sent to prison. His arms and legs were covered with tattoos of snakes. Tom avoided looking at him because he made his stomach turn and he frightened him. "I don't belong here" he thought "I'm not like him." Finally at four forty-five the guard came to Toms cell unlocked the door cuffed Tom's hands and said "Let's go Tom your lawyer is here." "It's about time" Tom replied the guard led him to a room with a small window a table and two chairs on each side of the table facing each other. The guard took off Toms handcuffs and went to stand beside the door. Elliot Blackwell was seated at the table. Tom sat down on the opposite side. With attitude Tom said "You're a half an hour late Blackwell." Elliot slid his glass down a bit looked at Tom and said "I didn't realize you had another engagement this afternoon Mr. Kincaid?" Tom sneered "I'm not paying you to be a smart ass Blackwell I'm paying you to get me the hell out of here." Elliot smirked "And that is what I am going to do Mr. Kincaid so keep your pants on."

Elliot liked to make his clients sweat that is why he made it a point never to be on time when visiting his client in jail for the first time. He wanted to establish his authority of being in control from the beginning. Elliot was over six feet tall with a mass of curly auburn hair perfectly styled. He had deep set green eyes his large nose gave him a ferocious look. He was wearing a grey pin striped suit white shirt with a grey tie. His clothes were tailored to fit him perfectly. He had graduated first in his class from Harvard Law School. His partner John Stone had graduated second in his class also. John and Elliot met their first year in law school and became best friends as well as study partners. They had planned to open their own office as soon as they passed their bar exam. Both of them passed on their first try fifteen years ago. They started small but grew quickly now their firm employed a dozen attorneys, five paralegals and eight secretaries. Their office was equipped to accommodate everyone's legal matters. Elliot only handled criminal cases. He was a bachelor and married to his job. Looking at Tom he said "Let me ask you this Tom and don't lie to me. Did you kill your sister?" Tom got angry "No I swear I did not kill my sister." "How did the gun get in your car then?" "I don't know someone must have put it there." "Do you have any idea who would try to frame you by placing the murder weapon in your car?" Tom thought for a second "No I don't" "Okay now for the art collection. Did you steal the paintings?" Tom sighed "Yes I did" "I believe you are being honest with me." Tom looked at Elliot "Mr. Blackwell I am being honest. You've got to get me out of here. They got me in a cell with a crazy bastard." Elliot looked at Tom. "I went to see the judge today to try to get him to set bail but he wouldn't do it." Tom huffed "Why the hell not?" "Because he feels you are a danger to society" Tom sighed in frustration "I've done some crazy things in my life but killing my sister wasn't one of them." "If you didn't kill Vicki we have to find out who did. Right now all the evidence points to you. Can you think of anyone who would want your sister dead?" Tom thought for a moment "I've thought about her second husband but he's in France. I can't really think of anyone who would want to kill Vicki unless." "Unless what?" "Unless killing Vicki was a mistake" Elliot raised his eyebrow "What do you mean a mistake?" "The bullet could have been meant for my cousin Sarah. Someone took a shot at her while she was riding her horse the shot missed her but her horse bucked and she fell off hitting her head on a tree. She was in a coma for two weeks. Sarah and my sister could have passed for twins." "When did it happen?" "July third" Elliot stood up to pace "Why wasn't this mentioned in your file?" Tom said with a smirk "How would I know you're the lawyer." Elliot thought for a moment "Who would want Sarah dead and why?" Tom was disgusted "I don't know." Tom started thinking to himself "I'd like to see the bitch dead of course I'm not going to mention this to Elliot." Elliot sat back down and gathered his papers together "Tom I'll look into this situation and see what I can find out. In the meantime you stay put." "Well that shouldn't be hard to do it's not like they are going to let me out anytime soon." Elliot put his papers in his briefcase stood up and said "See you soon Tom" Elliot knocked on the door for the guard to let him out.

Tom was escorted back to his cell. Once he was back in his cell his roommate said "How did it go pretty boy?" Tom ignored him and jumped up to his bunk.

At the Starlight Motel Maggie was getting dressed to leave she had been seeing Sean Delaney for three years. He was lying in bed watching her while she was getting dressed. He loved Maggie more than anything and wanted her to be his wife. "Maggie my love why don't you stay the night with me the room is all paid for" Maggie sighed "I should go home Sean" "Why you know how much I love to wake up with ye in me arms" Maggie sat on the edge of the bed he took her hand in his "Why don't ye marry me Maggie we could be so happy together" Sean was over six feet tall with red hair and blue eyes. He was a very strong man his arms bulged with muscles from working as a mason. He owned his own business he spoke with an Irish brogue. When he was fifteen years old he migrated to the US with his family from Ireland. Now at thirty six he wanted to marry Maggie so they could start a family of their own. "Sean what are we going to live on?" "I make a decent living enough for us to live on I've saved enough money for a good size down payment on a house that we could be comfortable in." "What am I supposed to do Sean keep working as a maid?" "No Maggie ye don't have to work at all. I can take care of you" Maggie groaned "We would be living like paupers I want more Sean I want to be rich." "I can't promise ye riches me Maggie but I love ye dearly and I promise I will take very good care of ye. We do not have to be rich to be happy." Maggie stared at Sean "How would you know Sean what it's like to be rich?" "I do a lot of work for rich people and ye want to know something Maggie. They have their boats, their jaguars and their society friends but most of the time they look very sad they never smile. I'm not saying all rich people are unhappy but many are. Money doesn't make ye happy. Ye need money to survive and be comfortable why than can ye not be happy with me? Ye know how much I love ye and I know ye love me too" Maggie frowned "It's just that I have lived and taken care of rich people all of my life I want some of what they have for myself." She kissed Sean on the cheek picked up her purse from the dresser and said "I'll see you later" and left. Sean turned off the light and thought "Why is she so damn stubborn if I didn't love her so damn much I would stop seeing her." He closed his eyes and fell asleep. While Maggie was driving home in her blue ford escort she asked herself "What is wrong with me? I love Sean yet I can't for the life of me settle for the life he is offering me why is it I always want more. I am so damned jealous of Sarah. She's beautiful and she's always had everything she's wanted. I wish I had someone to talk with. If my mother wasn't so involved with her precious Sarah maybe she could find some time for me. She always has good advice for her when she has a problem maybe that is why I hate Sarah so much. This hate and jealousy for her grows like a sickness inside of me. God help me I don't like what I am becoming." Maggie pulled into the servant's driveway and went into the house.

On Sunday afternoon Sarah and Evan were walking hand and hand along the ocean's edge in the water. Evan was trying to find a way to approach the subject of Julie. It was a beautiful day the sun's rays made beautiful reflections on the ocean. A dozen little sand pipers were chasing the waves. They looked like they were skating when the waves came in they would fly off and start again after the waves left the shore. The sandpipers all seemed to be around at low tide. Sarah asked Evan "Aren't they the cutest little things?" "Evan smiled "Yes they are I believe they are putting on a show for us." "I never thought of it that way" Sarah smiled. Evan didn't want to upset her they had such a wonderful weekend he had bought tickets for the musical "Auntie Mame" Which they saw on Friday night and after the show they went home and made love until sunrise. Saturday they rode their horses, swam and had a picnic at their private cove. Later that night they ate at one of Evans favorite restaurants Henri's Sarah enjoyed the food and the atmosphere again that night their passion took over. Finally Evan decided to bring up the subject of Julie he knew no matter when he brought it up Sarah would be upset but he had to do it. Evan suddenly stopped walking Sarah holding his hand stopped also she looked at Evan "Everything alright Evan?" Evan looked at Sarah with such a sad look it worried her "I would like to discuss something with you but I don't want to upset you. You know I would never do anything to intentionally hurt you." Sarah got a sick feeling in the pit of her stomach "What is it Evan?" Evan replied "It's Julie" Sarah wasn't expecting that response she said "Julie?" Evan sighed "There is something about that woman I don't trust. I really can't put my finger on it; I just want you to be careful around her." Sarah sighed in relief "Sweetheart she's my best friend. Does it bother you that she wears so many different wigs? Most men would probably think that's strange. But you see she doesn't have much of a choice her own hair is so thin and fine she can't have it styled. I feel so bad for her. I know she goes clubbing every weekend when she doesn't have a date. But that's not a reason not to trust her." Evan turned to face Sarah "No none of those things matter Sarah. It's something else maybe I just worry too much where you are concerned because I love you so much. I'm sorry I mentioned it." Sarah smiled at Evan "Like I had said earlier I'm sure once you get to know her more you will love her as much as I do." Evan tried to mask his disappointment "I'm sure I will" he said. Sarah smiled again "It's getting late we should head back for dinner"

Evan tugged at Sarah's hand "I'll race you!" They laughed as they both started running Evan reached the top of the stairs first. Sarah came up next all out of breath she said "You cheated you had a head start" Evan chuckled "Well I couldn't let you beat me!" He tickled Sarah and she started to laugh 'Cut that out" She said in between laughing and breathing "We will miss dinner at this rate." Evan laughed and pulled Sarah to him and planted a kiss on her lips. "Okay let's head in" They ate dinner and retired early in the evening knowing they had to be up early for work the next morning.

Chapter Twenty Four

Sarah got ready for work and decided to miss breakfast so she could beat the traffic. She got into her car and took off for work. Sarah thought "What a wonderful weekend I had with Evan. I can't believe how lucky I am. I love him more and more each day. This must be how granny felt when she met grandpa. I remember one night when I was sixteen years old granny and I was sitting on the swing on the back porch. Granny told me how wonderful their honeymoon was I can hear her telling me now." "You know Sarah it took a couple of weeks to reach England we spent most of our time in our suite in bed. I can't imagine what the other passengers thought about us. But really I didn't care I was so in love with your grandfather he was such a magnificent lover." Blushing I had said "Granny!" "Well he was dear once we were in Europe he did take the time to show me the sites" I remember granny laughing at that point "When we returned to Boston I was pregnant with your mother she was born here at the Haven. Your grandfather was by my side throughout the whole ordeal. When she finally made her entrance there were tears in your grandfathers eyes. Your mother was such a beautiful baby with her blond hair and blue eyes. We named your mother Mary after the ship she was conceived on "The Queen Mary" your mother was such a darling baby and so smart she never gave us a bit of trouble. Three years later your aunt Sabrina was born she was the complete opposite of her sister. She had jet black hair and big black eyes. She had so much hair when she was born I actually put a barrette in her hair. She was a very difficult child. She was fussy and she cried a lot. I tried everything but nothing seemed to help" Sarah thought "Now that I've seen granny's mother aunt Sabrina looked just like her. It must have been troublesome for granny sometimes to be reminded of her mother while looking at her daughter. Come to think of it Aunt Sabrina had a lot of her great grandmother's ways she couldn't be bothered with her children she was never with them. She gave birth to them and then left them with a nanny. She married well twice and spent most of her time in Europe. It's no wonder Tom and Vicki turned out the way they did never having loving parents. I was so fortunate both of my parents loved me. Granny had also told me that when my parents met at medical school it was love at first sight for both of them." "Sarah" she had said "It seems when we meet the one we are destined to be with we know the minute we set our eyes on each other. That is the way it happened with your grandfather and I. It happened to his parents also. I wish you could have known your grandfather he was such a wonderful gentle man and a very good father. He ran his business from home so he could spend more time with his family. He never raised his voice come to think of it I don't remember ever having an argument with him." Sarah remembered smiling at her grandmother and saying "Your eyes light up when you speak of him granny. It must have been very difficult for you when he died." "You don't know how hard it was for me Sarah" I was eighteen years old when we had this conversation I remember saying to granny "How did he die granny?" Granny had a sad look in her eyes when she answered me. "We were living here at the time and we had just made love." It was hard for me at that age imagining my grandparents making love granny continued "Before he went to sleep he told me how much he loved me and how happy I had made him. He kissed me goodnight we snuggled up together and went to sleep. When I awoke the next morning his arm was still around me but he felt cold. I tried waking him up but I couldn't then I realized he was dead. I started screaming Alfred the butler came running in and I pointed to Matthew. He picked up the phone in our room and called the doctor. I don't remember much about anything else the doctor kept me sedated. Your mother God bless her stayed with me for four months until I finally snapped out of it. She'd only been married a year and was living in the Beacon Street house in Boston. Thank God your father was a very understanding man." "Daddy always thought of you as his second mother. Did you ever think of getting married again granny?" "No my sweet Sarah I could never find another man like my Matthew. I know he is waiting for me when it's my time I'll join him and we'll be together forever." Sarah thought "I know from Simon that you are with your Matthew granny and very happy. I feel the same way you did about my Evan." Before she realized it she was parking her car at the office. "My God" She thought "I don't even remember the drive here. Well at least I'm safe and sound." Sarah gathered her things lock the doors and went to the office. When Sarah walked into the office she greeted Nora "Good Morning Nora" "Good Morning Sarah I have an important message for you. Julie is taking some time off she will be gone until Thursday." "Did she say where she was going?" "She decided to go the Realtor's Convention in the Bahamas" Sarah smiled "Good for her she can use some time off. I'm going into my office to finish up my bookkeeping" Sarah smiled at Nora and went into her office she closed the door behind her. Sarah went over to where she had left her paperwork on Friday. She opened the bottom draw and threw her purse in it. She sat at her desk and before long she was immersed in numbers. The month of June went fine she put that aside. As she did the month of July there were too many discrepancies something was wrong it just didn't look right. She took her large calculator out of her desk drawer and started calculating all of the deposits that had been made during that month. She thought "something doesn't look right" She buzzed Nora "Yes Sarah" "Would you please bring me all of the files on the properties that closed in July." "Sure thing I'll bring them right in" "Thank you" "You're welcome" A few minutes later Nora walked in with the files and handing them to Sarah said "Here are all the files you asked for. Do you need anything else?" "How many closings did we have in July?" "We had ten closings none of which were co-brokes" "Thank you Nora" "You're welcome Sarah." Nora left Sarah's office. Sarah started to add all the commissions together while she was adding she noticed that twenty thousand dollars hadn't been deposited "How can this be I'll have to speak with Julie when she comes back from her trip. She's the only one besides me that handles the check book I'm sure there's a logical explanation." She finished what she could of July making a note to talk to Julie. She buzzed Nora "Yes Sarah" "I was just wondering did Julie leave the name of the hotel or room number that she was going to?" "No I'm sorry and I didn't think to ask. Do you want me to find out for you?" "No that's okay it's nothing that can't wait until she is back."

The rest of the week flew by Sarah couldn't believe that today was Friday at six pm Sarah called Evan to let him know she wouldn't be leaving the office until eight she'd be home by ten. Sarah then called home to talk to Mrs. Johnson. Maggie answered the phone "Hello" "Hi Maggie it's Sarah could you please tell your mother I won't be home until ten" "Okay I'll give her the message" "Thank you" "No problem goodbye" Sarah hung up the phone and decided to try Julie again she had left numerous messages for her since she had been back and still hadn't heard from her. She dialed Julie's number and once again she got her answering machine she left another message "Hi Julie it's me again. I hope everything is okay. I just wanted to let you know that I will be leaving the office tonight at eight so I can get home by ten. I'll be here at the office if you call." Sarah hung up the phone and thought to herself "That is strange I would have thought she would have called me by now just to tell me about the convention. I hope everything is alright with her she's starting to worry me." Sarah checked the clock as she was finishing her paperwork it was eight she hurried and put everything away grabbed her purse out of the drawer and went to lock up. Checking before she walked out the door that she hadn't missed something she locked the door and left. Sarah got into her car and decided she was going to take the back roads it was a nice night. After Sarah had driven for an hour she thought to herself "I should have taken the highway I forgot how dark this road is at night." She glanced at her clock to check the time it was nine o'clock another hour and she'd be home with Evan. Looking in her rear-view mirror she could see another car coming up behind her. She thought "At least I'm not on this road alone" A short while later the car behind her was getting closer Sarah frowned "What's wrong with that driver he's almost on my rear end" Sarah was determined that she wasn't going to speed up especially on these roads however she wanted to put some distance between her and the other car so she pressed on the gas increasing her speed to get further away. Looking in her rear-view mirror she saw the car had kept up with her "What the hell is wrong with that driver doesn't he get these roads are treacherous at night. I am not going to speed any more than I already am" All of a sudden Sarah felt a jolt "What the." The car behind her had just hit her. "My God he's trying to run me off the road maybe my uncle didn't die like Tom told me maybe it's him trying to do this." "Looking in her rear-view mirror Sarah couldn't tell if it was man or a woman driving because it was too dark to see. Again her car jolted Sarah then pushed down on the gas pedal trying to get away. She was so scared her body was shaking there was no other road to turn onto to escape only dangerous curves and drops. Her car was speeding around the curve when she felt another jolt from behind she couldn't drive fast enough to get away. Sarah gripped the wheel so tight her hands were perspiring her face was drenched in sweat. "Dear God she prayed Help me Simon I need you. Please help me!" Suddenly the other car was on the other side of her pushing her car toward the edge of the road. Sarah looked over quickly and saw the driver "Oh dear God in heaven it can't be you. Now I remember where I saw the button" The other car made a hard swerve into Sarah's car she lost control and her car hit the guard rail and went over the cliff. The other car sped away yelling "Goodbye little miss rich bitch" As Sarah's car was rolling down the cliff Sarah hit her head on the steering wheel knocking her unconscious. Suddenly the car stopped it landed on the roof. Out of nowhere came Simon who opened Sarah's door unclipped her seat belt and pulled her out of the car. He pulled her out seconds before the car burst into flames and suddenly exploded. Simon thought "I know someone will come looking for her. I'll stay with her until they do."

It was midnight Evan kept looking at the clock he was beside himself wondering where Sarah was the more time that passed the more worried he got. He had called Julie and got her answering machine he left her a message asking her to call him at the Haven no matter what time she got in. He tried Sarah's home number it just rang and rang he hung up and dialed the office and got the answering service who said Sarah left at eight. Evan was sitting at Sarah's desk Mrs. Johnson kept bringing him fresh cups of coffee "Any news yet Mr.

Evan?" she was worried sick that something had happened to Sarah "No I can't seem to find anyone at home. Mrs. Johnson you wouldn't happen to have Nora's home number would you?" "No I don't Mister Evan I'm sorry" "That's okay Mrs. Johnson" She left him to continue his search. Evan decided to call Chris at the station "Newport Police Department Sergeant Dinsmore speaking" "Is detective Jennison in?" "No sir he went home about three hours ago. Is there something I can help you with?" "No thank you I'll give him a call at home." Evan disconnected and then dialed Chris's home number the phone was on the fifth ring "Come on Chris pick up" Evan was desperate. Finally after the seventh ring Chris half asleep picked up the phone "Hello" "Chris, it's Evan" Chris glanced at his night table clock it read one am he sat up "What's wrong Evan?" "I'm sorry to wake you up Chris but Sarah's missing and I can't find her." Chris pushed his hair away from his eyes "Are you sure she's missing Evan?" "She called me at six told me she was leaving the office at eight and would be home by ten and it is now one am and she hasn't arrived home yes, she is missing." "Have you tried calling anyone to see if they've heard from her?" Evan was frustrated "Of course I did I have called everyone I can think of and I haven't been able to reach anyone. I'm afraid something has happened to her. For God sake it only takes two hours to get her from her office" Chris sighed "What road does she usually take to come home?" "She usually takes the back road" "Where are you now?" "I'm at the Haven waiting for her" "I'll be there in a half hour and we'll go check the back road do you have a flashlight?" "Yes in my car" "Bring it I'll see you shortly." As Chris was throwing on his clothes he thought "I hope she is alright" He grabbed his police spotlight and went out to his car. A half hour later he was in front of the Haven Evan was waiting outside as Chris stopped Evan opened the door and jumped into the car. They set out for the back road.

Chris had been driving for fifteen minutes when he asked Evan "Why does Sarah take this road especially at night it is a dangerous road." "I don't know I can see how bad it is I have never driven this way I always take the highway." Another twelve miles down the road Chris noticed a broken guardrail "Evan look to the left there is a broken guard rail I'll turn around let's take a look at it okay? Be careful getting out of the car I'll leave my emergency lights and flashers on. Be careful going down Evan it's very steep" Evan shined his flashlight at the bottom as he swayed the flashlight left and right he spotted something. He aimed his flashlight on the spot. "Chris I think there is a car down there and it's smoldering I'm going down" "It's safer if you sit and slide down the hill I'll bring my radio in case we need it." Chris and Evan worked their way down the hill Evan got there first he let out a blood curdling scream "NOOOOOO Chris its Sarah's car." Chris aiming his spotlight said sadly "I'm sorry buddy but I don't think she could have survived the crash. I'm going to call this in." Evan screamed "No Chris she's not dead if she was I would feel it." Chris grabbed Evan's arm Evan pulled his arm from Chris "Let me go Chris I'm going to look around." Chris said more firmly "There is no way she could have gotten out of that car." Angry Evan said "I don't care Chris please you have to help me look for her." Shining his flashlight Chris moved to the right following Evan. Simon saw Chris and Evans flashlights shining in his direction. "I knew you would come for her my son now I will send you a sign" Just for a few seconds Simon encircled Sarah in a white light just long enough for Evan and Chris to see it. The light went out and Simone disappeared. Chris yelled "Did you see that? What the hell was that?" Evan smiled knowing he had found his love "I'll tell you later let's go get Sarah." Chris shook his head this felt like something out of movie, he couldn't believe what he had just seen. He followed Evan they found Sarah on the ground with her head against a rock her eyes were closed Evan ran over bent down and placed his head on her chest. "Thank God Chris she's alive!" Chris brought his spotlight closer and knelt beside Sarah. Evan shined his flashlight on Sarah's face she moaned and opened her eyes as they came into focus she saw Chris and then Evan she wrapped her arms around Evan "Oh Evan thank God you found me." Evan asked "How do you feel Sarah?" Sarah reached up to touch her head "I feel fine except for this pain in my head" Chris asked "How did you get out of the car?" Sarah looked confused "I don't know all I remember is being pushed off the road I was calling for Simon to help me then I hit my head and that's all I remember." Chris and Evan exchanged looks before Chris said "Someone pushed you off the road?" "Yes" "Did you see who tried to push you off the road and who the hell is Simon?" Evan looked at Chris "I can explain about Simon later Chris I think right now we need to get Sarah out of here and home" Sarah looked at the both of them and said "I can't go home." Evan said "Why not sweetheart?" "I'll explain it to you and Chris in the car." Chris and Evan helped her up the steep hill trying not to fall in the process. When they finally were at the top Chris opened the car door and Sarah got in Evan went in beside her. Chris closed the door and jumped in the front. Evan spoke up "Chris please take us to my house" He turned to Sarah "Do you need to see a doctor that's a pretty bad bump on your head." Sarah lay her head back "No it's only a bump I'll be fine I'll put ice on it when I get to your house." Chris spoke up "Okay Sarah why don't you want us to take you home?" Sarah took a deep breath "Because Tom didn't kill Vicki but I know who did and I won't be safe if I stay at home." Both Evan and Chris asked

"Who killed Vicki?" Sarah told them who it was then said "How can we prove it all we have is a button we found in the garden" Chris said "Let's get you to Evan's house and we'll figure out what we can do."

When they finally arrived at Evan's house it was five am the servants were still asleep. Sarah had never seen Evans home when they drove up it didn't look like a house at all it looked like a castle. It was built of stone with turrets on each side of the house. She thought it looked distinguished. Chris pulled into the driveway and stopped the car. He and Evan got out of the car Evan reach over and opened Sarah's door helping her out. He helped her to the front door. Taking out his key he unlocked the door and pushed it open for Sarah to go first. Once inside the house Evan led them to the living room. Evan said "Make yourselves comfortable I'm going to go get Sarah some ice to put on that bump. Sarah and Chris sat down on a maroon leather couch. Sarah looked around the room it was furnished with two matching leather chairs on each side of the stone fireplace. Over the fireplace was a painting of Evan, his mother and step-father. Evan was a teenager when it was taken. They all looked happy together. Evan walked back into the living room handing the ice-pack to Sarah "Are you sure you don't need to see a doctor?" Sarah smiled "Thank you for the ice-pack this will be just fine. Seeing a doctor isn't going to make a difference he'll just say to put ice on it." She took the ice-pack and placed it on the bump she grimaced from the pain. Evan noticed "Are you sure you are alright?" "Yes I'm fine but I am starving I haven't eaten since breakfast." Evan smiled "Then why don't we go into the kitchen I'll make us some coffee and see what we have to eat. Come to think of it I'm hungry too I haven't eaten since lunch yesterday." They followed Evan into the kitchen. He turned on the light. Chris and Sarah sat at a square maple table in the kitchen. Evan put on the coffee then checked the refrigerator. He found some chicken taking it out of the refrigerator he said "How does chicken sandwiches sound?" They both replied "That sounds good" Evan took out sliced tomatoes, lettuce, mayonnaise, milk and bread. He set it all on the table. Chris got up and searched the cabinets for plates and cups. Evan took out the silverware, napkins and sugar. After everything was on the table Evan went to get the pot of coffee and poured each of them a cup. He sat down and they all made themselves sandwiches. Chris was adding sugar to his coffee when he said "Evan I don't want anyone to know Sarah's alive." Evan finished what he was chewing and said "She can stay here for now. She can have my room. When the servants get up I'll give them two weeks off with pay they could use a vacation anyway. There will be no one here accept Sarah and maybe my mother I'm going to call her to ask her to come and stay with Sarah." Chris replied "Good" Turning to Sarah he added "I'm going to make it look like you were killed when your car went over the cliff and blew up. I want everyone to believe you are dead. That is the only way you'll be safe." Turning to Evan he said "You my friend will have to play the bereaved lover. You'll come with me to the site of the accident. I'll call my office and have my men meet us there. We'll go through the whole procedure treating it like an accidental death. As far as anyone will know Sarah was killed in an unfortunate accident." Sarah put her head down she was obviously upset she said "It's too bad we have to do this." Chris sighed "I know this must be terrible for you but it's the only way we can do this otherwise it is your word against the killer. We have no other proof this is the only way we can trap the killer." Sarah looked at Chris "I know" Evan placed his hand on Sarah's "Everything will be alright sweetheart you'll see. Now I'll clean up so the servants won't know I had company." Chris helped Evan clean up when they were finished Evan took the ice-bag and added more ice handing it to Sarah "Put this on your head. When you go to bed if you need medicine for your headache you'll find it in my bathroom medicine cabinet. I think it's time you rest I'll show you to my room." Evan took Sarah's hand and led her to his bedroom. When they entered the room Sarah took it all in she thought it looked very masculine. He had a high Cherry wood four poster bed, with a matching dresser, armoire and two nightstands. Over the fireplace was a painting of his horse Baron. "Sarah I know you probably want to shower however it would be better if you slept first. I'm sure you are exhausted." He opened his armoire and took out one of his pajama tops and held it out to her. "You can wear this to bed" Sarah started to undress Evan walked over to her "Here let me help you" Evan gently lifted Sarah's top over her head Sarah smiled "Thank you." She took off the rest of her clothes folded them and slipped on Evans nightshirt Evan said "When I leave lock the door behind me. I'll call you later when it is safe for you to come out of my room. I'll ring the phone twice and hang-up then I'll ring one more time that way you'll know it's me." Evan smiled "You look pretty sexy wearing my pajama top" Sarah sighed "I don't feel very sexy right now" Evan sighed "I can only imagine how you are feeling. Just rest sweetheart and don't worry Chris and I will take care of everything and don't worry. I love you." Sarah tried to smile "I love you too" Evan gave her a kiss on the cheek and left the room. Sarah locked the door behind him. She suddenly felt overwhelmed and exhausted. She turned off the light pulled down the covers and got into bed. She placed the ice-bag on her head and fell asleep.

As the servants awoke and came out of their rooms Evan gathered them all into the living room while Chris waited in the kitchen "Good morning everyone I just wanted you all to know that as of this moment you are all on a much needed two week paid vacation. It's my way of thanking all of you for your service. I'm asking that you all pack what you need and either go visit family or whatever it is you want to do. Also I need some time alone. I hope you all enjoy your vacation." The servants smiled and left to do whatever they had to do. When the last servant left Evan went back into the kitchen looking at Chris he said "It's all clear they are all gone." Chris got up from the table "Let's get this done then. Are you ready?" "As ready as I'll ever be just a minute I want to check on Sarah before we leave." "Okay I'll be in the car." Evan walked up the stairs to his room with his key he unlocked the door just as he thought Sarah was sound asleep with the ice-pack on her head. He lightly walked over to the bed and gently kissed her cheek. He opened the drawer to his side table taking out a notepad and pen he scribbled a note to Sarah for when she awoke. Leaning the note against his lamp he looked at Sarah one more time then left the room leaving the door unlocked. He locked the front door behind him as he headed for Chris's car.

When Chris pulled out of Evan's driveway he said "Okay Evan what the hell is going on? What did we see tonight? Who is Simon do we need to bring him in for questioning?" Evan chuckled "Would you like it answered in that order?" "Do not be a smart ass my friend" Evan laughed "It's a long story and you probably aren't going to believe me" Chris raised his eyebrow looking at Evan he said "Try me" Evan sighed "It all started when someone took a shot at Sarah and she fell off of her horse. She stood up and was brushing herself off she looked down on the ground and saw herself laying there and thought she was dead. She said the words out loud a voice behind her told her she wasn't dead she was in between worlds." Chris slowed the car down and looking at Evan he said "You are giving me the creeps." Evan looked over at Chris sighed and said "Please just listen Chris I know this all sounds out there but it is all true. I just need you to keep an open mind and you wanted me to tell you so I am." Chris nodded "You're right but it still gives me the creeps go on." Evan continued "There was a bright light and a man in a white suit was standing in the center of it. The peculiar part is the man looked just like me." Chris interrupted "Evan, never mind go on" Chris thought to himself "If I didn't know any better I'd think he lost all of his marbles." Evan continued "Sarah asked the man if she was going to die he told her no. He was here to help her. He told her his name was Simon" Chris shook his head in disbelief "You mean the same Simon you were talking about?" Evan answered "Yes the same Simon so you won't be questioning that witness." All Chris could do was laugh Evan laughed too and then continued "He told her he was sent here to bring her back to her grandmothers past." Chris asked "Why her grandmothers past?" Evan getting impatient said "I'm getting to that part Chris" Chris nodded "Okay, Okay I'll just listen" Evan continued "Her grandmother never spoke of her past it was just too painful. However she now knew that was a mistake and needed Sarah to know about it. She felt this would help Sarah decide whether to sell the Haven or keep it. The way Sarah explained it to me was as if she was right there she could almost touch her of course she couldn't. She told me it was like taking part in a video but not being able to participate or change anything that was happening. It was very difficult for her. I'll just give you a brief summary of her story Chris. Sarah's grandmother's name was Monique she had a little brother named Pierre. When their father passed away they were still very young. Their mother beat and starved them. The brother died when he was eight of pneumonia complications caused by malnutrition.

When her grandmother was fourteen years old her mother married her off to the iceman." Astonished Chris asked "Iceman" "Yes in those days they had iceboxes and the guy delivered ice." "Okay go on" "Where was I oh yes living with her new husband and his family was as bad if not worse than living with her mother. Her husband was cruel and so was his mother. Monique was sent to the boot mills to work along with her sister in-law who was eighteen at the time. At home they both had to do all of the house work washing, ironing etc. The mother in-law did the cooking. Two years later her grandmother had a baby girl her mother in-law wouldn't give her enough food to eat and her grandmother was breastfeeding the baby a few months later the baby died of malnutrition. Her husband died a year later. He was knifed in a fight in a local bar." Chris was getting angry "Good the bastard deserved to die. Then what happened." "Her grandmother ran away the night he was buried. She took the train to Boston. On her first night in Boston she was mugged and almost raped lucky for her a man came by just in time to save her. He was rich and quite the gentleman. He ended up being her second husband and he was very good to her." Chris smiled "Happy endings good for her. You know Evan Sarah could write a book about her grandmother's life." Evan smiled and looked at Chris "So you believe everything I've just told you?" Chris frowned "Who the hell can make up a story like that? As I recall when we were in school you couldn't make up a story to save your life." Evan laughed "That's true and there's more" Chris said "More? Okay I'm listening." Evan looked over to Chris "Remember when I told you I found Sarah I felt connected to her and fell in love with her the moment I saw her." "Yes" Chris replied wondering where this was leading. Evan continued "While Simon gave her a message to give to his son. However he never told her his son's name. Chris this part is so incredible" Chris shook his head "The whole thing is incredible if you ask me" "When Sarah came out of her coma I was sitting by her bed holding her hand she kept calling for Simon. When she opened her eyes she called me Simon and asked me why I had changed my clothes. I told her I wasn't Simon. She didn't believe me. She repeated the message Simon gave her to make sure she had it right. As she was talking I realized she was talking about my father. What she was saying about my father no one else would ever know. I can't explain how I felt I've never experienced anything like this in my life. You see Simon is my father." Chris raised his eyebrows "You mean to tell me the light we saw this morning was brought on by your father?" Evan nodded "Yes Chris he's the one that pulled her out of the car and saved her life." "Chris looked at Evan "Evan if I didn't know you so well I'd swear you were crazy. This story is so unbelievable you read about people having experiences with angels up until now I didn't believe in that kind of thing. Now I have to believe there is a better place for us when we leave this planet." Evan nodded "I'll tell you Chris this changed my perspective about life. Now the most important thing in my life isn't all the money I can make. It's having Sarah by my side and spending more time with my mom. Having a family and cherishing them." Chris smiled "You've probably made enough money that you could retire now and have a good life Evan" "Yes I could and I plan on doing just that after this is all over." Chris looked serious "Evan before we left your house I put in a call to the station my men will meet us at the site.

Chris and Evan were the first ones to arrive. Evan looked down the cliff at the car he shuddered as he thought of Sarah being stuck in the car unconscious. He looked up to the sky and whispered "Thank you dad for saving the woman I love. I love you." Just as they were going down to the car Chris's men arrived at the scene. When everyone was gathered around the car Chris explained the details of the situation. The officers took notes. Chris specifically said that this was a covert operation and under no circumstances is anyone to talk about it outside the station. The men all agreed and Chris and Evan followed them back up to the road. Chris and Evan got back into the car and Chris picked up his phone and called all of the newspapers to report the accident when he was finished he looked at Evan "Sarah's name should be in the newspapers in the afternoon edition and probably on the six o'clock news. I hope you're a good actor Evan you are going to have to be very convincing as the broken hearted lover." Evan looked at Chris "Don't worry I was in all the school plays I can pull this off. I can't make up stories but I can act." They both laughed

Chris pulled into the Haven. Alfred was waiting for them at the door. Both men got out of the car and walked up the steps. Alfred spoke "Master Evan, Detective Jennison did you find Sarah?" Chris answered "Let's go into the house Alfred I would like to speak to everyone that's here at the same time. Please bring everyone into the living room." "Yes sir" Evan and Chris went into the living room while Alfred went to get everyone that was in the house. They sat down and waited for people to come in. Julie was the first to come into the living room she went directly over to Evan. She said "Evan I'm so sorry I wasn't home to take your call. I was staying with friends as soon as I checked my service and checked your message I called here and Mrs. Johnson told me what was going on. I came right over. Is Sarah alright?" Evan stood up abruptly and walked over to the fireplace. Chris stood and walked over to Julie. Please sit down Miss Tate your questions will be answered when everyone else is here." Julie sat on the couch and looked over to where Evan was standing something was wrong with him. Mrs. Johnson, Maggie and Alfred walked into the living room Chris asked Alfred "Is this everyone that is here today?" Alfred answered "Yes" Chris looked at all of them and said "Please sit down everyone." Maggie sat on one of the chairs. Mrs. Johnson and Alfred who both looked tired from lack of sleep sat on the couch with Julie. Evan still standing by the fireplace with Chris now by his side said "I have some bad news. Sarah has been in a terrible accident" "Is she going to be alright Mr. Evan?" "I'm afraid not Mrs. Johnson. Sarah's car went off of a cliff and blew up she died in the fiery wreck." Mrs. Johnsons hands flew to her mouth tears were flowing "Oh my poor baby." Alfred placed his face in his hands and wept. Maggie sat there with no emotions showing. Julie started crying stood up and she tried to run out of the room but Chris had already been prepared in case anyone was too emotional to hear the rest. He reached for Julie "I know this is upsetting but there is more please sit for a little longer." Julie went back to the couch still crying. Chris continued "There is no body to be buried there was nothing left of Sarah but ashes. Evan has decided to have the funeral on Wednesday at Saint Paul's church." Evan took over "I'm sure you'll want to attend the Mass. I know Sarah had no other family except Tom and he is in jail. I'm taking it upon myself to make the arrangements." Mrs. Johnson wiped her eyes with her apron and said "I'm sure Miss Sarah would want you to take care of things Mr. Evan I know she loved you. I'm so sorry she was taken away from you." Evan had tears in his eyes "Thank you Mrs. Johnson." Chris thought "God he's good" Evan said he was going home to get some rest. He told them he'd take care of all the arrangements later. Mrs. Johnson asked "Should we have refreshments after the mass Mr. Evan?" "Yes I think that's a good idea Mrs. Johnson." Mrs. Johnson sniffling said "I'll take care of everything Mr. Evan" "Thank you" Evan replied Evan took his handkerchief out of his pocket to dry his eyes. Alfred walked them to the door and thanked them for coming. Once outside Evan said to Chris "I can take my car home now I'll talk to you later" Chris nodded and said "Evan are you okay to drive?" He wanted to make sure no one was looking out the windows or listening. Evan caught on to what Chris was doing so he replied "I'm okay I'll drive carefully. Thank you Chris for everything you've done." They got into their cars and left.

Evan arrived at home. He went straight to the kitchen to make himself a black cup of coffee. He took the cup into his office so that he could make phone calls. He sat at his desk took a sip of his coffee and picked up the phone. The first call was to his mother the phone rang twice and she picked up. "Good morning" She said "She's always so cheerful" Evan thought he answered back "Good morning mom" "What a pleasant surprise dear. How are you?" Evan sighed "I'm fine mom I have a favor to ask you. I know you are busy with all of your club activities and all but could you come and stay with me for a couple of weeks I really need you." His mother sounded concerned "I'm never too busy for my son. What's wrong?" Evan paused "I'd rather discuss it with you when you are here and not over the phone." "Where are you calling me from son?" "I'm calling from Newport mom." "Good I should be able to meet your sweet Sarah while I am there." "I'm sending my chauffeur to pick you up at three o'clock is that time alright with you?" "That's fine dear. I'll see you later today. I love you son." "I love you too mom." Evan hung up the phone. His next call was to the church the funeral was all set for Wednesday at ten am. His next call was to Nora. Sarah had given him her number before he left his bedroom. He picked up the phone and dialed her number he spoke to her for a few minutes he felt so bad that he had to lie to her. She was sobbing when he hung up the phone. Evan checked his watch it was eleven am and he was exhausted. He went upstairs knocked on his bedroom door and in a low voice said "Sarah?" Sarah opened the door to let him in. "How are you feeling?" Sarah answered "Better but you look like hell. I think you need to sleep. Why don't you change and get into bed with me I could sleep some more." Evan smiled as he walked in the room "That's a great idea" He took his clothes off climbed into bed and held Sarah in his arms they both fell asleep.

Chapter Twenty Five

Late Saturday afternoon Jake picked up the Newport newspaper tucked it under his arm walked into the package store and bought himself a six pack of beer. It was another nice summer day he didn't mind walking home. He lived in a small studio apartment in an undesirable neighborhood. He carried a 38 gun in his breast pocket but none of the riff raff in the neighborhood ever bothered him. When he got home he tossed the newspaper on his worn out easy chair. He took the gun out of his breast pocket and put it on the night stand next to his bed. He took his jacket off and tossed it on the bed. He pulled the six pack out of the bag grabbed a can from it and put the rest in the refrigerator. He flipped the can open and gulped half of it down and let out a large belch. He went over to his chair picked up the newspaper and sat down. The front page shocked him the headlines read "Sarah Saint James Killed" The Newport woman died when the trans-am she was driving rolled off of a cliff on route 66 in Rhode Island. The car burst in flames Miss Saint James never had a chance to escape. Jake went to the obituary page and found when and where the service would be held. He thought to himself "Holy shit she's dead I'm going to be a rich man. Kincaid is in Jail but he still wants to sell. Now that he owns the whole parcel I'm in like Flynn. My little friend came through." He got up and got himself another beer. "This calls for a celebration" he flipped the tab and gulped the whole can down. "Of course I'll have to pay my respects and go to the service. I think I'll splurge for a new suit I certainly can afford it now." He got himself another beer went back to sit in his chair he was dreaming about what he could do with the money.

The killer was also feeling very gratified while reading the paper thinking "This time there was no mistake Sarah is dead and two million dollars is looking very good. I deserve ever damn cent for a job well done. I think I'll give Jake a call to see if he's read the paper yet. I want to make sure he knows I was responsible for that little accident." The killer picked up the phone and called Jake they were having a long conversation.

Evans mother Kate arrived at five thirty. Peter the chauffeur carried her luggage to her room. She showed him where to put the bags. Peter asked "Will there be anything else Mrs. Taylor?" "Peter" She exclaimed "Where are all the servants?" "Mr. Taylor gave them all two weeks off." She thought that was strange but said "Thank you Peter." "You're welcome Mrs. Taylor" He turned and left the room. Peter was thirty-eight years old he was over six feet tall and had the physique of a body builder. He had dark brown curly hair dark brown eyes with long eyelashes. He had a scar over his left eye from a knife fight he was in when he was younger. He had been with Evan for twelve years. Peter travelled with Evan wherever he went. He made excellent money working for him. He owned a condo in New York and stayed in a hotel when he was in another city except Newport he had a room here in Evans home. Kate unpacked her suitcase and went downstairs to make a pot of coffee. In the kitchen she found Evan and Sarah eating bacon and eggs. When Sarah saw Kate she blushed she was embarrassed she was still wearing Evans pajama top. Kate said "I'm sorry I didn't realize there was anyone else here." Evan started to laugh he stood up and grabbed his mother in a bear hug "Come join us mom I want you to meet Sarah. Mom this is Sarah. Sarah this is my mother Kate." Kate smiled and went over to hug Sarah "I'm so happy to meet you my dear I've heard so much about you from my son." Sarah was still blushing as Kate said "Evan why didn't you tell Sarah I was coming" Evan smiled thinking nothing of it "I wanted to surprise her." Sarah raised her eyebrow and said "I guess you did letting me meet your mother in your pajama top no less" Kate smiled "Don't let that bother you my dear I always wore Philips pajama tops" Evan smile at his mother and pulled out a chair for her "Mom would you like a cup of coffee." "I'd love a cup" "Light with two sugars?" "That's right dear." While he was pouring her coffee he asked "Mom would you like me to fix you a couple of eggs with bacon and toast?" "I am a little hungry dear. Just one egg sunny side up and one toast please." Evan grinned "Coming right up" Kate pulled her chair next to Sarah she placed her hand over Sarah's hand "My son was right when he told me you were beautiful even wearing his pajama top" "Thank you" Sarah was still blushing however Kate made her feel very comfortable she could see part of Evan in her. Evan placed his mother's food in front of her. He poured himself another cup of coffee and sat across from her. While breaking off a piece of toast Kate asked Evan "Why did you send your staff on vacation while you are home?" Evan looked at his mother "Well mom that is the reason I wanted you here." Kate looked confused "I don't understand" Evan leaned towards his mother in a serious tone he said "Mom this isn't pretty but here goes. As far as everyone knows Sarah is dead" Kate dropped her toast and exclaimed "WHAT?" Evan continued "Someone tried to kill Sarah last night" again she placed her hand on Sarah's hand "This sweet girl but why?" Sarah replied "I didn't know who or why until last night when my car was side swiped and I saw who it was just before I went over the cliff." Kate frowned

"My God that's terrible you are lucky to be alive" Sarah sighed "Yes I am someone has been trying to kill me since the beginning of July" Kate felt bad "I can't believe this it's like a television mystery." Evan spoke up "Mom I think we should explain everything that happened to Sarah from the beginning. Do you mind Sarah?" "No of course not, tell your mother." Evan explained everything to his mother from the time Sarah fell off of horse until now. When he was finished his mother was crying. Evan got up and got a box of tissues for his mother. "Thank you dear" She took a few tissues out of the box wiped her eyes and blew her nose. "Excuse me dear the whole story is so unbelievable. But I believe every single word. I'm convinced you met Simon from what you said and the message he gave you for Evan. He was always such a wonderful man He was always helping someone in need. I can understand why he is one of God's angels." Sarah smiled "I can understand that too he was so good to me." Kate had a sad look on her face "Sarah it took me years to get over losing Simon he was my first love I never thought I could love anyone else as much as I loved him. Until I met Philip I was very fortunate he too was a wonderful husband and a good father to Evan. You must be very blessed my dear to be saved from death twice." Kate smiled at Sarah "Yes I have been very fortunate but now we have to catch this murderer. I really can't push my luck." They all laughed Kate said "At least you haven't lost your sense of humor and that is refreshing to see" Evan looked at his mother "Remember mother everyone thinks Sarah is dead. We have to keep it that way to keep her safe." Kate looked at her son "I know dear just tell me what you want me to do." Listening to them Sarah thought "How lucky I am to have Evan and his mother she is such a delightful person and she is beautiful" Kate was tall slim with short curly white hair. She had violet eyes that lit up when she smiled. As Sarah was still looking at her she thought "Six months ago I didn't know these people and now I can't picture my life without them." Evan, Sarah and Kate made their plans and everyone knew what to do.

Wednesday morning there was a big turnout for Sarah's Mass. Many of her customers and friends came to show their respect. They couldn't believe she was gone. Nora, Julie and all the agents from Sarah's office sat together on one side. Evan, his mother, Mrs. Johnson, Maggie, Alfred, Mr. Santos and Jimmy sat together in the first two pews. Jake was sitting in the last pew in the back. Chris was standing in the back of the church keeping an eye on everyone a few of his men were situated amongst the crowd and on alert. After the Eulogy the priest told everyone they were all invited to the Haven for a brunch. Jake thought "I might as well attend the brunch after all I'll get to see the inside of the place that's going to make me a millionaire." As the priest finished the final blessing he walked to the front of the altar and bowed. He turned and walked up the center isle to the back of the church. He greeted the people offering his condolences as they walked out of the church. Chris, Evan and his mother were the last to speak with the priest they shook hands and thanked the priest. They all walked out of the church together Chris looked at Evan and said "I'm on my way to pick up Tom" Evan gave Chris a look "Tom?" "Yes I got permission from Judge Watson to take Tom to the Haven for a few hours." Chris had explained the situation to the judge and he signed the release form Tom. Evan nodded "We'll meet you at the Haven." Chris gave Evan a nod and went to his car. Evan and his mother walked to the limousine Peter opened the door for them. Evan said to Peter "We are going to the Haven." "Yes sir" They drove off.

Sarah went to Evan's stables she found Baron. She went up and rubbed his nose "Hey there boy, want to take me for a ride?" Baron nuzzled his nose against Sarah's face. Sarah smiled "I guess that means yes" Sarah got Barons blanket saddle and bridle as she was putting them on him she talked softly. "I can see why Evan loves you. I can't wait for you to meet Midnight Blue I hope you love her as much as I do." After she finished saddling Baron she opened the stall and let him out. She led him out of the stable once outside she raised her leg up to the stirrup and climbed on Baron. "Okay boy let's go the Haven" Baron whinnied as Sarah led him to the Haven. When Sarah arrived at the Haven she went straight to the stables. She led Baron into one of the stalls she took off his saddle. She patted his nose and said "I'll be back in a while" she closed the stall door and walked out of the stable. Everyone was still at the service she let herself into the house and went right to her bedroom. She took a shower and got dressed. After she was dressed she sat down in her chair and waited.

Chris arrived at the prison. He walked in and went straight to the guard he spoke to the guard who led him to Tom's cell. When they got to Tom's cell he said "Well if it isn't the great detective Jennison" The guard unlocked the cell Chris said "Let's go Tom you are coming with me. I'm taking you to the Haven Sarah's will is going to be read today." "Why did the bitch leave me anything besides the Haven?" Chris frowned "Shut up Tom you turn my stomach. Turn around so I can cuff you and we can leave." As Tom turned and put his hands behind his back he thought "At least now I can sell the Haven and all the money will be mine. I'll have enough money to get myself out of jail. Money talks and I'll have plenty of it." After Chris placed the cuffs on Tom he said "Let's go" He led him out to his car. Tom started to say something snide and Chris interrupted "I suggest you just sit there and shut up. I don't want to hear anything you have to say. As far as I'm concerned you are nothing but scum. So do yourself a favor and don't say another word." Tom huffed they rode the rest of the way in silence.

When Chris arrived with Tom several of his men were already mingling with the guests. A large table was set up on the patio. Mrs. Johnson had outdone herself. She had prepared two large bowls of butterfly shrimp that sat on a bed of ice with small bowls of cocktail sauce on each side. There were also plates of assorted finger rolls, Swedish meatballs and other various finger foods plus an assortment of delicate pastries. Evan stood at the entrance along with his mother and Julie to greet the guests. When everyone had arrived Chris asked them all to gather on the patio. Evan and Julie joined them. Kate stayed behind to wait for the attorney. Evan made it a point to speak to all of Sarah's agents and friends many of her friends were so upset about her death they couldn't eat they just drank coffee. Chris walked over to Evan and said "Excuse me Evan could I see you for a moment?" "Sure please excuse me" Evan walked away with Chris. Chris turned to Evan and quietly said "I wanted to show you who Jake Lamark is. See the guy in the grey suit standing in the corner stuffing his face." Evan turned to look where Chris was indicating he said "Yes I see him" Chris said "That's him" Evan looked at Jake carefully he turned to Chris and said "I don't know why but I have a gut feeling that Jake should be present when the will is read." Chris nodded "I'll make sure he's there Evan" Evan said "The guests are starting to leave I'll say my goodbyes while you start gathering the others to go into the office for the reading of the will Attorney D'amour should be here momentarily" Chris looked at Evan "Ok I'll start gathering the low life." Evan nodded and walked over to the guests to say his goodbyes. Chris walked over to Jake "Mr. Lamark" Jake looked at Chris "Detective Jennison what a great spread" He said while wiping his mouth with a napkin. Chris smirked "I see you're enjoying it." "Yes I am" Chris looked disgusted "Mr. Taylor would like you to stay for the reading of Sarah's will." Jake look surprised "Why did the little darling leave me something?" Chris shook his head "I really don't know but could you wait by the door while I gather the others than we'll all go in together we are just waiting for the Attorney to arrive." Chris went to gather the others that needed to be at the reading. When the Attorney arrived Kate brought him to Sarah's office. He took a seat at Sarah's desk. Kate said to the attorney "I'll let Evan know that you are here. Everyone should be gathered by now." The Attorney smiled and said "Thank you" after Kate left the Attorney started arranging the folding chairs so that everyone could fit in the office.

Kate went out to the patio to find Evan, when she found him she whispered "The attorney is here son" Evan nodded "Thanks mom I'll let Chris know." "It's time he's here" Chris nodded and said "Will everyone follow me please" He led them all to Sarah's office Chris had Tom sit in one of the stuffed chairs so he could be behind him. Nora, Mrs. Johnson, Alfred, Mr. Santos, and Jimmy sat on the folded chairs. Jake sat on the couch next to Kate. Julie took a seat in the other stuff chair. Evan closed the door and stood in front of it. He thought to himself "The stage is set." Attorney D'amour was sixty years old he had white hair, grey eyes and he was average height. He had been Monique's Attorney for thirty years. He had taken over when his father had passed away. Attorney D'amour thought "This is quite a group. I've never done anything like this before. However my father and I have loved and respected Monique and her granddaughter for years. There's always a first time. Well here goes." He cleared his throat. Tom thought "What's taking the old bastard so long?"

as he shifted in his chair. The attorney began "You are all gathered here today so that I can read Sarah's last will and testament to you. When Sarah made out her will she was of sound mind and body." Julie thought "Get on with it I want to see how much Sarah left me." Maggie was thinking "She probably left me her wardrobe." The Attorney continued "To my cousin Tom I leave my share of the Have as written in our grandmothers will. To Maggie, sweet Maggie I leave my home on Beacon Hill in Boston with all of the furniture and any or my personal things there that she wants." Maggie gasped and placed her hands in front of her face and wept. "To my secretary and my loyal friend Nora I leave my business, all my savings, trust funds and all the material things I have in the Haven." Julie stood up and screamed 'What the hell is going on here? All those things and the money and business are supposed to be mine. Mine you understand you old fool!" Everyone just stared at her Julie continued "You old bastard what did you do with the real will? I have a copy of Sarah's will in my purse." She opened her bag and took out the will waving it she said "I have it right here." She leaned over the desk and shoved it at the Attorney. The Attorney picked up the will glanced at it and said "I'm sorry Miss this is not her current will. Sarah had a new one drawn up two months ago." Julie stood up angrily "This is outrageous! I want to see that will NOW" As the Attorney was about to speak Evan opened the door and in walked Sarah everyone gasped except Julie as she was facing the Attorney and didn't see Sarah come in. Julie more forcefully said "Did you hear me I want to see that new will" at that moment Sarah spoke "There is no reason for you to see the new will Julie" Julie spun around shocked and gasped "Sarah it can't be you are dead." Sarah frowned "That's what you thought when you ran me off the road wasn't it Julie? You wanted me dead so you could inherit everything I was going to leave you. Why Julie? You make good money; you have a beautiful condo and money in the bank." Julie with venom said "You have no idea what it's like to be poor Sarah you always had everything you wanted." Sarah was not only angry but hurt she looked Julie straight in the eyes and said "So because of that fact you thought you had the right to kill me? You are nothing but a conniving bitch. I should have listened to my gut instinct the first day I met you. I felt you weren't a good person. Shame on me for not paying attention to my gut if I had Vicki would be alive today." Sarah sighed. Chris left Tom and approached Julie 'Julie Tate you are under arrest for the murder of Vicki Dixon and attempted murder of Sarah Saint James." Julie looked at Chris "Wait a minute I was hired to kill Sarah I'm not going down alone Jake" Jake stood up and tried to make a run for the door Kate stuck out her foot and he fell flat on his face two of Chris's men grabbed him and he looked at Julie and yelled "You lying bitch!" "Oh no you don't Jake" As she looked at Chris "He offered me two million dollars to get rid of Sarah because her cousins were willing to sell the Haven but the dumb bitch Sarah didn't want to sell." Sarah looked disgusted. Chris turned to his men "Read these two their rights and take them downtown" He sent a sympathetic look to Sarah who had tears slowly forming in her eyes. Two of the men took Jake out another man grabbed Julie and said "Let's go sister" Julie looked at Sarah as she was leaving she stopped and asked "How the hell did you get out of that burning car Sarah?" Sarah looked at her with disgust "I'll let you think about that while you rot in jail Julie." As she walked out the door Julie said "It would have been nice having all that money" Sarah shook her head and thought "She is demented" Nora got up walked over to Sarah and hugged her "I'm so sorry Sarah I had no idea that was how she felt." Sarah looked at Nora "Thank you Nora I'm sorry for this charade but it was the only way we could catch Julie. Why don't you stay awhile I'll see you after in the kitchen." Nora nodded "Okay I'll see you in a bit." Maggie went up to hug Sarah "I'm so glad you are alive" and she really meant it for the first time Maggie felt good inside and she finally realized having money wasn't everything especially when people are willing to kill you for it. She thought to herself "Sean is right I can be happy without being rich" After Sarah hugged Maggie back she turned to the rest of the room and apologized to her servants for making them go through all of this. Mrs. Johnson spoke for all of them "We are just happy you're alive and well, Miss Sarah." Sarah smiled "Thank you Mrs. Johnson. Could you please make a pot of coffee I have more business to take care of and then I'll see you in the kitchen." "Yes Miss Sarah" Mrs. Johnson left the room and the rest of the staff followed her. Chris, Tom, Evan, Kate, and the Attorney were still in the room. Evan closed the door again. Tom stood up and said "You can take these cuffs off of me I'm free now. I didn't kill anyone." Sarah looked at Tom and with no feeling she said "You're not free Tom" Tom looked at Sarah in shock "What are you talking about Sarah?" Sarah frowned "I'm talking about Grand theft Tom fifty million dollars' worth." Tom shook his head "It wasn't that much Sarah." "Yes it was Tom. In fact it would be more than that if they had been sold at auction. Detective Jennison was able to obtain all of the receipts and that is the amount they added up to." Sarah walked over to where Tom was she looked disgusted as she said "You have a choice Tom you can go back to Jail or sign your share of the Haven over to me." Tom frowned "I don't have much of a choice now do I Sarah?" "No you don't. Included in the papers you are going to sign over to me there is a provision that states if anything were to happen to me you will never inherit the Haven. Also after you sign these papers you are never to set foot on this property again. If you do you will be arrested. Attorney D'amour has prepared the document and it is ready for your signature." Chris removed the handcuffs from Tom as he rubbed his wrists he walked over to the desk the Attorney handed him a pen and the papers showing him where to sign. Tom signed all the necessary papers. Chris, Kate, and Evan signed as witnesses and Attorney D'amour notarized their signatures. The Attorney gave Tom his copy. Sarah sighed "I never thought it would come to this Tom. I loved you and Vicki apparently you didn't feel the same way about me or granny for that matter." Tom looked at Sarah with a smirk "Love you hell no! As for granny she gave her precious Sarah everything you and this house can go to hell!" Sarah looked at Chris "Could you get him out of here please." Chris nodded "I'll be happy to. Let's go you can say goodbye to the house as you are looking at it from the road." Sarah and Evan turned to Attorney D'amour to thank him he smiled at Sarah and said "This was a strange one. However I am glad that justice was served and you are safe Sarah. Your grandmother would be proud of you." "Thank you" Sarah said with a smile. She offered to walk him to the door and he said "You stay put I can see myself out. Have a good day." Attorney D'amour stood and put his papers in his briefcase as he did that he said "I'll file these papers tomorrow Sarah and you will be all set." "Thank you again" He picked up his briefcase and left. Sarah walked into Evan's arms "Is it really over?" Evan hugged her tightly "Yes, love it is." Kate stood up and walked over to them "Sarah I'm so sorry you had to go through so much pain. But you came through this with flying colors. I know your grandmother would be proud of you." Sarah smiled "Thank you for all of your help Kate" "My pleasure my dear. Now if you don't mind I'm going to have Peter drive me home I'm a bit tired." Evan looked at his mother "That's fine mother" Evan hugged his mother and she left.

Sarah and Evan walked hand in hand into the kitchen to speak to Mrs. Johnson, Nora and Maggie. They were all seated at the kitchen table drinking coffee. Sarah said "I could certainly go for a cup of your delicious coffee Mrs. Johnson." Mrs. Johnson stood "Please sit down Miss Sarah you too Mr. Evan would you like a cup too or would you prefer something stronger after this ordeal?" Evan smiled "No coffee will be fine thank you." Mrs. Johnson poured two cups of coffee she brought them to the table and put a cup in front of each of them. She sat back down. After taking a sip of her coffee Sarah said "Again I am so sorry I had to put you all through this grief but there was no other way. We wanted to catch Julie and of course we didn't know Jake was involved. Everything worked out well. As far as Tom he will never set foot on this property again. The Haven now belongs to me and I will never sell it." "I'm so happy for you Miss Sarah" "Thank you Mrs. Johnson" Nora looked at Sarah "I knew Julie wasn't a nice person I tried to warn you." Sarah sighed "I know you did Nora so did Evan. When I was doing the books last week I noticed a large amount of money was missing I was going to speak to Julie about it Monday but of course I never had the chance." Nora sighed "It's hard to believe she wanted you dead Sarah." "I have a hard time believing it myself Nora. I trusted her so completely it's my fault really. I didn't trust her when I first met her I just had a gut feeling. There is an old saying that says something good always comes out of something bad." Evan raised his eyebrow "What good came out of this Sarah?" Sarah smiled and reached over to put her hand on Evan's arm "If she hadn't taken a shot at me we would never have found each other my love." They finished their coffee and Evan stood up "If you'll excuse us ladies we have some unfinished business to take care of." He took Sarah's hand and led her out the back door.

Sarah and Evan took off their shoes and walked on to the beach. They walked toward the water Evan looked at Sarah "Shall we go to our special place we haven't been there in a while?" Sarah smiled. "I'd love that" Together they walked to the cove once on the other side they held each other as they looked over the ocean. Sarah broke the silence "Evan, look a rainbow!" she exclaimed. Evan smiled "That must be a sign" Evan turned Sarah to face him he looked into her eyes. Smiling he reached into his pocket. Sarah gasped when he got down on one knee. Holding the black velvet box out in front of him he looked into her eyes and said "I have loved you since the day I set eyes on you. You are compassionate, understanding, giving, and most of all beautiful. My life would be empty without you in it. Sarah Saint James would you give me the honor of becoming my wife?" A tear slid down Sarah's face "Oh Evan I can't picture my life without you. I would love to become your wife." Evan opened the box. Inside sat a ten karat Cartier diamond encased with smaller diamonds around the top, set in a gold band. It took Sarah's breath away "That is beautiful" Evan took the ring and gently held Sarah's hand slipping it on her finger he said "Not half as beautiful as you are." He stood and wrapped his arms around her and kissed her saying "You have just made me the happiest man on earth." The both smiled held each other and as they turned their heads they saw the rainbow again it had gotten brighter. They both knew in their hearts that Simon and Monique were giving them their blessings.

I hope you enjoyed reading this book as much as I enjoyed writing it. Look for more action coming your way as we follow Monique's life in her marriage to Matthew in "New Beginnings" the second book in the Haven's Series It will be out sometime in 2018. Please leave a review and let me know what you thought about the book. I enjoy hearing from my readers. If you would like updates of upcoming books, or to leave comments please send them to my e-mail at: butterflywriter@comcast.net.

Also look for my new book "Angels Among Us" coming in 2017.

Thank you,
Estelle Falardeau

Made in the USA
Middletown, DE
27 August 2017